DREAM DAUGHTERS

COLIN MARTIN

authorHOUSE®

AuthorHouse™ UK
1663 Liberty Drive
Bloomington, IN 47403 USA
www.authorhouse.co.uk
Phone: 0800.197.4150

Published by AuthorHouse 07/25/2016

ISBN: 978-1-5246-3766-8 (sc)
ISBN: 978-1-5246-3799-6 (e)

Three daughters born, to a prophecy said;
To combat evil, again summoned to dread.
But a sisterhood sought, is not easily bred;
As the mother not see, the troubles ahead.
And evil conjured, will take its dead;
Unless the righteous, is united and lead.

PERSONAL ACKNOWLEDGEMENTS

The Three Girls

Thank you to the girls who I have used to model each of the three sisters for this story. I expect every girl's character is far different from each sister, but this reflection has helped me construct each triplet in hope that they develop in future stories.

Local people, friends and family

Thank you to all the people who have brought my debut horror-fiction novel *Dream Master* and have read its prelude, *Rain Maker*. I hope that *Dream Daughters* will compliment my earlier books so readers follow an entertaining and historic trilogy.

Authorhouse

Again, a big thank you the *Authorhouse* team who made possible the publication of my third horror-fiction novel. The main difficulty with *Dream Daughters* has been developing three contrasting sisters, but ones I would love to think as my own.

PART ONE

ONE

IT FELT AS THOUGH SOMETHING sinister had clasped her heart from behind; a cold, invisible hand that chilled her body to shiver. But she had learned how to suppress such horrid feelings, wanting only the warmth of fond memories. And now, before he left, she needed to envisage Carl one last time.

It was hard to recall how long he had been standing there waving, but now as Carl stepped back slowly into the darkness, Sarah remembered the sweet warmth of his kiss. Her heart pounded and her body tensed with emotion; a tingling, warm sensation shooting from stomach to groin. Yet somehow her legs felt immobile, frozen by a terrible, biting cold. And as mist rose above her feet, it seemed to envelope her whole body.

She glanced up, wanting to view Carl once more. But all Sarah's squinting eyes could see was his shadowy figure disappearing into the fog; a half lit hand blowing a kiss before it too vanished into the dark beyond the street lamp.

Feeling motionless, again she shivered. But with determination to shake the cold from her bones, she curled her nightgown about her waist and stamped her naked feet on the raised brick step of the doorway. However, as a tear escaped one eye and ran cold down her cheek, she could not help notice the mist now rise above her knees. Sarah cursed under a breath and turned to the light and warmth of the hallway, but noted how strangely it followed. Again she cursed, suppressing her nerves to peer over her shoulder with watery eyes, hoping to picture Carl one last time.

It seemed like shadows in the street were watching her; spectral shapes in the fog converging to whisper nasty rumours, or were they closing in to provoke insult. Sarah shook her head in defiance, curls of her darkening blonde hair sticking against heavier tears. Again for a moment she felt her legs paralysed, but kicked the swaying door open to jump inside the warmth of the hallway. Quickly she spun round, shutting the door against the inflowing mist, dismembering fingers from a vaporous crawling hand.

Inside the hallway, once again Sarah shuddered, but tingled to the reassuring warmth and light of the room. Yet now it was her observations that raised questions. What was she doing in Carl's home? Surely it had been years since she had been here? In fact, had she ever spent the night?

Although somewhat comforted, all felt so strange. Knowing that Carl was instinctively tidy, the kitchen was in a mess. Above her head and littering the walls of the hallway, were the usual cheap, unsavoury pictures of birds. And then entering the somewhat claustrophobic lounge, the room was decorated with dated décor; corners littered with books, sleazy excuses of ornaments dotted everywhere, and beside the fireplace was that tattered, old writing desk. The only thing with style (and probably of some value) was that old dresser he had in the bedroom – the one with that ornate but creepy, oval mirror. Yet her body warmed to recollect such fond memories here. Or was this some optimistic illusion?

At first it was the fall in temperature that agitated Sarah, but staring about the room with glazed eyes, she noticed the mist of her own breath exhale before the lights grew dim. It was not until they flickered off and on again in quick succession that her spine stiffened. Then it was a sound from behind that made her jump.

Sarah spun round, her eyes widening with fear. Fallen from the fireplace and now lying on the floor, was a framed picture of her and Carl. She took a step closer, but paused momentarily to pick it up, noticing how a crack along the glass had separated the couple. *Strange how it cracked on falling on soft carpet*, she thought, *or had it hit something beforehand?* Baffled, she placed the frame upon a nearby coffee table and turned slowly to notice a reflection in Carl's television screen.

It was not just the intense blackness filling the reflection of the room behind that stunned her, but the sudden cries from her babies lying in their cots in the bedroom. Afraid to move, she watched how the reflected figure formed into the shape of a religious habit, like that of a monk in a black robe. But as she turned to observe the reality of its reflection, it was something contrary to any holy man.

Although the swirling mass of the black figure blurred and reformed, she could now distinguish its hellish form. Somehow she knew that this abomination of evil had killed past friends. And now it stood wavering before her, its arms outstretched and blocking the way to save her children. From beneath a heavy, black hood appeared a powdery white face. It was not exposed as that of a naked skull, but had pale skin, shiny yet withdrawn. At first she saw it's taut, dark nostrils and a crescent mouth grinning at her with dagger-like teeth, but as the head tilted back, a pair of deathly black pupils glared from glistening white eyeballs. As its eyes turned to focus on the cries from the bedroom, the face shimmered through the dimming light. Although dumbfounded, Sarah found the exasperation to release her scream and the hellish eyes of the Dark Ghost glanced back her.

'You'll not have them,' Sarah bellowed, trying desperately to find movement in her legs. 'They're my girls and one day they'll vanquish you!'

But the Dark Ghost simply intensified its grin at Sarah and floated teasingly into the flickering light of the bedroom. She sped forward, finally finding her inner strength. Or was it the horrific thoughts of what a demon could do to such innocent children? She staggered and flung herself at the door, but hit hard against it as it slammed shut. She pounded on the door with one hand whilst testing the handle with the other. Begging for it to be opened, she wailed for her babies to be spared. But the door held firm. She heard the cries of her three triplet daughters intensify as if the thing was teasing them with its ghastly, elongated fingers.

Tears flooding her eyes and feeling her heart about to burst, Sarah grasped the crucifix about her neck and called to God; begging that the merciful One spare her children. She howled her words at the door, ordering for the evil to be expelled, but her ears deafened to the cries of her babies. And now they were squealing.

Shouting her last prayer and slamming her shoulder against the door, suddenly Sarah fell into the bedroom. Whatever evil power had prevented the door from opening, it had now disappeared... along with the Dark Ghost.

She pulled herself upon all fours and then squatted on her haunches to look about the room. No sign of any demon… no sign of cold or flickering lights… the warmth had come back? And quiet… no noise… nothing but a deathly silence.

No noise… but had her babies been taken, or been killed?

Sarah raced to her feet as fast as her tired limbs would allow. Her heart melted with joy to see all her three daughters lying parallel in each cot. Neither were crying, no pain, no anxiety, each baby girl with eyes wide open, just simply apprehensive to who was staring down at them.

For a long moment Sarah crouched over each cot, ensuring each girl was safe and warm under blanket. It was not until she released the crucifix from within her clenched hand that she saw the indentation in her palm. At first she was content, sanctified by its shining, silver image, but then came the numbing pain. She etched a half smile to ignore the pain. It was certainly better to suffer a little pain with prayer than be succumbed by such tormenting evil.

She stroked each girl's cheek, calling each by name and then whispering words of comfort. Yet were her words to console her children or were they to provide her own personal reassurance? Glancing away from her babies, Sarah searched the room, again becoming apprehensive. She was right to become fearful, as again it was growing cold.

Suddenly the bedroom light flickered off and on and Sarah shuddered. Again the overhead light flickered against its shade as now the room grew icy cold. Looking down at her babies, Sarah winced as a deep and distant voice echoed about the room.

'He died saving you,' deep voiced words expressed with sarcasm, and then sniggered, 'before any of his *precious* ones could ever know…'

Sarah stared about the bedroom, her eyes glazed by tears as she squinted through the wavering light. The room was fearfully getting dark as laughter echoed from all directions. As the laughter faded, Sarah glanced at her three crying babies. That horrid evil laughter had gone, so was it the biting cold that upset them?

Puzzled by how all three babies were reaching up to her simultaneously, Sarah noticed a ring of bright light glow about them. With their cries now deafening, she glanced at each in turn with bewilderment, but realised they had become scared of something above. Slowly Sarah's head tilted to face the ceiling.

Spreading like a pool of spilt black liquid upon the ceiling, the spectre of the Dark Ghost formed with ethereal tendrils reaching all corners. Growing with more depth, its body spread flat against the ceiling, it expanded larger to gradually conceal most of the bedroom light. Its malicious fronds reached the walls, until directly above her, its cold face of death appeared to grin at her.

'No…!' Sarah bellowed, 'You'll never have them…'

As Sarah felt her heart jump into spasm, the last thing she saw, was the Dark Ghost assail her from above. Its chalky white face gleaming as much as it's taut, dark lips opened to reveal glistening serrated teeth. But it was the deathly black of its pupils, against the white of its eyes, which stabbed such a hellish glare into Sarah.

👁 👁

At first she thought it was the sound of her children wailing in agony, but as the spectre of the Dark Ghost dissolved, there was only one scream, and a familiar voice.

Sarah shot forward but felt a firm hand stop her. As her sweating body dissolved of frenzied heat, so did the image of her horrific nightmare. She felt hands now grip each shoulder as her vision melted away. Slowly as she blinked, the concerned face above her came somewhat familiar.

'Emily…' Sarah croaked, 'is that you?'

TWO

EMILY STARED FRETFULLY DOWN AT her mother lying in the hospital bed. In all the years that she had visited Sarah in the institution, she had never witnessed her mother being aggressive. But as Emily arrived, she found her mother frantic; wavering arms above her head and pulling at her bedclothes as she tossed about wild.

Emily called her mother's name persistently, composed but with authority.

'I'll get a sedative.' Emily heard a voice call from behind.

'No!' Emily directed, 'She's calm now... she's better.'

The burly nurse stooped over Emily. She perched herself against the bed to reach over and grasp at Sarah's shoulders.

'Never known her be like this,' the nurse said with deep, nasal speech. 'She'll need restraining by the likes...'

'No,' Emily interrupted sharply, 'she's just having a bad dream!'

Momentarily the nurse stared at Emily with scorn, but then grasped for straps concealed beneath the bedstead.

'Miss Layton has not had such bad dreams since you were born young lady,' the nurse declared, trying repeatedly to locate the strapping belt, 'or was that her fine husband?'

'My father, Carl... my real father,' Emily started to explain but recoiled, disturbed that history could do nothing to help her mother now. 'What's it of your concern?'

'Nothing... just that he got people killed,' the nurse murmured, stretching her weight low, trying to brush Emily aside. 'Probably why poor Sarah here's, gone a little....'

Although the nurse restrained from finishing her sentence, Emily resented what the nurse was proclaiming. Especially being a woman of her profession, and in front of kin, even if the place *was* for such people?

Glancing back to Sarah, feeling her slump back against the bed, Emily removed the supporting hand from her mother's shoulder to clench the nurse's wrist.

'No, she's not mad,' Emily corrected in a sharp tone. 'And she, my mother, doesn't need such restraint.'

The nurse looked questionably at her wrist, and realising the nurse's expression, Emily withdrew her grip.

'Look, she doesn't need those things,' Emily insisted, her voice now somewhat more considerate. She pointed to how her mother was now slumped against the pillows. 'Besides, I'm here with important news.' Emily noticed the nurse look her up and down keenly and then stand tall. 'Please, look, she's waking, and there's not long for my visit.'

'Should've got here earlier then,' the nurse remarked sarcastically, but turned after taking pity on Sarah's condition. 'You've got ten or so minutes,' the nurse announced after consulting her watch. 'And as you've been told before, push the buzzer should –'

'Yes, the large, red button,' Emily intercepted, 'the one above her head.'

The nurse quickly examined the instruments she had wheeled in on a table, before glancing back at Emily.

'I know your mother is not as bad as some here,' the nurse commented whilst pausing to wheel out the table, 'but precautions need to be maintained.'

'Yes, miss... I mean nurse,' Emily agreed, her hands now clenching around one of her mothers. 'If she panics, gets upset, or shows any signs of...' Emily could not spit out the word 'violence' but nodded. 'I'll ring the buzzer.'

Hearing Sarah blubber incoherent words to her daughter, the nurse paused momentarily to study her condition. But after struggling to render a smile, the nurse left the room to wander slowly down the hospital passage.

'He's coming for you again,' Sarah murmured, her hair wild and stuck to her face by sweat, 'but this time it'll be evil itself... and you and them will be in danger!'

Emily realised her mother's voice was increasing with hysteria and so squeezed the pillows to raise her head.

'Mother, my dear, be quiet,' Emily said, trying a soothing tone. 'You've been dreaming... a nightmare by the looks...' Emily clenched her mother's hand tight and stooped over to observe her close. 'And we don't want *that* nurse back do we?' Emily saw rationality return in Sarah's eyes. 'Besides I have news.'

'You're not safe until all are together,' Sarah muttered, her eyes roaming to examine the door. 'See that's what happened before... when you were babies.'

Emily glanced away from her mother's sight to hide the escaped tear, but could not restrain her composure anymore. She held her mother's head firm with one hand and peered close.

'But that's why you're in this *place* you fool!' Quickly Emily swivelled her head aside to brush away a heavier tear.

'But I told you,' Sarah blubbered, 'it's what happened.' Sarah paused, waiting for Emily to once again face her. 'He came to kill you. It was a good job I was there!' Sarah paused to reflect on the past event and looked aside. 'Not that I was any use. But you had the strength to defend against such... even at that age?'

'But look, stupid,' Emily stared hard into her mother's eyes to show her annoyance, 'such a cock and bull story is what's keeping you here... stuck in this place... even if, as you say... it's the truth?'

'It is,' Sarah asserted, 'but it won't be Daniel next time, it'll be something –'

'But that's what you need to change!' Knowing she had rushed from work and had little time, Emily felt her anger mounting. 'That's why you're in such a place like this?' Emily paused to ensure she had her mother's full attention. 'Mike's worked with friends... colleagues at his work... solicitors and so forth.'

'Is he looking after you?' Sarah questioned, oblivious to Emily's attempt to explain important news. 'You looking so thin... Rachael says you swim harder these days.'

'Mom,' asserted Emily, trying hard to refrain from shouting. 'Mike says there's a way to reprieve your case. Maybe even get you acquitted.'

'Get me out of here,' Sarah questioned, but smiled; her once young looks now showing signs of age, 'and finally get to see all three of y' together?'

'I doubt that mom, but we'll see.'

Emily did not want to give any false hope that she could find her sisters, as it was difficult enough to keep a work-life balance. Besides, Emily had been separated from her sisters as a baby. And since been adopted and raised by Mike and Rachael, for their sake, she did not want to dig up the past. But like her mother, there was something hereditary that desired resolution; a deep compassion that niggled at her like a bad itch, not knowing what it would have been like to grow up and play with identical sisters. Emily shook the thoughts churning though her mind to concentrate on what her adopted father had said.

'Look mom,' Again Emily scanned her wristwatch, but gained Sarah's full attention. 'Mike tells me that after being in here for so long, you have a chance to a re-trial…. And without too much trouble, apart from tonight of course, you can…'

'I've been a good girl, have I?' Sarah interjected grinning, but gazed at her medical cabinet. 'Not that many rewards come much my way?'

'But this is a chance,' Emily reassured, squeezing both hands around her mother's. 'Tell them at this re-trial, that over time in here you remember more clearly what happened… that you stabbed Mr Whittaker in self-defence… and to protect us… and pushed him –'

'But it was you three that turned the knife on him… protected me you did?' Sarah clenched Emily's hands firm. 'Such a strange and powerful light turned his wrist. It plunged the knife and sent him flying… I was there, I saw it!'

'Oh for fuck's sake mother,' Emily rolled her eyes. 'Yes mother, as you've told before, but it's…' Emily took a deep breath. 'It's not deemed practical… or fucking possible to the court now is it? You protected us and so stabbed Daniel.'

'So how come no fingerprints on the knife?' Sarah questioned coyly, turning her head aside. 'It happened… I'm not crazy.' Sarah whimpered, remembering the ordeal, but suddenly faced Emily to change subject. 'I don't like it you swearing. That's coz o' Mike. Carl would never been so…'

'Mom,' Again Emily argued but subdued her annoyance with control. 'Believe me, if you don't plead self-defence after all what others have been to get this, then... then... I give up.'

'Okay, my dear,' Sarah felt distressed to see more tears in her daughter's eyes. 'If I change my story to this that Mike has, you'll get me out of here?'

'Yes,' Emily affirmed, 'but you've got to believe it... no more this past story of us protecting you?'

'Okay, I'll do it,' Sarah affirmed, but paused to think, her thumb and forefinger cradling her chin, 'but on one condition.'

'What's that?'

'You start finding those sisters of yours...' Sarah reached one hand up against Emily's mouth to smother her reply. 'So I may finally see all my daughters together again?'

'But, we've talked all this through before and...?' Still Emily's words were stifled by her mother's hand, her hazel eyes glimmering with annoyance, reflected by the powerful lights above.

'Don't matter,' Sarah now became resolute, something Emily had not seen for a long time. 'Rachael tells of this new internet thing... people searching people.' Sarah's hand now stroked Emily's long black hair, slowly curling it at the bottom.

'What, social networking?' Emily deduced, surprised at her mother's knowledge. 'They have that in here?'

'No, well, they do,' Sarah paused to scrunch up her nose and rub her one eye, 'but I don't know how to do stuff like that now do I... not after being in here anyhow?'

'Surely it's not all that bad?'

'Well, I'm sure that that nurse helped herself to those marsh mellows you bought last time.' Sarah clenched a fist in anger.

'What? Well I'll be...'

Sarah grasped Emily's wrist to pull her near, almost rising up from the pillow.

'But don't worry,' Sarah winked an eye. 'Bring that, your favourite ice-cream next time, as I'll be having it without her knowing.'

Again Sarah winked in sight of her daughter, but what made Emily smile was how her mother seemed to have regained that sparkle in her eyes.

'Rum-and-raisin ice-cream it is then,' Emily said in secret before standing up from the bed, 'and some of those biscuit wafer things?'

Sarah grinned to change the conversation, wriggling deep into her bed after adjusting her blankets carefully.

'When will they be visiting again?'

'Who?' Emily replied.

'Mike and Sarah of course.'

'Very soon,' Emily avowed, her dark eyes twinkling beneath the bright, fluorescent lights, 'especially now he has a chance to get you out.' She checked her wristwatch to realise that visiting time had finished minutes ago. 'I must go and tell them of the good news…' Emily winked. 'That my mother is now deemed sane.'

Sarah etched a smile but turned over, her face now exposing melancholy. Was it her daughter's last comment, or the regret of how only one, her eldest daughter came to visit?

THREE

DANIEL CURSED UNDER A BREATH and glanced about the dark corners of the room, the only light cast from a small, shaded desk lamp. And as he stared into the foreboding shadows surrounding him, he felt a sudden chill.

Maybe he was still scared, even after all he had been through; the left of his face burned from the mansion fire, scarred and disfigured like his upper body. Or was it the fact that he had now been disabled for more than fifteen years? But it was not just the physical violence. He had been scrutinised by lawyers and all kinds, trying to attest his innocence to a revenge killing.

No, there was something else haunting him – a tormenting, indescribable horror.

At what he had witnessed during his years as the doctor's aide, he was afraid to indulge into such affairs, but knew he had to go on. He had to understand the doctor's research – the delicate notes he had salvaged from the fire. Besides, it was the only thing that kept him resolute – kept distant the loathed memories of past treatment and constant medicines – helped disregard his inability to walk, having to wheel about the place, blistering his already hard-skinned hands. Maybe so many years of cursing his disability had turned his mind – had provoked thoughts of revenge and murder, wanted something evil to avenge rancorous desires. Or was it purely his way to avoid suicide?

Turning over another partially burned page, one he had examined countless times before, he sighed heavily. How much longer would it be before he could understand the ancient symbols and language he had now been studying for years? Was he missing some translation key, vital notes torn from the doctor's diary some twenty years ago by that pesky journalist? Was it simply some other research that he had overlooked, had yet to comprehend, or stuff that had perished along with most of the doctor's legacy?

He turned another page with his scarred hand, and wishing he had all the answers, cursed again. He remembered how affluent, intellectual and travelled the doctor had been. Daniel Whittaker had never visited any coastal shores of England, never mind the distant, tropical shores of the West Indies. He had now past mid-forty, but felt his body much older. Once he was fit and burly; a sturdy henchman to service the doctor's land and property, to frighten off trespassers and discourage strangers from learning about the doctor's occult society. But now he was a cripple and felt he had never been educated enough to fathom out all this shit.

To what Daniel had deduced through exhaustive research (after learning new technologies like the internet), the doctor's notes often referred to three powers that could combine to refute his commands of the Black Art. But at first it was not these powers that the doctor feared: three mystical animals that promote the natural good in humans, linked somehow to religions in the Far East? What the doctor feared most, and justifiably, was the reprisal from his bloodletting ceremony that summoned evil?

Daniel stared at the large, open book, his eyes glazed and wide but oblivious to the inscription, his mind elsewhere. Again he visualised the horrific scene of the fiery hand burning and torturing the doctor – his master burned alive on his very own doorstep. He remembered the panic – rescuing the book and diary, recovering his shotgun – all he could carry before escaping the fire, and then running with blistering pain through the woodland, only to glance back at the receding fireball and that strange fog bank.

It was guilt that consumed him now, bearing down on his shoulders like lead weights. Maybe he could have stopped to save his master from the blaze? But no, he knew the truth. As the magic circle did not protect Doctor Schroeck, then surely the fire demon would have killed him anyhow? And all this that lay on his desk would be nothing but ash. He too, would certainly be dead, nothing but a forgotten ghost?

No, Daniel thought, he had survived to go on. Finish the task his mind had been bent on for years. He would seek revenge, but not physically as his hunch had driven him to do all those years back. He would study much in memory of his master, learn the ways of black magic and invoke evil spirits to do his bidding. But what was this force that the doctor had investigated – a composition of white magic that could oppose him?

Daniel's thoughts were disturbed by quick knocks on his apartment door. He glanced up, again perturbed by how darkness flanked the doorway. Swivelling the lamp in direction of the door, he squinted to observe it more clearly. Again a quick succession of knuckles rasped the door from outside.

'Daniel, you in there?' a woman's voice called agitatedly.

'Amanda?' Daniel cleared his voice, his first attempt sounding feeble. 'Amanda, is that you out there?'

'Of course,' she replied with sarcasm, 'who else you get coming to y' door?'

'Well you can't be sure these…' Daniel muttered, searching about his desk.

'What?' came a high-pitched reply, 'Open the door, won't you?'

'Can't be sure these days, now can…?' Daniel babbled, fumbling with books and papers that littered his desk, his announcement silencing. 'Can't find the blasted…'

'Come on,' the voice beckoned, 'it's fucking freezing out here.'

'Stupid woman,' Daniel whined, but raised his voice after finding the remote-control receiver. 'It's locked, but wait… got it!' Pointing the gadget towards the door, he pressed a button. 'It should be open now!'

'What?'

'Come on in,' Daniel announced. 'It's open now!' He continued to talk, but mumbled to see light expand across the floor from the opening door, 'Unless you want to freeze out there?'

'What's this, a bloody interrogation room?' The silhouette of a slim woman questioned, shielding her eyes from the bright light as she approached.

'Sorry,' Daniel said, swivelling the lamp to shine back upon the desk. 'Don't like it too bright in here, as you know, but…'

'Then why have it so fucking dark you fool?' Amanda Burley's face came in view, her nose twitching and her dark eyes scornful and evil against the shadows. 'Why not put on the main light?'

'Coz, I don't like to see…' Daniel paused, pulling the hood of his fleece over his head, adjusting it to hide the left side of his face. 'Hate strangers seeing my face… their disgust.'

'But Mr Whittaker, I'm no stranger?' Amanda slithered her way towards the desk, pushing away Daniel's hood before propping herself up against the desk, her buttocks pressed against the edge. 'You've been in my hands now for… hmmm, how long?'

'Don't do that!' Daniel snarled, replacing the hood. 'Yes, lady… Miss Burley, you may know me, but that's no excuse to play –'

'But who's the beauty and who be the beast, Mr Whittaker?' Amanda interrupted, her lean legs taut as they crossed, her dark tights stretching her black, short skirt at the thigh. She watched him glance at her keenly, knowing how this forty-year-old woman could still arouse such men. But as she knew, Daniel was far than some gentleman. 'But isn't it news you seek Daniel, not pleasure?'

Again he scrutinised her up and down, her slender figure somewhat alluring in such office attire, but he was busy and snuffed aloud. 'I'm busy, can't you see?'

'Yes, with this crap again,' she ridiculed, moving the lamp aside to shuffle her hands through paperwork. She picked up one flimsy folder to examine its contents. 'And yet you learn nothing more. The doctor's notes make some sense, but that book… the one with those old drawings…'

'Ancient inscriptions, symbols… hieroglyphics,' Daniel described proud of what he had learned, but suddenly caught onto Amanda's mockery. 'So what makes *you* think you have right to go through this stuff?'

'I'm a reporter aren't I? Well more of practicing lawyer type.' She etched a smile as she placed down the folder. 'And you should be glad that you've got the likes of me, and my friends, to look after your interests.'

'My interests,' he retorted, but concentrated on duties at hand. 'What interests?' Daniel was becoming tense. Was it because Amanda always made him feel nervous, or was it that he was tired and had enough of research for one night? 'Why visit so late Miss Burley… sorry Amanda?' He knew she disliked being so formal. 'Any later and

I'd have bolted the door… not just locked it by remote.' Daniel sat astute in his armchair with arms folded to give her his full attention, but was conscious not to reveal his face. 'So what is it that is so important at this hour? Could you not come earlier?'

'I do have many other engagements my dear Daniel,' she remarked, pacing around the desk to stand tall in front. He could now see how aged her face looked against bright light and that her dark hair looked somewhat bedraggled with hints of grey. 'So I rushed to see you as best I could. It's a fare distance between my country house and this city you know.'

'So what is it you have to tell,' he sniggered whilst trying to continue, 'before you have to get back before the ball ends… and you're carriage becomes some pumpkin?'

'Ha, ha, very funny,' she amused, 'for you that's quite good. This research must be paying off… academically that is.' Amanda glanced down to notice Daniel stare back up at her, part of his disfigured face exposed from underneath the hood. A lump clogged her throat; his disfigured face looked more grotesque in such light. She turned away to scan documents littering the desk. Clearing her throat, she began to reveal her news.

'Well, let's see…' she paused, biting the end of a pen and staring at the ceiling to concentrate. 'Your friend Miss Layton, Sarah Layton, of who you have such a close relationship.' Daniel knew Amanda always took a sarcastic approach when disclosing important information. 'Well now, how do I put it… after all that I, and such powers I control, have done to ensure your friend stays under lock and key, we may now have a problem?'

'Problem,' Daniel snapped. 'What type of problem?'

'Let's put it simply now shall we?' her voice slowed. 'She has another re-trial.'

'But she's had one before and we've dealt with it?'

'I've dealt with it you mean?'

Daniel looked again at the research, thinking her news nothing special.

'But according to influential friends I've spoken with,' Amanda continued with vigour, 'Sarah is now to plead self-defence. And with new methods that give technological evidence, along with a different and unflavoured jury, well she could –'

'How could she?' he interjected. 'It is the truth, as I told you before. But how such a ridiculous story sounds to any jury, must prevent any chance of...'

'But self-defence is different,' she snapped, 'especially after all the time she has spent inside... and with good merit to her name?'

'But she plunged the knife into my...'

'*She* plunged the knife?' Amanda disputed. 'Not some powerful force?'

'It happened. I know it did. You know it did!' His anger was becoming evident. 'But it was her story, not mine... and it got her banged away... I was the poor bastard that suffered!'

'So how did a knife in your chest get you so,' Amanda paused to reflect on such a sensitive matter, 'receive such crippling injuries?'

'You know how, I've told you before!' he snapped, but stuttered his words, trying to continue. 'Some bright power twisted my wrist, pushed at my own hand clenching the knife... but not just that... that power threw me back against the wall, amongst the cupboards, the book cabinets...'

'And that crushed you enough to...?'

'No they were forced upon me,' he said, his eyes rolling with bewilderment. 'The furniture crushed me like I was some insect. A power even *she* could never have...'

'But I guess the defence will premise that.'

'Do what?' Daniel asked.

'People provoked to such extremes, can do such unbelievable acts.'

'Move heavy furniture from yards away?' he derided frantically. 'Push it enough to tip over on a man?'

'Well not, maybe not that, but...' Amanda looked to the floor, bemused.

'It's not that Sarah, I got to worry about anyhow?'

'Oh no, and then who?'

'You'll think it ridiculous. But call it a hunch,' Daniel said, his hands outspread to stipulate the doctor's research, 'but according to all this, the first thing I learned years back, was about three powers of good… that if combined, could combat the evil he summoned…' Daniel began to stutter. 'I believe it could defeat a physical attack as well as something –'

'Wait there just a minute,' Amanda stressed. 'Are you telling me to believe that three little babies could, I mean, that they inflicted such damage to you in order to protect their mother?' Amanda paused as a chill overcame her. 'So Mr Whittaker, you didn't go to kill Sarah but her…' Amanda covered her mouth; for once she was stuck for words.

'Miss Burley, some things are worth the risk,' Daniel defined, breaking an uneasy silence between them, 'especially if you're put in my shoes. This is not simply revenge, but a chance to master an absolute power… to reunite the dark coven… maybe perform tasks that go further than wheeling a bloody wheelchair about.'

'Sorry Daniel,' Amanda stated, pausing to show pity, or was it the shock to his recent confession, 'but surely no power can grant miracles.' She tried best to avoid discussing his disability, focusing more on her own interest. 'But if you find such power, I'd be –'

'Interested?' Daniel interjected, slamming his palms down upon the large book. 'But woman, you've seen the doctor's power?'

'No, Daniel, I did not,' she disputed, neglecting the fact that she had indulged in such sexual depravity. 'All I saw was some stupid pendant and the fact that Doctor Schroeck had fraudulent wealth, had influence on high cliental in society, and ran some perverse astrological society.'

'No, you stupid woman,' he snarled, 'if you read the doctor's notes and study this book, you'd see an old ritual to the Black Art; a ceremony of blood sacrifice that he learned from those strange islands in the West Indies. Some members of the old secret occult communion contested his powers, and guess what happened to them?'

Amanda's thoughts snapped back from the sin she had engrossed in all those years back, 'They got killed?'

'Not just killed woman, but torn apart.' Amanda chilled to the glare in Daniel's eye. 'Evil spirits summoned to do one's bidding.'

'And it's all in there?' Amanda's curiosity came from a new height. 'All that the doctor did... what you've learned... it's all ready to pay off?'

'No, not fully,' he stated, taking a moment to reflect. 'Remember what happened to the doctor?'

'Burned to death... trying to escape the fire in his mansion.'

'No, he was fine when he stepped outside.'

'Then, what happened...?'

'Haven't I told this before?'

'No Mr Whittaker, you always get... side tracked?'

Daniel looked perplexed, trying to recall if had indeed told the full story. And then he studied Amanda's face to see if he had her attention.

'With the spell contained in the pendant broken, and being the conjurer, the doctor's blood had been spilt to summon evil. That's why he...' Daniel paused to reflect on his master's work. 'But now, after studying all this, I'm sure that I'm onto something... a way to summon the evil by bloodletting, as the doctor did, but protect oneself so –'

'So it doesn't take *you* instead?'

'Yes, exactly,' he replied, staring hard into one dark corner, envisaging the doctor's burnt corpse.

'But how do you make such dark and evil powers do your bidding?'

'I'm not sure,' he admitted, 'but it has something to do with the incantation... the doctor was working on cursing a victim's personal belongings to get them –'

'Killed?' Amanda interrupted, but paused to raise her own acuity, 'Like putting pins in a voodoo doll?' She looked uneasy, her forehead furrowed against the light. 'But did he get this to work?'

'I've not discovered anything yet that suggests he did,' Daniel slumped to admit. 'But a lot of this has yet to be...' He opened his hands. 'And I'm not entirely the best person, even after all this time.'

Amanda stooped over the desk, inquisitive to the drawings in the large book, but noticed her host become intimidated.

'What's the matter?' Amanda moved away to one side, watching her host reach across the desk.

'Get me those tablets would you, woman,' he said grimacing, 'this fucking pain has come back.'

Retrieving a plastic container from beneath books, Amanda handed it gingerly to her host, surprised at how the cripple snatched it so discourteously. She stepped back to watch Daniel quickly load his mouth with a number of pills and then pull out a bottle from a nearby draw. But as she observed this was something a little stronger than water. After screwing the top back onto the small whisky bottle, he slammed it back into the drawer and glanced up at her.

'Don't look so surprised,' he whinged, 'I haven't got a spinal injection 'til next month.' Detested at how her face revealed pity, he barked out instruction. 'Make yourself useful while y' here… get that book from over there… the one with dark green binding.' He watched as Amanda pointed out the books, until a final nod of his head. 'Bring it here… look at the page marked.'

Amanda placed the book on the desk, but stood tall, wanting to change the subject. 'Look, Daniel, I came here tonight to go over Sarah's retrial… how to approach it, contest this new technology and the evidence it brings, maybe see what friends of ours can help to –'

'But I leave *that* in your capable hands,' he interrupted, 'I'm sure what I pay you is quite adequate?'

'But should Sarah receive bail… or get acquitted… then what?'

'It's not Sarah to whom I am concerned.'

'But what if she seeks revenge,' Amanda questioned vigorously, 'hires someone or tries to get back at you herself?'

'Then why, woman,' Daniel's tone rose to a new sharp level, 'do you think I have researched all this?' Amanda silenced to listen to her host's slow revelation. 'Yes I seek revenge although I believe Sarah was not wilfully the culprit. But to do any of this… to master this great and dark power, as did the doctor years back… repercussions have to be avoided… hopefully eliminated.'

'Then avoid doing all this, don't get involved and you won't be harmed?'

'But the power of this does not just avenge, but gives wealth… you've seen yourself what the doctor had. And besides… what choice have I stuck in this fucking wheelchair?'

Amanda had lost her fortitude to contest Daniel's deluded mind, but had to put one last question to him.

'So what's stopping you from becoming this master of the Black Arts… a practitioner as powerful, if not more powerful, than the doctor?'

'Three witches of Mother Nature.' Daniel wriggled in this wheelchair and squinted, watching Amanda's face expand with surprise. 'The last of the doctor's research continually reverts back to old folklore… animals in the Far East that hold secret powers that can combat the evil of man… powers, if combined, can negate such invocations of evil, and…' Daniel held up his unmarked hand and outstretched his forefinger to stipulate his point, 'can cause disastrous repercussions for the practitioner… maybe such virtuous and holy powers have no pity to inflict death on one whom…'

Amanda was confused, her speech wanting to deliver many questions, but her mind contemplating what to ask.

'I know that the doctor was well educated, well actually very intellectual… and quite convincing, but…' Amanda paused in her interruption, again considering her question. 'But what animal, or beast upon this planet, could be noble enough to work magic against such dark forces?'

Daniel smiled and requested her to open the book she had previously placed on the desk.

'Open the book at the page marked,' Daniel requested. 'It's all there about the three animals, or noble beasts as you described them.' He frowned, his voice conveying confusion. 'So close to humans, but I have no clue to their relation to witches.'

Amanda fingered to the pages embedding a bookmark and opened the page under a long fingernail.

Her laugh was the first thing that startled Daniel. And as she muffled her mouth with fingers, she glanced from the page to see Daniel stare hard at her. She looked down again in disbelief.

Sketched in dark ink were three monkeys: like her, the one to the right was covering its mouth with its hands. The middle one covered a hand over each ear, whilst the first covered each eye with a hand.

'But these are the Three Wise Monkeys?' Amanda derided between her chuckles. 'These have nothing to do with witches, let alone oppose dark forces of the Black Art?'

'Do they not?' Daniel said, knowing something she did not. 'It is not what they are, but what they do?'

Amanda stood amazed, her hands now fingering the page, her mouth slightly agape. And then she read aloud what was inscribed above the illustration.

'That into the good of man, one shall: See No Evil, Hear No Evil, or Speak of No Evil.'

FOUR

Emily looked up from the documents scattering the left of her keyboard to notice her friend Angela busy at the end of the office. Puzzled to what she was doing, Emily frowned, but gazed back at the computer screen.

Having lots of articles to draft before implementation, she knew how much she was behind already. And the editor would obviously have to pass them before she could assign any for publication. A number of clients were now becoming pedantic, nuisances who wanted articles neat and accurate, but still requiring her personal flare to outsmart competitors.

She was proficient and intricate with the design software, but first it needed a basic draft, based on the correct facts and background story. Although she could skilfully elaborate on words for optimum effect, this was nothing without hard evidence. It was the research she hated, always getting headaches in times like this.

Angela Nielson was different. Her friend had graduated in law and had employed research through years on her degree. But Emily knew she had been appointed by soft option. Mike had put her name forward, and although he worked for the company no longer, he was still quite an influential figure. Plus, he had helped in many more ways than just adoption; helping with swimming lessons, homework, talking about friends, and once protecting her from that troublesome boy from the class a year above. Sarah said Mike was different to Carl – her true, biological father, and as friends, she wondered to how they got on, worked together on the computers back then? How did they get into the journalism business? Mike had always described Carl as a natural talent working with computers. Some of it, Emily thought, she had inherited, but obviously not all.

Maybe she took too much of a brash attitude when it came to computers, not focusing enough on training workshops, using visits to external agencies as an excuse to escape work. Or was Angela a bad influence, wanting to check out other office talent? Indeed the last guy, visiting from the local university to train them about 'typography and graphics' had been, how did Angela describe – a hot dish?

Emily eluded thoughts about her social life, knowing she needed to concentrate on her current workload: one murder investigation for a local newspaper, several fashion show reports that now awaited photographs and a ghost-hunters explicit for a magazine – one she thought as an excuse to expose a fake psychic, or was it some magician? Luckily she had worked late last night, completing most of the fashion reports, again her swimming having to wait. The ghost-hunters research was done at home. Strangely this was something she felt quite enthralling – better than reading that new novel before bed.

However, the murder investigation, she had not even started the research? Only glancing over what she had been given, making sure the email included all enlisted. She bit the end of her pen, thinking of how much another coffee was going to necessary.

Emily got up, dispensed a coffee from a local drinks machine and headed back to her desk. Looking back over her shoulder, she pondered to why Angela scampered about like some startled mouse.

'Watch where you're going young lady!' a stern voice yelled.

With hot liquid almost scolding her chest, Emily did not see the woman who had bumped her.

'What the…' Emily gritted her teeth to prevent her from swearing. 'Sorry, but… what the… well you could at least…?'

Emily watched in disbelief as a slim, middle-aged woman in dark office attire paced astutely down the corridor, not once looking back to apologise. She swore under her breath and cricked her neck to look down at her coffee-stained blouse.

'Fucking bitch!' she moaned, putting down the cup of hot liquid, 'Best one on today… had to be didn't it… not the old pastel blue?'

Angrily she strode off to the ladies toilet, only to be joined by her friend Angela.

'What's happened to you?' Angela asked peering at Emily's half open blouse. 'Being eyeing up the new guy who writes those sports columns?'

'No, some fucking bitch bumped me on the way to my desk,' she replied, rubbing wetted kitchen towels against her stained blouse. 'But best of it, I apologised, but she never did.' Again Emily swore to release her frustration.

'Was it some dark-haired woman, slim… about forty?'

'Yes, something like that.'

'Had a robust walk, as if posing down a catwalk?'

'Yes, that's the one… most definitely.'

'Well,' Angela disclosed, sliding around to face Emily, her back against the washroom mirror, 'that'll be the woman for interview.' She paused, watching how Emily's face screwed up with displeasure. 'I know coz I served refreshments in the boardroom… tea, coffee… biscuits and such like.'

'Don't make me anymore angry,' Emily snapped. 'But an interview you say?'

'Well I guess it's been hushed up a bit,' Angela studied Emily through the mirror, 'but it's about new management.'

'I've not heard anything about job recruitment,' Emily quizzed, her eyes narrowing to show contempt. 'Not that the likes of us would hear anything about it!'

'Miss Burley, her name,' Angela revealed, blinking profusely as she always did when revealing secret information. 'I didn't get her first name though.' Whilst watching Emily rub more her blouse, she beckoned. 'Looks good for her age, don't you think?'

'So how come you know so much about that bitch?' Emily questioned, now examining to see if coffee had strained her bra. 'Hope she'll not work here. I'll rather quit than work under the likes –'

'But Ems, you shouldn't hold a grudge against anyone 'til y' know them?'

'I don't care,' she snarled, looking to see if her blouse reflected any stains in the mirror. 'I have a bad feeling about her. Don't ask me why, but… call it my…'

'Second sight again… those visions?' Angela interjected, her eyes rolling behind round spectacles, her auburn hair falling to one side as she tilted her head.

'Instinct my friend, call it intuition if you may?'

'All that again,' Angela ridiculed softly. 'You want to concentrate more on hard facts to get your stories out. Aren't you behind?'

'I worked most the evening last night... missed my swim.' Emily turned her eyes from her reflection to look directly at her friend. 'But you'll help today, won't you?'

'I guess so, but later.' Angela glanced at her wristwatch. 'Shit, I'd better get back in there after the interview... I've been asked to clean up!'

'And do something else for me, won't you Ange?'

'What's that?' she asked, seeing a smirk come on Emily's face.

'Pour some hot fucking coffee over that bitch before she leaves?'

'As I told you Ems... bad vibes... you shouldn't hold a grudge.' Angela turned to wink before exiting the washroom. 'It was probably just an accident. Being so busy, we get them all the while in this place.'

'Okay Ange, I retract about pouring coffee over her smart head.' Emily grinned as she tided her blouse. 'But do try and get her first name, eh? It'll be good to know what new boss we might have.'

With light reflecting against her spectacles, Emily did not notice Angela's eyebrows rise slowly before she disappeared from the washroom.

Emily looked back to her reflection in the mirror and contemplated. Was she really developing some nasty streak, or was it just an everyday accident on which she was overreacting? But maybe it *was* something more? Reactions were part of that uncontrollable anger that made her nose bleed... those dizzy spells that only Angela knew about? But to things like this, she had reacted on instinct in the past, and generally, she was never far wrong.

Angela scuttled up between the isle that segregated workstations and peered over the partition to Emily's desk. At first she was oblivious to Angela's announcement, having research on mind as well as brooding to how different her friend looked without spectacles.

'Her name is Burley!' Angela disclosed in an exaggerated whisper.

'What,' Emily frowned, nudging close to hear.

'That woman in the interview,' Angela stated, leaning against the partition to repeat. 'Her name is Burley!'

Angela watched as Emily clicked to expand another window on the computer screen. Quickly into a search on a social media website, Emily typed the surname incorrectly.

'No not Barley,' she rectified. 'Burley... Amanda *Burley*!'

As Emily corrected the misspelt surname and conducted a search, Angela announced her request to have no involvement in such an affair. But as Emily scrolled down, examining profile after profile, Angela glanced quickly at the screen.

'But Ems, my guess is she's not like us.'

'What you mean?' Emily concentrated on the screen, scrolling as fast as she could but not missing a picture.

'Maybe she's an age that doesn't use social media?' Angela supposed, viewing nervously the people in work before placing the tray on the corner of the partition. 'Probably doesn't use computer stuff like us either.'

'Of course she would,' Emily corrected, 'managerial job here, well, she's got to know...?'

Realising that her search had been unsuccessful, Emily glanced over to the director and manager's office, and finding them empty, smiled mischievously. She glanced at Angela and grabbed the coffee jug from the tray. After filling quickly her half empty cup with replacement liquid, she returned it before typing quickly into another search.

'You're not supposed to use that one for private stuff,' Angela warned, her face flustered. 'The auditors can trace such like through that search.'

'But what do they know which is company research and what is private?' Emily sipped at the replenished hot liquid. 'Besides this page lists only historic articles... stories that have been reported by us or some other...'

'What is it?' Angela asked, wondering to why Emily stopped talking.

'Hey, this one looks top.' Angela knew Emily's extravagant use of words initiated that she had found something interesting. Or was it something she was not supposed to?

'I've got to get this stuff back to the staffroom,' Angela stuttered, pointing her thumb back over her shoulder. Covertly, she did not want any involvement with misconduct at work, the money meant far too much now that her boyfriend had been made redundant. 'Besides it's all got to be washed, dried and put away.'

'But look,' Emily announced her interest following another click of the computer mouse, 'there's a story that refers to that woman here.'

'Sorry Ems, but there's cups to do from this morning,' Angela's voice trailed off along the office corridor. 'Besides, how can you know it's the right woman?'

Emily browsed with overwhelming interest, a personal vendetta grasping hold of her. She had sifted through countless sites before, but this was research on a different level. As online connections came ever more personal, she could feel something turn over her stomach, her hands were twitching, her eyes dry and sore. And there it was.

As she clicked on one hyperlink, she was confronted with the past. It shot through her like a bullet. Why had she not thought of this before? Why had she not researched about her real father's death, or to how her mother had really got stitched and banged up in some institution for the criminally insane?

But there it was now. A webpage detailing a report following the case of a Daniel Whittaker: an already disfigured and scarred individual, prosecuting a Sarah Layton for grievance bodily damage. Emily read on, her blood hastened by the bias of the report, published by this woman, Amanda Burley.

On confrontation with Mr Whittaker visiting Miss Layton's home on goodwill, and taking into consideration the unfortunate visual disfigurement of the defendant, Mr Whittaker was attacked and suffered knife wounds and was crushed by heavy furniture. This unscrupulous deed was obviously instigated by Mr Whittaker's unfortunate appearance, but was carried out with immense strength and vigour by the accused. Having admitted such a delusive statement and admitting uncontrollable anger, the accused has been proved to have such irrational violence, to leave the defendant paralysed and confined to a wheelchair.

Emily's hand trembled to the fact that the woman she had just bumped, had but twenty years ago, expertly exaggerated the facts to ridicule and dishonour her mother, enough to convict her for what Emily had all along deemed as self-defence. But now they had new technological methods. And providing Sarah changed her statement, revised evidence could retrial her mother and so get her acquitted?

Nonetheless, this could not hide the fact that her biological mother had been put away almost all of Emily's life. She was not able to visit Sarah but after work, sacrificed her social life and had to rearrange other commitments to be with her. And gone were her so-called sisters; split from birth because all of this.

Emily sifted through the web pages she had opened in other windows, closing irrelevant ones, but sending all to print which she thought relevant.

Unaware, someone behind was watching. Fortunately, it was only a colleague, but one full of anxiety.

'You can't print all that,' Angela stuttered, clearly fretful. 'Those might get picked up by one of the managers?'

At first Emily's heart jumped, and then she recognised the distraught voice.

'Relax, there all out... the director and such like.' Emily knew inside that her quaking had not just come from being startled by her friend, but her blood boiled from rage. And it was soon unleashed.

'Where's that woman?' Emily stood, her face flushed and eyes wide with anger.

'Who,' Angela questioned, her voice quieting after seeing Emily's wrath. 'You mean the woman for interview?' She paused to swallow hard. 'That woman named Amanda... Miss Burley?'

'Yes,' Emily demanded, her body stiff, 'this Miss Burley... where is she now?'

'She's just finished interviewing,' Angela stated slowly. 'She'll be leaving soon know doubt?'

'Then I'd better get after the bitch.' Emily marched around her friend but felt a restraint on her arm.

'Don't get causing trouble Ems,' Angela affirmed gripping her arm. 'Please we don't need any trouble.'

Snatching away Angela's wrist, Emily strode in direction of the boardroom, her friend left bewildered and flexing her stiff fingers in pain.

'Oh, in a rush somewhere, Emily?' a voice asked, a small, plump body blocking her way to the boardroom.

'I... I just got to go...' Emily pondered on her excuse, 'toilet sir.'

The editor's face calmed from agitation to a friendly smile before acknowledgment procured a different expression.

'Funny coincidence,' the editor said, fingering the last strands of hair to conceal his balding forehead. 'Strange really, but...' He conveyed a more direct explanation after seeing Emily restless. 'The lady I've just interviewed... she knew something of your father... your late father that is... Carl Aston?' The editor stepped back, not sure if Emily's eyes regarded him with curiosity or malice. 'A Miss Burley... Amanda Burley? She came to interview and knew something of him.' He took another step back as Emily stood over his stumpy body. 'I guess she'd know Mike as well, your –'

'Where is she now?' Emily interrupted, peering down at him with an uncomfortable stare he had never seen from her before.

'The interview finished five minutes ago, so I guess,' he took stance, remembering his authority, 'so I guess that she would be heading home, or at least back to her other...' His unfinished sentence came from watching Emily shoot down the corridor to the end of the office.

Emily marched through the heavy fire doors, not knowing that they fell back into Angela, who was hot on her heels in pursuit. Emily stood at the top of the staircase, clenching the handrail to peer out the window and into the car park below. Emily caught sight of Amanda as she made her way to her car. *There she is the smug bitch*, Emily despised. *She's too old to flaunt that sexy figure, but swaggering her way... to what? Nice car you bitch. Bet you've not paid for that!* Emily noticed Amanda press the mobile alarm to her car, the indicator lights flashing as she heard a short, sharp bleep. *Fucking see that you'll suffer someday bitch,* Emily cursed, *like my mother has for all these years. Call that justice?*

Emily's sight of Amanda was wavering, as if a shimmering heat had descended on the car park outside. As the woman strode provocatively to her car, a bright light filled Emily's vision. And although she could see her surroundings in the haze, another vision was emerging. She held tight onto the handrail, her breathing now heavy, waiting for the unsteady feeling to subside. Once more her legs grew weak, her body a sway. She fought against the tumbling sensation, but how long could she last? Again she felt that tingling sensation before the onslaught of heat, and wished that soon it would pass. But that was not to be. As an image came distinct through bright light, all she could do was hold on and grip her clammy hands as tight as possible onto the handrail.

There she was; the vision of a little girl at a party, pulling down balloons that celebrated someone's birthday. And although she felt happy, she wanted more. She shook the long curls of her dark hair, determined not to let go, but felt hands all over her. She grasped at the two balloons, her little, clammy hands gripping the stretched surface. And although she hated the rubbery sensation, she would not let go. Closer to her chest she hugged the balloons, not letting them be taken by the other hands.

And then a sudden, bright light erupted; a sensation that exploited her vision and tensed her body. Within the eerie silence of her vision, she sensed the most deafening explosion, each balloon bursting simultaneously, the tight release of compressed air caught only by imagination. But unlike the instant escape of air, the envisaged sound continued. Until that is, something else disturbed her senses.

Angela held Emily as steady as she could. She did not want to slap her friend across the face, but knew it was necessary; it had worked successfully once before. But what troubled Angela this time was to how rigid her friend had become, how Emily's eyes had opened so wide, enlarged pupils staring into oblivion. It scared her to lash out, but like before, it had worked.

'Emily,' Angela cried, 'Emily, are you alright?' Still Emily swayed uneasy like a ragdoll under her grip. 'I heard some noise out there and then you were like this?'

Angela shook her friend, trying best to revive her from her dizzy spell. Once Emily's hands had released their grip from the handrail, Angela carefully sat her down. As Emily's legs collapsed from underneath her, Angela tilted her body to lean against the wall, some distance away from the stairs. Asking repeatedly if her friend was all right, Angela cupped Emily's head, gleeful to notice her senses return. At first Angela watched her head straighten, but then after her eyes focused, a word slurred from Emily's mouth.

'What happened...? I... I heard an explosion... exploding gas... air?'

'It's okay now, Ems,' Angela affirmed, but came puzzled to Emily's description.

'I was holding them, as if in control,' Emily's eyes still wondered, trying to gather focus. 'Then some sudden explosion.'

'It came from outside,' Angela suggested, standing to take look.

'No, it was the balloons,' Emily stated, her pale face still expressing uncertainty, 'they exploded.'

'No, I'm sure it came from outside,' Angela reaffirmed, returning to kneel close to support Emily's shoulder. 'Anyway that's irrelevant. Are you okay?' Angela noticed that Emily had taken focus on her. 'Gave me quite a scare there my girl... being at the top of the stairs and...' Abruptly Angela stopped talking to notice a stream of blood escape Emily's nostril and run close to her mouth. 'Ems, your nose is bleeding. That happened last time, didn't it?'

Emily raised her still unsteady hand and fingered clumsily her mouth. She brushed her top lip with her forefinger and gazed down with still bleary eyes. Blood smeared her finger and extended across her hand. She looked ungainly at her friend.

'What's happened Ange?' Emily slumped back, kicking out her legs beneath her. 'Did I pass out again?'

'Yes, but we had best not let...' Angela glanced around, hoping nobody had seen them. 'Let's get you to the washroom again. Already stained y' shirt with coffee... don't want blood on it too.'

Angela helped Emily to her feet and although unsteady at first, they paced slowly to the washroom, hoping nobody in the office would notice.

'If you ask me,' Angela tried best to comfort her friend, 'I think you've stressed yourself over this woman. I know it's about your mother but, can't you let it go... for now at least?'

'But that woman helped send my mother away.' Again Emily stopped to finger her nose for signs of blood. 'She helped get her banged away in that...'

'Your mother got sent there because she tried to kill a man.' Angela interjected without thinking.

'It was self-defence!' Emily snapped, pulling away to check for more blood.

'Sorry, Ems, but it's not what I heard, and the court ruling was... as you know?'

'If you don't want to help, then don't,' Emily snapped, distraught to see more blood on her finger. She paced toward the washroom but stopped. Turning slowly to acknowledge her friend, Emily conveyed her appreciation. 'Thanks for what you did back there, but I'm going to get my mother out, even if I do it alone.'

'Look, I'm sorry that you're like this,' Angela said taking a step toward her, 'but if those things keep happening, don't you think you should...'

'I'll be alright,' Emily asserted, opening the washroom door.

Cautiously Angela followed her friend. Surely they had to talk things over as Emily was one of her closest friends.

FIVE

EMILY WAS OBLIVIOUS TO THE cars racing past, but knew the street was littered with people, some engrossed in conversation, others alone and like her, probably using their lunchtime to escape work or browse shops. Hunched forward with elbows on knees, she sat staring at the cracks in the pavement below, her mind elsewhere. What was this vision she had? Why was she at a party? And to what significance were the balloons? Her mind throbbed to the roar of the explosion and remembering the consequences, she touched her nose. No blood.

Actually it was Angela's idea to get some fresh air, sit on a park bench to eat lunch. Her friend had made the excuse that it would do Emily good, but perhaps Emily's little scare had frightened Angela a little too much. She looked up, observing to how the light blue, early autumn sky had overcast, and although a hazy sun burned through thin cloud to give warmth, Emily chilled to the cold breeze that had stirred since morning. But it was something to expect now, she thought. Since Monday, she had felt the change. Not just the temperature, but also some grasping cold that she could taste in the air. And again it would be here tonight, and next morning, the days becoming shorter and probably more dismal. For a moment she studied the row of shops opposite, cars and people – nothing but shapes in motion.

She glanced at her friend sitting alongside. Angela too, was silent in thought. Parts of her long, auburn hair shone a sandy colour in the daylight, her plump body looking even more cumbersome as she sat eating. And without her spectacles, Emily regarded her different, a spoilt schoolgirl lacking etiquette and decorum. But she was her friend and probably the closest Emily had.

'Look, I'm real sorry you know,' Emily cleared her throat. 'What happened in there is something I don't want to happen again.' She paused to see Angela face her. 'But I don't want doctor's involved... not until I can't handle things myself.'

'I understand,' Angela acknowledged. 'I promised last time, didn't I?' Angela recognised Emily's inner smile behind her taut lips. 'But maybe you should get away a bit... you know from work...' Angela watched in disgust as a drunken tramp mouthed obscenities to the car that braked to avoid him. 'Maybe get away from this place? I'm getting to hate this area.'

'It's not that bad really,' Emily muttered, 'there are lots of memories here, places to see, and places to eat, drink... with friends like you?' Emily paused to reflect on other responsibilities. 'Besides, I have a commitment.'

'Yes, your mother,' Angela identified, trying not to interject sarcasm. 'Maybe that's why you need to get away from here... well at least for a while.'

'Not at the moment,' Emily stated, commandingly. 'Like I said, mother has a chance to get acquitted and I've got to be here for that. Besides, even though it sounds sad, that crap at work, it helps me forget about all the other stuff.'

'Well what about those sisters you had,' Angela knew she stepped on coals with this subject, but munched away on crisps, unperturbed. 'Where are they? Do they not have any duty to your mother... or want to find out who she is?'

'We were separated after what happened,' Emily restrained her annoyance. 'You know that.' She pondered upon her mother's constant wish. 'Why should it be me that finds them? I'm only the oldest yes, but only by minutes?' She glanced over her shoulder, back at the office building. 'Besides, I've got to keep this job... it's shit at times but... well, Mike got it me and.'

'I've got no sisters,' Angela slurred, washing down crisps with coffee. 'No brothers either... and I get by?'

'Yes, but you got Josh? And he's more understanding than most.'

'Then, maybe, Miss Layton-Aston, you should find yourself a partner... a husband?' Angela rolled her eyes. 'Find that special boyfriend you've dreamed of?'

'That type is not around here,' Emily stated with scepticism, eyeing the passers-by, 'that type of guy is met on holidays and such like, not a place...' Emily paused to question the conversation. 'Is that why you've bought me out here, to lecturer me about boyfriends again?'

'I bought you out here to get lunch, remember?' Angela was resolute, but agitated at trying to find a lighter. 'Settle that mind of yours. Relax by having some fresh air.'

Emily watched Angela light the end of a cigarette, short bursts of smoke taking to the air after one long inhalation.

'That's a funny way of having some fresh air?' Emily prompted.

'Well I find it calms my nerves, especially when I've got to look after friends and so forth.' Angela smiled to convey her cynicism as friendly banter. 'God knows what my friend would've done to that poor woman should she have got hold of her?' Angela puffed away, her subtly subsiding. 'Making yourself a right idiot in front of everyone by having funny turns in the office... just to get sympathy off the boys.' Angela glanced at Emily, first her mind in alternative thought, but now curious to what her friend had in hand. 'On the other hand... that might be a good...'

At first, Emily etched around the edges of the large sketchpad, the pencil at a slant and being sharpened by her shading effects. 'I've got other methods to relax,' but suddenly Emily froze as if recalling some unnerving, past event, 'even if at sometimes... even I frighten myself.'

'You'd be better off having some drags off this, than doodling on that thing.'

'But I haven't had one of those since...' Emily looked to the floor in thought.

'Then maybe it'll help?'

'No, those things make me go giddy, and you know what happens...'

'Yes, maybe at first, but... not like, well maybe it'll calm your nerves.' Angela swapped the pencil for her half-used cigarette and at first Emily just sat and watched it burn. 'It'll be out soon, so a few puffs won't hurt you.' Angela stooped down to look into Emily's face. 'I'll help with stuff this afternoon... I promise... and maybe 'til late. I haven't got to meet Josh 'til late anyhow.'

'Don't want to start up again do I?'

'I guarantee you don't.' Angela increased her concern. 'But after what you're going through, with work and y' mother, well...?'

Emily hesitated, the smell intoxicating but somehow enticing, the smoke stinging her eyes. Maybe it was its aroma after drinking coffee... the mustard on the ham roll?

'What the hell.' Emily swapped the cigarette to her left hand, and taking the pencil with her right, took slow, careful inhalations.

Initially the smoke scathed her nostrils and throat, but then as the bitter taste subsided, it transformed into something more soothing. Her eyes grew wide as her body tensed, and for a moment that fearful sensation returned. But soon she felt relaxed, maybe too much. A peculiar feeling came over Emily, but there was no resentment, no animosity. Slowly Emily began to draw.

Angela talked as Emily drew; reminiscing the last time she and Josh had dined together. It was not until Angela saw that the cigarette had burned away, that she paused to remove it from Emily's fingers. After Angela's enquiries to Emily's welfare were flouted, she stooped to look up at her friend's face.

Emily's face was placid and pale, her eyes wide but unfocused, as if not seeing what she was drawing. And as Angela discarded the burned out cigarette, she gazed upon Emily's sketchpad. The pencil flew back and forth across the page so fast it was as if it was in control; that some unnatural force was guiding Emily's hand.

For a long minute, Angela sat in disbelief, pondering on whether to grasp Emily's hand; she had never seen Emily draw like this in all the years they had been friends. Watching in bewilderment to how quick a drawing developed below Emily's fingers, Angela sat transfixed. But now she noticed small beads of perspiration appear around Emily's dark hairline, that her nose and cheeks became shiny pale. Thinking back to how Emily was just hours before, Angela panicked and clasped at Emily's drawing hand.

At first Emily did not flinch, her hand cold, still and limp, only clamminess felt about the palm. Softly Angela enquired if Emily was all right, but without response she took the sketchpad, watching Emily's hands fall loose between her legs.

'Ems, that's uncanny.' Angela stretched her arms out to look at the picture from a distance. 'God you must of only seen her for a second, but the looks are uncanny. It's that Amanda, right... the one who came for interview?' Replacing her spectacles, Angela regarded the picture more closely and raised her eyebrows even further. 'I knew you could draw, but my God... that's an uncanny resemblance.'

'Ange, I'm sorry, but I've got that headache again.'

Angela glanced up from admiring the pencil portrait of the woman and looked with concern at her friend. Emily was rubbing her eyes.

'Ems, you're best out here in the fresh air.' Angela now regretted letting Emily finish off her cigarette. 'I'll not have another 'til we finish your stuff later. And we'll just sit for another ten, 'til you get yourself sorted.' But Angela came inquisitive to her friend's unusual talent. 'I didn't know you could draw people... portraits?'

'I can from memory,' Emily was still a little sluggish. 'People from a glance, a dream... people I've not seen before... when I was young I saw faces of men... horrible men with knives.' Her eyes turned to notice the sketchpad Angela held. 'My mother believed I saw murders... the childhood pictures were visions of them... like what my father had.'

'How come you're so good at drawing?' Angela's curiosity to her friend's talent ignored the fact that Emily despised the things she had drawn as a child, that such memories still haunted her. Mike and Rachael had put her talent down to an overzealous imagination, but she had got nosebleeds then. Checking her nose, luckily this time, it was not bleeding. She caught the end of Angela's question, something about school.

'I've been good at art since school; you know that, I told you so.' Emily took the sketchpad from Angela to examine her own handy work. 'And some pictures from the past still haunt me now.'

'How come?'

'Sketches I made were...' Emily shivered; the air a sudden colder. 'Pictures from secondary school, from...' She did not want to recall the blackouts she had back then. 'The visions I had were scenes...'

'You drew scenes... of places in your past?' Angela looked at her expectantly.

'No, things that I believe came true.'

'Like bursting balloons... at that party you pictured?'

'A little more sinister than that, I think.' Emily turned away and placed the sketchpad into her handbag. She wanted to discard the past, forget her mother's suggestions to why she had such talent. Quickly she gulped down the last of her coffee. Sadly it was cold.

'I wonder if y' sisters share such talent?' Emily knew Angela was reflecting upon her artwork, but she shivered again, contemplating to whether triplets did share similar abilities. Did her two other sisters have different talents, have similar interests... in fact, did they even look like her? Surely they must do, she thought. All twins... triplets look the same, don't they?

Angela babbled more questions, but Emily stood up to announce that she was fine. Noticing a jewellery shop across the street, Emily pondered in getting three identical necklaces. Maybe it was hope, something to admit she wanted a reunion. Or was it a way to force her to do this... to finally meet up with her long lost, triplet sisters?

SIX

Quickly Jack followed George into the jewellery shop. He had seen the dark-haired girl browse outside his friend's shop before, but she had never ventured inside. Near the entrance, Jack pulled George back by the arm and pointed with his other hand to the girl in question.

'That's the girl, George,' Jack whispered, watching the girl examine a nearby window display. 'The one I told you about... works in those offices at that freelance journalist place across the road.'

'What the little stumpy one?' George questioned disparagingly, annoyed at being restrained. 'She's cute alright, but a bit short for me.'

After managing to free his arm from Jack's grip, George dashed behind the counter and acknowledged a work colleague, who eyed them curiously.

'No the dark-haired one... slim, but athletic...' Jack winked evidently. 'The one I've been wanting to...' He paused to hear Angela call Emily's name; asking her to look at some other necklaces on display. 'That's a start!'

'What is?' George was still annoyed; he was trying to compose himself for work after their lunch.

'Her name is Emily,' he said quietly. 'Nice name Emily.' Over his shoulder he covertly scrutinised Emily before returning his gaze to George. 'It's nearly as nice as her body, and that pretty face.'

'Look, why don't you just go and ask her out?' George snarled; annoyed to how Jack snubbed the other shop assistant, who was trying to get his attention. Hearing his work colleague's request, George disregarded Jack and turned to him. 'You may go for your lunch now if you wish. I've had mine and I'm back now.'

For a moment George watched his work colleague smile, but then noticed him frown as if troubled.

'George, my friend,' Jack suggested mischievously, 'I've got a better idea.'

Jack tried to join the two shop assistants behind the counter, but the work colleague blocked his way, confessing to George that he had not checked or balanced the till.

'That's all right,' George acknowledged, 'I'll see to it. You just go to lunch.'

'Yes, my friend,' Jack repeated, watching the shop assistant regard him objectionably, obviously annoyed that Jack had no authority. 'You go to lunch. George and I will watch things here.'

Waiting calmly until his work colleague had vacated the shop, George then erupted with frustration.

'What on earth do you think you're doing behind here?'

'You've got to do the till haven't you?' Jack stated. 'I heard your work colleague say?' Again he winked, looking quickly to admire Emily as she moved nearer. 'And you said the boss wasn't due 'til late.'

'That's not the point,' George declared with a hint of scepticism. 'You can't just pretend to be shopkeeper when you feel like it. Besides you do not know what –'

'Can you tell me please,' a voice interrupted. 'There's a crucifix in the window and...'

Emily regarded Jack with suspicion but had to admire the twinkle in his deep blue eyes; somehow they were wide with excitement, but distant and dreamlike. She frowned and turned her attention to George, but Jack nudged his friend aside to stand between their gaze.

'Yes my dear,' Jack intervened, his smile invigorated by Emily's beauty, 'a crucifix in the window you say... you want to... to look at it closer?'

'I'm sorry to ask, but do you work here?' Emily quizzed, observing to how strange a shop assistant should be dressed different, and look so nervous.

'Just started today,' Jack pretended. 'Does she need help too?'

'No, she's like me,' Emily followed Jack's gaze to see Angela point out other items of jewellery. 'We're just browsing really, but I do like one.'

Jack glanced back at George to see him roll his eyes and shake his head, but Jack secretly pleaded with his friend, visibly crossing his fingers and praying in silence beneath the service counter. Again shaking his head, but this time in denial, George handed over a small set of keys.

Like an ecstatic, young child, Jack skipped around George to open the glass window cabinet, but the real shopkeeper whispered stern conditions to end his petty endeavour.

'Watch what you're doing with those Jack. Give them back before you know who returns.'

Jack stopped to listen, but was eager to continue in his task. However, whilst composing himself to approach the girls, he also heard George declare from behind, that item numbers were required to process purchases.

Thrilled but nervous that he had finally found courage to speak to this beautiful, dark-haired girl, Jack strode forward. But taking every step was as if his body had been laden with lead, his knees quivering whilst heavy feet sank into a muddy floor. And finally, as Jack observed Emily close, he stopped to digest the hypnotic beauty of her hazel eyes. Emily's eyes twinkled as they turned to view Angela, her voice sweet but authoritative with her request. Jack shuddered again when Emily fixed gaze with him; her eyes gleaming like dark jewels. Jewels, he thought? Yes, this girl had repeated her request – to examine more closely an item of jewellery – a silver crucifix in fact. But Jack's thoughts were elsewhere.

'Are you listening?' Emily asked, her eyes narrowing. 'Did you hear me?'

'Sorry, yes my dear,' Jack pretended he was attentive. 'Sorry, yes, I was thinking what number it may be.'

'What number it may be?'

'Yes, Miss... the number?' Jack stood close enough to stroke Emily's gorgeous face, some inches below his. 'Yes Miss, you see,' Jack took focus to where Angela was pointing, it being a suitable distraction. 'The necklace you want should have an item number. We need that to do purchase, Miss err?'

'But I want to hold it first... check it over if possible?'

Exhilarated, Jack watched Emily walk over to her friend. She too pointed to the glass cabinet, both of them announcing the number in synchronisation.

Jack ambled forward and fumbled in opening the relevant glass panel. Awkwardly he joked to how each key looked the same (even though they did). But before getting too flustered, luckily one key turned the small metal lock. He reached in and carefully retrieved the necklace, its weight heavy, even for a relatively small piece of silver. He turned to Emily, and finding hidden courage, asked to fix it around her neck.

'No, please, I just want to feel its weight,' Emily requested, a half-smile etched on her face. 'It's not just for me?'

Jack regarded her curiously. This time it was not just to admire her beautiful features. Noticing her soft and delicate fingers spread wide as she reached out, he carefully placed the necklace into the palm of her hand.

'Well, just this one,' Emily rolled her eyes and glanced at Angela before looking back at Jack. 'I want three really, but that's for hope of...' She paused to think. Why reveal her secret desire to such a stranger – a newly appointed shop assistant – even if he was somewhat handsome?

'You want to buy them for friends?' Jack stated, before studying her face more diligently. Obviously if one was for her, then... 'You want one for yourself... and the others are for sisters?' Somehow the inkling had come to Jack. They were not for a mother and grandmother, not for daughters. Bloody hell, he thought, this girl has sisters? Older or younger... surely they must be just as gorgeous?

Jack watched Emily hold high the necklace; twirl it inquisitively about her fingers, observing its reflection in her dark eyes. Angela repeating to shout the item number severed Jack's thoughts. He mused to see Emily feel the weight of its chain against her wrist before offering it back. Like Angela, she announced the jewellery item number, but with a personal tone of interest.

From behind the counter, Jack could feel George's eyes burning into his back. Indeed, his friend had been viewing him from the sales room all the time.

To get any more information other than this beautiful girl's name, he would need her to complete a sales order. Obviously he could try on his charm, but to get a sale, well that was another thing. But one necklace would do it, maybe make the sale of the day, let alone three?

Jack excused himself and took the crucifix necklace to George in the sales room. Unfortunately, after verifying stock, they found that it was the only one available.

'I'm sorry Miss...?'

'Emily.' Knowing that Angela was not far away, her eyes widened with concern. 'Call me Emily. Not that you don't know my name already?' She smiled mischievously as if Jack's true intention had been exposed.

'Yes, Miss... Err, Emily,' Jack smiled, but frowned to reveal his concern. 'This necklace you want is the only one available and it's a show piece.' He detected by her face that the news had saddened her. 'But if you want to order three, we can have them ordered in no time.'

'Can't I just have that one?'

'Sorry, but I've been told it's a show piece.' Suddenly Jack's pretence as a salesman overwhelmed him; he thought now of the big sale. Or was it the strange way this girl injected vitality? 'It's in the window for display only, and you did say you wanted three?'

Emily looked to the ground, momentarily contemplating a decision.

'Simply fill in an order form,' Jack was trying his best sales pitch, but with other intentions in mind, 'provide your email, or best, your mobile number and...' He glanced behind, noticing George busy in the sales room.

Emily's eyes searched the floor until they noticed Angela, who continued to browse the shop. For a while her eyes wondered again about the floor before fixing their gaze upon the order form held in Jack's hand.

'So why display an item if it out of stock?'

'Well, we'll text you,' Jack replied but corrected. 'No sorry, the shop computer, will text you once your stock has arrived.' She stood unconvinced, curling strands of black hair between her fingers. 'It saves having too much jewellery in stock, what with the burglaries we've been having around here lately... you know how it is?' Jack became astonished at his own charade.

'Well it is such a nice piece.' Emily stepped towards Jack but paused to contemplate. 'Ordering three isn't going to be cheap, but...?' Decisively she swiped the order form from Jack's hand and turned to walk off, but stopped halfway, looking back. 'You were right you know,' she stated, 'they are gifts for my sisters, but only if we can hook up sometime?'

Jack stood in silence, only glancing back now and then to monitor where George was. As Emily rifled her handbag for a pen, he became delighted in watching her smile back at him. But then she was writing and so Jack reversed to lean against the counter, admiring to how sensual her legs looked in such a tight skirt. And he was near to completing his task: not only to get her mobile number, and/or email address, but maybe the shop's best sale for the day?

Suddenly Emily felt a nudge.

'Ems, that man,' Angela questioned quietly next to her. 'The one wanting you to purchase that necklace...?'

'What about him?'

'It's just come to me now.'

'What has?'

'He's no shop assistant.'

'No, is he not?' Emily stopped writing, but realised she had almost completed the paper order form. 'Then who is he?'

'I'm sure he's a science lecturer or someone like that... from the university?'

'Is that right?'

Admiring Emily's rear as she talked quietly to her friend, suddenly Jack was jostled.

'Jack, forget what you're doing,' George told, desperation in his voice. 'He's coming back with the boss. I'm sure that bastard has tags on me!'

'But I'm so close to a sale and have nearly –'

'Go now you fool... out the back way.' George stammered, his voice fearful. 'Go now or I could lose my job!'

Jack panicked as he recognised the shop assistant walk in the front door with a fat but astute man – according to his formal dress, clearly this was George's boss. Quickly he made for the rear exit but some dark-haired girl blocked his haste. With the paper order form slapped against his chest, Emily stood angry, her firm hand holding him there.

'Aren't you forgetting something my boy?'

He did not hear her questions – the fright and panic of the situation somewhat capitulated into silence as he adored the sincerity in her eyes. And it was not until he withdrew the form from her fingers that he could escape her gaze – he had never experienced her face being so close – almost near enough to kiss such sweet lips. As he looked down at the form he felt no longer captivated by those hazel eyes, ones adorned by overhead light. He felt the form crumpling in his hand, Emily's soft and delicate fingers now squeezing tight around his.

'Sorry boy, but you make a lousy shopkeeper,' Emily squeezed tighter his hand. 'Maybe you should forget this sale, but...' She paused to smile, as if a totally different character had emerged. 'If you really like me that much, why not just be a man and ask?' She winked as abruptly Angela giggled. 'I might just have given you my number?'

For a minute Jack stood bemused, but looked to his hand as Emily's released her grip. As the two girls backed away to find their way out the shop, Jack peeled open the crumpled order. Indeed, not only an order for three crucifixes, but an email address and mobile number of an Emily Layton-Aston.

Unfortunately, the beautiful girl had not completed the required signature for there to be a sale.

SEVEN

'OPEN THIS FUCKING DOOR,' AMANDA ordered, the side of her fist pounding Daniel's apartment door, 'before I break it down!'

She awaited a reply... nothing.

Again she banged on the door. As it was broad and thicker than most, it held firm like a fire door; the pounding only reverberating within the surrounding frame.

'Come and open it, you stupid man!' Amanda paused to hear a muffled voice come from inside.

'Who's there?' a startled Daniel awoke to watch his whisky glass roll on its side against the floor. 'Is that you, woman...? Amanda?'

'Who else would it be?' Amanda yelled sceptically. 'Come to talk about that research. I've got an interest in it now.' She leaned back against the wall, her voice lowered to just above a whisper. 'A real interest now *this* has happened.'

'Wait one moment.' Daniel pushed his wheelchair around, trying to pick up the tumbler from the floor. 'It's a bit late for a visit, isn't Miss?' He managed to retrieve his drinking glass and wheeled himself to a nearby cabinet. 'Why come so late?'

'I had problems Daniel,' Amanda sighed heavily, 'transport problems. Somehow both my front tyres decided to go flat... fucking faulty valves or something?'

Accustomed to the sound, again she heard the door unlock by remote control. As she turned the handle and slowly opened the door to dimmed light, a voice instructed.

'Woman, kindly do not swear in public.' Daniel was seated some distance away in the shadows. 'I might not have many neighbours, but the ones I do, moan about everything that happens around here.' He edged his wheelchair closer to the door, a desk lamp casting the only light. 'Close the door before anybody has chance to...' He turned his attention to a nearby bottle of whisky and half-filled a tumbler held upright between his thighs.

'No bloody lights in here again you morbid fool.' Slowly Amanda took a few paces forward before closing the door behind.

Without light floodlit from the hallway, again she noticed to how dark the room had become. 'This place is as gloomy as the fucking day I've had.' Leaning back against the door, she sighed.

'Want a drink?' Daniel sniggered, holding the whisky bottle aloft. 'There's ice in the freezer.'

Taking a gulp of the neat spirit, he chuckled to himself, obviously thinking Amanda would never touch his stuff. But as she approached, he could see the darkness around her eyes and the anger in her face. And then she swore, muttering words that cursed somebody.

'I'll have a shot,' Amanda said to Daniel's surprise, 'with ice that is.'

'Must have been a bad day,' Daniel stated, adjusting his desk lamp to enlighten Amanda's face, or was it to conceal his own features? 'You've never had any from me before, but I guess there's always a first.' Lowering his face, he scratched at the greying bristles on his chin. 'So what causes a solicitor to turn to drink?'

'Bad day,' Amanda said sternly. 'Fucking car problems... but that's not the all and end of it.' She moved close to Daniel, aware he was studying her, his one eye glaring up at her from beneath his hood. 'So I'll have a neat bit first.'

Stooping over Daniel, Amanda quickly snatched the glass from his hand, and in one gulp, finished the remnants of the spirit.

'Hey woman, that was mine,' Daniel barked disapprovingly. 'Get y' own, you know where stuff is!'

He wriggled awkwardly in his wheelchair, pushing on one wheel, turning it to watch her disappear into his kitchen. He lifted the whisky bottle to eye level and swirled it around, examining to how much liquid remained. Suddenly he felt it being snatched from his grasp.

'What the hell...'

'It's fucking disgusting in there,' Amanda affirmed, her face showing contempt with what she had just seen. 'Thought you had carers in or someone like?'

'Not got the cash or the time for those folk these days.' Daniel narrowed his eyes and then searched her body. 'Where's my glass?'

Amanda slammed his glass on the table and slipped in a couple of ice cubes from a fresh glass.

'Don't need them with it,' he said, watching her pour a less than adequate level of whisky into the glass.

'But you can't keep having this stuff neat all the while,' Amanda told, helping herself to the same in the fresh glass.

'Got nothing else to look forward to, have I my dear?' Daniel's voice again echoed remorse.

'Not if you keep downing it like that!' Amanda watched him gulp at the glass, the ice cubes barely melted before the glass came empty. 'You're not the only one with problems, even if they be different?'

'So my dear,' Daniel asked slowly, a hint of sarcasm in his voice. 'What is it that makes *you* have a bad day?'

'After that ridiculous interview at that stupid little place,' Amanda scorned, 'I returned to my car only to find the front tyres flat.'

'Why on earth would you want to be interviewed at a freelance journalist?'

'Well apparently, one of those sisters works there and...'

'And you wanted to find out more about her?'

'Yes, exactly,' Amanda confirmed her suspicion. 'She is definitely one of the Layton-Aston sisters... the triplets you tried to...' Amanda could not finish her sentence; even by her ruthless standards, Daniel's past attempt at murder was deemed barbaric.

'Both tyres flat you say?' Daniel broke the silence.

'Yes, both front ones,' she retorted, 'at the same time.'

'Did you in any way piss off the sister that works there?'

'Well, maybe... I accidently spilt coffee over her.' Amanda finished off her glass of whisky, but frowned at Daniel's question. Placing both hands on the arms of his wheelchair she stared directly down at him. 'What's that got to do with it?' But Daniel simply grinned. 'You think *she* let down my tyres... on purpose?'

'Maybe, my dear,' Daniel grinned wider, 'maybe, otherwise?'

'But she couldn't have known who I was?' Amanda changed the conversation to stop aggravation taking hold of her. 'Besides, the mechanic that towed my car to the garage said that both valves burst... probably about the same time.'

'It's very rare for both to go at the same time.'

'That's what the garage said.'

'Then it sounds like foul play.'

'You suspect foul play?' Amanda questioned cynically. 'So this sister Emily, while I was being interviewed, planted dynamite in each valve, replaced the caps and exploded them on my return.' She clenched her fists and slammed each down against Daniel's padded arm rests, 'And all because of split coffee?'

Daniel cringed and wiggled in his wheelchair, annoyed not only to Amanda's anger but also to the fact that his whole face had come exposed. He pulled at the wheels of his wheelchair enough to remove her grip and then pushed himself behind his writing desk. Again he returned the hood to cover his face.

'Probably just coincidence,' he declared, 'a faulty service or something?'

'Faulty service my arse,' she argued, 'that's a top car, serviced by a top garage, only a month ago.' She paced heatedly over to his desk, noticing his sudden defiance. 'You know something don't you?'

'Like what, my dear?'

'You seemed interested until...' Again Amanda realised to how she so fervently released her anger. 'It just gets me so wound up again thinking about it.' She pointed inadvertently at the window. 'There's something about that Emily that is a bit odd. Black eyes like a shark – not deep brown and beautiful like mine.' She paused to reflect on their abrupt office collision that morning, but saw Daniel stare inquisitively up at her. 'If you know something Daniel, you would tell it me, wouldn't you?'

Daniel shifted awkwardly about his desk, trying to gather papers, photographs, differing files and a large, decrepit book. And then he hesitated to open the doctor's old burned and blemished diary. But seeing the anguish in Amanda's eyes, he knew she needed resolution, wanted some radical explanation. Yet all he had to go on was what he had learned and the suspicions he had gained over all these years. But was the doctor right, could he pursue revenge on some assumption fabricated from research? Well he had spent so many solitary years trying to fathom out parts of the doctor's research, and even though he wanted the power for himself, maybe it was time to share his findings, get a different perspective?

He trusted Amanda to some extent, but to expose the last research of the doctor – to be sniggered at for believing in such hypothesis – to have to share his ultimate goal? But now he was convinced that Amanda had experienced some unnatural force from the eldest triplet. That a power, whether being good or evil, could seek revenge, even if flat tyres seemed rather vicious to avenge a bit of split coffee?

Daniel looked up, his thoughts suddenly broken by Amanda's voice.

'You're not listening again,' she scolded.

Daniel held up his hand in gesture for her to be silent.

'You remember what we talked about last time?'

'Yes, I remember... something about those three monkeys?'

'Well, the ceremony the doctor did,' Daniel was trying to put it bluntly; he could not remember if he had explained this before. 'Well he used his own blood to draw the evil to the cursed stone, and whoever held the pendant, they...' Amanda swallowed hard, her throat suddenly dry. 'But you see, should the stone get destroyed and the curse lifted, the summoned evil would not go back empty-handed, it would still finish the task... the conjurer now being the cursed... the victim.'

'Yes Daniel, I'm sure you've explained this before.' Amanda rolled her eyes and sighed. 'Play with fire and you'll get your fingers...'

'Exactly,' Daniel intervened, eager to continue. 'And like many witches spells, the doctor feared this insecurity. And so he furthered his research.' He paused for one moment, Amanda poised not sure if all this was significant. 'Hoping to find solutions to such a problem, he indeed found another problem.'

'How's all this to do with...?'

'I'm getting to that,' Daniel interjected angrily, 'should you let me finish?'

'Sorry, go on...'

'The doctor found through his research, as noted in this diary and that old book, that there could be born to tribute Mother Nature, three people, each having powers that if combined could neglect the doctor's dark magic... a combined force enough to break his spells and cast evil against him... a white magic that promotes common good in man so no evil deed is sought.'

'Argh, now I think I get the picture,' Amanda construed. 'You think that those sisters protected themselves against harm... your evil deed... and that explains...' She opened her hand to reflect on his disability. 'But they were only babies, and...' Again Amanda silenced to cringe and repeat. 'So that's why you went to... all those years ago?'

Daniel spoke as if thinking aloud and not hearing Amanda.

'So look at what they could do if adults, against that power I wish to get from the doctor.' He stared hard at his guest. With the light from the lamp, Amanda's eyes glistened wide with surprise.

'But how can there be any relation to monkeys and those sisters, even if all three still be alive?'

'They be alive, I know it.' Daniel confirmed but frowned, stabbing his forefinger at notes and drawings in the doctor's diary. 'But surely, aren't these animals male?'

'Why would they be male?' Amanda retorted. 'If there weren't any females, the species would soon become extinct.' Again she rejected starting an argument based on gender and surmised, 'But these are simple animals, not witches... humans that can read out spells and shit like?'

'Not all magic spells require a verbal order my dear.'

'What do you mean, not verbal?'

'Magic, good or evil can be inherited.' Daniel leaned forward, his disfigured hand clenched as a fist. 'And surely, it is not the gift that commands a good or evil act, but the person who bestows it.'

'And what type of gift gives that Emily the right to burst my tyres?' Amanda became satirical.

'Telekinesis my dear; haven't you heard of that?'

'But that's stupid. No-one has the power to move things by thought.'

'Then you've not researched what I have,' Daniel voiced. 'You've not researched stuff like me... all this is not just the doctor's work.'

'Think what such a powerful gift could do.' Amanda voiced her thoughts, her mind elsewhere.

Daniel eyed her frustratingly until she glanced down to notice he had more to say.

'Yes, but according to my research, unless it's embraced correctly, such a power can harm its owner.' Amanda watched him flick through the doctor's diary. 'The doctor conjured evil to do his bidding by using a bloodletting ceremony. His blood sacrificed to a summoning stone gave him command over such devilish creatures. But as it was broken, he paid the price.'

'Yes Daniel,' Amanda intervened, 'you've told this before, but what use is it now without such a stone?'

'Well, I know I'm not as literate as the doctor, but for his legacy and after all these years of research, I believe the ceremony can be re-written, or maybe made to work with another stone... a warlock's stone.'

Amanda rejected her delusions of having a power such as telekinesis, but deliberated on other ways to control the rich piers that once sponsored their dark coven and other people she wanted to overpower, or simply deride.

'It sounds meddlesome to delve into such dark powers Daniel.' Amanda faced Daniel to express her concern. 'Doing such like may get you killed.'

'What else have I got? How else can I attain such power to avenge?' He pointed to the door inadvertently. 'That woman, look how she left me?'

'But it's a bit drastic don't y' think, sending some demon to kill that Sarah?' Amanda sniggered but gradually felt remorse. 'Besides, she's been in that institute for nearly twenty years!'

'And *you* don't feel the same against this Emily,' Daniel inferred, 'knowing she burst your tyres like that?'

'That girl has no such gift.' Amanda folded her arms tight in denial. 'If she has, it'll be bloody hard to kill her.'

'Then let something else do it for you.'

'What, one of your demons?' Amanda stood erect with scorn, her eyes narrowed to peer at Daniel's research. 'I'm somewhat cleverer than you my dear, so that is why I wouldn't delve into such insidious shit.'

Daniel snatched the nearby, empty whisky bottle from the edge of the desk and paused for a moment to see ice cubes melting in his glass.

'Then tell me my good woman.' Daniel's exposed eye inspected Amanda curiously. 'How are you going to become this powerful and wealthy woman you've being promising yourself for all these years.'

Amanda took a few steps back and regarded the cripple as insolent.

'Ambitious women, like myself, have other, more subtle ways that can be just as effective.' She paused to look at her wristwatch, surprised to how late it had become. Before striding to the door, she turned to announce, 'You could've asked your belated doctor friend all about that!'

EIGHT

CENTRED IN A SMALL MEETING room down a corridor from the court, Emily looked at Sarah across an oval table. Again her mother was silent; quietly watching the lawyer spread folders across the table, the elderly woman sorting through particular documents. Although brightly lit, the room seemed confined, especially with such a large wooden table.

She was glad that her mother had changed her statement, but although the lawyer in their defence had argued credibly, she was still apprehensive. Unfortunately Sarah had stuttered in telling her story of how, after taking Daniel Whittaker as some intruder, she had, in a fit of rage, assailed him with a knife. Sarah had started shaking as she retold the past, saying it was all but a blur, but Emily hoped that her mother's anxieties to lie would be construed as a nervous reaction to recollect the incident. She had seen her mother cry many times in the institute, but these tears revealed a different pain. At first Emily thought they came from her refusal to plead guilty, but as the lawyer had argued that Sarah acted in self-defence for her and her three babies, she realised they were tears of loss; her mother regretting not having a chance to bring all daughters up together. And of course there was Daniel's paralysis. How could a woman, having three baby daughters to look after, gain enough strength to move furniture to crush a man? But with Daniel being disfigured by fire, surely seeing such a frightful sight would panic any woman? And what was he doing in her home in the first place?

Emily wanted a convincing and professional opinion.

'Miss Chapman,' watching the lawyer sort documents before her, Emily cleared her throat, 'with my mother's change of statement, now that we deduce what really happened after all these years...' Emily saw the lawyer peer at her over narrow, elongated spectacles. 'Do you think the jury will question Daniel's paralysis?'

'You mean the way it happened,' the astute, elderly lady leaned forward, 'to how Mr Whittaker sustained such spinal injuries?'

'Well, yes. And to why he was there in the first place?'

'He said he went there to resolve discrepancies Sarah had with him over your father's death, but I don't play that.' The lawyer paused to contemplate. 'But to Mr Whittaker's paralysis, well, I think Sarah did well to convey how shocked and horrified she was to have confronted an intruder when in charge of you as babies... especially a man so hefty and disfigured.'

'Yes, mother,' Emily clasped Sarah's hand, her mother looking agitated. 'You did well to recall what happened, but after *such* a long time.'

The lawyer smiled thinly before revealing concern. 'One question however, is to why the knife, if it was from the kitchen or even if it was Mr Whittaker's... it had no fingerprints on it?'

'But whosoever knife it was... and being self-defence,' Emily conveyed her own opinion, 'surely it was that which caused Daniel's paralysis?'

'Medical evidence shows here that the knife was blocked by the sternum or central rib cage. So spinal injury, unless having some association with the nervous system...?' The lawyer's face screwed up to neglect the theory. 'I doubt it anyhow and it's superficial. Prints were smudged by sweat from your mother's hand.' She paused to reflect and then thought aloud. 'Yet analysis showed nothing of Sarah's DNA?' Before either could contest or intervene, the lawyer continued in her deliberation. 'What is of more concern, should the jury be convinced that Sarah has served enough time to recollect the incident correctly, and after good rehabilitation of course, is how she moved such heavy furniture to fall against Mr Whittaker?'

'But didn't you just argue that –'

'Yes, I suggested that Sarah, having suffered such trauma with the loss of Mr Carl Aston, after seeing an intruder and one conceived as a perpetrator to his murder, was enraged to protect herself and her children. And so your mother infused such anger into an insentient temper that gave her unusual strength to move furniture, enough to fall upon Mr Whittaker... that she did this without knowing... in a rage of anger. These things have been known before.'

'Have they?' Emily was curious.

'Yes, in here are many such cases,' the lawyer flicked through a folder to reveal several case studies. 'One here describes that, after seeing flames start, a father was so enraged, he rolled an upturned car in order to save his daughter. Apparently, he tore his hands and arms in breaking the back window, but never remembered any pain.'

After scrutinising the lawyer for some time, Emily noticed her mother turn to her and smile.

'So it's the jury that needs convincing?' Emily questioned, her attention focusing back on the lawyer.

'And the judge,' the lawyer added. 'But it's a bit late for that. We've already argued our side, so let's just hope –'

'Ladies, I believe you are required,' a voice announced as the door opened. 'The jury has reached a verdict.'

Emily enclosed her hand around Sarah's, her mother gazing up at her to observe the security guard peer around the door. As the lawyer stood to acknowledge the security guard, Sarah glanced back at Emily, her eyes sincere, but her words a mumble.

'The bright halo flung him against the wall... the bright light.'

'Please keep with *this* story mother.'

'What did she say?' Acknowledging the security guard, the lawyer misheard their conversation.

'She wants to finally see the light,' Emily rephrased. 'Get acquitted and be rid of this nightmare.'

The lawyer frowned at first, but then smiled. 'We best get down there.'

Sarah stared about the courtroom, thinking to how large it had looked before. But now it seemed to be closing in on her. In the noise and bustle it was hard to think, but she recalled the old wooden landscape encompassing the room, the engraved markings below the magistrate's bench, the tall panels of the witness box, and the line of balusters before the jury.

In flashes, the ornate scenery brought back images of the doctor's mansion, where she had learned that Carl had saved her. And before that; when they had met by accident in the study, both of them searching for answers. Although their inquiries were different, both concerned the doctor. No her memory was fine, even after all the medication, the accusations and rehabilitation. She knew exactly what had happened that night, but hung onto Emily's story. For some reason she had renewed faith in her daughter; that maybe one day, after her acquittal, she would see all daughters together again.

Sarah's thoughts were broken by a tighter squeeze to her hand, Emily reaching over to also embrace her neck and whisper in her ear.

'Hold tight now mother and believe...' Emily was also nervous; Sarah could feel it in her daughter's hands and voice. 'Believe that this will bring us properly together... forever.'

As Emily retreated to her seat behind, Sarah glanced at an also anxious lawyer. The elderly woman smiled thinly, her spectacles glimmering from light above.

'Remember to stand for the judge when verdict is called,' the lawyer said whilst winking. 'Courtesy will work in your favour my dear.'

As the lawyer sat back into her seat, Sarah noticed eyes staring back at her from across the courtroom. Sitting beside a hooded man in a wheelchair and in the prosecution box, was a dark-haired woman about her age. It was obvious that the disabled man was Daniel, but who was that stern-faced woman?

Suddenly from around the courtroom an order for silence was called.

Feeling apprehensive with palms sweating, Sarah glanced back at Emily. Her daughter shifted nervously in her seat, squinting to observe Daniel's lawyer for the prosecution, but she was disturbed by another call for silence.

A deathly quiet gave the room heavy air, a sense of foreboding. All the jury had taken their seats and the judge entered to take his place to oversee all. As the court session started, nerves took the better of Sarah, and so she was oblivious to a lot of formality. But as Emily took hold of her shoulder from behind, the judge requested the jury read its verdict for the trial.

A pensive, elderly gentleman with white balding hair stood from the front of the jury box and cleared his throat.

'We the jury have deliberated this case with much thought, and in the matter of grievous bodily harm, we find the defendant Sarah Layton guilty. But after taking Daniel Whittaker, the prosecution, as an intruder into her home, declare that Miss Layton acted in self-defence for both herself and her children.'

As questions whispered about the courtroom, Sarah could feel Emily's hand squeeze tighter. The inquisitive whispers grew louder.

Suddenly the judge's hammer reverberated the bench.

'Thank you, the jury,' the judge announced. 'I too have deliberated on this case with much thought and have now come to sentence.'

Sarah rose with trembling legs after being nudged by her lawyer. The judge requested that Sarah stand, but noticed she had already done so. Quickly she glanced behind to notice Emily cross her fingers.

'Miss Layton, you have been proven guilty of grievous bodily harm in relation to your own confession and that considered by members of the jury. But to many years of good behaviour you have served in rehabilitation, I believe this has given you time to recollect the incident in question and so reflect on the injuries you have caused the prosecution.' He paused to swallow, seeing Daniel uncover his hood. Next to him, hard-staring eyes glared up from the prosecution desk. 'And taking into account that Mr Whittaker was mistaken as an intruder that night, invading the defendant's home without invitation or cause, I grant Miss Layton release under the following conditions…'

Abruptly a voice erupted from the prosecution desk as Daniel punched his fist into the air.

'She made me like this…' he screamed. 'I've had to suffer this shit now for years… pain and medicines… only went to hers to find out what happened…?'

'Silence… please, silence by all!' the judge commanded, hearing additional voices grow loud. 'Please, lawyer for the prosecution… control your delegate.' The judge waited for Amanda to console Daniel, but the disabled man twisted angrily in his wheelchair, his voice muttering words of contempt. The judge continued. 'I will now read sentence…'

Sarah looked from the disturbance at the prosecution desk to watch Emily's hand slide into hers from behind.

'Miss Layton, although your previous statement of the night in question gave some concern to your mental health, examinations through years of rehabilitation have deemed your reaction to harm the prosecution as an uncontrollable fit of rage.' The judge paused to look directly at Sarah, to get her attention. 'And so Miss Layton, providing you satisfactorily complete six months of reassessment and attend medical examinations when necessary, you are granted freedom to walk from this court in hope that you will not return.'

The judge's hammer closed his sentence and he acknowledged the jury to thank them for their services.

Sarah could not release her breath until the tight hug on her body was released. She could not see anything until the kisses that smothered her face ceased. Then as she felt Emily bounce, she stared about in bewilderment. Emily's eyes sparkled with delight, as tears of joy streamed down her cheeks. A hand of congratulations was held out before her as her eyes met those of her lawyer; her face also pleasured to win the case.

In the noise and turmoil, Sarah glanced across the courtroom to notice Daniel disclose his annoyance, his fist again reaching to the sky, his emotions letting loose, now not conscious to how exposed his disfigured face had become.

'They'll not get away with this… I assure you of that…' Daniel's cries became quashed by the noise in the court, only the security guards now trying to keep order.

Placing a hand on Daniel's shoulder, he looked up to see Amanda, her eyes fixed hard on Sarah.

As Emily retreated from thanking their lawyer and helped her mother put on her coat, Sarah noticed Amanda mouth something to Daniel and quickly march over.

Obscuring Sarah's view, again her daughter hugged her tight, but felt Emily's grip being wrenched away. Sarah watched in dismay as Emily was pushed aside as Amanda's hands grasped at her.

'You might be happy now bitch, but you've not seen the end of this!'

Emily stood perplexed, shocked by the dark-haired, angry woman accosting her mother.

'Get your hands off her,' Emily demanded. 'Who the hell do you…?'

For a while Emily did not recognise the woman grabbling with her mother, but by the time she had intervened and a security guard had parted them, she remembered her face. However, it was too late to respond and seek revenge for split coffee; the security officer was now marshalling Sarah out the defence box. And Emily must be with her mother now, especially after such good news. Maybe, in contrary, this woman had not seen the end of her?

Wording her displeasure, Amanda pushed away another security guard who had intervened and marched back to the prosecution box. Ignoring Daniel, who heatedly voiced questions, she felt her fingers ache and her hand burn with pain. Amanda opened her hand to notice a large coat button wedged in her palm. At first she frowned at the object, but gradually an evil grin stretched across her face.

Quickly Emily caught up with Sarah, her mother slowly being escorted out the courtroom.

'Mother,' Emily was fretful and clenched at her mother's arm to stop her for a minute. 'Do *you* know that woman?'

'I didn't at first, but,' Sarah paused to recollect, 'she's not just a lawyer, or some associate to that Daniel, but an evil woman… I believe she had something to do with my friend's death.' Sarah poised to hold her head, her tears of joy suppressed by bad memories. And then she looked up. 'Do you know her?'

'Not met her until… last week.' Again a strange wrath stirred within Emily. 'She had a job interview at our place. But to what I knew, we weren't recruiting… not for managerial roles anyhow?'

'Avoid her if you can my dear.' Sarah declared, annoyed at the security guard pulling on her arm.

'Yes, I don't want coffee spilled over me again, do I?'

'What?' Sarah swivelled her head to face Emily after acknowledging the security guard.

'Don't worry mother, she'll get her comeuppance.' Emily took her mother by her arm and followed the security guard out of the courtroom. 'For now, let's celebrate your freedom!'

NINE

'How's your mother, Emily?'

'She's fine Ange... just got to go through some formalities before she's finally released.'

'And then where's she stopping?'

'The small box room at mine,' Emily replied slowly, her concentration mainly on the computer screen. 'It's going to be tight, but for medical reasons they agreed she'd be better off with someone for a while.' She faced Angela in an open-handed gesture. 'And me being family...?'

'Good job *my* parents don't live far.' Angela waited for a reaction, her feelings fraught, but her friend did not respond. 'Think I'll be staying with them this weekend.' Still Emily glared at her computer screen, her concentration undisturbed and vexed. 'Me and Josh, well...'

'You've had another argument?' Emily assumed, knowing Angela's old trait to seek attention. 'But you're always arguing?' She paused to look up from the screen. 'And the next thing you'll talk of is how good he was in bed.'

'But this was something else...'

'Yes, and as you've done before,' Emily smirked, 'you'll sort out y' differences in bed.' She paused to reflect on her friend's relationship. 'At least you've got someone to talk things over, even if things do get heated.'

'You think I worry too much?'

'Yes, like me, you worry too much.' Emily's sympathetic voice turned to words of discontent. 'And who the hell is this?' She glanced at Angela standing at her office desk and pointed to the screen. 'This is your fault, you silly cow... getting me to sign up to this.' Emily continued cynically, her voice imitating Angela's squeaky voice. 'Try this popular social media site... you'll get men crawling at y' feet... you'll get a date in no time.' Emily changed her tone to voice sarcasm. 'More like desperate foreigners trying it on to get over here?'

'How do you know they're foreign?' Angela quizzed, suddenly realising the site Emily was browsing. Fascinated, she moved quickly to peer over Emily's shoulder, but at first took note to who in the office could see them.

'Look at this one here,' Emily said in agitation, but quietened her voice, not wanting her condemnation to be overheard. 'You can tell by his bad English, the way he repeats things and his come on.'

'He's not that bad actually... quite a hunk.' Angela took charge of Emily's mouse although she still held it. 'Let's look at his profile.'

Emily watched as an image of a French man appeared, his features more revealed by an enlarged passport type picture. Angela screwed up her hose now she saw more his facial features, but what were more disturbing were his posts.

'He's a bit direct for someone who's never met you?'

'But according to this, he has.' Angela turned to see the anxiety in Emily's face. 'Look, here he said he liked me close up. That it was better than the show?'

'Bloody pervert!' Angela's face contorted even more. 'Show, what show?' With her mouth agape, Angela again faced Emily from studying the man's profile. 'You've not posted pictures or video, have you?'

'No, of course not. Don't be stupid. I've only been registered a few weeks.'

'Then why does he call you Helen? Is it some nickname?'

'I don't know. I don't know any of them.' Emily continued, her voice croaking somewhat. 'But he's posted things before... about taking me out... something about English girls have more curves... are more outgoing... have bigger –'

'Yes I get the picture.' Angela interrupted, shifting to take Emily's seat. 'Let's take over a while and see what other posts you have, and where they come from.'

'Be my guest.' Emily stood with arms folded, her eyes rolling, but was still inquisitive to who the men were. 'I think all posts come from western Europeans... most I think are Dutch.'

'Yes your right,' Angela asserted, her social media expertise examining several profiles. 'You know, I've always wondered what it be like to date a European guy.' The plump girl's carefree attitude changed after reading one other profile post. 'Blimey, who's this dirty bastard... telling you of how long his...?'

'Manhood,' Emily intervened, watching Angela cover her mouth. 'I know which one that is. He's one I definitely want to delete!'

'Quite handsome though,' Angela stated, moving the mouse wheel to enlarge his picture. 'Apparently, he's from Amsterdam.'

'They're all dirty bastards from over there.' Emily cringed.

'Not all of them. Actually some are quite nice.' Angela glanced up to see Emily view close the social media profile. 'I've been over, although it being a long time ago.'

'He's probably being nice to get you in bed?'

'Like your friend in the shop?' Angela surmised.

'Oh, that prick.'

'Yes, but didn't you admit that he was quite cute?' Angela swivelled around on Emily's chair. 'And I saw how impressed you were with his stunt.'

'He said he worked there.'

'I told you, he works at the college or university... some young lecturer in computers or something like.'

'So why try and pull off a stunt like that?'

'My guess is that he likes you.' Angela winked. 'He likes you a lot.' She pointed to a friend request on Emily's social media profile. 'And do you want to do something about it or shall I post a blind date with one of these foreign sharks?'

'Do that and we be friends no longer?'

'You'll be employees no longer if the manager see's you on *that* site.' Gary was a new, young employee and had come to give Emily a message. 'Not that it's any of my business, but there's a call for you Emily... ring Glenda on reception.'

Emily brushed Angela aside to reach the telephone, her back turned to indicate her want of privacy.

As she watched Emily dial the reception desk number, Angela quickly scrolled to the top of Emily's social media profile. Secretly she clicked the button to accept Jack's friendship request.

'Yes, this is Miss Aston-Layton,' Emily declared, 'you have news about my mother, Sarah Layton?'

Angela's face smirked as she tweaked settings on Emily's profile.

'Yes, I see, but I thought her assessment wouldn't be finished until...'

Angela stood tall from Emily's chair and gingerly returned to her own.

'Well, what time can she be picked up?'

On her own computer, Angela examined Emily's profile through her own to see if changes were now visible.

'I'll be glad to, but need to clear it here at work.' Emily glanced over her shoulder to see Angela back at her desk. 'I guess it should be okay, but have you a number just in case?'

Angela closed the browser that viewed Emily's profile and grinned.

'Guess what?' Emily bounced with excitement. 'They've released Sarah... I can pick her up in an hour.'

Angela's wide grin turned to a smile. 'Why that's great, maybe your fortune has changed for the good... next you'll be dating fellas.'

'Don't push my luck too far now will y' Ange.'

Emily rushed from announcing her arrival at the reception desk to hug her mother. As Sarah stood from her seat in a brightly lit waiting area, Emily could see tears flood her eyes. Even the attending nurse, who had seen many residences reunite with family, had been taken aback by their affection. But procedures had to be followed.

'She's allowed to go as long as she's got enough medication.' The small, round-faced nurse continued in a strict voice, hoping her instructions were clear. 'There's enough here for a week, after which the doctor here will reassess the need for particular medication. Some I think will not be necessary later on, but she needs to return next week.' Emily parted from Sarah to look down at the nurse who prodded her with a curled envelope. 'All instructions for return assessments and daily dosage of medication are described in here. Make sure she adheres to them. I need your signature here my dear.'

The stern-faced nurse watched Emily sign the form, her rosy cheeks revealing a smile, her eyes too, conveying sympathy.

'Look after Miss Sarah. She's been quite good to us these past few years.'

'I will,' Emily agreed, turning to watch Sarah hug the nurse. 'But I know she'll certainly not miss this place... especially once she sees how I've got things set up for her back home.'

As they strolled with bags out of the waiting room and through the reception, Sarah turned to the waving nurse and voiced her concern.

'What about my other stuff... clothes and such?'

'They'll all be cleaned, ready for collection soon.' The nurse stepped forward, not wanting to shout. 'We'll phone when they're ready. You'll collect them, won't you Emily?'

Emily acknowledged the nurse and ushered her mother to her outside car.

It was cold that late afternoon, the approaching twilight anticipated in the air. But to Sarah, the brisk gushes of wind were ghosts of that place being blown from her body, her freedom captured in the smell of early autumn leaves fallen beneath her feet. And as she kicked at the large sycamore leaves, thinking the coloured blanket resembled some patchwork quilt, she stopped Emily to catch her attention.

'This place, where I'm going,' Sarah asked, 'has it got a nice bed... a thick, warm blanket?'

Emily nodded and smiled. 'We'll get whatever makes you feel at home.'

Emily placed all bags in the car boot as Sarah took the passenger seat. As she took the driver's seat, Emily shivered and looked at her mother. Sarah gazed oblivious at the gravel drive ahead, overhead trees enshrouding it, but looking naked now they had shred most of their leaves. Emily was just about to start the engine when Sarah turned to ask Emily a question.

'One day all of you will be united again.' Sarah took Emily's hand that gripped the steering wheel. 'I want to see you all together again, as you were as babies, but *you* deserve it most.'

'It wasn't your fault mother,' Emily interjected, clasping her hand on top, 'Mike and Rachel agreed to take me in. What with Rachel not being able to...?' Emily cleared her throat. 'But the others, maybe they've got on well... probably doing well?'

'Probably is not an answer.'

'One thing at a time mother,' Emily looked up at the sign that overhung the entrance to the institute. 'We've had to be devious to get this far... to get you out of that place.'

'I hated lying like that,' Sarah muttered, her face solemn, 'especially when what I said before, I knew was true.'

'So some bright, fantastic energy turned the knife into his chest and threw him across the room.' Emily was wondering now, if she had taken on some uncalculated responsibility. 'What did happen if it wasn't self-defence?'

'I don't want to remember.' Sarah looked at her hands; they were trembling. 'I hated to lie in that court... all those people judging me after admitting I hurt him.'

'Then tell me one thing, before I drive this car home.' Emily concealed her tears with anger. 'Why would that man want to harm us as babies, eh? Tell me that?'

'Please don't ask coz I don't know.' Sarah peered up at Emily from staring at her hands. 'All I know is that something saved us from harm that night... and it wasn't me.'

'Then what was it?'

'Let's not go on about it.' Sarah rubbed her face with nervous hands. 'Let's just get home.'

'Do you know something you're not telling me?' Emily looked sincere. 'Have you kept something from us all this time?'

'No my dear, I would never do that.'

'So, no more surprises... you promise?'

'Yes, I promise,' Sarah sighed heavily and took in a large breath. 'No more talk of that past as long as you promise to try and find your sisters.'

'Like I said mother,' Emily sighed also, 'One thing at a time.'

TEN

AMANDA SLAMMED DOWN THE PILE of paperwork on her desk. Again it had been another long day, so she was glad to be home. After being queried to why Daniel had visited Sarah in the first place, she could only speculate. The real truth of his intent so many years ago had to be kept secret; a compromise made between them, long before Sarah's acquittal.

Her canvass bag too, was heavy. This contained library books that she had borrowed from Bristol's central library. She could not take all the ones she wanted, but for the weeks ahead, the books that she had loaned would help with research. And later, she would conduct her own investigation. But for now, she needed two things; a stiff brandy and that cigarette.

As she sipped at the bowl-shaped brandy glass and her cigarette burned resting in a heavy, glass ashtray, Amanda spread her research into two piles. To the left of her laptop, she piled all library books; ones she had found most closely related to the occult and witchcraft. To the right, she spread copied notes from Daniel's research.

It had been impossible to persuade him to lease the doctor's book, and so took Daniel with her, him clinging onto the volume as though his life depended on it. And whilst she copied most pages, she noticed a keen eye not once let it out of his sight. As she was unsure to the importance of the doctor's diary, notes and letters, Amanda had photocopied them all. Such important or relevant documentation could be scanned and made digital later.

Whilst waiting for her laptop to boot so that she could log in, Amanda took a long drag of her cigarette. Unlike Daniel, she was proficient at research, even if this was somewhat different to law.

After driving him home, she now realised to how much he was bent on revenge; his disposition overwhelmed by bitterness, wanting Sarah and her siblings dead whatever the cost. Initially, she had only agreed to help Daniel with his research, to stop him doing something he would later regret. But in continuing her own investigation, Amanda felt the affluence of having such evil knowledge niggled at her like some incessant craving. It was as though some invisible demon was scrutinising and enticing her to understand this dark and formidable force.

She had flicked through all her library books, and although some were shamefully interesting, they disclosed nothing but general information on a wide variety of topics. Apart from one on witchcraft rituals, none were anywhere close to what she had learned from the doctor. As she realised the doctor's practise was somewhat unique from years of research, Amanda turned to the internet. But here, she got lost in an array of online forums, occult groups and websites leading to profanity. By accident, she did find some interesting links on medieval witchcraft, an influential history on witches and warlocks, plus ancient occult practices that cursed people and objects. But these too came to an unsightly end.

For half-an-hour she delved into the doctor's past, but apart from some journal papers he had wrote and had published, her internet research comprised mainly of the man's wrongful conviction of murdering a young boy. However, investigations after his death outside his gutted mansion, found he had being manufacturing and selling fake historic artefacts and paintings; that indeed, the doctor had black-mailed many wealthy and affluent individuals within this local community, some of which had strangely disappeared, or had come to some disastrous end. Amanda read more into this doctor's conviction, her interest somewhat intensified by the mention of some cleric's name of Aston; a Steven John Aston, who's adopted son was also killed during the mansion fire. Apparently the young man, a Mr Carl Aston, had judged the doctor unscrupulous, and so got unfortunately caught in the mansion fire during investigations. Amanda read more on the page, but then decided to save the hyperlink to her browsing favourites. As this was but newspaper history, she could copy and print it later. She pushed down the screen of her laptop, thinking her research on the doctor's occult practice was going nowhere.

She turned to the spread of research on her right and flicked through the copied notes from the doctor's diary. She had skimmed through the diary before and questioned Daniel about the notes and diagrams, but always felt like Daniel was hiding something. He admitted in not fully understanding the translations to the ancient inscriptions of Latin, but somehow knew the procedure of the summoning ceremony?

By the time she had finished her brandy and was lighting her third cigarette, Amanda felt herself being drawn into this malevolent, dark stimulus. She pieced together parts of a jigsaw she had not understood before; realising the difficulties the doctor had in translating the ancient language. Somehow he had transcribed the bloodletting ceremony from an association he had discovered between Celtic mythology and dark voodoo magic performed in islands of the West Indies. This, Amanda now realised, was what had taken up most of the doctor's life.

Doctor Joseph Schroeck had used ancient records from another book to help translate the old Latin. And copied (by illustration from this book) into his own notes, was a decorated pendant; a warlock's stone, or *call* stone, used in the ceremony for summoning evil. Although somewhat confused, Amanda continued to gather from the doctor's notes, that the ceremony to summon evil to this dark stone (made from black onyx) came from translated voodoo curses discovered during studies in Haiti and Tobago. Indeed, Amanda came intrigued to read a letter of correspondence between the doctor and an accomplice in Ireland.

Difficult to read from its photocopy, but mostly from a nervous hand, the doctor described the success of his research; having found a method to control an evil curse, one he had worked on for such a long time. In sketchy detail, the doctor described that, whoever held the warlock's stone after conducting the bloodletting ceremony; a malevolent evil would hunt down the bearer and kill them. Amanda read on to understand that the onyx stone had not always been cast in decoration, but that this was done to disguise it. As the doctor continued to humour himself in his letter to the real value of such an onyx stone, Amanda realised the doctor was in fact scared and in fear of his own life. Described in worsening scrawl, he tells his partner to sell artefacts back home so he can very quickly return on a safe ship back to Ireland; as unless he leaves soon, the primitives of

Tobago will find out his true intentions, and for such crimes against their religion, he could be executed.

Amanda read on but her concentration was wavering. Maybe it was the brandy, too many cigarettes, or the fact that she had skipped lunch only to have a snack. She examined the letter, the date faded and so searched for the envelope. She was intrigued to how long ago all this had happened, but unfortunately it had not been copied. She took a last drag on her cigarette and doused it irritably in the glass ashtray. She rummaged around, skim reading quickly other letters, photocopied notes, and then with a last attempt to deny she was exhausted, flicked again through the doctor's diary notes.

She pondered on her conversation with Daniel in her car home, but slowly another headache returned. Surely he would not try anything without asking her first, even if he had been so high rate. With the warlock's stone destroyed, he had no way of conjuring evil, let alone set such malevolence on Sarah. Besides, he had only a basic understanding of the bloodletting ceremony, and the pronunciation of Latin words would surely come out wrong.

Thinking all was too much for one day, she sighed and put down the cigarette packet and folded her arms to cushion her weary head. She could feel her forehead throb against her folded arms, but more was the ache from heavy eyelids.

Startled, Amanda awoke to see the room still and quiet. It was not the fact that she had been frightened, or had suffered a nightmarish dream, but a chill of realisation came over her; some of the words Daniel had said, the deadly threats he had voiced. She now remembered how he had cursed Sarah back in the library?

Surely he was not mad enough to try anything was he?

Without any response from his telephone, Amanda gulped at a glass of water, before making for the door.

ELEVEN

EMILY THANKED MIKE AND RACHAEL for coming, waved her goodbyes, and then shut her front door. As she wondered admiringly into her lounge, she contemplated on the good memories she had with her foster parents, but noticed Sarah gaze solemnly at pictures lined above the fireplace.

'It was good for you to see them again,' Emily stated, 'out of that place that is.' But Sarah was not listening. 'Pity they couldn't stay a while longer and have another drink.' Emily watched Sarah get up and stroll over to pick up a framed picture from the mantelpiece. 'Never knew you lot had so much history... things to catch up on.'

Sarah stood insensitive, her hands trembling a little.

'You okay mother?' Emily saw Sarah examine the picture of her with Mike and Rachael; the day she won gold at swimming during her last year at junior school. 'They're great don't you agree, but you're still my *real* mother. I appreciate that even more now that you're here.' Emily paused but continued, unperturbed by Sarah's silence. 'Mike and Rachael are fine with everything now.' She took a deep breath. 'It's not like I'm that age anymore, now is it?'

'At that age, I hardly saw anything of you,' Sarah croaked, her hands nervy to place back the picture.

'But surely Mike and Rachael told you all that happened,' Emily quizzed. 'How they looked after me?'

'Pity they couldn't have all three.'

'Look mother,' Emily sighed again, the celebrations and alcohol wearing off for some reason. 'You knew their circumstances... and I was the eldest.'

'I know Rachael lost her job and so could look after you, but Mike had difficult times after losing...' Sarah could not mention Carl's name, his death still a hurt to her as well as Mike, but Emily quite understood. 'And not being able to have children of her own,' Sarah clenched her fist, 'you'd think all three of you could've been brought up together?'

'We've discussed this mother,' Emily sighed, her voice tense. 'It's the past. And what is done is done. It just brings squabbles between all of us.'

'I know it's not their fault,' Sarah cursed, slamming her fist against her thigh. 'If only that stupid bastard hadn't broken in that night.'

'They said the door was open,' Emily stated without thought, maybe the alcohol had not yet worn off?

'You know what I mean.' Sarah mumbled, her eyes beginning to weep.

'So why did that Daniel want to murder you, or us as babies?'

'I don't know, but...' Sarah enticed Emily to sit down beside her. 'Days have become months, months into years, and over time in that place I have recalled something old Aunt Evelyn said years ago.'

'Aunt who?' Emily interrupted.

'Carl's aunt... a very righteous woman... her sister's past was corrupted by that doctor.' Emily edged close to listen inventively to Sarah's in-depth description of the past. But Sarah cut short her story, eager to convey her own belief. 'I think, like Evelyn and maybe her sisters, that each of you have a gift... something I felt when I gave birth to you.' Sarah pondered to take Emily's hand. 'And each of you being triplets, you have this gift split between you.'

'But the only gift I seem to have mother, is to draw.' Emily picked out her sketchpad from her bag beside her new sofa bed. 'I drew this after bumping into that woman.'

'That's the one at...'

'Yes an uncanny resemblance, if I may say so myself.' Emily paused to contemplate, watching her mother inspect the drawing with much curiosity. 'Yet I can't remember much about drawing her, or seeing her in fact? I literally just bumped into her that morning.'

'I don't think that be the gift that saved you.' Sarah placed the sketchpad on the sofa bed between them.

'Saved me?' Emily enquired.

'Yes Emily, I know it may be hard for you to understand, but now were out of that place, I can tell you the truth... the *real* truth.'

'Oh, about that great halo of bright light... the one that froze Daniel's hand, turned his knife on him, and threw him across the room?' Emily's voice expressed not only sarcasm, but also irritation. 'We've covered this before. It has nothing to do with having *gifts*?'

'Maybe not,' Sarah looked glum. 'We'll not know until we find Effie or Ellen.'

'They may no longer be named that.' Emily pretended to neglect the fact that she was indeed curious about her sisters. 'And to having gifts, well it's all a bit stupid, don't you agree?'

'Effie May and Ellen Louise.' Sarah stated, staring earnest into Emily's eyes. 'That is what I christened them, but since adoption, you could be right, they could be known as...?' Sarah raised her hands to open them to gesture. 'But one thing will be sure...' Sarah's face grinned with admiration. 'They'll surely be just as beautiful as you my angel.'

Feeling Sarah caress her hand and detecting her mother's sincerity, Emily placed her hand on top to ask a question.

'So you named me Emily... it's not what Mike or Rachael gave?'

'I had you christened Emily Rose, and asked the adoption agencies to keep all girls names as they were christened.'

'So my sisters, Effie and Ellen, they should still have the same names?'

'Maybe,' Sarah yawned, 'if, when adopted the agencies kept their promise, but how was I to know in that place? They only told me the parents' names and some sketchy background story. And I was confused then, too distraught by what happened.' Sarah stretched her aching limbs and cradled her head in the corner of the sofa bed. 'But I'm out now and...' Again she yawned, Emily following suit.

'So it isn't coincidence that all our names begin with an e?'

'No, I named you all that way,' Sarah smiled, 'the same letter as Evelyn and her sisters names began with. Elizabeth and Eleanor were the other sisters. Somehow it all relates to mother earth... mother nature.'

'Yes, and like myself, this mother must be tired. It's surely been a momentous day, but an exhausting one.' Emily swivelled to refill

Colin Martin

their two sherry glasses from the sofa bed and offered one to Sarah, 'But maybe another, just to finish off our celebration?' Emily looked to her mother and smiled to find that she had already nodded off.

She turned to put one glass down, but sipped at the other; her thoughts somehow numbed by alcohol, but her mind full of memories. As she watched flames dance in the gas fire, she recalled times at school, most enshrouded by the parental governance of Mike and Rachael. But as she attended college and scuffed two years at university, she began to realise how independent she had been all along. And now she grasped that it was her lonesome trips to visit the institute that brought all this on.

At first Emily could not understand the negative and uncompassionate behaviour from her biological mother, but as she grew into being a teenager and talked with girls of similar background, she had discovered things along the way. And these had not just been secrets about Sarah's past, but more importantly the pressure Mike and Rachael had put on themselves.

By the time she was ten, she would perceive when Mike and Rachael were to argue, and so travel to visit her mother. She thought it best the institute staff question the dedication she had to her real mother, than to witness commotion back home. Mike had never hit her since she was young and disobedient, but as an anxious teenager, it was getting harder not to reveal her promised secret. Every day she pledged that one-day she would disclose her foster parent's quarrels to Sarah, but for some reason it had never occurred.

Maybe by the time she had left school, she had found a way to ignore it; having Sarah, a now more considerate and loving person who showed great appreciation for her visits. And by the time she had left college to study at university, Mike and Rachael were practically out the picture. But she would never forget the many times Mike had saved her from boys that were attracted to her; one constantly following her home to beg her to go out with him. Rachael, herself had virtually dragged Emily to school to argue with the headmaster; that some girl had bullied her once she had become involved with this other girl's past boyfriend. And of course it was Rachael that

78

pushed her hard through sport and athletics; found that she had a natural and fast swimming technique.

After some difficult affairs during college and university, Emily could handle herself, but she could never give up her dedication to visit Sarah. When Mike had got her the junior journalist internship, she never looked further than to do work. As for love, Emily looked no further than that from her foster parents and of course, Sarah. Indeed, as she had found her footing in the company, and now had her own property, her relationship with Mike and Rachael had come close again. But maybe this was because they all wanted to get Sarah acquitted?

Emily sipped again at the sherry and turned to look at Sarah, her thoughts on-going. *But she is out now and here with me. Mike... Rachael, I will keep you close like a special aunt and uncle, and maybe they'll help me find these long lost sisters, but Aunt Evelyn, who the hell was she? Mother Nature... nobody believes in that stuff anymore?*

Suddenly Emily heard Sarah yawn and exhale. She finished her drink and faced her mother to watch her wriggle uncomfortably against the corner of the sofa bed. Carefully Emily placed a flat cushion between Sarah's head and the sofa bed, and then drew a blanket up level with her mother's neck.

For a moment Emily stared at Sarah, her mind full of distorted memories. She turned and smiled before taking the glass of sherry intended for her mother. In one gulp Emily finished off the sherry, and considering her other sisters, whispered, 'one thing at a time.' Slowly she ignored her troubled thoughts and rested her weary head in the opposite corner of the sofa bed.

Suddenly Emily awoke, her drowsy mind shocked by some vision. At first her heart raced and she felt sick, as though her dry throat would convulse and vomit the undigested party food. But slowly, as her eyes focused on the room and she took deep breaths, she gathered herself, her body and hands now only clammy from previously sweating. At first she could see the gas fire flames dance before her, but as the vision returned, she grasped at the sketchpad, hoping that drawing her fear would eliminate it.

Quickly Emily picked out a pencil from her bag, somehow knowing the funny light would enshroud her again. Soon, without vision and study, Emily's hands scribed the paper in frenzy; her eyes glazed peculiarly, her breathing heavy, and her limbs twitching fretfully.

It was not until the table lamp lit up the room that Emily's drawing frenzy stopped. At first with her eyes blurred, Sarah asked if she could go to bed and get a proper night sleep. But as Sarah's vision cleared, she noticed her daughter sitting still with her hand poised against the sketchpad.

Ignoring her request, Sarah watched Emily stand; her body unstable and the sketchpad drop from her hand. Not yet awake, Sarah grasped the sketchpad from the floor, asking to why Emily dropped it. But as Sarah observed Emily more clearly, she could see that her daughter's eyes were fixed and staring.

'Emily... my Emily,' Sarah queried warily, 'are you alright my dear?'

After rubbing her eyes, Sarah scrutinised her daughter again, worried to how she stood unsteady. Suddenly Emily dropped, her body slumbering back upon the sofa bed. Again Sarah asked if her daughter was all right, but there was no answer. And so Sarah examined the sketchpad, curious to know what she had drawn.

'I'm okay now mother, I think.'

It was not the delayed and slow reply that made Sarah shiver all over, but the hideous drawing her daughter had sketched so unwittingly.

'How come you've drawn *this* Emily?' Sarah enquired, her voice revealing revolt. 'It's so hideous and...' Sarah's throat clogged as her body went cold.

'I don't know,' Emily replied, her senses now returning, 'it's just some creature I envisaged... something from a horrible vision I just had.' Emily faced her mother. 'I do them unknowingly... sometimes out of anger... sometimes fear.' Suddenly she realised to how pale her mother had become. 'I know it's hideous, but it's usually me that turns pale. That's what Ange says anyhow?' Emily realised that there was more to Sarah's silence. 'What's up mother?'

'Well you should fear this thing,' Sarah trembled as she crept close, her voice croaking. 'I dreamed this horrible apparition when I was in that place.'

'Maybe it's true then,' Emily teased. 'Maybe mother and daughter do share psychic talent... horrible dark ghosts included?'

TWELVE

AT FIRST HE WOULD NOT open the door, but as Amanda had argued incessantly with Daniel's neighbour, the fat landlord had responded to their call. But as the landlord stood poised with the key to Daniel's flat, he again doubted Amanda's frenetic behaviour.

'It's so late miss, and we all know that Mr Whittaker likes the drink?'

'But something has happened to him, I know it!'

'And you've tried the phone?'

'Yes for God's sake,' Amanda shouted, pointing to the neighbour at the end of the corridor. 'So has he, and there's no response!'

The big man screwed up his chubby face and looked towards the neighbour. From some distance he could see the frail, elderly man sheepishly nodding his head, his encounter with Amanda not as gracious as he first thought.

'I just hope you have good cause for this call out miss.' The landlord put the key in the door and pressed a release button on a keypad beside. 'We don't tolerate disturbance around here, especially when it's late.'

'Will you just open the fucking door,' Amanda sighed, her arms folded and supporting a canvass bag. 'Check things out and I'll be on my way.'

'Don't tolerate swearing either,' the landlord muttered as he swung the door open. 'Just check on him whilst I wait... and then we can all be on our way.'

Amanda brushed past the fat man and slowly entered the room. Again it was shadowy, the only light cast from a distant desk lamp. But strangely, the lamp was on the floor. And then she saw how ransacked the room was. Indeed Daniel was not the tidiest of people, but the place looked as if it had been robbed.

Amanda edged closer to Daniel's large and sturdy desk, half of its usual contents littering the floor. She squinted to scrutinise the room, her dark eyes eventually coming back to focus again on the desk. She leaned forward to examine the extent of disorder behind the desk, but saw something else. At first she recognised the large, timeworn book that once belonged to the doctor; the one Daniel never kept from sight. But as she inspected closer, she saw a hand clenching the book. Amanda peered closer, her upper thighs pivoted against the corner of the desk for support. It was then that she recognised Daniel's overturned wheelchair, his body slumped against it and stretched upon the floor. Slowly Amanda stepped around the edge of the desk to see Daniel's body in full view.

'Is he in there?' the landlord broke the silence to startle Amanda.

'Yes, yes he's here,' Amanda shouted, deliberating whether to investigate the horror she saw. 'But wait a minute will you?'

She had hoped just to see Daniel collapsed by consuming the contents of another whisky bottle, but as his body came into full view, she froze.

Although his body faced Amanda, Daniel's limbs and head did not. The hand holding tight the book was twisted backward, the elbow joint snapped and arm pulled from the shoulder. The other arm, Daniel's scarred and disfigured side was even more mutilated; the hand lacerated and shattered from the wrist in his attempt to defend, his arm strangely elongated as if dislodged from its shoulder socket.

Stepping gingerly around Daniel's outstretched body, Amanda could see in the shadowy light, his scarred and deformed head. It was not just that his full disfigurement was revealed, but his face was elongated, his mouth stretched downward as if melted wax, somehow capturing his gasp of terror. His glazed eyes too were frozen in a glare that exhibited such fear. And against a blue tinted, pale face that shone like a cold night moon, Amanda was repulsed.

She almost retched, but again heard the landlord question.

'Wait one minute,' she asked, eagerly pulling the doctor's book away from Daniel's grasp. 'The place looks like it's been robbed.' But Amanda now realised that this was no murdering thief, but something else.

Amanda stepped away slowly from Daniel's corpse, trying best to neglect the image she had just seen, but pictured him by memory. Placing the book carefully in her canvass bag, she mused at the window. He had always opened that window after she had visited, as he had never liked her smoking, but never stopped her. She presumed he had never opposed certain things in his secret affection for her.

Quickly Amanda acted on hearing the landlord moan from the doorway, and so as he came in, she gathered what she could from the desk and floor. First she took the doctor's diary and then a tattered notebook; maybe then those letters. But as the landlord questioned to what she was doing, she simply ignored him and pointed.

'He's over there,' she announced, stepping back toward the window with a handful of letters. 'Looks like some robbery, and they've...' Along with the diary and notebook, Amanda shoved the letters in her canvass bag and pretended to care. 'I don't know what they've done to him but... I think he's dead.'

The landlord peered over the desk quickly before glancing back at her, 'Don't you think you'd better call the police, than take his stuff?'

'He wanted me to have it,' Amanda forced tears from her eyes, looking to the floor to inject memories. 'Carry on with his research he did... he told me to fulfil his master's legacy.'

Amanda wriggled her way towards the door but the landlord caught hold of her arm.

'I'm no detective, but I'm sure you can't take stuff from a crime scene.'

'Only a murder scene,' Amanda pretended, pulling away from his grip.

'So has he been murdered?'

'I'm not sure, but he looks...' Amanda ejected more tears. 'Why don't you check behind the desk yourself... *you* phone the police...? I'm too distraught.'

The landlord let go of Amanda's arm to walk and peer closer over the desk.

Amanda reached into her pocket for her car keys but pulled out a disc-shaped object, thinking it a large coin. In her palm she noticed the button she had pulled from Sarah's coat. As the landlord stepped carefully around the desk to examine Daniel's body more close, Amanda grinned, a deceitful thought overcoming her. Quickly from her other pocket she retrieved a handkerchief and cleaned the button. As the landlord stared back at her, she noticed his face go pale.

'I'd better get the police quickly,' he said slow, 'never seen anything like it.'

'Yes, mister, I would do that, and quickly.'

As the landlord glanced back to take a last look at the murder scene, Amanda flicked the cleansed button from her handkerchief, to watch it bounce beneath the desk.

The landlord swung around to ask Amanda for her mobile phone, but found that she was gone. He raced to the doorway only to be greeted by the curious neighbour.

PART TWO

THIRTEEN

WITH A WORRIED EXPRESSION EMILY opened her front door.

'Emily,' a deep masculine voice enquired. 'Are you Miss Emily...' the detective paused to look down at his notepad, 'Aston-Layton?'

'Yes,' Emily replied, viewing the tall black man inquisitively, his hair shaved almost to the skin on his head. 'I am Emily, who wants to know?'

'Well actually Miss,' the detective looked over Emily's shoulder, as if to peer into her hallway, 'I'm following an investigation in which I need to speak to a Miss Sarah Layton, who I believe is your mother... your biological mother?' He paused again to read his notepad. 'I was told, since her release from the Wiltshire Rehabilitation Centre that she's been staying here?'

'And you are?' Emily pondered on just who the man was.

'Sorry Miss,' the detective grinned, realising he had not shown any identification. 'I'm Detective Nathan Lawrence, and I need to speak with your mother, Sarah Layton.' After showing his identification, the detective replaced it inside his wallet, before sliding it back into his trouser pocket.

Emily spun round, not letting go of the door as it was half open, but also using her foot to secure it. She called for Sarah several times before returning to face the detective.

'What is this all about officer?' Emily was concerned. 'Sarah is somewhat of my responsibility now, so if you don't mind...?

As Sarah joined her daughter to peer around the door, the detective announced the shocking news.

'I've come to question you Miss Layton.' He cleared his throat. 'Miss Sarah Layton, I require information about the murder of a Mr Daniel Whittaker?'

Sarah and Emily looked at each other in shock; the detective realising that their surprise was genuine.

'Murdered,' Emily requisitioned. 'Daniel Whittaker murdered, but surely...? The detective looked at each woman in turn. 'But what's this got to do with us?' Emily changed her tone, something she always did to cover up tension. 'Surely you don't think...? She paused before ridiculing the detective. 'Oh, so you think my mother killed Daniel in a revenge killing, something she planned as soon as she got out, is that it?'

'No Miss Emily. That is not the case.' The detective shrugged off her cynical remark, somehow knowing she was emotional. 'But if we can speak inside, I'll try to be brief, and get the information I need.'

Emily looked around to see her mother nod and walk back into the lounge.

'I'm sorry, detective...?'

'Nathan... Nathan Lawrence.'

'So sorry, but with all the court proceedings and paperwork...?' Emily held her forehead for a while and then rolled her eyes. 'Won't you come in? I'm forgetting my manners. Maybe I can get you a drink, coffee... tea?'

'No, thank you, I'm fine,' the detective said, pacing into the lounge and looking at its décor, 'but thank you again for your hospitality.'

'Then take a seat?' Emily prompted, pointing to one opposite an anxious Sarah.

'No, I'm fine miss,' he declared, 'I think better when I'm standing.'

Sarah observed him cautiously, regarding his last remark as some introduction to an interrogation method. Her eyes followed him about the room, observing everything he examined.

'So you've been stopping here with your daughter since leaving the institute?'

'Yes Mr Lawrence, I mean detective,' Sarah answered sheepishly. 'Only the other day did I finally...'

'Yes Miss Layton, I am aware when you got released,' the detective interrupted.

Sarah sat quiet until Emily joined her side to offer a mug of tea.

'My mother has been here for three nights now.' Emily caught hold of the conversation. 'I give her medicines as ordered and so forth.'

'So she was with you last night?' the detective directed his question to Emily.

'Yes, we were both home together, after my foster parents left.' Emily sat on the arm of the armchair beside her mother. 'We had a little celebration for Sarah's release.'

'But what has this got to do with that Daniel,' Emily observed her mother look up at her as she spoke. 'Surely you don't suspect...?'

The detective turned his back on them to look directly at the extinguished gas fire.

'Miss Sarah,' the detective again cleared his throat, 'do you happen to have a button missing from a coat of yours?'

'But what the hell has that got to do with –'

'It's okay, puppet,' Sarah intervened, getting to her feet. 'I'll take a look.'

Emily eyed the detective narrowly and weaved her fingers through her dark hair, another thing she did when tense. She watched him again circle the room, wondering to what he knew, or the things he wanted to know. Agitated, she took another sip of her tea.

'There are two of them missing,' Sarah announced fretfully as she came back into the lounge. 'How did you know?'

The detective slowly pulled a small cellophane bag from his own coat pocket, its transparency exposing a single button inside. As the two women realised a similarity, they stared at one another in bewilderment.

'So how come you've got one?' Emily questioned.

'And where's the other?' Sarah followed to enquire.

The detective came over to take the coat and verify the match. It was only when he found that another button was missing did he reply.

'I'm not sure about the other button.' Again the detective cleared his throat. 'But this one was found during a primary investigation at Daniel Whittaker's residence; the place of his murder.'

'Well I don't know how it got there, coz Sarah was with me here all last night?' After all the work Emily had done to get her mother acquitted, she knew she had to control her temper. 'We had a home-coming party, like I told you!'

'So, Sarah,' the detective turned his focus to Emily's mother, noticing how she clenched her hands nervously. 'How do you think one of your buttons got to Mr Whittaker's crime scene?'

'I don't know,' Sarah responded with anger, but her voice breaking. 'It's the first I knew that they were gone. Maybe I lost them the other day, but I'm not sure.'

'Can't we do this some other time?' Emily noticed Sarah getting distraught. 'She's not really had time to settle in.'

'When was the last time you knew the buttons were on your coat?' the detective pried, ignoring Emily's request.

Emily stood to stamp her feet, trying best to control her indignation to intervene.

'I remember undoing all buttons to take off that coat when we were in court... the day I got acquitted.'

'And when did you first know they were missing?'

'I didn't know until now, not until you asked me to fetch the thing!'

Emily could see that her mother was getting restless, her voice and hands nervy. And because of her busy morning, Emily had forgotten to give her mother the prescribed medication.

'Can't you lay off her for a while,' Emily interjected, 'she's not yet had her medication.'

'Sorry to say Miss Emily, but it sounds like you've not started very well with your responsibilities, have you now?'

'And what would you know about that?' Emily played again with her long hair. 'Lord, why are people of authority so quick to...?' She stamped her feet like a distraught schoolgirl. 'Why you're worse than that solicitor woman harassing us!'

The detective turned around from studying framed pictures upon the mantelpiece, to squint at Emily, his eyes quickly studying Sarah before returning to Emily.

'You wouldn't be referring to a Miss Amanda Burley by any chance, would you?'

'Yes,' Emily spluttered her contempt for the solicitor, 'that be that horrible woman who accosted us.'

'She's horrible, spiteful and evil, that –'

But the detective's question interrupted Sarah's scorn, 'She accosted you?'

'Yes, Mr Lawrence,' Sarah disclosed. 'Emily had hardly had chance to rejoice with me before that woman squabbled with us in court.'

'We won the case fair and square,' Emily added, 'the judge's sentence final, after hearing the verdict of the jury that is.'

'And yet I hear that the woman is highly regarded as a solicitor,' the detective muttered, scratching his chin in thought, 'and circles in good community.'

'A black widow spider weaves a web to lure its prey, but to a lot it is invisible.'

Emily turned from hearing her mother mutter, to face the detective.

'So have you met this solicitor woman and seen how nasty she can be?'

'Funny you should mention that,' the detective said, fingering with the button within its package before replacing it back into his coat pocket, 'but earlier this morning I questioned Miss Burley about some property of Daniel's that the landlord said she took after finding him murdered.' The detective flicked through his notepad. 'Interestingly, Miss Burley also told me, that through history Sarah has always held a grudge against Daniel for being an accomplice to her partner's murder, a Mr. Carl Aston?'

'That's not the truth,' Sarah professed. 'Mike said Carl saved me from… and Mike saved me from fire!'

'Look mister,' Emily's composure had snapped. 'Don't bring up that stuff as it really upsets her. Can't you see she's distraught already?'

'I'm only doing my job miss.'

'Yes and we've answered your question… we were here all last night!'

'Are there any other witnesses to prove this?

Emily stared at the detective as she comforted her mother, her eyes narrowing with resentment.

'Ask my foster parents,' Emily affirmed with a harsh tone. 'As I said, they were here most of last night!' Emily turned to hug her mother after seeing the detective write in his notepad. She faced the detective again, disturbed at how he studied the room. 'Now if you don't mind mister, Sarah needs her medication and I have house work to do.'

'Will it make her drowsy?'

'What, the medication?' Emily was flustered. 'It will make her sleep awhile, but what has that got to do with things?'

'Well, when she feels up to it, maybe later today,' the detective tried to convey sincerity in his voice, 'we'd like her to make a statement down at the station... the police station in Bristol Road.'

Again Emily awaited acknowledgement from her mother, and after some whispering, Emily agreed.

'She'll have a walk down there late this afternoon, so I can pick her up after work... is that okay?'

'Yes, thank you Emily, but one last request?'

'And that is?' Emily rolled her eyes before glancing at her mother.

'Can I take that coat for analysis,' the detective asked pointing at Sarah's overcoat. 'I'd like to make an exact match between the buttons?'

'Do as you wish young man,' Sarah said, 'if it proves our innocence to you.' Sarah leaned forward, her eyes staring hard at the constable. 'But remember one thing young man... and that is to never trust that woman.'

'Again you scorn that solicitor, but why?'

'Solicitor or not,' Sarah renounced, 'that woman cannot be trusted... that woman is evil.'

'Sarah, the only evil stuff she has, is some stupid research she claims Daniel left her.' The detective chuckled to himself. 'And a few books on witchcraft, borrowed from the central library.'

FOURTEEN

She glanced about the room, trying to find inspiration; or was it the fact that picturing Daniel's mutilated body was so distracting. Even though the police were baffled to how someone, or something, had got in to murder Daniel, Amanda knew fore well to what had happened. But she had only heard about the stories of hideous creatures, ghosts and apparitions, the evil that could be summoned. At first it all seemed so incredible, but now?

She stared down at the doctor's notes, her head a vast ocean of unanswered questions. Maybe she had to admit that such research was more than a challenge, that Daniel must have found a way to summon evil before her knowing. Or maybe he knew beforehand, but wanted to keep it secret? Yet she was way more intelligent than some stupid, past groundskeeper, some alcoholic bent on avenging some woman for his disability. But Daniel had found a way to summon evil; the fact that some hellish fiend had mutilated him was proof. And what was more disconcerting, was that if Daniel had the answers, by now the police would have his research. Even as Daniel's solicitor, Amanda could not contemplate approaching the police, not until the murder case had calmed down somewhat.

Maybe then, using contacts she had in the right places, Amanda would find answers; vital information Daniel had gathered. Yet something niggled at her like some incessant itch; the want of this ancient knowledge to harvest dark forces, a way to ascertain indescribable power and gain wealth beyond her wildest dreams.

Amanda fetched her near extinct cigarette from the heavy, glass ashtray and dragged on its last remnants before stubbing it out. As she came back to reality with her thoughts, she was stressed to ponder over things Daniel had said, but hoped something might shine a light on the burden of documents littering her desk.

She considered another brandy but had to reject the desire. Determined, she would research more about Latin and its association to religion, witchcraft and ancient history, before approaching the bottle. Maybe she was not ready to learn about this seductive, dark power, and certainly would not make the same mistake as Daniel, especially if intoxicated. There were other ways to get things done. Yet her ploy to get Sarah arrested had been foiled.

As of yet, she had heard that Sarah had been suspected, but was primarily a lead in police investigations. Surely with Sarah's coat button found at Daniel's murder scene, it was obvious that she should be arrested? Suddenly, after picturing again the horrific crime scene, Amanda realised to how mutilated Daniel's body had been. What kind of thing can do that to a human, even one already disfigured like Daniel?

Maybe there were other, more subtle ways, to avenge Daniel's murder and settle a score with Sarah, but this could get police bothering her, maybe detectives prying into her personal history. How could she cover her own back? *One day*, she promised herself, *I will find a way to call on dark forces to do my bidding. But up until then, its research, and finishing the translations Daniel had worked on prior his death.*

She looked again at the doctor's notes and to the key translations Daniel had worked on. Online research had proved helpful, but some leads were blocked and forbidden, restricted or cumbersome to interpret. Apart from some part-confidential and historic library resources, a lot of researches led to false witch cults and sexual promiscuity. However, with what she had remembered from past conversations with Daniel, and by using the results he had gathered, Amanda knew she had to decipher Latin words that the doctor had inscribed from an old Celtic language. With reference to the doctor's diary, he had found an old religion that incorporated similar rites between Irish and Celtic folklore, to voodoo practiced in particular islands of the West Indies. She had read this before, but noticed how the doctor had arranged letters to be part of a key.

The ceremony he prescribed was predominantly formulated on ancient Celtic folklore, but the witchcraft ritual of 'bloodletting' was a personal sacrifice practised by witch doctors. After all her recent study, Amanda now gathered from the doctor's notes, and to what Daniel had interpreted, that blood sacrificed to a warlock's stone, or 'calling stone', would invoke evil spirits. And with the correct ceremony, the conjurer could summon demons upon the earth to do unholy bidding; set creatures of the underworld against mankind. But as told to Amanda by Daniel, there was no longer any warlock's stone.

Again Amanda came to a dead end, but one obviously Daniel had seen his way through; how to conjure such evil without this 'calling stone'? She had not noticed if Daniel had sacrificed blood to summon evil that night, but with what had happened to him, she knew the precautions he had taken beforehand had not worked – that without some protective circle or magical precedence, he would be slaughtered by the evil he invoked. How could he be so stupid, or was his measures of precaution overwhelmed by such an evil entity? She had read some on the doctor's methods of protection, but reckoned Daniel must have relied on trying to command the evil entity by words of the ancient language. Obviously, that had not worked.

She read again some central pages from the doctor's diary, his pressured inscriptions emphasising their importance. Three or four pages described the blood sacrifice and its significance to the invocation. Further pages then described the doctor's ideas to protect oneself from such evil; that mercury, salt, water and sulphur were effective, but not so much as a sacred circle, especially like that used in the Sabbath. And that only the words of supremacy would send evil back to hell.

Amanda read on to find leaves of folded paper she had not seen in the diary before, ones she had not copied. After reading, she gathered that these were notes the doctor had added later. She found that the doctor was researching a way to protect himself from the blood sacrifice ceremony, should the 'calling stone' spell be broken. As she read on she learned that the doctor had practiced the 'bloodletting' ritual using other things, but after using hair, saliva, urine and semen, only once did hair prove positive. But it was blood that was life, he described devotedly; that it was blood that supplied life by oxygenation, stimulated sexual arousal, flowed love and hatred around the body, and that human blood was a delicacy to drink for devils and demons.

Suddenly Amanda's concentration was averted to the ring of her mobile phone. As it blasted out some whimsical tune, she regarded the caller with surprise.

'Yes, professor,' the number had been recognised, 'what gets you to call this late at night?'

'I've just heard about Mr Whittaker's death,' the professor told, his voice somewhat anxious. 'Investigators are puzzled by how it happened, how anyone could've got in?'

'Yes professor, it is but a mystery.' Amanda grinned to view the research on her desk.

'I know what you are doing,' the professor stated, 'and can only suggest you don't delve any further in stuff like that.'

'Like what professor?'

'That of which the doctor did?'

'But professor, you attended the ceremonies like I did all those years ago,' Amanda's voice was again cynical, 'and enjoyed our late evening escapades. I believe you came quite highly rated in our *astrological* society?'

'I'm only giving you prior warning Miss Burley,' the professor's voice lowered with sincerity. 'What happened to Daniel is I believe the same as the doctor. And I think should you continue –'

'The doctor got burned from his mansion fire?'

'Believe that if you wish my dear.'

'Anyway Mr Grayling,' Amanda snapped back, 'I don't profess to have the level of knowledge the doctor had... not as of yet, anyhow.'

'Well my dear,' Professor Grayling paused. 'I can only hope you don't delve too deep in things that should be left alone.'

'And why not,' Amanda asked before surmising, 'maybe you'll find this research interesting? It's quite up your street.'

'You've researched enough to...?'

'Well Daniel had got so far, but obviously his aptitude was not right.' Amanda averted from research that was puzzling her. 'He wanted Sarah Layton dead, but looks like it reverted back around. Probably didn't do it right.'

'The ritual, you mean... the ceremony?'

'But I guess until this research comes clear, things will have to be done in a more subtle way.' Amanda paused, acknowledging the professor's heavy breathing was due to unease. 'Sarah Layton isn't going to get off that lightly, or her pretty little daughter. These car crashes can be somewhat accidental, but quite inevitable.'

'But my dear Amanda,' the professor said with conviction. 'Why be like Daniel and be so fixated on the woman. Such dirty tricks could get you into trouble, even if we share such accommodating contacts?'

'What and your little artefacts business haven't dirty fingers?'

'That's different, it don't harm anyone?'

'Doesn't it,' Amanda spat out venomously, 'what about those who loose thousands due to forgeries?'

'Most of that stuff was salvaged from the doctor's mansion, only some were replicated.' The professor sighed heavily. 'Besides, I have a more reputable career now my dear.'

'Yes, but that nice country manor didn't come cheap, even if you bought it some years back. Auctioned off most stuff to buy that house then, did we?' Apart from static, the phone was silent. 'Talking of the doctor, we must get his dark coven going once more... just to support his legacy, and that of Daniel of course.'

'Miss Burley, I think you have other ideas?'

'I would if I could understand the late doctor's notes.' Amanda stopped abruptly, her voice expressing surprise. 'Why professor, you have a reasonable knowledge into languages don't you?'

'What if I do?' the professor said. 'If you're talking about that ancient text, well I...?'

'Surprisingly, professor, I was.' Amanda intervened to convey a tone of incentive. 'Why this ancient Latin is right up your street... I could do with help to unravel these key translations.'

'Then maybe I should take some lead on this.' The professor cleared his throat to continue. 'Besides, we were like brothers, me and Joseph.'

'And why would a professor like *you* want to harness such dark power?'

'Well it's a man's job, you know, being the lead.' The professor's voice came over strong. 'The doctor would have wanted a *man* to be adjudicator, someone of stature, like himself.'

'Why is it men have this gender discrimination?' Amanda snarled. 'Why is everything questioned comes down to gender?' She spoke on before the professor could intervene. 'Daniel said the same stupid thing about his wise monkeys?'

'Daniel's what?'

'Never mind professor,' Amanda asserted, 'just something of research.'

'So you'll want help with that research?'

'Maybe, I'll see.' Amanda wondered to how naive the professor could be.

'I could get copies and advise you of my own translations?'

'Professor, I'll think about it.' Amanda was too involved in this research to pass it on, but maybe she could use the professor's knowledge, even if only a little. 'Tell you what Mr Grayling, you pay that offshore account the sum we discussed, and we'll look into this together... maybe get that old astrological society back?'

FIFTEEN

EMILY SPUN ROUND TO SLAM shut her car door and lock it. As she turned back to face the long pavement leading up to the police station, she paused momentarily. Noticing the time on her wristwatch, she continued quickly up a number of steps and followed the pathway until it reached a level, open area where paved slabs had replaced most grass.

Muddled to find the main entrance, Emily turned full circle, her eyes examining all the buildings around her. As there were many routes to different doors, she searched the area for signage.

'If you're looking for the main entrance,' a voice announced, 'it's that way.'

Emily turned briskly, the voice from behind startling her. Two hands reached out to grab her arms. She looked up in bewilderment until her gaze met that of Jack, the annoying but handsome man who pretended to be shop assistant. In the fading light, but enlightened by a lamp above, Emily saw his eyes twinkle blue. His brown hair appeared darker in the twilight, his height somewhat taller, but most of all, she felt the strength of his grip. For a moment her eyes fixed on his and she could not look away. But then she realised her purpose there.

'If you're after the main entrance,' Jack said, pointing in a southerly direction, 'it's that path down there my dear.'

'Thank you mister,' Emily tried to regard Jack as a stranger. 'I'm already late so...' She pulled away, desperate to meet her mother, but found Jack tugging on one arm.

'Hang on a minute,' Jack could not understand Emily's timidity. 'I met you at the jewellers and you seemed interested then?'

'Interested? Interested in what?' Emily pulled again on her restrained arm. 'Interested in getting stuff for my –'

'Sisters,' Jack interjected. 'Yes, you wanted three similar crucifixes, one for each.'

'But you didn't have any in stock, so could you please…' Emily diverted her gaze at her arm as she could get hypnotised by those alluring blue eyes. 'I'm already late to meet my mother.'

'What about the date you posted,' Jack asked, 'made me a friend so we could talk?'

'I don't know what you're talking about mister, but please let go of my arm.'

'But it's you… Emily?'

'You have the wrong woman.'

'You're Emily,' Jack stated adamantly, 'Emily Aston-Layton.' He paused to get her attention, her eyes now observing his sincerity. 'I've been trying to get your attention for ages and being a little shy, I…' As she stood, her face full of bewilderment, Jack was amazed at how beautiful she looked. He cleared his throat and looked straight into her dark eyes, trying best to keep his composure. 'But when you said that you were interested… asked me to agree our friendship online, well I…?'

'I'm sorry mister, but I…?'

'Jack,' he interrupted, smiling, 'my name is Jack Torrance. You posted for me to agree our friendship online?'

'I've done nothing of the sort,' Emily stated, finally pulling her arm free. 'I hardly use such social media, unless…?'

'Unless what, Miss Emily?'

'Unless…' Emily fingered with her mouth whilst thinking, 'my friend at work has done it for me?'

'You didn't agree it yourself?'

'No,' Emily's annoyance changed to empathy. 'I'm sorry but I think my work friend has done it without me knowing.' Emily looked around, still desperate to meet Sarah. 'You know the one who came in the shop with me?'

'The little, stumpy one…?'

'By God don't let her hear you called her that, or she'll have…' Emily squinted in the distance to see Sarah striding quickly towards her.

'They were George's words, not mine.'

'George?'

'The shop keeper, my friend who let me...?'

Emily stepped away from Jack to greet her mother, quickly saying goodbye to leave the man dumbfounded. But Sarah turned to face Jack after giving her daughter a hug.

'And who's this, Emily,' Sarah pried, 'a friend of yours?'

'No, not really, mother... more a case of mistaken identity.' Sarah edged close to Jack. 'He was helping with directions.'

'My name is Jack my dear.' He put out his hand to greet Sarah, 'I work at the university. I'd really like to get to know Emily more.'

Emily turned her mother away from Jack and ushered her along the path, only glancing back once to acknowledge her thanks. But in that one, personal and secret moment, she caught her last glance of Jack's handsome but bewildered face.

'Hope to see you again my boy.' Sarah announced, Emily pulling her along.

Jack stood deflated, the thought of Emily liking him gone, shot down by the truth; that her friend had played some stupid trick with their online profiles.

'Come on mother, I've got news.' Emily could not glance back again; she had other things on her mind.

'But he's cute,' Sarah said winking an eye. 'He reminds me of Carl... got nice eyes and smiles like him.'

'How can you remember mother,' Emily questioned, whisking Sarah quickly down steps to her car, 'it was years ago, and you've not got a single picture?'

'But I have you know,' Sarah said putting a forefinger up against her lips. 'But don't tell that to Mike or Rachael.'

Emily positioned Sarah beside the passenger door of her car before ambling round to the driver's side. She stood for a while to stare over the rooftop, bemused to why her mother did not get in. Instead Sarah's grim face watched another car pull away quickly and race up a side street.

'What is it mother?' Emily glanced back over her shoulder to look in the direction of Sarah's stare. 'What's wrong?' But her mother grabbled with the car door, muttering to herself as she seated inside. 'What's wrong mother?' Emily grabbed Sarah's arm after seating herself behind the steering wheel.

'You didn't see that car did you?' Sarah said ominously. 'I'm sure that evil woman was driving it.'

'Who, that solicitor,' Emily glanced again out the window, 'are you sure?'

'No, but,' Sarah rubbed her eyes, her face weary. 'It certainly looked like her.'

Emily paused to acknowledge the anxiety on Sarah's face, but she had good news for her mother.

'Never mind that woman mother, I have good news.'

Sarah turned her eyes from the road and watched Emily's hands comfort hers.

'What news?' Sarah now stared at her daughter. 'What news could be better than having evidence that I didn't murder Daniel Whittaker?'

'Mike has given a statement?' Emily had forgotten to realise that the detective had grilled her mother.

'Yes, and so did Rachael, so yours will not be needed.'

Emily poised, her face dumbfounded. But then she clenched Sarah's hands tight, rejoicing that her mother's innocence was again substantiated.

'Why that's great news,' Emily affirmed. 'So we can now finally get all that shit behind us.' She recoiled back into her seat to start the engine.

'So what's this *other* good news my dear?'

Emily drove the car out into the road after checking the wing mirror, her mind focused on traffic. But then after turning a corner, she comprehended to what her mother had asked.

'Oh yes mother, I know you won't know much about online stuff but...'

'I'll have you remember girl,' Sarah interrupted. 'I did a bit in that institute.'

'Maybe, but not to the extent of research I've had to do.' Emily glanced away from the road to see her mother perplexed. 'It's taken some searching and telephone calls, but I've found Effie!'

'My second... you're middle sister?' Sarah's face lit up. 'Effie May?'

'Yes, its great news that she's okay and all that, but I'm afraid...' Emily paused to realise that Sarah had only just been released from such a place. 'Apparently, after being adopted when we were babies, her foster parents found something wrong with her.'

'Something wrong with her,' Sarah became angry. 'What kind of something?'

'As an infant they thought she had just adopted imaginable friends, like a lot of children do, but...'

'Go on,' Sarah implored, not realising Emily had paused to navigate a tighter turn.

'Well their local doctor thought the same too, but it went on into her being a teenager,' Emily glanced again at her mother to recognise her disgruntlement, 'well it went on that they thought she was speaking to herself, but after secret tests, and tests in hospital, she was found to be doing things that these *invisible friends* had told her to do.' She paused to watch her mother's head drop. 'It came to a point where the foster parents hardly had her at home.' Emily glanced again at Sarah, knowing that what she had found out next would upset her more. 'And when she was found cutting her arms...?'

'My Effie, cutting her arms,' Sarah babbled, 'for why?'

'The doctor wouldn't disclose too much on the telephone, even if I told him who I was.' Emily changed gear and accelerated; the road ahead straight. 'Apparently she had collected a bunch of knives, hiding each about different places around...'

Suddenly Emily felt a vibration in her pocket before her mobile phone blurted out a ringtone. Awkwardly she pivoted one leg against the steering wheel to prise her mobile from her pocket.

'Yes this is Emily.' Suddenly she recognised the voice of Detective Nathan Lawrence. 'Yes she is here. I picked her up from the station about ten minutes ago.' The detective asked if Sarah was all right. 'Yes, why, what's up?' Emily responded, but missed some of his dialogue. 'Hang on Mr Lawrence; I'll put you on hands free.'

Both Emily and Sarah could hear the mobile phone from a dashboard recess, but had lost half of his sentence. However, they gathered that the detective had located Sarah's other coat button.

'Where did you find it?' the mother and daughter asked simultaneously.

'Well Miss Emily, I remembered you telling me about Sarah's scuffle with Miss Burley and so searched the courtroom. At first I found nothing, but quite accidentally bumped into one of the cleaners who service the courts. She emptied a hoover she had used over the past couple of months, and inside the bag was a button matching Sarah's coat. Obviously a direct match has to be verified.'

'So Mr Lawrence, how did the other button happen to be found at...?

Abruptly Emily's mobile dropped to the floor, the words of the detective becoming incomprehensible. It was not that Emily had driven over a bump or scathed the car's underside, but something had shaken the car from the floor. And now, as Emily braked to fumble around her feet to reach her mobile, the brake pedal had no pressure. Several times she tried desperately to find pressure against the pedal, but the brakes failed to apply, the pedal flimsy and loose.

As Sarah started to panic and ask questions, Emily neglected her phone and sat up straight to observe the road ahead. Without brakes, the car was accelerating down an incline. And although the road was wide and straight, near the bottom were embankments that lead up to a bridge. Even if she could turn the car onto the bridge and hope the flat would eventually slow down the car, the abrupt turn might tip them over.

Her mother squabbled beside her. Anxious, Sarah's arms shot up to grip the roof, her body braced for an inevitable accident. Continually she roared questions to why Emily could not brake, but her daughter did not reply.

Emily glanced at each side of the street, looking for some way to slow down the car; this was their lives that were in danger. Suddenly she thought not of the brake pedal again, but that of the handbrake.

Emily wrenched on the handbrake, but it too came loose after something suddenly snapped. Again she pulled on the handbrake, but it's once taught wire was now broken, or somehow detached. Her mother's frantic behaviour added to Emily's hysteria, her mother shouting and screaming as Emily inadvertently steered the car wild. She glanced at the sides of the road, the pavements littered with people. What could she do but try to turn the car from going down the embankment and drive along the bridge?

As Emily swerved the car from side to side, trying to beat off her mother's panic attack, horns and shouts bellowed Emily's ears to intensify her mayhem. And now, yet fifty yards away was the embankment, and Emily was heading straight for it. If she swerved the car towards the bridge, surely they would end up at the bottom, the car a wreck and them...?

At the last moment, before the overpowering light, Emily recalled only trying to turn the steering wheel. Within the centre of the light, the chaos she heard from outside was somehow quashed, the voices and horns and panic a dim. Then she envisaged the squeal of brakes against the wheel plates, the mechanics of the brake shoes tight against metal. And the tighter she tensed, the tighter she felt the car brakes squeeze. In her imagination of sound, Emily's head pulsated as if it were to explode, but felt her whole body turn. But how could she, unless the car had turned with her?

Surrounded by an overpowering white light, Emily held firm onto the seat, her fingernails almost braking in gripping the car seat material. Suddenly she felt her body stop from the turn and her senses settle. And as her vision returned to nothing but a bright light, she came dizzy, her eyes blurred but enough to welcome the sight of the road again.

As Emily's sight became clear, she was now puzzled to how her car now faced backward; somehow a handbrake turn had twisted the car 180 degrees. And luckily this had also stopped it from going down the embankment. Noticing Sarah slumped back into her seat, Emily looked out the passenger window and up the road they had just come down. Somehow Sarah's side of the car now faced the middle of the road, but they were safe, or were they? Was this some dream you have during some dreadful accident? Would Emily wake up after it all in hospital?

'Emily?' a familiar voice shouted. 'Emily, are you alright?'

Emily turned her aching neck to see her mother glaring back at her.

'Yes mother, I think so, but my neck...?' Emily lifted a heavy hand to massage the back of her neck.

'Then what was that?'

'Then what was what?' Emily still only saw a vague image of her mother.

'The car turned at the last minute and I was sure we would...' Sarah gazed at Emily like someone crazed. 'But then I saw that bright light about you, like the one...' Sarah held a hand to her mouth. 'Like the one when you were just...' Sarah gasped to notice something else about Emily, but something now, quite real. 'Emily your nose... it's bleeding.'

Emily reached up her hand to wipe beneath her nose. As she pulled away her hand and looked to her forefinger, indeed it was blotted with blood. And now she could taste that sickly, copper tang in her mouth.

Emily sat up to examine her face through the rear view mirror, her head still a little dazed. Just like the time Angela had picked her up after imagining sounds of exploding air, Emily again had a nosebleed. She now questioned that surely this was not just some medical condition, some result of anxiety or stress? And she had nosebleeds before, totally ignoring what might have led to them. Thinking whether the handbrake had worked or she had turned the car by steering, Emily was now convinced that something else had saved them. Maybe Carl was looking down on them?

Perplexed by thought and shaken physically, Emily did not notice Sarah open the passenger door, but heard her mumble something about being safer outside the car. Emily leaned onto the passenger seat, trying to get her mother's attention.

'Mother, get inside,' Emily called, 'you'll be in the middle of the road!'

It happened within a flash. The car that had been travelling fast up to the bridge had swerved but caught the open door. Catapulted in a spin, Sarah was flung with the car door, along the wing and onto the road.

Emily could not understand her immediate reaction, but instead of checking on her mother, at first she searched the car to find her mobile to call an ambulance.

It was later, in the ambulance ride to hospital, that cold, nervous tension overwhelmed her body.

SIXTEEN

Upon a hospital bed, Emily held tight her mother's hand. By the bandaging around Sarah's other wrist, Emily knew that it was bones in that which had been fractured by the accident. As she looked gravely up at her mother's bruised and lacerated face, she could only imagine her dismay; the elation of being acquitted with murder and free after years at the institute, to be in hospital again, but this time for physical harm.

Although Sarah had been in hospital overnight, an earlier phone call had told Emily that all tests were not done. And as like with all car accidents, it was internal bleeding that could be problematic.

'Don't look so worried my child,' Sarah pondered trying to manoeuvre her other hand on top of her daughters, 'I think the worst of the pain had gone.'

'But why didn't you listen,' Emily croaked, her eyes already swollen with tears, 'I told you to stay in the car, but you...?'

'I was scared my dear.' Sarah's eyes exposed her sincerity. 'Not just because of the accident, but to what happened.' Sarah paused for a moment, noticing bewilderment on Emily's face. 'It was the same to what happened the night I tried to stop Daniel getting to you, and I thought it was the three of you that turned his knife against him. But now, I know it was you that brought such bright light... but with power from your sisters.'

'That's stupid mother, and you know it.' But Sarah could see by Emily's face that her daughter had no other answer, especially for the giddy spells. 'But how could I have done such a thing, and as a child?'

'I think Mike and Rachael should tell you stuff about the past, things they've probably kept from you as being your guardians.' Sarah looked around the room, puzzled to where her friends were. 'But tell me my girl, where are Mike and Rachael, as it was good of them to bring you?'

Emily turned at the bedside to take sight of her foster parents at the ward desk.

'I think they're talking to the doctor,' Emily told, pointing to the desk outside the ward. 'They said they wanted to know what medication you're on.'

Sarah squeezed Emily's hand to get back her attention.

'But what happened to your car?'

'It has been picked up and is at a local garage,' Emily replied, 'but it may have to have a new door.'

'Have they said why it wouldn't stop... to why the brakes failed?' Sarah asked, but Emily shook her head. 'I told you I saw that Amanda. Maybe she did something –'

'Don't concern yourself with that woman,' Emily intervened, 'the main thing now is to get you better and back home.'

'Maybe I'm safer in here,' Sarah muttered.

'Maybe, but we've not gone through all that paperwork to be back at square one... to be visiting you back in hospital again, now have we?' Emily paused for a moment to see a tear fall from her mother's eye. 'Is it just the wrist, or have they said...?'

'They're not sure yet, and I'm on sedatives for the pain.' Sarah looked down at the bed, Emily not sure what to say. But then she found something to please her mother.

'I told you I had found Effie... Effie May,' Emily said, the tone of her voice optimistic. 'Well I got a visit booked to see her tomorrow.'

'A booked visit,' Sarah asked puzzled, 'to where?'

'She's in some hospital, been there since childhood or as a teenager. She had learning difficulties and –'

'Yes, I remember now, you told me in the car, before...'

Emily could see that her mother was anxious, either by the accident, or that she thought of her second daughter as some degenerate.

'But it'll be okay,' Emily praised. 'We'll get her home too, you'll see!'

'I am truly glad you've found her and that...' Sarah's voice trailed off. 'But I am worried for all of us.' Again Sarah paused to see Emily bemused. 'I'm sure that evil Amanda has something against all of us... especially with what happened to your car.'

'But why think it was her?' Emily asked, but continued to answer her own question. 'You reckon you saw her just before, but surely it was just an accident... some failure in my brakes.'

'I don't think so,' Sarah muttered. 'Mike told me and Rachael things after they investigated your father's death.'

'You mean my real father, Carl?'

'Yes my dear, the man I made love to, that made you three girls.'

'Then what has he got to do with this Amanda?'

Suddenly a figure approached to disturb their conversation.

'Rachael's giving the doctor more information on your medication,' Mike announced looking directly at Sarah. 'But until certain tests are done, the doctor is not sure to how long you'll be in here.' Mike looked down at Emily sitting beside the bed, her eyes inquisitive. 'What is it my dear?'

'Sarah said you know things about my real dad,' Emily asked, 'things you found out about his death after some investigation.'

Emily observed the way Mike stared at Sarah, as if they shared some guilt.

It was Rachael that broke the silence between all three.

'Just come in to say my goodbyes as we must get going.' Rachael kissed Sarah on the forehead, but stood tall at her bedside to ponder on the silence. 'What's up, have I missed something?'

'No, it's okay,' Mike announced, ushering her from the bedside. 'Just get to the car and we'll drop Emily off at ours first.'

'But why, she lives nearer?' Rachael turned to ask.

'It's about time I gave her those things from the past,' Mike said calmly. 'Things I think she can figure out for herself.'

'What do you mean?' Rachael asked.

'Yes, what do you mean?' Emily repeated eagerly, reaching to grasp Mike's arm.

'We've kept a shoebox,' Mike disclosed, looking down at the girl he had fostered most of her life. 'It's full of old stuff... letters, photos and other bits and pieces. Mainly all the shit Carl kept to himself.' Mike recognised that curious gaze in Emily's eyes. 'Maybe we've kept this stuff from you for too long. Even Sarah hasn't seen some of it.'

For a long moment there was silence between them, until Rachael demanded that they needed to go. Emily stood but felt her arm being tugged back.

'Maybe knowing your father's past will help you understand my dear,' Sarah said, grasping at her daughter's sleeve, 'but for now, get me something of Effie... I'd love to see what she looks like.'

Upstairs, Emily sat on her bed, her curiosity restless to open the shoebox. And yet she paused, wondering to what delving into her real father's past would bring. Nervously she undid the ribbons banding the box like some Christmas present, but paused again to open the lid.

The first thing she noted was the musty smell; the stuffy stench of the box increased as she sifted through the contents and laid them on the bed beside her. Most of the box contained letters parcelled back into their envelopes, but there were faded, old photographs. These pictures, Emily gathered after reading some of the correspondence between Carl, her father, and an Aunt Evelyn, were of this aunt with her two other sisters.

And there were photographs. One was of a frail, ill-looking woman pictured with a strange looking man; his evil glare emphasised by thick eyebrows above dark piercing eyes. And on another photograph, the same sister again, but pictured this time with some clergyman. Surely that was not her grandfather, was it? Or was it the sharp-looking gentleman in the previous picture; a man who's appearance somehow made her skin crawl.

But Emily's concern came more to the look of this sister, a woman identified on the back as Eleanor. Not only did Emily learn from letters by Evelyn that there were three sisters, Elizabeth, Eleanor and Evelyn, but that Eleanor, Carl's mother, had died giving birth to him as she was a frail but gifted woman, gifted in the way of clairvoyance.

As Emily sorted through each letter, she skimmed only their contents, her impatience wanting to learn fast about the past. But suddenly she stopped half way through one letter, to realise what Sarah had said about all sisters having their names begin with the same letter. Back then there was Elizabeth, Eleanor and Evelyn. And now she was Emily, and her sisters were Effie and Ellen.

As Emily read the letter in full, she realised that Sarah was right; that all sisters were named after Mother Earth, as some celebration to the ways of Mother Nature. She read notes of research that explained that generations of sisters past were regarded as witches, but to the good of mankind, and that one day they shall inherit saintly gifts to warn mankind of the seductions of evil; that the righteous man will see no evil, hear of no evil word, or to speak of any evil to their fellow man. Emily looked up, her eyes searching her bedroom, thinking that she had heard of something familiar to this, but was eager to read on.

She read letter after letter, some of the past coming clear, but some still dark and mysterious. She found another photograph near the bottom of the shoebox, the fact that it was colour proved it to be more modern. And before she could recognise the two young couples in the photograph, she found the last item at the bottom of the shoebox. The birth certificate confirmed her unusual perception; the priest in the picture, a Reverend Steven John Aston, had himself adopted Carl. But unlike Emily, Carl, her father, did not know his biological father. Or did he?

After packing all letters back into the shoebox, Emily placed all photographs together on top, but missed the coloured photograph beside her. As she reached to examine it, she shuddered to the ring of her mobile. Quickly she grabbed it from on the bed beside her and looked at the number displayed. It rang again, but she paused to recognise the caller. As it rang again she had no recollection of the number but answered the call.

'Yes, Emily speaking.'

'Hi Emily, sorry to bother you, but it's Jack... and I was wondering...'

Emily hung up. Not only was she annoyed that he had disturbed her at this time, but to how she had been so stupid to leave him with her number at the shop. And she was annoyed with Angela, to how she had intentionally sent a friendship request on the social media site without her permission. What importance was a relationship now she had got her mother acquitted and was going to visit her other sister tomorrow? All she needed now was to find Ellen Louise, and for that she could use her laptop.

Emily tucked the shoebox under her bed and sat again upon the bed to examine the colour photograph. Dating it back to the early nineties, she recognised three in the picture. Although a lot younger, it now being almost twenty years on, she recognised Mike and Rachael cuddled together, and then Sarah beside a man, holding his hand. This guy she deduced was Carl. And Sarah was quite right; he was quite a handsome fellow.

She took the photograph along with her laptop downstairs and after making a mug of tea, cuddled into her favourite armchair. After placing the photograph on the arm, she booted up her laptop, sipping at the tea as she waited to log on to the internet.

For nearly an hour Emily searched records using different websites, trying to trace the name Ellen Louise Aston-Layton, but the only positive results came from historical adoption records that stated the female baby was adopted by a quite wealthy family on the outskirts of London; that her foster parents had a country house, but commuted to the city to conduct business. And all that Emily could trace of Ellen during her childhood was her sister's admittance to a boarding school due to complications between her fostering parents. Emily had found out that by the time Ellen was at boarding school and in her late teens, the fostering parents had divorced but agreed to pay all education fees to see Ellen through boarding school. Until the age of nineteen, Emily found nothing until she stumbled on passport records that told Ellen had left the country eighteen months back, but had never returned to England.

Again Emily shuddered to the ring of her mobile, but seeing it was Jack's number again, she ignored it.

Emily stared back at the display on her laptop, the screen showing another failed search. She pondered on how to find her youngest sister, but came annoyed to all that she had learned. Would she have been better off not knowing all she had found out today? What significance did her name have, or that of her sisters? Was it just coincidence that they were three sisters born just like Elizabeth, Eleanor and Evelyn, and that they were triplets?

Emily looked into the dark corners of her lounge and felt the silence of the room close in around her. With Sarah in hospital, again she was alone. She logged into the social media site and saw posts by Jack, and another post by Angela, asking if Jack had asked her out yet. She almost slammed shut her laptop screen against the keyboard, but turned her head away, swearing under her breath. Then she noticed the photograph on the arm. Why did she bring it down?

Emily picked up the photograph to study it more closely, at first smirking at the clothes they wore. But slowly, as she saw how happy they were all together, she felt truly deserted and alone. Maybe this Jack was a good man, and Angela's interference was not just some coincidence. But was she prepared for such a relationship, or any relationship, come that?

Not sure whether it was her loneliness, or the fact that she had admitted to herself that she needed some help, Emily picked up her mobile and redialled the missed call.

What the hell, she thought. Won't hurt just to get a little help? Besides, I need a lift to see Effie.

'Emily,' Jack said with delight, 'you've answered my call.'

'Hi Jack, yes I'm sorry I've been a bit mean…'

'Mean,' he joked, 'I was about to give up on you, what with your friend posting that message and…'

'Yes, I'm sorry for that too,' Emily interrupted. 'But I need a favour, and you're…'

'The last one in the world you could think of?'

'No, actually you've been nothing but kind to me and…' Emily paused, realising how difficult dating could be after not being with someone for years. 'Well you know about what I told you about me having sisters?'

'Yes, that is what the three crucifixes were for, weren't they?'

'Yes, well,' Emily cleared her throat. 'I need someone to take me to meet my sister Effie somewhere out in the country.'

'Where does she live exactly?'

'I'm not sure, I've not been there before, but it's an institute on the outskirts, north-east of Bristol.' Emily paused to find the address on her laptop. 'I haven't got the exact place now, but I'll find it out and –'

'You've never visited her before?' Jack interrupted overwhelmed with curiosity.

'No, you see, it's the first time I will have met her.' Emily looked at a picture of herself on the social media site, pondering to whether Effie would look like her. 'We were separated as babies and were all fostered separately.'

There was a silence at the other end of the line.

'I'm sorry about that Emily,' Jack told sombrely, but picked up a cheerful tone to continue. 'Then how can I refuse such a beautiful lady in distress?'

'You have a car?'

'But of course my dear,' but Jack put on a serious voice. 'However, there is one condition, and you may find it rather gruelling.'

'What's that?' Emily asked with surprise.

'You'll have to come on a date with me.' He paused for a reaction, but there was silence. 'Don't worry Miss Emily; can I call you Miss Emily? Maybe it'll just be a talk at a café, or maybe a meal at one of those quaint pubs somewhere in the country?'

'We'll see,' Emily told quietly, before raising her voice to make arrangements. 'Meet outside the jewellers… nine in the morning?'

'Then it's a date my dear.'

SEVENTEEN

AT THE RECEPTION DESK, THE doctor retrieved and opened a folder containing history and medical records of a patient. Typed in capital letters on the front of the folder, Emily could see the name *EFFIE MAY ASTON-LAYTON*. From a paperclip holding documents together, he peeled a photograph and handed it Emily.

'These were your sister's adoptive parents. When she became a teenager they eventually admitted she was too much to handle.'

'She was violent?' Emily questioned, looking up from the photograph.

'No,' the doctor frowned, 'by the contrary, she was quite docile; probably the imaginary people she talked to quashed her audacious side as a young girl.' The doctor took back the photograph to examine for himself. 'It was then that they approached us. At first they just wanted tests done at the hospital and so forth, but out of the security of her home, her behaviour got worse.'

'How come,' Emily enquired, acknowledging the doctor as he indicated for her to walk with him, 'What do you mean by worse?'

'As a child she had imaginary friends and like any parent they'd think their child would grow out of it. But later as she became a teenager, she had many behaviour problems, some that medication or tests could not resolve.' The doctor turned a corner, but paused. 'Maybe I should just let you read this, or take certain copies home. But I think it best you see her for yourself.'

'Yes, of course, I've come to see her, but,' Emily grasped the doctor's arm to stop him, 'I'd like to know why she was like that, or if she is like that now?'

'I'm afraid she was diagnosed of having mental and behaviour problems even before she became a teenager. And when she reached puberty, she was having conversations with imaginary people, having convulsions and panic attacks, drawing patterns over floors... circles that she sealed, sat inside and would not come out.' He looked at Emily in dismay. 'At one time our local priest visited the institute over several days. He thought he saw symptoms of hallucinogenic possession, but she gladly accepted his faith, worshipped the man like her own father and even kissed his hand.'

'Symptoms of what?' Emily did not fully understand his medical terms.

'Not to worry about that now, we're nearly there.' The doctor stopped and turned, holding up the folder. 'I'll do prints of stuff I can give you.' The doctor held Emily's shoulder strong with one hand. 'She's been quite good over the past years, maybe by her twenty-first she'll be quite a normal lady?' The doctor smiled thinly, but this gave Emily concern. 'Down the corridor and she'll be in the visitor's room, on the right.'

Emily acknowledged the doctor's directions with a smile, but paused to watch the man disappear back towards the reception area.

Stepping gingerly down the corridor, Emily past room after room, some empty, some with patients. One woman, in the last room before the entrance to the visitor's area, was sipping tea loudly through a straw. Blue, but cloudy eyes glanced up at her as the elderly woman stopped to drink. Emily froze for a moment, the eyes curious to who she was. Would her sister give such a hostile reception?

Emily turned the corner after seeing another but smaller reception desk opposite. As she edged her way slowly into the room, she found a circle of heavy armchairs surrounding a low table. But these were all empty. It was not until she examined the corners of the room, that Emily noticed a lighter chair; it's back turned and a figure with shabby dark hair seated and leaning forward.

'Effie,' Emily called with a croaky voice. 'Are you Effie my dear?'

The girl turned to face her and looked up, but did not speak.

For a second Emily thought she saw something of her own reflection, but as she studied the bemused face that looked shyly to the ground and then back up at her, Emily saw a difference. At first the girl's face looked pale and gaunt, but Emily realised to how it matched such a thin body. Was it that she had such a frail frame, or did the clothes they supplied her the smallest of a large size?

Although Emily recognised that this girl had to be her sister, it was Effie's look that required attention; a long, plain face without makeup, a sad mouth with thin lips, and shabby, emaciated hair, with strands reaching her knees by her elbows.

'You are Effie aren't you,' Emily's voice was a little more assertive, 'Effie May?'

'Yes,' the girl said timidly, 'that is my name.'

'Then you'll be my sister, if you have the surname *Aston-Layton*.'

'I believe that is true,' the girl said quietly as she looked again at the floor, 'and you do look a bit like me.'

'Yes you do, but you could be prettier if you did something with...' Emily reached forward to feel her hair, but Effie backed away, her eyes wide like a startled horse. 'I'm sorry if you disprove, but...' Emily reached into her handbag and pulled out a circular mirror, coated in a thick, pink coloured plastic. 'But look at yourself my dear, with a little makeup you'd be chased by all the boys.' Emily tried to amuse her sister, but Effie's eyes just looked confused. Anyhow, who was Emily to preach on having men; she had only just got Jack to bring her here on the promise of a date.

At first Emily just noticed how the light from the mirror reflected against Effie's hazel eyes, but then her sister grasped the mirror and then touched her hand. For a second Emily felt an overpowering sense of dismay, years of neglect and sorrow in her heart, as if electricity had shot through their hands to transfer information. Emily looked straight at her sister as Effie glanced up. Emily knew her sister was a triplet and so the same age, but observing how she reacted and talked, it was as though Effie was a couple years younger.

'I look awful I know,' Effie said retracting to hold the mirror, but Emily grasped her hand; it was fragile, cold and thin. 'But it's no good me trying to better myself.'

'Why not,' Emily questioned, 'you should at least look after yourself?'

'In here?' Effie blew in contempt. 'Besides they'd not let me have such things.'

'What, this mirror?' Emily ridiculed. 'You can have it Effie... call it a gift.'

'It's not that.' Effie took the mirror and handed it quickly back after examining it. 'We're not allowed things that can cut us.'

Emily looked at her cosmetic mirror all over, perplexed by the fact it was encased in thick plastic. 'But it's not got sharp edges?'

Effie watched as Emily rolled the mirror in her fingers. 'The mirror inside could crack and break.' Effie tried not to focus on the object as she spoke in a quiet voice. 'The edges would be sharp.' Nervously Effie scratched at the sleeve covering her arm. 'Besides I better not get caught with it, even if it be a gift from you. This place has rules I must...'

Effie went quiet and Emily was unsure what to say, but hated to see such unkempt hair.

'But your hair would look nice if...' Emily struggled for words, 'if it wasn't so shabby.'

'I've not been sleeping well.' Effie snapped but calmed herself by rubbing vigorously her thighs.

'So why is that,' Emily probed, 'is it this place?'

Effie looked bashful, her flowery cotton dress ruffled by her actions. She was about to answer Emily when a figure disturbed them.

An elderly man, his eyes grey like his thinning hair, sat next to Emily on one of the armchairs. As both sisters looked at one another, the man spoke aloud.

'Don't want them and won't have them.'

Both girls frowned as the man looked at each in turn. As they looked back at the man, they noticed him spit pills into his hand and search the low table. Disgusted but feeling pitiful for the man, Emily pulled a small packet of tissues from her bag and handed him one. Immediately he snatched the tissue and looked behind before placing the salivated pills into the tissue. Quickly he screwed it all into a ball and threw it to the corner of the room.

'You'll see they won't have me, won't y' girl?' The man pointed at Effie. 'Come and torture and try to kill me they do, the bastards, but not if I'm awake this night.'

Suddenly hands grabbed the man from behind, pinning him against the back of the armchair.

'So this is where you've got to Ernie,' one nurse announced, the other coaxing the patient up on his feet, 'had y' tablets already have we?'

The other nurse moved around, apologising to the girls about their predicament, but the sisters saw the man wink as he proclaimed, 'Of course I have, I've had what y' gave me!'

But then another nurse tapped one of the two on the shoulder to show her the screwed up tissue she had seen thrown to one corner.

'Who's a naughty boy again, eh, Ernie?' the nurse watched the man's face distort with disappointment. 'I'll wash them down myself this time, shall I?'

The man struggled and nearly sent one nurse flying over the armchair, but once all three had him in grasp, they marched him out the room.

'No, you know they'll hurt me,' the man screamed. 'Get me while I sleep!'

Emily turned to Effie, but paused to ask as her sister looked on the man with such pity. Eventually, Emily spoke to get Effie's attention.

'I don't like to pry, but what's wrong with –'

'He's like me, he hears voices,' Effie snapped, but calmed by twirling her hair. 'But poor Ernie is quite mad.'

'He hears voices?' Emily was disturbed not only by her sister's comments, but the fact that Effie curled her hair the same as she did when nervous.

'The story is, the one I've heard,' Effie spoke in a low voice as she leaned forward, 'is that Ernie was an author and sold hardly any of his books. He didn't even get any reviews or something like that.' Effie pushed herself to the edge of her seat. Emily was not only engrossed in her story, but also pleased that she was holding a conversation. 'He hated it so much, he ripped up his next book and set it alight to curse all who read his books. Now in his sleep, he swears he hears those who criticise his books, the ones he cursed, and that one day they'll haunt him forever.'

'What a sad story.' Emily knitted her fingers together to feel her palms sweaty against each other. 'The man is obviously and positively mad.'

'But I too have heard people talk about him.' Effie said quietly, looking out into the corridor.

Effie's comment hit Emily like a heavy rock; the fact that as long as her sister remained in this institute, she was either already, or was going to be the same as that author. But the doctor had said Effie was improving, had over the past few years improved dramatically. And now, as her sister was just opening up and confiding in her, Effie would pull the trigger and shoot down hopes Emily had to get her out.

For a long minute, both sisters looked upon the floor. Emily wandered if the small wolf spider crawling along the carpet towards her sister would make her flee, but Effie looked in her own world. Suddenly Effie looked up and Emily caught her gaze.

'You probably think me mad too, what with hearing voices, but I know why they talk to me.'

Emily sat quiet, her mind trying to find reason to her sister's condition.

'All I want,' Emily cleared her throat. 'All I came here to do is to try and get you out, so Sarah, our real mother, can finally see you. But if you keep up this charade?'

'But they *are* real, maybe not to you or anyone else, but I know they are there, I hear what they say.'

'That's why I promised our mother to get a picture of you,' Emily tried to neglect what stupid pretence her sister believed, 'so to make her happy and that we'll *all* be together again.'

'They are voices of dead people,' Effie confessed, talking quietly and confidently as if Emily would believe her. 'I know this, because that fat, spotty woman in that stupid purple hat came to give thanks to those who work here. But he told me who killed him.'

'Killed,' Emily questioned, the attempt at ignoring her sister's antics wearing off. 'Who's got killed?'

'Her son, but of course,' Effie sat back and wriggled into the uncomfortable seat. 'He's nice to talk to, but I can't stand his mother. That's why I won't tell!'

'So you know the murderer of somebody's son and...' Emily changed her line of questioning. 'Was the murderer arrested... were you right about who it was?'

'No, he's still out there.' Effie grinned, but finally showed conviction. 'But the woman is so horrid... so horrid... she used to hit Charlie.'

Emily sat back in the chair she had pulled up to sit beside Effie, her thoughts constantly trying to find a way to get her sister's trust. But she *had* confided in her, even if Effie's story about this murdered son was somewhat unbelievable. And maybe it was something she had not disclosed before? It was time to question her sister from a different angle.

'Do you have a picture of yourself Effie,' Emily edged her seat close to her sister, 'one that is recent, but not in this place?' Emily paused to see Effie's mind wonder. 'It's for Sarah you see, our mother. She so wants to know what you look like.'

Effie fingered with her mouth to think. 'The only one I think would be from the identification records of this place.'

'I'll ask the nurse to get me one next time.'

'So you'll be visiting me again?'

'Well yes, of course, if I'm to get that picture.'

Effie smiled thinly, but her face saddened as she spoke quietly. 'I've not had a photograph taken out of this place since school.'

'So how was school?' Emily thought she had something to gain Effie's interest.

'I didn't like school.' Effie placed her hands between her thighs and dropped her head. 'My parents back then never understood the friends I made.'

'School friends,' Emily presumed light-heartedly, 'girls from your school?'

'No the friends I talked to at night.' Effie circled her head around as if her neck ached, or was it that she was annoyed. 'They said I followed them talking and walking the house at night, but

I don't remember. They said it was just some sleepwalking thing. I guess they never liked me as I was strange... not like other children.'

'You're not the only one who's a bit weird, might I use that phrase.' Emily smiled but had no response from her sister. However, at least Effie now showed some interest. 'I have harsh visions, a bit like sleepwalking, but they last no longer than a minute, and the pain brings on headaches. I even have nosebleeds.

'You've had these at school?'

'Yes, I had some bad ones at school.' Emily watched Effie's eyes stare with deep curiosity. 'In my last but one year, there was this bully girl. I think she hated me because I was nicer looking, but anyway, one day in class I nodded off.'

'Interesting lessons, like Mrs Cartwright's?'

'Yes, well, once I nodded off, I had one of my visions, like a dream to describe it. And in this dream, blood ran all down this bully, from her head, eyes, nose, mouth... you name it.'

'Was it a dream?'

'I was asleep in class, but it was a vision and must have happened within less than a minute.' Emily could see Effie was now well interested. 'Well I felt wet on my face and woke up to find the bully had spat paper through a pen at me. And as I wiped it from my face this girl got up and was taunting me about blood running from my nose. Indeed there was blood on my hand.'

'You had a nosebleed because of the...'

'Yes, but then as the teacher asked the bully to sit down and my headache came on, I could see the bully's skirt dampened with blood at her rear. And slowly she had her first ever and heaviest period. Blood trickled down the inside of her leg at first, and then it came heavy. By the time all girls had finished laughing and the teacher was holding her steady, the girl collapsed and groaned in pain.' Emily paused to recollect the past, but Effie's eyes were wide with interest. 'And all the time, all I could think about, was how much I hated her.'

'What happened next?'

'We were both taken to the nurse, me for my nosebleed and her for her period.' Emily looked at Effie as if she was her junior. 'You do have periods right, been taught what to do in here?'

'But of course I know that stuff,' Effie snapped, again rubbing her thighs vigorously up and down. 'I'm not that stupid, just because I'm in this place. I was taught that stuff at school as well you know!'

'Then why, if you're not stupid, are you in a place like this?' Emily could not believe she had barked out a question like that, especially at their first meeting. 'I'm sorry, I didn't mean it like that, I just want you to be out of here and back home with our real mother.'

'That's okay,' Effie replied quietly, 'but what if the girl's bleed was just a coincidence? Maybe you didn't make it happen by this vision thing you said you have?'

Emily sat quiet, her body chilling to recall many other visions she had at school, and the consequences that followed. Emily's thoughts were severed as Effie grabbed her wrist.

'What's wrong,' Effie asked with genuine concern, 'were there other times?'

'Yes my dear, many, some I can only now realise the outcome.'

'Then your visions are like my voices.' Effie held Emily's hand tight. 'Please believe me as I know they are voices of the dead. They not just talk of the past, but warn of things to happen.'

'Pity they couldn't have warned me about my car accident.' Emily found herself mumbling.

'What is it you said, your car?'

'Not to worry my dear sister, but it's good to finally see you. And now I can tell mother all about you.'

'Do I look like mother?' Effie asked slowly.

'Yes, I guess we all do, and have something in common. And as sisters, mother says we all share different gifts. Maybe these things are what she said, but my nosebleeds are just stress they say. The doctor tells these visions I have are probably just something brought on by stress.'

'I fear what some say about me,' Effie said, her voice quaking, 'one voice told me that my mother was in danger, but I thought it my foster parent.'

'Maybe it was the accident?' Emily went cold, her hands almost shaking. Could it be true that Effie has some sort of gift? But unlike her, Effie's madness in talking to dead people got her locked up

125

in this place. No, surely like the doctor said, it had to be some delusional state that hopefully her sister would grow out. But she was like her, almost twenty-one. Pointing to a figure in the doorway and asking who the man was Effie cut Emily's thoughts.

'That man standing there, is he waiting for you?'

Emily swivelled around to face the doorway entrance of the corridor.

'Yes my dear Effie, that's my friend Jack. He's offered to help as my car...'

It was then that Emily stopped talking. As Effie pointed towards Jack, her sleeve had been pulled back and Emily could see numerous scars along her arm and around her wrist. And now in the light, Emily noticed dark red blemishes at the end of her fingers.

'Sorry Emily, but the nurse says visiting time is up.' Jack announced, standing above the two sisters, his eyes examining the room. 'It was up nearly ten minutes ago and I have things to do.' From searching the room, Jack's eyes finally settled on Effie, and although somewhat skinny, he realise to how much she looked like Emily. Like Emily's, it was Effie's dark eyes that attracted him as they sparkled to glare up at him. But not for one second did she blink. 'So this is your sister Effie?' Jack asked smiling. 'There's certainly some resemblance, but looks like she needs to get out of here and get some good food inside her.'

'Don't tease, it's only our first meeting, isn't it Effie?'

Effie smiled at her sister, but fixed her gaze again on Jack.

It was not until Emily stood up to follow Jack out into the corridor, that Effie grabbed Emily's sleeve. Perturbed at being held back, she looked down at her sister's anxious eyes.

'You'll come again?'

'Yes of course Effie, I'll be back, sooner than you think.'

Effie smiled, her eyes glistening as they looked over to watch Jack disappear.

'Will Jack come too?' Effie retracted her grip and sat on her hands like a child. 'He's nice your friend... he's cute.'

Emily smiled back and waved her goodbye, and then raced into the corridor.

'Wait up handsome.'

'You think me handsome now do you?'

'No, but my sister does.'

'What, Effie?'

'Yes, but she's not the one hoping to get another lift here tomorrow.'

'What for, I thought you had to book appointments?'

'You do, but I've got to see that doctor again, ask him something about Effie?'

'Why what's wrong with her now, apart from being in a place like this?' Jack sniggered, but searched the reception desk before looking back at Emily. 'Mind you, it is supposed to have a great reputation.'

'Did you see Effie's arms and wrists?'

'No, I was hardly in there a minute or two… why?'

'She's got scars all over them, as though she's cutting herself.'

'She's self-harming you mean?'

'Yes,' Emily looked anxious, 'that's why I want to come back tomorrow.' Emily held Jack's shoulder firmly. 'Besides I want to get a picture of her for mother.'

EIGHTEEN

With urgency Emily raced up to the doctor after seeing him finish his duties at the reception desk and grabbed his arm. The doctor turned to look down at Emily, his face apologetic to the receptionist, but annoyed with her.

'Oh, yes Miss Emily,' the doctor pulled her away from the desk. 'I must disprove of you insisting to see me at such short notice.'

'But I did telephone?'

'That's beside the point. It is highly irregular. You must book appointments.' The doctor lowered his voice to continue, conscious that the receptionist may be listening. 'I can let you see Effie for a couple of hours, but I am a busy man.'

'But it is you I really need to talk with,' Emily stared with seriousness, 'if only for a few minutes?'

'What about, exactly?'

'It's about Effie,' Emily swallowed hard, 'she has scars on her arms and wrists?'

'Argh, so you've noticed already.' The doctor guided Emily to a secluded spot but not far from the reception. 'That's why we take precautions in things they can have.'

'But surely if she stops here, she'll get worse?'

'On the contrary Miss Emily, she's in great hands here.' He stopped to talk, his eyes observing the whole room. 'And she's come a long way since her foster parents disowned her as a teenager.'

'Was it because they couldn't control her?'

'Not exactly, but...' the doctor paused again to look about. 'You know that I told you Effie sleepwalked, talked to voices and drew circles to protect her from nasty voices... people she claimed were dead.' He took a deep breath. 'Well what I didn't tell you, was that those circles she drew on the floor, were from her own blood.'

'She self-harmed?'

'Yes, but no,' the doctor saw that Emily looked baffled. 'She cut herself not to alleviate stress or anxiety, but to follow the instruction of the voices she heard... dead people who said others would come to take her, even kill her.'

'She painted a circle around her to protect her... in her own blood?'

'Yes, so you can see why when her foster parents found her doing this, well that's why –'

'She was admitted to this place?' Emily finished the doctor's sentence.

The doctor nodded in agreement, his eyes now somewhat more sympathetic.

'I can have copies of her historical records done for you, but I thought you might find some stuff a bit...'

'I don't care Doctor Hampton,' Emily played with her hair in annoyance. 'Look I've gone to the trouble of finally getting my true mother acquitted from a murder she never did commit, to be at home with a promise that she'll see all her grown up daughters together one day.'

'Sounds rather sweet,' the doctor ignored Emily's determination with scepticism. 'I truly hope you have some luck with that.'

'Yes and so do I, but to help push things along with getting Effie out of this place, I've written an official letter to grant responsibility of my sister.' Emily had already started to anger. 'And I've had my mother, Effie's true biological mother, sign it!'

The doctor took the letter waved in his face and paused to read it.

'Nicely put my dear, but to get your little sister Effie out of this institution, you'll have to go higher than some personally orchestrated document.' The doctor moved out of the loom of Emily's angry face. 'I'm afraid my dear, you'll need some power of attorney over your sister, or at least go again through court proceedings.'

'But surely it is my responsibility to get back my sister... until our mother is well enough... especially after those foster parents disserted her?'

'I can sympathise with you my dear, but,' the doctor shrugged his shoulders, 'until then, Effie stays under this roof and in our protection.' He moved to her side, glancing back at the reception desk. 'Could you, or your foster parents, give her constant attention, should she begin to self-harm again?'

'To get my sister back home, Mike and Rachael will do what is necessary,' Emily said assertively, 'And so will I.'

'What if Effie reverts back inside herself again,' the doctor surmised, 'walks your place at night, hearing and talking to voices whilst you sleep?' He added with a smirk on his face. 'You'd have to keep knives and cutlery hidden... keep her under constant surveillance?'

'Look Doctor Hampton,' Emily interjected stubbornly. 'I believe my sister is worth a life out of this place, and I'm going to see that she gets it.' Emily continued; her temper now at boiling point. 'Not only that, but that one day, she comes home to her real mother, and all her sisters...'

Suddenly Emily felt a vibration in her pocket and could hear a recognisable, but muffled ringtone.

'Yes, this is Emily.' She pulled the mobile phone closer to hear. 'Who is it?'

Watching the doctor edge slowly over to hover around the reception desk, Emily gathered that a mechanic servicing her car had questions.

'Yes, if it doesn't cost too much to have another door put on, well...' But Emily wanted to know what *had* happened to her car. 'But why did it not brake before my accident?'

'Well after bringing in the car from where it was left,' the mechanic explained, 'the car had a number of things wrong; that I do believe weren't part of the accident, but certainly caused brake failure.'

'Sorry, but I don't follow,' Emily admitted, 'I'm not particularly mechanically minded, but you say things were wrong with it before my accident?'

'Yes, miss, err...' The mechanic paused to read from a list. 'Firstly, the front brake liquid pipe was half slashed by something like a craft knife so pressure would decrease as liquid escaped. Secondly, the handbrake wiring must have been tampered with to break so easily under pressure.' The mechanic paused to sniff and clear his throat.

'But the thing that confused us all was that we needed to prise the brake shoes from the wheel before we could even move the vehicle. I don't know how the brakes could've stopped the car as the cable had snapped?'

'Well if you don't know I'm sure...' Emily got side tracked into thinking, the mechanics voice nothing but a drone.

Emily realised then that her mother could be right. Sarah was adamant she had seen Amanda that time Emily had picked her up from the police station. And if this vile woman knew Emily's car from being parked at work, had tampered with it after spotting it that afternoon? Emily squeezed her mobile, unintentionally her anger tightening her fingers. Maybe she was right about this hateful woman; her gift of visions etching a drawing to warn her of her wickedness, an evil her mother had professed.

'Do you want all that done,' Emily's thoughts were broken by the mechanic's repeating and loudening voice, 'and a full service, miss?'

Emily agreed to the full repairs of her vehicle, and because of the time and labour, the mechanic directed her onto the garage's car hire service, so whilst her car got fixed, Emily had a vehicle at her disposal.

Emily ended the call after noting details with a pen and paper. Before she could put most things away and back into her handbag, the doctor returned.

'Miss Emily, sorry for my conduct and I do sympathise, but,' the doctor raised his eyebrows showing he was earnest, 'although Effie is a lot better than years back, and has showed no signs of self-harm for some years now, she, in my mind, still requires particular medication, even if it just be sedatives... something to make her sleep and stop her hearing the voices.'

'Doctor Hampton, I have decided to go ahead with my mother's wish, as I know Effie would be safe with us at home.' Emily pointed her pen at the doctor. 'And one day all three sisters will be back once again with their biological mother.'

'Don't you know it's rude to point?' a voice distracted Emily's dispute with the doctor.

Emily glanced around to see Jack staring at her with eyebrows raised, but another voice cut the temporary silence.

'I hope your friend is also not here to see your sister, as I can only grant one visitor at such short notice.'

'That's okay doctor,' Jack announced, touching Emily's shoulder in acknowledgement, 'I have work at the university but can pick her up from here later.'

Emily approved Jack's arrangement with a smile, but was again blocked by the tall doctor, who handed her a photograph.

'Here's a photo of your sister,' the doctor announced wearing a thin smile, 'but sorry Emily, because of other patients, only an hour or two at the most?'

Knowing Jack stood close enough to hear, Emily replied, 'I'll wait in the canteen when finished. Jack, pick me up from there later?'

'Yes, okay Miss Emily,' Jack had overheard the doctor's discourse and thought it amusingly suitable. 'I'll pick you up later should you survive that canteen.'

'Why what's wrong with it?'

'Just don't try the coffee,' Jack advised, 'it looks and tastes like mud!'

NINETEEN

AMANDA HAD SIFTED THROUGH ALL the research she had either misplaced or disregarded. She could not help but wonder if the police had withheld any of the doctor's original research. Although the investigation had come to some conclusive end, the burglary of Daniel's flat was no way an explanation to the way he had died. The horrific image of her mutilated colleague was gradually disappearing, or was it because she had other things of her mind?

Usually Professor Grayling was glad to see her, but on her last visit he had been somewhat vindictive. Maybe the old man was coming to terms that he could not please women anymore, especially a mature but erotic lady like herself; one in which some younger men would struggle to satisfy. But tonight she would drown her need for such sexual pleasure with brandy and her favourite cigarettes.

As she gazed into the empty bowl of the brandy glass, she stubbed out another cigarette, her eyes now beginning to sting. She rubbed her eyes, blaming their soreness on the smoke. But she knew her obsession to uncover this dark, hidden power had captivated her to study into the late hours. If she could only find something that stood out from all the mishmash she had read; research that pointed her in the right direction, so she could safely control such dark forces.

Amanda looked around the room of her apartment, thinking of how the décor could be changed, but came subjected to the dim of the walls and shadows that haunted each dark corner. Fearful, she changed her thoughts to that of her conversation with the professor. He disliked her having all of the doctor's research and all that which she had collected from Daniel's flat. But she rejected his claim, gritting her teeth to recall him saying, *a man like me should be in charge of all that*. The professor, like Doctor Schroeck, was indeed an intellectual man. But like all men, he was a fool. Now it was time for a woman to delve into these Black Arts and reap power from this dark force.

Amanda admired her conduct whilst visiting the professor; she had calmed herself sufficiently to avoid starting an argument.

Not only that, but she had worked her charm on him, in order to get him to study the Latin she needed help with. It was because of her suspicion to the man's true intention that Amanda would always be ahead of his game. However, she could not deny the fact that his knowledge of Latin and ancient languages was essential to uncover the secret of the Black Art, that which Daniel and Doctor Schroeck had learned. And of course he would know something of the hieroglyphics, the Celtic and runic symbols etched in the old book. To her, even though she had learned a lot in the past year, the sketches and drawings, the ancient language inscribed, were nothing but gibberish. Surely there was some easier method to attain such dark power, something simple she had overlooked. But for now, and in her own interest, the professor would be her closest companion, but someone kept at arm's length.

Suddenly Amanda's thoughts were distracted by a knock on her apartment door. She ambled over, expecting another knock, but when she opened the door, there was nobody there. She frowned as she leaned out to look down the corridor. With annoyance she slammed the door and scratched her head, but felt something under the heel of her shoe. Bemused to see a large, brown envelope, she knelt to pick it up. It was not as heavy as she first thought.

Back at her desk, Amanda used the doctor's sacrificial knife to open the envelope. Quickly she twisted her desk lamp at an angle to examine the contents. Inside, there was another small envelope.

Amanda sat down to open the smaller envelope. It was from the professor. The letter described intense study that had kept him up all night. But with research so compelling, he could not put it down. At first Amanda sorted through the professor's study about the etched drawings of the old book, and eventually onto translations of some of the ancient language. But it was when she pulled out documents returned by the professor that the question hit her. Why does the conjurer sacrifice his or her own blood?

She read on to find that the professor had done some translation work of the doctor's bloodletting ceremony and had noted down his invocation in phrases of English. Impatiently, Amanda rifled through Daniel's notes and found his somewhat more pitiful interpretation of the invocation spell. But in essence, they matched. The ceremony again described that of a bloodletting, a sacrifice to call on dark forces, but to the unfortunate holder of the warlock stone, it resulted in death.

But without this onyx stone, how did Daniel control the evil? Simple, Amanda assumed; he didn't. As she read more into the research and translations send by the professor, she came convinced that Daniel's attempt to bypass the warlock stone and use a hex like spell from the West Indies had backfired on him. Undoubtedly Daniel had been killed by the evil, the one, he himself had summoned. Not just because he had sacrificed his own blood, but the fact that he had failed to find a method to control the evil, or at least a way to protect himself.

Amanda took a long drag on another cigarette after again seeing the brandy glass empty. She pondered on another refill.

Taking into account all that the professor had sent, along with Daniel's notes, the doctor's past research, and her own investigation, she again speculated to why the conjuror had to use their own blood?

It was as if a dark veil had been lifted from her; Amanda's confusion to all this research simplified to some technique she should have grasped from Daniel's death.

And, as her mind teased with the simplicity to it all, her face shone in the light of the desk lamp. Strands of hair fell over one eye as shadows enhanced the dark of her eyes and mascara, the gleam of her pale, powdered cheeks; all made her look as if she was staring into the oblivion like some demented but devious maniac.

With her new, simplistic idea of using Sarah's blood as some experimental test, Amanda's evil grin exposed her tightly grit teeth, surrounded by stretched lips gleaming with dark red lipstick. With the delight to finally avenge, her dark eyes glistened from the glow of the desk lamp, to stare eagerly into the darkness.

TWENTY

Striding down the hospital corridor, Emily was deep in thought. At first she did not hear a voice call her name, but as it repeated, a hand held her back. As she stopped and turned around to display annoyance, her face scrunched to see Jack.

'Emily, you didn't say you were in an accident?'

'Well if you saw my body,' Emily exclaimed, 'you'd see the bruising.'

'Yes, well, I did see some bruising on y' arms after picking you up to see your sister, but...' Jack glanced at a patient being wheeled by. 'I didn't want to ask and thought you might –'

'Well some people have other things on their mind,' Emily snapped, 'and have others to consider!'

'Like you're mother, you mean,' Jack specified, trying to stand Emily still to face her. 'I hear she was in the car with you.'

'And who told you?'

'You're sister, Effie.'

'And when did you make it your business to see her?'

'I made an appointment.'

'For why, you're not family?'

'Let's say, I'm a concerned friend.' Jack smiled; again Emily looked even more beautiful when annoyed. 'Effie quite likes me.'

'Is that so?' Emily pulled his hand away from her arm. 'So if you can't date one sister, you'd try it on with the other more innocent one?'

'It's not like that,' Jack told, but Emily strode infuriatingly towards the exit. 'Emily, I can explain, I thought you'd want a lift?' Jack saw her disappear around the corner, but shot after her. 'I came to see how you were,' he announced trying to hold her back as he caught up with her, 'and your mother.' Jack paused to catch breath. 'How is she?'

'She's not too bad actually, considering...' Emily saw the concern in Jack's eyes and for a moment she was hypnotised by them. 'The scans prove she has no internal bleeding or damage to organs... just a

136

fractured wrist.' She looked down at the concrete steps of the hospital entrance and then towards the car park. 'The doctor says she'll be out in a couple of days. Just a lot of external bruising'

'Well that's good, isn't it?'

'Yes, I suppose so,' Emily squinted at him as the sun shone out from a cloud.

'Then why so sad,' Jack asked looking to the sky, 'looks like it's going to be a beautiful day, for this time of year that is?'

'Mother is not the only problem you know.'

'Why, what's wrong with Effie now,' Jack assumed, 'I heard the doctor praise her chance of discharge?'

'You did?'

'Yes, so why the glum face?' although nervous, Jack felt he had hooked the fish he had always wanted to catch, and unless he started to pull on the reel, it would get away. 'Can't I see that beautiful smile again, like the one at the police station?'

'Funny you should say that?'

'Say what,' Jack inferred, 'about the police station?'

'Yes, well it's there that I realised I have another problem.' Emily paused to think. 'Well mother suspected her first.'

'Suspected who,' Jack frowned, 'I don't follow?'

'I'm sorry,' Emily stood beside Jack, his height shadowing the bright sunlight from her eyes. 'At first mother believed my car was sabotaged by some disruptive, evil bitch from her past, and at first I didn't believe her.'

'And so your car ended up...' Jack struggled to find the words, 'the accident?'

'Yes, I think this woman did it.' Emily thought of her mother. 'Sarah is adamant that she did it.'

'Do you have proof?'

'The car shows damage before the accident,' Emily explained, 'before it is fixed that is.' Seeing Jack's bemusement, Emily presumed that he was not convinced and so wondered off to her car. 'Never mind, I guess it's not your problem.'

'I must admit, it seems a bit of a drastic thing to do, even if this woman is such a bitch?' Jack followed to watch Emily open the door of a small, red car. 'So I guess you'll not want my delightful taxi service anymore?'

'No Jack, the garage have hired me this one.'

'What,' Jack scorned, 'that shitty, little thing?'

Seated behind the steering wheel, Emily wound down the window.

'It'll get me around for now.'

Jack leaned against the roof of the car to peer down at Emily, deliberately to show a sad face. 'So looks like I've been booted out of my driving job then.' He held a hand to softly stroke Emily's cheek through the open window. 'And probably won't see such a beautiful client again.'

Although Emily came quite aroused by Jack's touch, she brushed away his hand.

'You said she likes you, so do Effie a favour and get her out of that place?'

Emily started up the engine of her hired car.

'She's nice like you,' Jack divulged, 'but it's the sister *Emily* I want to take on a proper date.'

Emily smirked at Jack's comment before replying.

'Get poor Effie out of that institute and I'll think about it.'

As Jack watched Emily drive off in her small, red car, he chuckled to himself. He thought back to how he had considered the idea before, but wanted it as a surprise to win over the girl he always wanted.

TWENTY—ONE

AMANDA TOOK ONE LAST LOOK at herself in the mirror before heading out into the brightly lit corridor. She had taken long enough to adjust her nurse uniform and examine the identification badge that her contacts had made. In the ladies washroom she pretended she wanted to look convincing, but knew she hesitated because of nerves. Yet she had done far worse tricks than this before.

Slowly and cautiously she wandered down the corridor to the main reception desk of the hospital, her mind reiterating everything she had planned. As the receptionist twisted around to face her, it was time for her to act.

'Sorry, but I'm quite new and have the evening to morning shift.' Amanda cleared her throat feeling her voice lacked conviction. 'But I need to know the ward of a Miss Sarah Layton... car accident I believe?'

'Oh, yes... nurse?' the elderly, white-haired receptionist squinted at Amanda's identification badge.

'Nurse Jones... Beverley Jones,' Amanda smirked.

'You must be new,' the receptionist declared, 'not seen you before or noted you on the system?'

'It was a different receptionist on recruitment.' Amanda smiled but her heart raced, hoping her uniform would convince all she met tonight.

The receptionist turned to face Amanda after typing a search into the computer and announced the ward to where Sarah was located.

'Unusual to have mature nurses on recruitment these days, usually they're students and such like.' The receptionist eyed her curiously, but smiled. 'Better come down around midnight, just before I go, I'll get everything sorted on your record.'

Amanda smiled, but her insides loathed the woman already; she could see how falsely the receptionist pretended to like her. But the feeling was mutual.

Stepping away, Amanda again heard the receptionist call for her.

'Oh, Nurse Jones, if I was you I'd get rid of that lippy... the old bulldog is in charge of that ward tonight. She's old school. Not that that is a bad thing.' The receptionist turned to a colleague hovering over the desk. 'In my day, when I started, we couldn't wear anything... lippy, mascara, earrings. Today they get away with murder, only cover wedding rings because of health and safety.'

Amanda acknowledged the receptionist, but as the woman discussed more with her colleague, she slipped away to find stairs to the third floor.

Gradually as more staff accepted her disguise, Amanda came confident in her pretence as a nurse. Strolling down to Sarah's ward, even a couple of young doctors admired her body; she noticed the men turn away to snigger as she twisted to catch their gaze. But this was not the time for a virile, mature woman to entice younger men; she needed to concentrate on her mission, to get a sample of Sarah's blood and get the hell out of there without getting caught. She only prayed that the stupid, old bitch at reception would not identify her later.

Following the signage above, Amanda came to the ward where she had been told Sarah was. Around the corner and at the entrance to this ward, was another reception. Luckily at this time, just before visiting hours, it was empty. But she had been told this was the best time, as there was either a change in shift staff, or nurses would be busy giving patients medication. Pausing at the reception desk to enter the ward, Amanda thought about her own pretence of medication; setting her instruments on a tray so they could be hidden under a cloth. First, she would sedate Sarah using chloroform, and then get a sample of her blood by hypodermic needle and syringe.

Amanda entered the ward and gently sneaked down between beds. Apart from an elderly man opposite Sarah, all were asleep. Quickly, but as quietly as she could, Amanda swept the surrounding, overhead curtains about Sarah and examined her from a distance.

Inspecting her body more closely, Amanda noticed Sarah's bandaged wrist, but hurriedly checked to see whether she was asleep.

As her eyes were closed and her body relaxed, maybe Sarah had already been sedated? But Amanda could not leave it to chance. She dripped a generous amount of chloroform liquid so it absorbed into her handkerchief and placed the small bottle into her breast pocket.

At first Sarah did not feel the handkerchief smother her mouth, but as her eyes shot open, she began to panic and tried to pull it off. But holding it firm, Amanda pressed it over nose and mouth, her other hand trying to steady Sarah's swivelling head. And as Sarah's body tossed to wriggle free, a voice shouted to add to Amanda's turmoil. The voice called again as she struggled with Sarah, but knew that the body had to be under proper sedation. The voice called a third time, Amanda deducing that it was the patient in the bed opposite; this old bastard was trying to upset her mission.

It was either that the old man awaited a response, or that Sarah had quietened and become flimsy, but for a moment the silence haunted Amanda. Suddenly she heard the old man start to wail again.

Amanda marched through the bed curtains and out towards the old man, her anger controlled. But if other nurses or a doctor interfered, her assignment could be ruined.

'What is it?' Amanda cried.

'I need fresh water for my tablets,' the old man said staring at his bedside cabinet. 'This jug is empty.'

'I'll get it in a minute, so please be quiet!' Amanda commanded. 'I've got to see to this lady first and then...'

Amanda turned to quickly disappear between the curtains, where she discharged her anger on slapping Sarah's face. Obviously there was a reason for this; Amanda needed to know if Sarah was properly sedated, but took pleasure in doing so.

Disregarding all emotion to concentrate on her task, Amanda placed the needle upon Sarah's arm. Nervously, she pierced the vein as instructed by the online medical video. But what about cleaning the area first, like she was shown? *Fuck it*, she thought, *this bitch is going to die anyhow!*

Slowly as she pulled on the syringe, thick, red liquid filled the bottle and for a moment all was going to plan.

Suddenly Amanda was startled by the shrill of a bell that rang a couple of times, but calmed to know that it just meant that visiting hours had just started.

With her face grimacing to examine how long blood took to collect, Amanda anticipated, *just another few seconds, a little more and it is done.*

But as she withdrew the needle to put the contents into another small bottle, the curtains swished open.

'Why are the curtains closed?' a voice asked. 'What's wrong with...?'

Amanda turned to face Mike as he entered between the curtains, the syringe held high in front of her face. Amanda had no time in bottling her sample, but peeled off the needle before bundling the syringe into her handkerchief.

Although many years had passed since spying on her, by the time Mike looked again upon Amanda's face from observing the syringe, he truly recognised who she was. It was then that Mike reached to grasp her by the arm, knowing Amanda's malicious intent. However, as he tried to stop her escape, a knee came up between his legs.

Amanda shot out between the curtains, her momentum catapulting a bemused Rachael to the shiny hospital floor.

'Get after her man!' Mike bellowed. 'Rachael, stop that nurse, it's...' But Mike was in too much pain to explain. Besides, Rachael herself was clawing her way back upon her feet.

Rachael pulled back one curtain to glare first at Mike and then at Sarah.

'For fuck's sake Rach, get security,' Mike yelled. 'Get them to arrest that nurse!'

'But why Mike,' Rachael stammered watching Amanda's figure disappear out of the ward, 'what's she done?'

'Don't ask, just believe me and do it,' he demanded. 'Get after her!'

For a number of seconds Rachael was confounded, but saw her husband wave vigorously for her to get going. After momentarily steadying herself against Sarah's bed, Rachael raced out the ward and ran in pursuit of the fake nurse.

Although encumbered with pain, using the bedside metal bars as leverage, Mike crawled to his feet. Leaning heavily against the bedside, he fingered at first to clear Sarah's hair from her eyes and then examined them. Amanda had either, somehow totally anesthetised her, or the worst scenario, just murdered Rachael's best friend. Standing more tall and confident, Mike reached out to Sarah's bedside cabinet to retrieve her drinking glass. Clumsily he almost knocked the glass to the floor, but grasped it as it circled on its side. After gaining a little more confidence in his footing, Mike knelt over Sarah and placed the drinking glass near her mouth. At first and from a distance, it was hard to check, but eventually his trick showed that Sarah's breath had misted the glass, and so at least, she was still breathing. Again Mike opened Sarah's eyes to examine them, but was disturbed by a familiar voice from behind.

'I lost her down the stairs,' Rachael barked but came short of breath, 'that nurse you was on about!'

'Then what about security?'

'There's nobody at the desk!'

'Then find somebody,' Mike shouted with scorn. 'It's a fucking hospital, there's bound to be somebody about!'

'But that woman was just a nurse, wasn't she?'

'No, it was Amanda,' he disclosed, holding the metal bars tightly, 'she's done something to Sarah.'

'How can you be sure?'

'It was Amanda, believe me,' Mike growled, his eyes staring back at Sarah, 'pretending to be a nurse, but why?'

'But you hardly saw her,' Rachael questioned, her eyes frightened as they studied Sarah, 'and that was years ago?'

'Believe me, it was her,' Mike growled, his eyes too, staring back at Sarah. 'Have her checked over Rach, I'm going to find...'

'What's going on here,' a nurse asked, pulling more of the curtains aside. 'What's with the commotion?'

Turning to face the nurse, Mike bellowed, 'Some bitch has poisoned Sarah!'

'Excuse me?'

'My husband thinks that a woman, pretending to be one of you, has...'

'The woman had a needle and so could have poisoned her!' Mike interjected, leaning on the bed to move along.

'And what's wrong with you?' the nurse questioned Mike's incapacity to walk unsupported.

'I caught her doing something to Sarah and the bitch...' Mike omitted his temporary disability to focus on Sarah. 'Look, forget about me... get our friend here checked over will you?'

Mike made his way to lean against Rachael, before watching the nurse conduct a series of checks.

'She's been anesthetised alright.' The nurse checked Sarah's breathing and caught hold of a smell. 'Her face smells like she's been chloroformed.'

'But she had a needle,' Mike announced, 'a syringe?'

The nurse swivelled her head to ask, 'Who?'

'That woman,' Mike yelled, 'that nurse who kicked me!'

'No need to shout,' the nurse replied, 'I'm just enquiring.'

'But the security here is a fucking joke!'

'Look,' Rachael intervened, pushing Mike back behind her, 'can't you just get my friend checked over by some doctor... to see if she's been poisoned or something?'

The nurse hovered over Sarah to check her eyes, her pulse, and her skin.

'We'll get her admitted to an examination cubicle as soon as possible.' The nurse looked at each of them in turn. 'You'll either have to leave or wait in the visitor's rest room.'

Mike and Rachael held each other as the nurse unlocked the brakes on the feet of the bed as guided Sarah towards the entrance. Other visitors were now arriving and came perplexed by the patient now being wheeled for examination; their rush to visit an unfortunate loved one blocked by the hospital bed.

Watching Sarah's unconscious body being wheeled away, Rachael started to cry, but Mike lifted her chin to have her look up at his face.

'I'll get after that woman myself if need be.' He wiped escaping tears from Rachael's eyes. 'If anything happens to Sarah, she'll not just have our feisty Emily to deal with, but me too.' He looked to the entrance to catch his last glance of Sarah and surmised. 'I wouldn't be surprised if that bitch had something to do with Carl's death.'

Rachael reached up to turn Mike's head to look in her direction.

'Should we tell Emily about this?' she asked sombrely.

'Of course, we have to,' Mike stared angrily down at his wife. 'She's our adopted daughter.' Mike held Rachael's head in his hand, guiding it to weep against his chest. 'Besides, she's only just managed to get Sarah out of that bloody institute?'

TWENTY—TWO

EMILY WAS ALREADY OUT OF breath by the time she reached the reception desk of the institute. For someone who was a regular swimmer, she had struggled to run with so much excitement. But maybe it was the exhilaration of hearing such good news that made her heart beat so fast.

As she slumped against the reception desk, she turned to see the expectant face of the receptionist.

'Can I help you miss?'

'Yes, thank you, just a moment.' Emily took several deep breaths to calm her fatigue. 'I came as soon as I heard.'

'Heard about what my dear?'

'It's about my sister, Effie.' Again Emily paused to take breath. 'Doctor Hampton phoned about half an hour ago, stating that she can be released.'

'Doctor Hampton you say?'

'Yes, he told that Effie could be discharged providing she has the right medication and care under some observation period.'

'Just a minute, I'll check for you,' the receptionist advised whilst dialling a telephone number.

'I can't believe it,' Emily coughed, joking with joy, 'it's only been but a week since I first met her and...' She paused to clear her throat and then sniggered. 'We've not been together as sisters since we were babies... but now this is happening.'

The receptionist could hear Emily voice her jubilation, but moved away to focus on her telephone conversation with the doctor.

Impatiently Emily paced up and down in front of the reception area, eventually stopping to place her handbag on top of the desk. As one hand held the straps of her handbag, the other played with her hair, fingers curling strands of hair in reaction to nervous tension. She was just about to ask the receptionist about waiting, when a voice came from behind.

'Miss Emily,' Doctor Hampton announced, 'why you got here quick.'

146

Emily turned around to face the doctor, her fingers paused in play.

'Well it's great news you gave me,' Emily replied, her hazel eyes glistening with joy. 'Wait until mother finds out about this.'

'I hear you had a slight car accident?'

'Yes, what of it?' Emily thought his statement disparate.

'Well, I also heard that your mother was in the car with you when it happened.'

'Yes, so...?'

'Not a very good start for someone expected to care for a sister when she puts her own mother in danger?'

'It was an accident,' Emily disclosed, her eyes searching the ground, a little remorse in her voice. 'Well it was more of a misfortune.' She paused to watch the doctor's eyebrows rise with scepticism. 'My mother is glad to be finally acquitted. She would never hurt anyone intentionally. And I'd do anything for her, like I will my sister!'

'Then it's a good job someone trusts in you and that you have such an influential friend in psychology.'

'What do you mean?'

'As I said over the phone, it's a trial period,' the doctor reiterated, opening a folder to check notes inside. 'And as I said to this colleague of yours, Effie will need medication and close observation in case –'

'What colleague?' Emily interrupted; stamping her feet at thinking the doctor was teasing her. 'What friend in psychology?'

A call to the doctor made his head turn to look down the corridor, and Emily's eyes followed suit.

At first Emily could only see an elderly nurse holding a large suitcase, but as another figure came into view, Emily could see it was Effie. Her sister held the nurse's hand but was reluctant to follow, her eyes scared and searching the place as if it was all new. But somehow Emily knew that her sister was not frightened of the place, but to where she was going. Maybe, since being institutionalised, Effie had never been outside, except that which they called a garden?

Emily felt her heart warm as Effie spotted her and etched a smile. She could not contain her emotions any longer and sped down the corridor to hug her sister.

'I can't believe this is happening sis,' Emily announced, hugging Effie tight, 'I've only visited a few times and...' She paused, knowing tears had escaped her eyes. 'You'll finally get to see mother, our mother... Sarah!'

Emily pulled away but still held Effie by her arms. For some reason Effie looked unemotional, somehow perplexed and anxious, her arms held tight to her sides.

'What's the matter sis,' Emily asked her face full with concern. 'You're not going to miss *this* place are you? Besides I've cleared the small room, it'll do for now.'

'It's not that,' Effie croaked, watching the nurse put down her suitcase. 'I'm glad to be leaving.'

'Then what is it?'

Suddenly another voice disturbed their conversation.

Goodbye Effie,' the nurse said, holding Effie's shoulder tight with her hand, 'hope you like your new home.'

Effie acknowledged the nurse and accepted her kiss with a smile, but Emily could see that her sister was still perturbed by something. As she watched the nurse walk in the direction of the doctor, Emily looked Effie straight in the eye.

'What is wrong Effie,' Emily questioned sincerely, 'is it leaving this place?'

'No, it's not that, but...' Effie paused to move close to Emily and whisper. 'I gave your mirror to that author and shouldn't have. He could hurt himself.'

'Why give it to him?'

'He kept putting his hands over his ears and wouldn't listen to anyone.' Effie's eyes grew wide with fear. 'He told me the voices were from ghastly shadows that would come for him... horrible people who hated his writing.'

'So why give him my mirror?'

'I told him, when I knew he'd had his tablets, that as long as he cannot see such shadows in your mirror, that they weren't there to hurt him.'

'Did he believe you?' Emily asked, but paused to notice Effie think twice. She felt awful to watch Effie come quite distraught again. 'Never mind,' Emily reassured, 'the author can have the mirror. Besides, it's covered in thick plastic so it will be hard to break. Just hope he don't get caught using it.' Seeing the doctor approach, Emily winked at her sister. 'If he needs it to do as you told, surely he won't break it.'

Emily embraced Effie again to whisper in her ear.

'Actually I'm quite proud of you sis.' She hugged Effie tight. 'It's a good deed you have done.'

But soon the doctor's voice broke Emily's excuse to embrace.

'What's this,' the doctor announced, 'surely you'll have enough time for sisterly affections when you get home?' The doctor looked directly at Effie. 'You have a good sister there Effie, so be good for her and take the medications that I prescribe.' He turned to Emily wearing a thin smile and instructed her to visit the reception desk before leaving. 'Effie's release papers are at reception and will need a counter signature. Her prescriptions for the first week are there too.'

'Counter signature?' Emily questioned, but watched as the doctor ignored her to order the nurse to take Effie's belongings out into the hallway.

Emily turned to watch the nurse escort her sister along the corridor, through the entrance, and out into the car park. She turned back to follow the doctor to the reception where she held out her hand to stop him.

'What do you mean... a counter signature?'

'Well Miss Emily,' the doctor turned to disclose, 'medically there's mine, and as a relative there's yours, but psychologically the other responsibility is that of your somewhat persuasive friend.'

'Psychologically,' Emily had forgotten what Angela had told her in the shop, 'what friend?'

'Why did he not tell you,' the doctor almost laughed. 'You came with him the first day, but he appointed to see little Effie again afterward.' Emily suddenly realised to who the doctor was referring as he spoke his name. 'Jack I believe his name is, but he's a doctor in psychology and so forth... at the university I believe. He has some persuasive colleagues.' The doctor paused, somewhat bemused. 'I thought you knew as you were friends to Effie May?'

'So he managed to get her out?'

'Sort of,' the doctor paused to recollect. 'This lecturer, your friend Jack Torrance, drafted up official documents to release Effie with an agreement to terms that as a man of psychology, he would conduct and report medical and psychological observations of your sister for one year. Good behaviour and so forth could make it less.' The doctor paused again to reflect. 'He must have some significant contracts to get this release sanctioned at such short notice.'

As the doctor came to the end of his sentence, Emily recollected her conversation with Jack in the car park not long ago. But surely Jack could not get Effie released in that short time?

The doctor could see that Emily was perplexed, even when signing the paperwork and retrieving Effie's medication, but briskly took the pen away.

'I hope all goes well Emily,' he stated before rushing away to his duties. 'You owe a lot to that friend of yours.'

Emily looked at the paper bag filled with medication and with handbag over her shoulder, walked slowly to the entrance where she took a minute or two to lean on the stone archway.

Emily surmised in thought.

How could Jack have gotten Effie's release papers approved so quickly, even if he is some big name in psychology at this so-called university? She looked over to see the nurse drop Effie's cases near her car. Inside she was amused at the petty requests of her sister, but pondered again on Jack's intention. *Was this the friend she had promised to date on Effie's release, or was this observation period Jack's idea to get to know Effie better? After all, they were so close alike, in looks that is. But didn't he say it was the sister Emily he wanted. And he did do that stupid pretence of being a shop assistant to impress her. Well that is how Angela took the prank.*

Emily chuckled to herself, but still couldn't shake off the fact that Jack had annoyed her and still did, even if he did have such gorgeous blue eyes. She had to admit that she was nervous to date this man. Indeed she secretly liked him, but maybe it should stay that way?

Deep in thought, Emily did not see her sister approach to ask.

'Why Emily you look sad,' Effie reflected her sadness too. 'Are you not happy that I go home with you now?'

Emily broke from her thoughts and melted to the words of her sister.

'No, Effie, of course not, I'm delighted to get you home, it's just...'

'Why, what's wrong then,' Effie was close to tears. 'Am I going to be too much to... you already have mother to look after, and with the accident?'

'No Effie it's not that,' Emily stubbornly wiped escaping tears from her eyes. 'I guess I've taken on a lot in such a little time, but it's to get us all together again.'

'Then why the sad face?'

'It puzzles me to how Jack got you released so soon,' Emily gasped, her face twitching and hands shaky. 'I don't know the guy well enough to know his real intent?'

'Does it matter how he got me released,' Effie said stepping back to look on the place with eyes of resentment, 'even if I be nervous with leaving?'

Effie watched Emily grab keys from her handbag and stride along the gravelled driveway to her car. Like a little schoolgirl, Effie blew out air in contempt and ran after her sister. As Emily was placing Effie's luggage into the rear of her car, Effie grabbed Emily's wrist to get her attention.

'I think Jack is nice and handsome,' Effie confessed, 'I cannot tell why, but I feel he is someone special.'

'Then maybe *you* should try and date him,' Emily said secretly biting her tongue, thinking of how Effie looked years a younger sister. 'After all, we are similar in looks and obviously the same age.'

Emily placed the last of Effie's luggage into her car and slammed shut the boot. With car keys in hand, she was about to take the driver's seat, but saw Effie look sadly at the floor.

'You okay Effie,' Emily asked openly, 'to go home now that is?'

It was not the response Emily had expected.

'But I thought Jack was your special friend. As for me, he's only trying to help.'

'He is Effie, he is, more than I deserve.' Emily etched a smile. 'But we won't let him know that, will we?'

At first Effie stood bemused, but casting aside her innocence and naivety, she deduced Emily was playing some sort of game.

TWENTY-THREE

EFFIE WATCHED EMILY PUT DOWN her luggage by the rear of the car but came confused to why her sister had suddenly stopped unloading. Apprehensive to see the smallest of her suitcases unsteady against Emily's knees, Effie stared in the direction to where her sister was looking.

Slowly Emily placed the last suitcase down upon the pavement but did not take her eyes off her front door. As she squinted against the last beams of sunlight, she eventually made out the silhouette of Rachael standing in the doorway, her foster mother anxious.

With Effie trailing to carry the smallest of the suitcases, Emily watched Rachael's expression change as she approached. Although her foster mother was smiling and exhibited happiness, Emily knew she was hiding something.

'Why Effie, it's nice to finally meet you.' Rachael stepped outside to take Effie's case. 'Emily showed us the photo, but to see you...' Rachael turned after pecking a kiss on Effie's forehead to follow Emily inside.

'Don't concern yourself with the big cases, will you Rach?' Emily retorted.

'We have more important concerns than suitcases.' Rachael glared at Emily but saw Effie glance up as she sheepishly stepped inside. 'But I'll tell you later.'

'Tell me about what?' Emily said, trying to close the door against a suitcase blocking the way. 'What concerns?'

'Not now Emily, later!' Rachael's eyes burned into Emily's to make her appreciate that with Effie present, this was not the right time.

At first Emily stood dumbfounded to what Rachael was trying to convey, but filled with sympathy to look upon her discomforted sister; Effie standing uneasy with hands together, staring down at her smallest suitcase.

'Don't worry puppet,' Rachael said, dragging other suitcases nearby, 'we'll get you sorted in no time.' With all Effie's luggage inside, Emily managed to close the front door and hear Rachael instruct Effie where to take her things. 'Yours is the small room down the hallway and on the right.' Rachael turned to Emily for confirmation. 'That's right isn't it?' Emily nodded her approval and so Effie turned to take her smallest suitcase down the hallway, her eyes nervously searching her new home.

'So what's this important concern you have?' Emily asked, trying to keep her voice low.

'Like I said,' Rachael instructed, lifting one of Effie's heavier suitcases, 'I'll tell you later, when...' She jerked her head in Effie's direction; both of them watching Effie carry her suitcase timidly into the small room.

'No,' Emily had become fed up of kept secrets, 'Tell me things now... you've kept enough from me in the past!'

'You want to know what Mike told me,' Rachael snapped, gripping a suitcase handle hard with anger, 'after what he witnessed at the hospital?'

'Hospital,' Emily repeated, her voice clogging. 'Nothing has happened to Sarah, has it?'

'No, not really,' Rachael was obviously troubled by the news of her friend, but turned it into sarcasm, 'only that Mike found some woman pretending to be a nurse, trying to inject Sarah with something!'

'What nurse... what stuff?'

'He asked me to get security, but nobody was about. I chased after her but lost the woman down the stairs.' Rachael rolled her eyes. 'To me she looked just like any other nurse there, but according to Mike...?

'Then who was she?' Suddenly a chill overcame Emily as she surmised who the culprit might be.

'Mike said it was some woman from the past.' Rachael put down the suitcase, her anger subsiding. 'It was some woman that Carl had told him to spy on years back.'

'I think I know who the woman might be.'

'You do,' Rachael again rolled her eyes, but stared seriously at her adopted daughter. 'Then what do we do?'

'Where's Sarah now?' Emily demanded, holding Rachael's shoulder firmly with one hand. 'How is she?'

'She's had tests and everything seems fine.' Rachael remembered to what Mike had requested after their escapade at the hospital. 'She's in isolation with security keeping observation.'

'Then I'll make sure she comes home as soon as I can and that she is safe back here with us.' Suddenly Emily realised her plan for the next day. 'I was hoping that Effie could visit tomorrow.'

'But what if Sarah has to stop in isolation longer?' Unexpectedly Rachael felt a hand tug on her sleeve.

'Are you going to bring my other cases, or shall I...? Effie looked first at Rachael and then at her two remaining suitcases in turn. Both Rachael and Emily stood silent and then looked at one another. Effie knew something was wrong after overhearing some of their conversation. 'What's wrong with Sarah... what happened?'

'It's nothing serious,' Emily told, trying to reassure her own doubt. 'You know Sarah's in hospital because of the accident...' She tried to speak positively, knowing Effie had been fretful about moving all day. 'She'll be out soon and will be delighted to finally meet you... it'll be a nice little reunion.' Emily forgot herself in talking to a sister that had been somewhat unconnected with the outside world. 'No, fuck it. We'll have some nice party. And I'll invite Jack. How does that sound?'

Effie looked at Emily and then at Rachael, her eyes tired and face contorting to hide a yawn.

'I never thanked Jack,' Effie stared at the floor, 'for getting me out that is?'

'Never mind about that now,' Emily announced, marshalling Effie to walk on before picking up both suitcases. 'What you need is that medication I've been told to give you before bed.' As Emily followed her sister into the small room she had cleared that morning, she observed to how matted Effie's dark hair was and how sluggishly her skinny body walked.

Emily sat Effie on the bed and promised her a long hot bath the next day, and that she would curl her hair before visiting Sarah. But for now, as directed by Doctor Hampton, Effie was to take medicines with food and get plenty of rest.

'I'll get you some of my favourite chunky soup,' Emily assured, smiling to try and eradicate all of Effie's troubles although her mind buzzed with her own. 'And a toasted baguette... you'll like that!'

'With lots of butter,' Effie asked in earnest, 'they don't give much in that place?'

'Why of course, but I only have margarine.' Emily winked before nudging her sister slightly. 'But do me a favour and make sure you have that tablet before bed.'

Effie looked to the floor and then at her suitcases.

'What about them?'

'Oh, don't worry yourself about them,' Emily assured, pushing them to one side to sit on the bed, 'we'll unpack them in the morning.'

'But what about...?' Effie pulled at her sweatshirt and then tapped the pillow, her hand resting there to appreciate its comfort and softness.

'You're about the same size.' Emily disregarded her sister's degeneration in weight to reflect on height. 'So you'll be fine in one of my cotton nightdresses, they're about the right length.' Again Effie saw her sister smile. 'And they're nice cotton, soft.'

'Can I have another mirror,' Effie asked, her hands pressed nervously together in her lap, 'like the one I gave the author man?'

'Why you have no need to use one,' Emily conveyed, pointing to a small dressing table opposite, 'that's one that Sarah had years ago and...'

'But I want one to take to bed,' Effie explained.

Emily looked at the oval shaped mirror tilted on Sarah's dressing table and then back at her sister.

'Why it's a lot larger to see your reflection than one of my...' Emily paused, her face creasing to reconsider her sister's true mental health, but knew she had to play along kind and would probably have to make many sacrifices. 'It's not for doing make-up or for combing your hair, is it Effie?'

Somehow a glint in her sister's eyes told Emily that she was right. And when Effie observed the size of the dressing table mirror with wide eyes, Emily remembered what her sister had told about the author and the talking shadows. Maybe Effie was scared of shadows too, looking for their reflection as they spoke to her? For a moment Emily's heart sank, but gradually she realised that she must do all she could to keep her sister happy; that now with Effie out of the institute and here at home, she would soon see her mother. The thought of having all three reunited made her smile. Emily's thoughts were broken by Effie's soft question.

'Do you have one like before,' Effie squeezed hard the soft pillow, 'it's just... but won't matter if you don't?'

'As a matter of fact,' Emily spruced herself up with excitement. 'I have one other the same, although a different colour.'

'Not pink?'

'No, I bought a pack of three,' Emily paused to recollect. 'The last one of the pack I think is black.' Emily looked at her sister. With eyes like her own, she knew the look of gloom. 'You don't like black?' Emily watched her sister shake her head to agree. 'But your hair is almost black, like mine?'

'That's different.'

'And your eyes are hazel like mine.'

'Yes, but that's different too.'

'But we are sisters and will have a lot in common.'

'Maybe,' Effie looked at Emily and then at both of them through their reflection in the dressing table mirror; she was obviously making some comparison. 'But that's just probably on the outside.'

Emily shook off her sister's disparaging words and concerned herself with what Rachael had said about Sarah.

'Look Effie, I'll be back soon.' Emily stood up from sitting alongside her on the bed. 'Get into that nightie and sort yourself out and I'll be back in ten.'

Emily smiled, but as she turned, she felt as though she could cry. Inside, she did.

Emily placed the bowl of soup and toasted baguette on the tray and for a moment glanced around the kitchen before settling her eyes back upon Rachael, who was drinking the last of her tea. Somehow things that Effie had said now haunted her, but at least her sister was home. Her mother however, was still in hospital and because of that, she needed some reassurance.

'Please Rachael, tell me again what happened.'

'I've told you twice already.' Rachael rolled her eyes. 'Mike recognised the nurse as that Amanda woman. We thought with her having that syringe, that she had already poisoned Sarah, but...' Rachael stopped Emily fiddling with a glass of water she had placed on the tray. 'Look, Sarah's had tests again and she's clear. In fact, the doctor has told us that her arm fractures should heal quite quickly. She's a strong one.'

'She needs to be if that cow is after her.'

'But like you said, she should be safe in isolation,' Rachael repeated to convince. 'Her room is practically opposite the ward's reception, and security patrols it regular.' Rachael paused to etch a smile. 'You know what Mike is like, after laying into them lot, they're sure not to disappoint!'

Emily smiled thinly before looking at everything she had laid out on the tray. Again she stared about the kitchen trying not to release emotion and cry.

'I've just got to give Effie this and I'll be with you,' Emily told, walking out of the kitchen and down the hallway.

As she turned the corner, Emily saw her sister sitting on the bed. Agitated, Effie glanced up, but seeing that it was Emily, she grinned slightly.

'I like this nightie,' Effie revealed, touching the frills that ran down to her waist. 'Like you said, it's so soft.'

'Glad you like it.' Emily said, putting down the tray. 'And I have something else for you.'

Brushing aside her cardigan to reach inside a deep pocket of her denim skirt, Emily pulled out another round, cosmetic mirror. It was just like the pink one Effie had given the author, but black.

'Now my little sister,' Emily tutored, 'it's time to keep your end of the bargain and eat up all this, but first you must have this tablet.' Emily stood above Effie sitting on the bed, her high-heeled shoes making her ever taller, her naked legs slender but voluptuous in comparison to Effie's. With one hand holding a glass of water, Emily opened the other, a large tablet in its palm.

Suddenly Rachael called to Emily from the kitchen; on hearing the doorbell ring, Rachael was going to answer it. As Effie gave Emily back the glass after taking the tablet with water, Emily shouted back that she would go. Once Effie saw Emily dart out the bedroom and into the hallway, she swallowed the rest of the water, but slowly spat out the large, white tablet into her hand. Effie searched the small bedroom to find somewhere to hide it, but for now, a pocket in her nightdress would do.

As Emily met Rachael at the front door, she told her foster mother that she would answer it. As they both thought it was only Mike anyhow, what was the rush?

After hearing the doorbell ring again, Emily briskly turned the inside doorknob to open the door wide. Standing there was not Michael Mackenzie, but Jack Torrance.

'Oh hi Jack,' Emily was clearly surprised, 'I thought it was just our Mike coming to collect Rachael.'

'No, well, sorry,' Jack said, looking to see Rachael peer around at him, 'I just wondered if Effie had been released.'

'Yes she has, and thank you,' Emily was agitated by Rachael prodding her in the back and whispering comments.

'Well don't keep the fine gentleman outside,' Rachael announced, winking at her secretly as Emily turned in annoyance. 'You could at least invite him in for a bit?'

Emily returned her eyes on Jack, his feelings warmed by her attractive smile.

'Sorry Jack, yes please come in,' Emily said feeling awkward. 'But I've given Effie food and a tablet that should make her sleep.'

'That's okay,' Jack replied, stepping into the hallway and turning back to face her. 'Well, as long as she's alright.' Jack looked about the hallway, his determination trying to win over. 'But it's you I'd like to see actually, maybe have a talk?'

Emily felt herself blush. If it was not Effie, then what was this man going to *talk* about?

'Don't mind me guys,' Rachael said, disrupting the gaze between them. 'I'd better be off soon anyhow.'

'Not just yet,' Emily held Rachael by the arm before looking back at Jack. 'Would you mind waiting in the lounge Jack, just while we say our goodbyes?'

Jack nodded and turned to step down the hallway, looking first into the kitchen before noticing the lounge opposite.

'Hey Emily, he's quite a cutie.'

'Rach, please don't tease,' Emily whispered putting a forefinger to her lips. 'Don't let on that I like him as I'm not sure about him yet.' She looked down the hallway to see if Jack had disappeared into the lounge. Seeing he had, she faced Rachael again. 'Besides I'm not sure of anything lately.'

'Well, I just think he's very nice.'

'That's what Effie said, but I hope he's not leading *her* on.'

'You think he likes her instead?'

'Maybe,' Emily looked perturbed. 'I don't know.'

'Well the way he's just looked at you, I think different.'

'You do?'

'Yes, I remember Mike having that look in his eye for me when we first met.'

'But what do I do?' Emily said tensely. 'With everything happening to get Effie here and now Sarah having trouble in hospital, how can I...?'

'Don't worry about things so much,' Rachael told. 'Enjoy yourself a little more.' She winked and jerked her head in the direction of the lounge. 'Look, Sarah is strong and safe in hospital. And if you're anything like your mother, well you have it in you to be here for both Effie and Sarah.' Rachael patted Emily's cheek with the palm of one hand. 'Besides, should you need any help, you've only got to call on me or Mike. We're always here for you, you know that.'

Emily filled with emotion, thinking of how much in the past few months she had shunned her foster parents to be with her real mother. But Mike and Rachael had been rock solid; her foster parents bringing her up through school and collage real well. And in reflection to how her past could have been, or that she could have had a deprived upbringing like Effie, she was beginning to appreciate things even more.

'I'm so glad Sarah gave me to you and Mike to look after.' Emily hugged Rachael and blubbered with emotion. 'After how Effie has been looked after in that place, I feel so much for her.' She backed away to look at Rachael, her eyes already streaming. 'It may be tough to get all of us back together, but now I feel so determined, so passionate all about it... and I owe it all to you.'

'You owe that inner strength to your mother,' Rachael had neglected to cry in front of her adoptive daughter many years ago. 'Sarah's the one that had to be strong after losing Carl. Both of us just agreed to her wishes, and so that is what we did. At least you've found one sister to be united with.' Rachael held Emily's hand firmly with hers. 'What about the youngest?'

'I've not done enough research yet,' Emily said, wiping tears from her eyes, 'but I'll find her, I promise.'

'So I take it you know her name?'

'Yes, Sarah named her, Ellen Louise.' Again Emily had to compose herself from crying. 'But Sarah said that, although she was baptised as that, her name could've changed through adoption.'

Suddenly from outside, both heard a car horn.

'Well,' Rachael realised that Emily had a date awaiting her in the lounge, 'I better not keep you, or that nice man of yours.'

'He's not exactly mine.'

'Yes, well, we'll see, eh?' Rachael again patted Emily's cheek before moving toward the front door. 'But remember Emily, we'll always be here to help if you need.'

As Emily watched Rachael step down the path into the dim of oncoming twilight, a heartening warmth expanded through Emily's body. She waved at Mike in the awaiting car, but then remembered the visitor waiting in her lounge.

'Sorry for being a while Jack, but other things have been happening.'

'Apart from Effie coming out of the institute you mean?'

'Yes something like that.'

'Like what exactly?'

'I'd rather not say, but...' Emily paused to acknowledge that Jack was actually sitting on her large, comfortable sofa bed, his eyes staring with interest to what she had to say. 'I am very grateful to you for helping to get Effie out of that institute.'

'I suppose Effie wonders to how it all came about?'

'Yes and so do I?' Emily admitted.

'Well, obviously I got the ball rolling as so to speak, but it was colleagues at the university that disclosed the right way to approach such a case.'

'You talk about it, like it is some judicial thing.'

'No, it's not really, but procedures have to be...' Jack looked at Emily, his eyes searching her face, thinking if she could handle such responsibility.

'Look, I'm sorry. I must apologise again.' Emily rubbed her eyes and yawned. 'What kind of guest am I, eh?' She searched a nearby glass cabinet to retrieve two wine glasses. 'Fancy a drink or two?' She placed the glasses down on a low table in front of Jack and held one hand across her forehead. 'I certainly do... it's been a long day.'

'Then I must be imposing,' Jack declared, his voice somewhat tense. 'I just wanted to see if Effie was okay really.'

'I thought you wanted to talk,' Emily squinted, she nervous too, 'to me that is?'

'Actually it is you,' Jack sat back into the comfort of the sofa bed. 'Not just about this observation period for Effie, but...'

Emily awaited a finish of sentence but saw Jack wriggle agitatedly.

'I'll get the wine. It'll help us relax a little.' She looked at him and thought to how she must have sounded; was that some sort of come on? 'Firstly, you can tell me of how you got Effie out of that place.' Quickly she disappeared into the kitchen to search for that near full bottle of Spanish red wine.

Emily felt nervous in having Jack in her lounge, but at the same time she was elated to have him there. And with Effie probably now asleep, he was tonight's only company. A confident and gallant man, one with stunning blue eyes but somewhat dark, and that was not just his hair colour. But to the way Jack was now acting, she knew he too had nerves. Leaving the kitchen, again Emily thought the best solution to an awkward moment like this was to relax over a bottle of wine.

'You like red do you, Spanish?'

'Yes Miss Emily, that'll be great.'

Emily poured a more than generous measure of wine in each glass, but took hers to drink standing up, sipping little and frequently until Jack took his.

'So how did you manage to get my sister out?'

'Like I said,' Jack slurped at his wine a little, 'colleagues in psychology and medicine at the university, and one at the hospital, described procedures to get someone of Effie's background released on an observation period. Luckily, your sister has been quiet.'

'Quiet,' Emily probed, 'what do you mean, quiet?'

'Her demeanour,' Jack explained, 'her character... she's not had any episodes recently of...' Jack looked at Emily's eyes fretfully, 'what she had in the past. Over the past year or so her medical records report her of reformed character; a willingness to be taught, response to education, and importantly a reduction in medication.'

'So what's with all that stuff,' Emily asked, 'I've just given her a tablet.'

'Well that's just a sedative,' Jack affirmed. 'With a change to her environment... to where she sleeps and that, it'll help to keep her from being anxious and distracted.'

'You mean that she won't hear those voices?'

Jack looked to the floor and then back at Emily's hard staring eyes. With light twinkling against them, if they had not been so beautiful, he may have been unnerved.

'Effie's told you openly about her past condition?'

'Well sort of,' Emily admitted, thinking that Effie still had problems. 'She explained some of her past after I told her mine.'

'It's good that she confides in you, and so well at short notice.'

'Well, we are sisters after all.'

'Triplets actually I believe?'

'How do you know that?'

'I found things out after compiling a report for my colleague and medical physician; the man who helped with the release form.'

'He signed the release form?'

'Yes, on the agreement that I counter-signed another to monitor your sister. Otherwise it could've got complicated; getting social services involved and so forth.'

'Oh I see,' Emily sipped her wine more freely. 'So what is it that you have to do in this observation period?'

'Observe Effie,' Jack joked, but coughed to continue on a more serious note. 'No it's more reporting back after having weekly visits to check her aptitude, her medication, her...'

'Weekly visits,' Emily interrupted stridently, some wine spilling down her arm to stain her cardigan sleeve at the elbow. 'You've got to check on her here every week?'

'Well that's to what Effie agreed,' Jack stood to disclose. 'Why, is there a problem?'

'No, not really,' Emily pretended, 'but I may not always be here. And there are other things now?' Emily reflected on other problems to negate her feelings.

'Like what?' Jack asked, noticing more wine spill to run down her arm.

'Just my mother is in hospital,' Emily looked away to hide her nervousness, 'the car accident and other things related to it.'

'But I thought people liked to talk things over with taxi drivers?' Jack joked. 'Oh, but I was sacked from that job wasn't I? Maybe this new one may bring me closer?'

Emily turned from looking at the floor to gaze directly into Jack's eyes close up, his empty hand holding her wine glass steady. He could see that her eyes were tearful and so calmed his voice. 'But if you don't like me... don't want me or my help... then I'll...?

Emily had never felt such an emotional urge come over her, but could do nothing but smile at the handsome man a couple of feet in front of her face. For seconds she melted and could only blubber out her true feelings; that she indeed found him incredible.

'But I do... I do like you... more than I can let on... I just didn't know how...?'

Emily felt her arm being raised as Jack's strength pulled her close. Then, as if it was some erotic play, she felt Jack's tongue against her arm, the stream of spilt wine being sucked by his mouth, the warmth of his breath and lips against her skin. And then his mouth moved along her forearm to her wrist until her twitching hand split more wine.

Feeling his tongue against her skin, Emily moaned that he forgive her for leading him on. Momentarily she closed her eyes, saying nothing to enjoy the eroticism of it all. She felt her arms being lowered and the glass taken from her hand. The whole of her body was tingling and her heart raced as if she was to have another flash episode. But this was different. This was her final admission to years of denial, not to a temper filled, anger powered illusion.

However, it was like an illusion; a dream to how she found herself kneeling across the sofa bed, her hands gripping the armrest in support. With her high-heeled shoes somehow removed by accident, all her lower body was naked up to her denim skirt. And it was this that was being exploited. But now succumbed, Emily did not mind one bit.

With eyes closed, Emily could feel the warmth of Jack's tongue slide from ankle up to buttock and back again, his hands caressing and sliding along the silkiness of her thighs until they pressed her calves. Again Jack moved up and down, massaging as he went, until he touched the moist between her legs. At this Emily exhaled, to now feel fingers exploring inside her knickers until they found a parting in the wet.

Emily could not resist any longer and started undressing, pulling off her cardigan and blouse to throw them to the floor. She felt inside her bra, her nipples hard and erect like never before. With one hand propping herself up, she played between her breasts with the other, relishing her own touch, but knowing that between her legs, someone else fingered her. And she felt her knickers being pulled off, so raised her knees for them to be removed. Feeling them hang over one foot, Emily wriggled her toes to let them fall, but soon found herself distracted.

The warmth of Jack's mouth had now moved between her legs, the wet opening of her vagina being licked and sucked. As he played with the tip of his tongue, she could feel him frequently hit the spot. This injected an explosion about her groin, a sudden spread of heat through her stomach to give quiver to her hips. And now Emily felt the denim of her skirt being raised, folded over to reveal more of her buttocks. As Jack licked away with pleasure, she thought he was going to unbuckle her skirt, but felt it being pushed high against her hips. Before she could turn to remove her skirt, something hard had entered her from behind and Jack was motioning her buttocks forward and backward, his one hand pressed firmly against the small of her back.

'Let's put down the bed?' Emily gasped, but felt Jack hard inside her.

'No, my beauty, I'm...'

Emily could feel Jack motioning faster, and as his penis thrust full length in and out, she too felt herself climaxing, something she had not done for years. She felt herself begin to tingle all over, the heat between her legs throbbing, the wet of her vagina making a loud smacking sound. And then as Emily felt Jack explode inside her, she groaned loudly, her lungs gasping for air. For a minute, they knelt in their compromising positions, both gasping passionately for air, feeling the perspiration grow cold over their bodies.

'I wanted it the other way,' Emily panted.

'What other way,' Jack asked, feeling up to her breasts. 'Wasn't that good the way we just did it?'

'The best I've felt Jack, but...'

'Then how?'

'Naked,' Emily's voice croaked. 'Naked and down on this sofa bed.' She paused, feeling his hands stop sliding along her back. 'I want to feel you too?'

'Then we'd best get this off,' Jack said, unpinning her bra and watching her breasts hang loose.

'You're going to stay the night?' Emily asked suggestively.

'Yes, if you're up for it?'

'But you've only just...?' Emily paused to enjoy his hands cup her breasts.

'He'll be ready again soon.' Jack kissed Emily's shoulder whilst groping her breasts.

At first Emily knelt back to take off her bra, but then reached behind to feel for Jack's penis.

'But Jack, he's already going small?'

'Don't worry about him Miss Emily,' Jack said, trying to nibble at her ear, 'with a body like yours, he'll soon be ready to shoot again.'

'Is that so?'

'Yes my dear,' Jack said, his mouth now working around to suck at her breasts, 'and with Effie asleep, well, we can always play a little instead.'

'Get down this sofa bed and we'll see.' Emily stood to drink the last of her wine. She watched Jack pull off his trousers and boxer shorts, his shirt now also removed for her to admire his slim and muscular physique. 'Not bad for a university lecturer.'

Jack smiled before finding the lever to lower the bed and set to work. 'Do we need pillows and things?'

As he stood up to look around, a light blanket hit him in the face. For a second it concealed his vision of Emily, but after dropping on top of the sofa bed, Jack saw Emily undress. To watch her slowly remove her skirt and turn off a nearby lamp, his gaze came fixated on her. And when she crawled on all fours to slumber down on the bed, he was mesmerised. She dragged the dropped blanket up to comfort her elbows before looking up at him.

Her dark eyes glinted evil against the shadows of the room, but after admiring her amble breasts and curvaceous figure, Jack became aroused once more by this dark-haired, gypsy-looking girl. This was not just any girl he had dated from some local club, or even some attractive student he admired; this was *that* girl he had wanted for years. And now here she was, naked and gazing up at him from her sofa bed, her soft, silky skin glowing in the half-light, her wild hair cascading over her shoulders and between her breasts.

'Oh, Mister Jack,' Emily said, her eyes growing wide with excitement, her inhibitions long quashed. 'I think you were right about *him*.'

Unusually so soon, Jack could feel another erection come on.

'I don't know if it's that gorgeous body of yours Miss Emily, or those beautiful dark eyes, but...?'

'So what are you going to do about it?'

'I liked doggy,' Jack winked, 'but what would Miss Emily like?'

Emily awoke with a fright; her body cold but feverish, her hair laced with strands of sweat. Had she had a sudden nightmare vision, or had she been awake to have another flash episode?

The image was still unique in her mind; the deathly face as gaunt as a skull but covered in pale skin, its eye sockets dark to exemplify it's piercing stare, it's mouth a black crescent moon, opening to reveal silvery white, razor-sharp teeth. Was this the thing that Sarah had tried to describe? But in her mother's dream, this Dark Ghost had come for them as babies, in this vision however; the thing had come for Sarah?

Still trembling somewhat, Emily turned over to see Jack fast asleep. Although his presence helped calm her nerves, she shuddered to the cold. It was not the room temperature that made her shiver, but remembering the flash images of her vision. She had never had one asleep before, but again, maybe there was always a first time. Maybe it was a result of finally enjoying intercourse with an attractive and studious man?

Slowly Emily got out from under the blanket and carefully covered Jack back over with it. Recovering from a little giddiness as she stood, Emily replaced her knickers before putting on Jack's shirt. On her way to the kitchen, Emily did up a couple of buttons before standing at the kitchen window. She grabbed a tumbler glass from the sink's drain away surface and filled it with water.

After reviving her dry throat with gulps of water, she looked into the dark of the window's reflection. Petrified for a second, she almost dropped the glass after capturing a glimpse again of the Dark Ghost from her vision. It was as though it stood outside, or was it behind her? But this time it was not a vision, just her mind playing tricks on her. Trying to calm herself, she realised it was nothing, but then remembered again the harsh attack on Sarah; how in her vision, this thing had crumpled her up like some paper tossed to the waste bin.

Maybe this was all to do with what had happened recently; the assault on Sarah by that so-called nurse at the hospital, Effie finally coming home but Emily underestimating her responsibilities, and now Jack, developing a relationship with some man at one hell of a wrong time. Now Emily's thoughts made her head ache, or was it the effects again of having an episode?

Emily walked slowly into the hallway, frequently sipping at the glass of water until opening the door to her lounge. Before entering and for a while, she stood to watch Jack sleeping on the sofa bed, his shoulders broader than she first observed.

'Emily,' a voice whispered loud, 'Emily, I'm scared.'

Emily turned around, perturbed to see her sister walk up through the darkness of the hallway. But obviously by her look, Effie was more nervous than she.

'Hush, be quiet,' Emily put a forefinger to her lips, 'Jack's asleep.'

Effie's eyebrows rose as she peered around the door before Emily could close it.

'What's the matter,' Emily whispered loudly back, 'you should be asleep in bed?'

'I know but I can't sleep.'

'I gave you a tablet,' Emily scowled, 'it should make you sleep until morning?'

Effie retrieved the dried out pill from her nightdress pocket to show her sister.

'Why did you not take it?'

'I knew something was wrong.'

'What do you mean?'

'The voices returned,' Effie cowered as if truly scared of the darkness about her, 'and they were shadows in the mirror... truly this time, I swear.'

'You swear you saw shadows of dead people in that mirror?'

'Yes, at first I was scared, but...'

'But what Effie,' Emily had no time for games, 'but what?'

'They said they were like us, but sisters of the past, and...' Effie shivered to reveal what she had been told, 'that Sarah was in grave danger.'

'What sisters,' Emily was curious but unconvinced by Effie's little charade. 'Who were they?'

'I think one was called Evelyn,' Effie said thinking, a finger scratching her head, 'or was it Eleanor?'

In hearing the names that came from her sister's lips, Emily knew Effie could have never known what Mike had kept in the shoebox, and at that, Emily shivered uncontrollably, her eyes staring wild at her sister.

'What is it Emily,' Effie stood with arms wrapped around her. But it was not the cold that upset her; it was the reaction to what she had just said. 'I'm sorry for not taking the tablet, next time I will, I promise...' But Effie watched Emily rush upstairs.

Gingerly Effie followed her sister upstairs to her bedroom and watched Emily dress into jeans and boots before stepping into the room to question.

'What's up Emily, I'm sorry about not taking –'

'Forget about the tablet,' Emily snapped, 'just make sure you take them in future!'

'Then what is it?'

Emily pulled an overcoat around her but stopped in her rush at the stairs.

'Stay with Jack I implore you,' Emily stared harsh at her sister. 'Go back to bed and get rest, it may be nothing.'

'But where are you going?'

'I'm going to the hospital to see if Sarah is alright.'

'You believe me about the warning,' Effie asked, her face both amazed and frightened, 'from some Aunt Evelyn?'

'No, not at first, I thought it was just your imagination,' Emily paused, panting at the top of the stairs to recollect. 'But I just had a vision that Sarah was in danger, so both of us can't be wrong can we?' She hesitated again on the top stair. 'I do hope we are both wrong, you're supposed to meet her tomorrow... your true mother.'

'But surely they'll not let you in at this hour?' Effie shouted as Emily rushed down the stairs. Seeing her sister disappear, Effie followed down the staircase but paused half way to voice her thoughts out loud.

'But I hope Sarah is going to be okay?'

TWENTY—FOUR

At first it was the cold that made her wake, but as Sarah peered from beneath the bedclothes, the room darkened somewhat. For a long minute she lay perturbed by the decrease in temperature and crouched up tight to keep warm. But then she noticed to how the lights wavered, dimming before rapidly flickering on and off. Somehow she had seen all this happen before, but with such a stupefied mind, all eluded her.

Troubled, Sarah pulled back the bedclothes and stepped upon the cold of the hospital floor. *Surely it was not supposed to be this cold, and what was wrong with the lights?* As the cold of the floor sent shivers from foot to spine, she gazed about the room, rubbing her eyes to clear her vision. For a moment she gazed out the window; a strange fog bank rising above lights across the car park, gradually drifting towards the building.

Slowly she paced across the cold floor, her steps to reach the door weary and unsteady. Clenching the handle for stability, she almost jerked back to the cold of it freezing her fingers. And then she shuddered to notice a light blue gown her only clothing apart from bra and knickers. She searched the room with aching eyes and then looked down to examine herself, her legs and feet naked against the tiled floor below.

Again she shivered and the room dimmed to faltering light. Disconcerted by the increasing cold, Sarah turned from leaning against the door to attempt to open it. At first her nervous hands slipped to push down the large metal handle, but suddenly the door opened ajar against her weight. Using the handle to support her body, she circled around it until she could peer into the hospital corridor.

Looking to her right first, she noticed the corridor long and dark, but to her left, the corridor and ward's reception desk was well lit. She held onto the doorframe, rising up onto the balls of her feet like a ballet dancer to peer at the reception desk. Head down and asleep, she noticed a nurse to whom she called, but her throat was coarse and dry.

It was like a blast of artic air that made Sarah look right, and in seconds before being thrust back into the room, all she saw was blackness; a dense mist towering above her in the shape of some cloaked figure.

Splayed across the floor, Sarah levered herself up to test quickly the door; wishing her sight would clear somewhat. But as fear alerted her senses, she may have wished different.

Abruptly the door slammed shut and the lock turned. Within seconds, the dark mist outside was seeping through a gap beneath the door, to flow across the floor and towards her.

At first Sarah struggled to get to her feet, but after recalling the Dark Ghost in her dream, she panicked to reach the door. As she tried desperately to pull open the door, the metal handle had now become ice cold.

Remembering the thing that had attacked her babies in the dream, she was now terrified and so pulled more forcefully on the handle. Struggling to turn back the locking mechanism beneath, Sarah could see her breath exhale into the freezing air. But that was not the only mist in the room. Sarah turned as something obscured the light from behind.

Towering above her was the dark figure she had dreamed; cloaked hands mystically elongated and outstretched, deathly eyes staring from beneath a dark veil. And from the blackness beneath its cloak came voices of tormented souls hollering cries of torture and pain.

Sarah raced to the window and screamed at the top of her voice. But with her throat being choked of air and ears deafened by cries of pain, she did not know if she had screamed. The last she felt was some almighty power; deadly cold hands spinning her body out of control, fingers twisting and contorting her limbs. And then she was flying.

Emily screeched the car to a halt and raced towards the hospital entrance. After slamming herself against the weight of the heavy glass entrance doors, she felt her shoulder still throbbing as she approached the main reception. Emily paused to look at the receptionist from a distance; she knew that visiting hours were over and so decided it would be better to go on unknown. For a moment she paused, standing in the shadows of the waiting area like a statue, the lights here somewhat dim to that of the reception.

She searched the overhead signage to locate a direction to Sarah's ward, but had to squint in the half-light. And then she remembered: Sarah had been put in an isolation cubicle, a section on the north side of the hospital, located on the third floor. Emily concluded, if she got to the third floor, then surely she could find her way from there?

Noticing a stairwell giving access to all floors, Emily turned to sprint but a strong hand grabbed her arm tightly.

'What y' doing here miss,' a large, heavily dressed security guard asked, 'visiting hours finished almost four hours ago?'

Emily flinched, her anger flaring to find her task mired. She pulled with might against the black man's weighty grip but could not escape.

'It's no good trying to get loose miss,' he grinned, now grasping at her shoulder to calm her, 'you're not going anywhere until you tell me what y' doing here.'

'I need to see my mother,' Emily barked. 'I believe she's in danger!'

'Danger,' the security guard probed. 'What kind of danger?'

Emily wriggled but could not get loose.

'You wouldn't understand,' Emily stared at him hard, 'If I can just get to see her... if only for a second?'

The security guard was just about to reply when they both heard a distant scream. And in the seconds that followed, the noise of smashing glass sounded somewhere in the distance. At this the security guard loosened his grip on Emily's arm and she pulled free.

'What the hell was that?' Emily asked in fright.

'I don't know.' The security guard stared at first at Emily and then looked to the woman on reception. 'Did you here that Linda?'

'Yes, it sounded to come from upstairs.' The receptionist picked up the receiver of her telephone. 'I'll call Glenn.'

'Wait here while I investigate,' the security guard instructed Emily. But seeing the sturdy man stroll over to the lady at reception, Emily seized her chance to race for the stairs. Apprehensive to run, Emily hesitated but was shocked to hear another scream. This time, it was definitely from outside.

Hearing the security guard call after her, Emily bolted for the entrance and raced outside. At first she wandered about the car park's access road, bemused at a strange fog bank now dispersing, or was it retreating back into adjacent woodland?

Puzzled, Emily paced about the car park in bewilderment until she heard voices and heavy whimpering. Joined suddenly by the security guard, she searched his eyes before escaping to investigate things herself.

At first she came upon a scene where a knelt girl was whimpering, her boyfriend and another man talking aloud about what happened.

'I heard breaking glass, and the next thing, this...'

'She must have fallen from that window,' the other man replied, his voice clearly distressed, 'from the third floor.'

As she stepped closer, Emily heard the later part of the men's conversation, but could not see the victim; the girl obstructed full sight of the body.

'But the poor woman's body is twisted all over?' the girl whimpered.

'Must have come from the fall,' the boyfriend replied.

Emily stepped ever closer, her heart already thumping hard inside her chest, her mind rejecting the possibility – a woman... third floor... hospital... Sarah in danger...?

It was then that Emily saw the contorted body; a middle-aged woman sprawled upon the concrete of the car park, blood oozing slowly from head and chest injuries.

As she stepped gingerly about to view the woman's face, Emily fell to her knees.

It was Sarah.

PART THREE

TWENTY—FIVE

EFFIE WIPED AWAY HER STREAM of tears. Although she had never known her mother, she knew in her heart that Sarah had been special. Yet, no matter to how strong Effie felt for her mother now, the opportunity had been missed; their joyous meeting replaced by Sarah's mysterious and sudden death. She looked up from reading the plaque on the freshly covered grave, her eyes studying Emily and Jack in turn, the couple sometimes hugging but never parting hands.

Effie contemplated, that without knowledge of her other sister, she had no one now but Emily; her mother murdered by some dark evil her great aunts had spoken of. But they had warned too late. Emily had been too late. Maybe what had happened at the hospital could have been prevented?

But during the funeral, the look on Emily's face had said it all. Sarah had not died accidentally by falling out of some hospital window, or by some secreted suicide. She had been killed by supernatural causes, injuries that had happened to her before the fall. Mike and Rachael had attempted to question their friend's death, but Emily had been too distraught, telling them to keep their enquiries until after the service.

Although she had been told not to accrue any anger, secretly Effie promised her own revenge. It may mean pretending to take medication in order to consult shadowed voices, but Effie would make her own plans. For now however, she sobbed to observe nothing more than a carved name in a marble plate. Inside, her emotions stirred like crazy. She did not want to blame Emily for Sarah's death, but a strange rage circled through her veins like never before. Or was it her obscure curiosity?

Effie looked again to how Emily cried in the arms of her new friend Jack. Surely her sister was grieving more than she, as it was Emily who had fought to get Sarah out of that rehabilitation centre? She had learned that Emily had fought tooth and nail to get Sarah acquitted to some crime she had never commit. But how did this Daniel guy get paralysed from the waist down?

As fine droplets of rain began to fall upon Effie's face, she squinted to watch the couple free their embrace. At least Emily had Jack to confide in, she thought. But she had begun to feel that she was just in the way and would never have such friends. Apart from those that spoke to her through the mirror.

Effie heard Jack call for her to go over, but looked down at Sarah's grave. Emily called twice, but she ignored her. Noticing Emily approach in the corner of her eye, Effie stepped sideways, sheepishly glancing to see if her sister was angry.

'Jack called you. I called you,' Emily asked, her eyes red and swollen with tears. 'Why did you not come?'

'I never even got to know her.'

'Yes I know.' Sniffling with a tissue, Emily wiped her nose. 'And I was going to take you...' Emily coughed, her throat clogged with emotion.

'But I guess I'm not the only one who'll never get to know her.' Effie looked at Emily expectantly.

'You mean our other sister, Ellen?'

'Yes, at least I got to come and say goodbye,' Effie whimpered, but dried her eyes quickly in defiance. 'Is that her real name, Ellen?'

'Yes, Ellen Louise,' Emily said quietly. 'But she was adopted like both of us and so could have had her name changed.'

'But we didn't have *our* names changed did we?' Effie's eyes sparkled although the sky was overcast and dark. 'Didn't you say we were baptised or something?'

'Yes, and Sarah wanted us to keep our names as part of adoption, but with her in...' Emily paused to compose herself. 'Well, we just don't know?'

'You know where Ellen is?'

'No, not until I do research.' Emily looked back to see Jack walking slowly towards them. 'All I've found out is that Ellen was adopted by some wealthy family on the outskirts of north London.'

'I'd like to see her,' Effie looked again upon Sarah's grave, 'especially now to what's happened.' She paused to see Jack stand nearby. 'I never had true friends in that place, and to have two sisters?'

'But finding Ellen may be harder than finding you Effie.'

'I don't care, I want to find her.'

'Yes, so do I,' Emily admitted.

'But at least you've got Jack.'

'Who's got me?' Jack intervened after hearing his name mentioned.

'Nobody,' Effie huffed. 'It doesn't matter.'

Jack and Emily watched Effie stride moodily back towards Jack's car.

'What's up with her?' Jack questioned.

'She wants to find Ellen, our other sister.'

'The youngest triplet sister,' Jack spoke rationally to hide any emotion. 'But that's been nearly twenty years ago and you were separated as babies weren't you? She could be anywhere.'

'But we found Effie and she wants to find her. I want to find her.' Emily's composure was crumbling again. 'And after what's happened to...'

Jack took Emily again to comfort her, stroking her hair, feeling it now wet.

'Emily, you know I'll help in whatever way I can.' Jack pulled Emily's head from his shoulder to hold her face between his hands and reveal sincerity. 'I helped to get Effie out of that place didn't I? Maybe there will be friends at the university that can help trace Ellen through adoption sites or at least check historical records.'

'But I've already tried ones I know.' Again, Emily began to cry. 'I've got to find Ellen after this. It is what Sarah wanted.'

'Like I said,' Jack held Emily tight once more, but separated as the rain came heavier. 'I'll help, I promise, but first let's get back to the dry car.'

Effie wiped the condensation from the back seat window to watch Jack and Emily approach the car. For a moment they kissed and Effie looked away to smirk. Somehow she was still embarrassed to observe such a display of passion.

As Effie watched Jack and Emily take front seats in the car, she heard Jack tell of asking colleagues at work tomorrow.

'Ask who about what?' Effie squeaked from the back seat.

'Jack promises to help us locate Ellen,' Emily told as Jack started the engine. Watching him drive the car out from the grass verge, she continued to explain. 'Tomorrow he's going to ask friends at his work, people who can search historical records, missing people... things like that.'

'You're going to help us find Ellen?'

'Yes,' Jack replied, observing Effie through the rear view mirror, 'something like that.'

Although Jack focused on the road now exiting the cemetery, Emily knew he was thinking. And secretly Effie observed her sister from the back seat, wondering to how curious Emily was about Ellen. Emily browsed the passing countryside after wiping the misted side window, her thoughts alone.

For minutes all three busied themselves with personal thoughts until Effie broke the silence.

'I wonder if Ellen had a warning to what happened to Sarah.'

Emily twisted to glare at Effie, but heard Jack speak.

'What are you on about Effie?' he asked, lowering his head to view her in the rear-view mirror.

'Didn't Emily tell you of her vision,' Effie frowned hard, 'a premonition that Sarah was in danger?' Emily froze as Jack shook his head to hear Effie continue. 'That's why she left so late that night, to go see her at the hospital.'

'I told you not to say anything!' Emily snapped, but then glared at Jack. 'Stop the car. If she says anymore, she's walking home!'

'Don't be stupid, Emily,' Jack protested, 'we're out in the middle of nowhere.'

'Exactly, she'll walk if she doesn't be quiet,' Emily shouted. 'Stop the car now!'

'No don't... don't please Jack,' Effie pleaded, but the car jolted to a halt beside a tall grass embankment.

'Look Effie, if you don't keep it shut, you'll walk,' Emily instructed, twisting to face her in the back seat. 'You promised not to say anything?'

'I'm sorry Emily, but...' Effie cowered into the furthest part of the back seat, her hands pushing her black dress firmly into her lap. 'But didn't you say not to keep things from –'

'So what y' all keeping from me,' Jack intervened, turning to face each sister in turn. 'What about Sarah... what vision?'

'I don't want to talk about it.' Emily sat back into the passenger seat, her arms folded tight. 'Bloody blabber mouth back there.'

'So is that why you left that night,' Jack asked reaching for Emily's arms to unfold them, 'left me with Effie, until we had your call?'

'Well, I didn't want you to think I'm some...' Emily waved her hands around, her eyes rolling. 'Crack pot!'

'But I thought we promised not to keep things from one –'

'Shut it Effie!' Emily encroached.

'Well this is a good start isn't it?' Jack rested back into the driver's seat, his hands tapping the top of the steering wheel. 'Sisters arguing and keeping stuff from me!'

For a second or two Emily glared at him and then out of the window.

'Look,' Jack successfully peeled Emily's folded arms apart this time. 'If it's something to do with how Sarah got killed, then it's a good reason to share, especially if the police get involved.'

'But you'll think me...?'

'A crack-pot,' Jack inferred. 'Then convince me Miss Emily, because your mother certainly suffered some cruel death, if not murder?'

Emily sat quiet.

'Look, I don't believe in premonitions, foretelling the future and all that shit,' Jack paused to swallow. 'But whatever it was, if it could've saved Sarah's life, then it must be taken seriously.'

Emily turned to see Jack stare unpretentious.

'It scared me too,' Effie said quietly until her bravery won through, 'the voices were nasty people at first but then came the warnings.'

'What the hell is she talking about now?' Jack glanced at each sister in confusion.

'Okay Effie, shut up!' Emily instructed, taking one of Jack's hands to hold in hers. 'I saw it happen. After we...' Emily swallowed hard. 'Whether I was asleep or awake, I saw it happen.'

'You saw your mother get thrown out of a window?' Jack surmised.

'No,' Emily's eyes expressed fear. 'I saw her get attacked by some evil, dark ghost-like thing that crunched her up like some piece of paper. It was horrible.'

'And this was your... premonition?'

Emily did not know what to say, but Effie spoke for her.

'I believe that my sister, like me, has a gift... a special something that sees future events.' Effie watched Jack's eyebrows rise.

'Is this right,' Jack glared in disbelief. 'Is your sister right?'

'Well actually they're like quick, silent dreams... day dreams,' Emily said in a low voice. 'They're usually bought on by stress, anxiety, and give me killer headaches.'

'And she has nose bleeds from them.' Effie interjected, watching Jack's eyes grow even wider.

'So this premonition of Sarah being attacked by some ghost,' Jack stared into Emily's hazel eyes, the exposure of her secret uncomfortable but now displaying relief, 'some vision of evil attacking her... this was real enough to convince you Sarah was in danger that night?'

'Not at first,' Emily admitted, holding Jack's hand tight, 'but when Effie told that Sarah was in danger too...'

'And how did she know?' Jack turned his attention to Effie to express his sarcasm. 'You had a vision too?'

'No, someone told me,' Effie revealed adamantly, 'Aunt Evelyn at first but then Eleanor.'

'Who told you?' Jack stared at Effie, but heard Emily speak.

'Our great Aunt Evelyn died years ago when I was young. Mike and Rachael managed to get Sarah out of the institute to visit her funeral. And according to stuff left to me in a shoebox by Mike, then I believe Aunt Eleanor was our Grand Mother.'

After seeing Jack dumbfounded, Emily and Effie grinned at one another. But then after a minute, Emily also came puzzled, her eyes curious to look at Effie.

'But how did Aunt Evelyn know what would happen to Sarah?'

Effie sat back and spoke as if it was everyday knowledge.

'Beyond the grave, the deceased know much more than any of the living.'

At hearing the sincerity of Effie's comment, Jack and Emily stared at each other in disbelief.

TWENTY—SIX

AMANDA'S EYES GLEAMED FROM THE light of the desk lamp. After staring oblivious into one corner of the room, they focused again on the newspaper laid out beneath her. It was not until she had read the entire article about Sarah's unexplainable death that she started to grin.

And then her eyes searched each dark corner of the room, expecting some evil shadow to appear and request some sort of sacrificial payment. But unless invoked, she knew it could not. Now she knew how it worked, or at least decrypted a part of the magician's trick. But what were the consequences of not following procedures? Were there indeed any procedures to follow?

She turned the pages of the newspaper and folded it to toss it to one side. There were more important things to read now; research that could enrich her knowledge of what she had become devoted to. But unlike Daniel and the doctor, she did not want to go to hell – just exploit the evil power that dwells there.

Suddenly Amanda's concentration was disturbed by a knock at her door.

'Yes, who is it?'

'Miss Burley, it's Professor Grayling; I have the last of Daniel's stuff from his apartment.'

'It's open,' Amanda shouted, not wanting to get up from her desk.

She peered over to watch the professor enter slowly and close the door gently behind. Gingerly he stepped towards her, the light against his round spectacles obscuring his view of Amanda until he reached the desk.

'This is the last of the stuff he had,' the professor indicated, scratching his white stubble beard after putting down a book. 'Some of it you never copied so I thought...' He fingered with notes inside to show her.

'Well all that about three monkeys and Mother Nature, well it's all a bit stupid.'

'But I thought that Miss Burley, before I read these notes.' The professor stepped aside of the lamp to observe Amanda better. The old man stood astute, now scratching at his balding head. 'And to what I can make out of his research, it could oppose our little society.'

'Is that so?' Amanda said as she stood. 'But tell me something professor. I am more curious about what sacrifices we must endure to keep our little coven established, or at least secret?'

'Well like I said before,' the professor edged around the desk, still perturbed by the glare of the lamp, 'now that our Daniel has gone, and that another senior member died but months ago, then the old coven is two short of thirteen members.'

'But do we need to do all that stuff the doctor did years ago,' Amanda questioned, her eyes examining the book the professor had placed on the side of her desk, 'surely we only did that ritual to keep *him* out of trouble?'

'And maybe you'll need it to keep you out of trouble.'

'What do you mean by that professor?'

'I'm not stupid,' Professor Grayling leaned forward, using his fists as support upon the desk, 'I gather that Miss Layton's death came of no coincidence or accident.'

'You're only jealous because some solicitor woman has deciphered the doctor's magic, whereas you, a professor, after knowing the man all these years, has yet to decipher it for his own use.'

'The Black Arts should not be used for personal vendettas Miss Burley.'

'Oh, but did you try telling that to your doctor friend when he was alive,' Amanda stated irately, 'as he did the same to earn you and him personal wealth?'

'All I'm saying is that if you play with fire...'

'You're just jealous of the knowledge I know.'

'No, actually,' the professor pointed at her, 'I just want old customs upheld, so the entire coven doesn't suffer.'

'And you've friends in the pipeline I hear.'

'Yes, two actually,' the professor turned his back on her to walk and admire a picture on a wall of three angels. 'One is a young councillor, a rather wealthy man who is good at finance and has admirable contacts.'

'But isn't he the one who just wants to launder money through our offshore account for medical reasons,' Amanda scratched her cheek irritably. 'Oh yes, treatment to relieve his weak heart wasn't it?'

'It's a difficult operation, actually.'

'I'm sorry, but I doubt the man's commitment to our group. He's too much of an outsider.' Amanda stepped around her desk to join the professor near the picture. 'Anyhow, if he is wealthy already, why not pay for the operation himself?'

'It's not as easily as that.'

'What,' Amanda snarled with cynicism, 'he wants us to bump off some donor of the same age and blood group?'

The professor turned to stare at Amanda, thinking that she now had the power to do such a deed.

'We are two short to do rituals in our coven,' the professor said softly, 'but as I unfortunately don't like the man, I think you should visit him… check him out for yourself?'

'Oh, so why recommend this young man if he's gay,' Amanda jested, 'have you changed your ways too professor?'

'No I have not,' the professor strode over to the desk, obviously trying to subdue his anger. 'And it's about time I had some reward for sorting out all this mess. The coven would be nothing without me.' He pointed at her again. 'I should be the coven's newly appointed adjudicator!'

'Is that right,' Amanda sneered, seductively smoothing out her tight skirt, knowing the professor would be captivated. 'But a pretty thing like me needs rewards too. And not just knowledge to the doctor's secret.'

'An inexperienced and obstinate bitch like you should suck my dick at the next ceremony,' the professor derided. 'I should be the one…'

Suddenly a shoe heel hit him on the chest. The professor recoiled to the doorway.

'Get out, you old sod,' Amanda waved her arms in anger. 'I always said you were some pervert.' She removed another shoe to aim at him. 'You may be in control of the coven, but I'm the master and adjudicator now.' The other shoe bounced off the professor's shoulder.

'But I've always wanted a bit with you,' he said, Amanda not knowing if he was jesting or spoke the truth. 'Isn't that part of the ceremony, to show our wicked ways… to divulge?'

The professor turned for the door and felt something hit the rear of his ribcage. Without delay he raced for an exit and left the door ajar.

'Cheeky bastard,' Amanda said aloud whilst going to collect and replace her shoes.

As she picked up the book and the notes sprawled out from it, she recalled how long it had been since having sex; but to have it with *that* man, how horrible? Besides, the old bugger would probably end up having heart attack. But this new councillor, a young man; even if what the professor said was true? A little wine, as she was told he liked, a bit of female company? Even if he wasn't going to be committed to their coven, she could get something from him. Desirably she could kill two birds with one stone, as they say: please her lost appetite for sex and get Professor Grayling off her back.

Returning to her desk, she threw the book and the notes beneath the desk lamp. For a while she stood angry, pondering over the comments of the professor. But then she mellowed to think of steamy sex with the young councillor. And being a gay man, what a challenge that would be?

It was when she focused again on the notes sprawled across the desk that she saw how burned the edges were. She collected them all in hand to sit and examine. These were notes rescued from the doctor's mansion. These were his final research into the power of Mother Nature and its strange animal relation to three monkeys.

Not this again, Amanda thought. *This is why I didn't copy such crap from Daniel's place.* Amanda threw down the notes and chuckled to herself. *To why Daniel ever got engrossed in such shit, I'll never know?*

Amanda's thoughts came distracted by the vibration of her mobile phone. Feeling it tight in a back pocket of her skirt, she thought of sex again with the young councillor; do gay men ever use vibrators? And answering the call, she found it him. Talk of the devil, she thought.

'Hi, yes, hello Christian, how are you?' She squeezed to find comfort in the chair behind her desk, pondering whether to play with herself a little. 'Professor Grayling has just left. He said you had interest in our... society?'

'Yes, hello Miss Burley...'

'Please call me Amanda.'

'Well Amanda,' the man paused. 'I've talked with Professor Grayling and another associate to your... society, but sadly regret I think I'll have to decline the offer.'

'But Christian, subscription to our little group is more than discreet. Occultism isn't always what you think. It is more a gathering to the pretence of magic and merriment. Sexual foreplay, copulation and intercourse are only part of a ritual, should you wish to partake that is.'

'I would like to play along with you Amanda, but there are other –'

'This is no lonely hearts club or dating agency Christian,' Amanda barked to interrupt, but slowed her voice to become more sympathetic. 'Look I know of your preferences to other men, and I believe another in our group is the same. He also keeps this discreet within our society.'

'I appreciate the offer, but I would probably not subscribe for more than a year.'

Amanda almost lost her temper, knowing this man just wanted to launder money.

'This is not some yearly magazine subscription or some gym membership Christian,' she calmed to explain. 'This is a life membership society that meets every month or so for its own pleasurable ceremonies and becomes wealthy in doing so.'

'The professor told me all about what you do, and although enticing it may sound to a man like me, I still think I cannot go along, especially for a life membership.'

'I get it,' Amanda said sympathetically, 'I understand, as the Professor told me all about your condition. And our society can help with medical costs. The money you put in is not...'

'Yes, I appreciate your concern Miss Burley,' Christian's voice interrupted but came nervous and quake. 'I really do, but I don't like how my more than generous donations are being sent to some overseas account, especially through devious means.'

'But this is how we all do it to...' Amanda paused to console herself for explanation. 'You want enough for a heart operation? You want to meet men who are like yourself, and like me, you want wealth and power? Then my darling,' Amanda put on her sexy voice as her fingers played between her legs, 'let me come round and talk. I'll explain things that the professor probably neglected to discuss. We don't want anyone revealing our secrets, now do we? We'd all like you as a new member.' She stroked the right place beneath her knickers and almost flinched, her legs opening wide, tight against her skirt. 'I'll bring a bottle of your favourite around and well discuss this like men.'   .

'Would I make enough in a year to get an operation abroad?'

'If you show your commitment to the society...? Why yes.' Pushing out her knickers with her hand, again Amanda stroked the opening to her vagina in the right place. 'Let me play with figures for you and show you what we all do and how things work, and...'

'It all sounds great what the professor described,' Christian paused to hear heavy breathing at the end of the line. 'I just hope any extra stress doesn't burden my already weak heart. Until an operation that is, and then I'll need therapy.'

'Oh, we'll make sure you'll get whatever therapy you need my dear, and ensure a great recovery.' Amanda flinched again with pleasure but had to stop; it may ruin it for later. 'I'll come round and show you how we work things. All we ask is that you'll be a committed member of our club.'

'I'm still not sure.'

'Then I'll be around about eight,' Amanda instructed, wiping her wet fingers against her skirt. 'I'll try and remember the wine... it's one of my favourites too.'

Before she could hear any response from Christian, Amanda disconnected the call and smiled.

'Well baby,' she said aloud to incite her wickedness, 'let's get into *you* tonight. And if not persuaded, well a little blood test might persuade your heart to be in the right place?' Amanda stared at her mobile phone. 'We don't want ours secrets out now do we?'

TWENTY—SEVEN

'Is this the place?' Emily frowned to study the tall and narrow building through the car window.

'Must be,' Jack replied, checking again his street map after switching off his car engine. 'This is not the foster parents' address… my university friend said Ellen left them to come here.'

'Maybe she moved back after a while?'

'No,' Jack pulled out paperwork to show Emily, 'if she was still under their care, her parents would have filed back the change.' He sifted through a number of other documents. 'According to adoption records, young Ellen was fostered at several locations around the outskirts of north London, but this one, the one we're at now, was her last home.' Jack could see that Emily was unconvinced, but had nothing else to go on. He pointed to the document Emily held. 'According to that form, Ellen left her parents to be with a boyfriend. And as she was eighteen, after that, who knows?'

Emily pushed the copied adoption sheet back into Jack's hand and stepped out the vehicle. Standing back to lean against the car door, she paused to examine the building, disconcerted by how unkempt it looked. The path that shared two adjoined properties was uneven with broken slabs, the gate before the path was battered and almost off its hinges, painted brickwork had peeled and littered the space below, one upstairs window was cracked, and beneath, the front door was weathered with its bottom frame rotten.

Seems abandoned, Emily thought. *But how could anyone neglect such property, even if so small? With a little attention, surely it could be homely?* She had gathered just enough courage to open the front gate when she heard Jack slam his car door. She turned back; perturbed to see how he too looked pitiful at the building. Jack peered at her from some distance, wondering whether she really wanted to investigate.

'We've come this far,' she heard Jack call, 'and it's been a long drive.'

She turned back from his expectant stare to observe the house again.

Decisively Emily strode up the path to knock loudly on the front door, but later shuddered to think how her sister could live in such a place. What would she say? Was Ellen still with someone? What if her sister was married, had children, and at such a young age?

'What's it you want young lady?' A voice barked from the adjacent, neighbouring property. Emily looked up to see a man shouting down at her from his bedroom. 'If y' want the bloody place back you'll have pay up. Shouldn't have left so...' Suddenly the man paused to study Emily's face in full. 'Aren't you Ellen, Robby's girl?'

'No I'm not,' Emily shouted back up to the man, 'I think you mistake me for my sister, Ellen.' Emily noticed Jack stand close by. 'We're looking for her, can you help?'

Emily misheard the man's instruction as he closed the window.

'I think he's coming down,' Jack murmured.

Emily and Jack looked again at the terraced house before studying each other for their reaction. It was the man's voice that disturbed their gaze of curiosity.

'Apologies miss; I thought you were Robby's girl.' He acknowledged Jack inquisitively before turning his attention back to Emily. 'I've had no real interest in the place since they went.'

'You're the landlord?' Jack interjected.

'Yes mister,' the landlord confirmed after wiping his hands across his already soiled t-shirt. 'And your sister, along with her boyfriend, absconded without paying their last month's rent.'

'So you have no idea to where they went?' Emily enquired.

'You think I'd go chasing them if I did?' the landlord joked. 'Of course I don't know. They just left early one morning before I had chance to...'

'Did they leave anything?' Emily interrupted.

'Only a fucking mess,' the landlord sniffed.

'Can we have a look around?'

'You want to rent the place?'

'No,' Emily instructed, 'just to see if there's anything we can use to trace my sister's whereabouts.'

'I don't know,' the landlord said, scratching his half-bald head. 'There's probably only garbage in there anyhow.'

'So you've checked the place out already?' Jack assumed.

'Well I had to see if they left any money, or what they had in payment see. They left rent in arrears... a month short.'

'Then if I pay my sister's arrears, can we search the place ourselves?'

'Can't see why not,' the landlord looked at both of them inquisitively. 'But how you pay for y' sister's keeping?'

'I'll write a cheque,' Emily insisted, 'it's all I have on me but a card.'

'I'll take card payment and the place is yours for the day, how's that sound?'

After satisfying the landlord's curiosity as well as his greed, Emily and Jack had been given the keys to the house and found themselves searching rooms. Jack had started downstairs and for a while Emily joined him in the lounge.

It was a dismal place; the furniture was filthy and scratches covered the armchairs as if some cat had pawed its anger out upon them, the floor was littered with cans, sweet wrappings, pizza boxes, you name it. And obviously, one or both of them smoked; several items that scattered the place were used as ashtrays. At least there were no sign of spoons and needles, Emily sighed.

Watching Jack walk to inspect the kitchen, Emily stepped gingerly up the steep wooden staircase, amazed to how such a small property had ample room. Yet, leading up to a sudden turn onto the landing, she noticed to how narrow the stairs really were. Emily headed for what she deduced was the main bedroom, but peered to examine a smaller room on the way. Her assessment deduced that this room had been used to incorporate musical instruments. But now it had nothing but an old amplifier, broken speakers on high shelves, and shreds of music paperwork littering the floor. She hurried on to the main bedroom.

Gingerly Emily stepped into the bedroom; her first impression was how a large bed took so much precedence. And then she turned her nose up at the state of it. Emily could never live in a house so neglected. Could her sister Ellen be so different? At least Effie appreciated elegance and cleanliness as much as her. And reflecting on her sister since she had come home, she now thought Effie as a bit finicky. But here, this place was like some squalor; some poor, mistreated home, used by unloving residence, people wanting all the comforts in life without working for them.

Emily considered sitting on the bed but could not, the bedclothes bedraggled and musty. Viewing nothing but neglect and clutter on her first scan, she was about to exit the bedroom when something caught her eye. Pushed into the frame of an old dressing table mirror was a postcard showing snaps of a city. In fact, as Emily observed stepping near, it was Amsterdam. Curiously she plucked the postcard from the frame and turned it over to read the back.

Written badly in English, the postcard was indeed addressed to Ellen. It told her and her boyfriend to come and live in Amsterdam; to bring all that they have. This Dutch girl, verified by the name Beatrice at the bottom, told of being able to get her boyfriend a lead guitar role in her friend's band, and like her, maybe get Ellen a job working at a local café. Emily read on about how the girl described things as being so much cheaper in Europe, and that their lives would change for the better.

Suddenly Jack nudged Emily; she had not noticed him come upstairs.

'There's nothing downstairs that gives us a lead.' Jack noticed Emily holding something. 'Is that of any interest?'

'As a matter of fact,' Emily turned to face Jack with pride, 'I do believe it's a postcard to Ellen.' She placed it down on the dressing table and began to open draws. 'Take a look if you want.'

'Has it got an address?' Jack enquired, picking up the postcard to check.

'Yes, it's from a Beatrice in Amsterdam.' Emily paused in her search of the next draw down to grin at him. 'It might be hard to distinguish, but it's written at the bottom.'

'Yes it has,' Jack muttered, but put down the postcard to exhibit pessimism. 'However, the address could be deserted, like this place?'

'Why be so negative, Jack?' Emily frowned. 'And why be in such a hurry?'

'What are you doing now,' Jack countered, 'we need to get back?'

'Well I've only have one chance to search this place,' Emily responded stubbornly, 'and as you say, we've come a long way. So I might as well do a thorough job of it!'

Jack rolled his eyes after checking the time on his wristwatch. 'Guess I'll have another look downstairs. I'll wait for you in the car.'

Jack did not notice Emily even acknowledge him and so moaned his way quietly downstairs. Knowing she was obviously fixated in finding her sister, he checked the kitchen once more, but thoroughly this time. However, apart from kitchen utensils and cooking equipment, and of course general rubbish, all cupboards and draws proved empty.

'Still browsing mister?' the landlord asked Jack from the doorway.

'Yes, she's desperate to locate her sister.'

'She does look like her,' the landlord said, scratching his bristly cheek, 'but then again, it's been a while.'

'How long ago did they leave?'

'Be about a year now, maybe longer.' The landlord stepped forward to hand Jack a receipt stub. 'Good of you to pay the rent arrears.'

'Like she said, Ellen is her sister, although they've not seen each other since they were babies.'

'Why's that then?' the landlord asked, but heard Emily call from upstairs.

'It's a long story.' Jack brushed past the landlord to acknowledge Emily at the top of the stairs; she obviously did not know Jack had company.

'Would you be interested in renting this place,' the landlord asked, 'or know anyone that might?'

'It needs a bit of a clean-up first, don't you think?'

'Yes I know, I keep saying I'll get the wife around one day and both of us will have a go at it.' The landlord paused, hoping to ask about any possible tenancy, but Jack responded to Emily, she wanting to search a last room.

'Well do you know anyone that might be interested?'

'No, I don't think so,' Jack looked again at his wristwatch. 'Besides we're not from around here and have driven all the way from Bristol. I'll need more petrol before heading back.'

'There's a garage down the road, on the right before you hit the main highway south for the M25.'

'Thanks, I'll check it out.'

'My brother has a hotel not far from the garage if you and the lady friend want to stop over.'

'No, but thanks,' Jack was bumped by Emily who rushed down the stairs to run past, 'we have to get back before midnight.'

'How come?' the landlord enquired, again scratching his cheek.

Emily stalled to here Jack announce, 'Coz this one will turn into a pumpkin if we don't!'

Emily turned to thump Jack on the arm, 'Cheeky bugger!'

The landlord etched a smile after watching a wide grin stretch across Jack's face.

Jack turned to Emily to see her annoyed, 'Well it's been a long drive and now we go back with just some stupid postcard?'

'Maybe *more* my good man,' Emily smirked, 'maybe more.'

The landlord and Jack looked at one another after watching Emily race outside.

'What does she mean by that?' the landlord asked.

'Beats me,' Jack responded, but turned to follow after seeing Emily sit eagerly in his car.

Jack waved goodbye to the landlord and sat to start the car engine. 'What was all that about my good woman... *maybe more?*'

'I didn't want him to see that I took stuff.'

'But he's going to cleanse the place...' But Jack frowned as he pulled the car out into the road and touched down on the accelerator. 'What do you mean, maybe more?'

Emily waved the postcard before Jack's eyes, her confidence unperturbed. 'We have Ellen's address now and –'

'That's if she's still there with her boyfriend that is,' Jack interrupted. 'According to the date on that postcard, it has been more than a year since your sister and her boyfriend left.'

'It doesn't matter so much now anyhow.'

'Oh and why's that?'

'Coz I found more in one of those bedroom draws,' Emily announced excitedly, now waving a photograph before Jack's eyes. 'That's obviously Ellen on the left and that must be Robbie holding her!'

Jack took the photograph to examine whilst driving. He pinned it against the steering wheel to scrutinise the faces more closely.

'Yes, it surely looks like a younger you.'

'Well, we *are* all triplet sisters you know!'

'No, I mean that she looks more like you than Effie.'

'That's probably because poor Effie's so thin after being neglected in *that* place.' Emily paused for a couple of seconds before continuing. 'But that landlord...'

'What about the landlord?'

'It's just that he's given me an idea.'

'Like what?'

'Well, if he mistook me for Ellen,' Emily surmised, her eyes opening wide, 'then surely some picture on social media could mistake us as the same person.'

'I don't follow,' Jack glanced over. 'Surely you're profile has your name.'

'But those buggers on the internet,' Emily deduced, 'they don't know my real name, do they?'

Emily left Jack tidying the car and rushed to open her front door. Without hesitation she turned on the lights to find her laptop.

Jack shut firmly the front door and eventually found Emily sitting on her sofa bed and powering up her laptop in the lounge.

'I thought you said you were tired?' Jack queried, peering around the door, his eyes weary from the long drive.

'I must have nodded off in the car,' Emily admitted, the dark of her eyes gleaming from the bright screen of the laptop. 'Besides I want to see into this.'

'Then I'll make us some tea,' Jack declared, but received no response.

After a few minutes, Emily had powered up her laptop and was browsing her social media profile; the latest posts were from Angela, inquisitive about her relationship with Jack. But before that, scrolling down to see previous days, there were other posts.

'Where's Effie?'

Emily glanced up to see Jack handing her a mug of tea.

'She's stopping at Mike and Rachael's,' she replied, taking the mug of hot liquid. 'I've instructed them on what medication she needs and all.'

'Then she's in good hands and,' Jack paused to remember the first time they had made love, 'we've got the place to our own.'

'Yes, but,' Emily was engrossed in browsing the website on the laptop screen. 'I shouldn't be doing this as I'm so tired.'

'Then give it up, let's go sleep in your nice bed upstairs.' Emily did not answer, so Jack sat alongside her to sip his hot tea quietly.

'Filthy bastards,' Emily muttered. 'What the fuck is Ellen like?'

'Excuse me?' Jack peered over.

'You use this social media site?' Emily enquired, tilting the laptop screen in view, but ridiculed her own question. 'But of course you do, Angela got us in contact that way.'

'What about it?' Jack squinted at Emily's profile picture.

Emily tilted back the screen, wanting more to explain in her own words.

'Since I've uploaded my profile picture, a photograph of my face that is, I've been getting a number of posts from Dutchmen... at least I think they're Dutchmen? But I think they mistake me for Ellen.'

'How can they if your profile name is Emily?'

'Coz we look like one another, stupid. And I guess if you're in the line of work I think Ellen is in, they don't care what your name is.'

Jack sipped again at his tea. He had only started to use social media to get to know Emily, as lecturers were told to be careful in respect to students.

Emily turned to explain. 'Let's put it this way...' She cleared her throat. 'This one Dutchman posts a message asking if I still do online sex shows... something about live cams? And in response, another man messages that my performances are by far better in the flesh.'

'So she's more than some stripper at a nightclub?'

'Yes something like that. Must be short of cash if she...' Emily came confused to look at other posts, conversations in Dutch or another language indecipherable. However, there was a Dutch name mentioned that stuck in Emily's mind.

'So what do we do,' Jack sat back in disarray, 'go searching all the nightclubs in Amsterdam?'

'No you fool,' Emily became angry at his sarcasm but bit back. 'Not that *you'd* enjoy that!' She leaned forward to grab his hand. 'No, we start with the address on that postcard. At least it's a positive start. And then there are the photos.'

'Your sister, a girl just like you... dancing with her tits out, swinging her thighs around some metal pole, mirrors everywhere...?' Jack winked at Emily, but she knew he was only teasing.

'Me, some erotic dancer...? I'm definitely not that!' Emily moved aside, shutting the laptop before placing it on the floor. 'You wouldn't see me getting up to show all I have to those dirty buggers!'

'I don't know, you're probably a little taller than your sisters; those athletic, silky legs curling around a pole.' Jack reached to hold her thigh before moving to play with her hair, 'and that gorgeous, dark hair, swishing around?' He winked again. 'You'd make a killing in some place like that.'

'Would I...?' Emily looked him up and down, before noticing a bulge in his jeans. 'Doesn't look like I need to strip that way for you, does it?' But Emily frowned as she touched his jeans just above his hidden erection. 'But I thought you were tired?'

'I might be, but he's not,' Jack disclosed, winking.

Emily smiled, but paused to think. 'Well Effie is in safe hands.' She stroked around the zip area, seeing the bulge increase. 'And we might not get another chance after she comes back?'

'It's a pity to waste him,' Jack grinned, looking down at her poised hand before searching her face again. 'For some reason, he's not tired?'

Emily smirked as her thumb and forefinger pulled slowly on the zip, his boxer shorts bulging out, forced by Jack's stiffening penis below. And as her fingers played with the material below, suddenly Jack's erection popped out like some helmeted soldier standing to attention.

'Yes, he surely seems up for it,' Emily muttered before lowering her head.

As her lips parted to accept his hardening erection, Jack again wanted to feel the admirable weight of Emily's breasts. At first he fumbled with her bra, but eventually it sprung free, his hands now groping at her breasts as they hung loose beneath her sweater. And he had to play more with them; Emily's head was now moving regular, her mouth accepting more of his erection, his top button undone. She played now inside his boxer shorts, her fingernails tickling his scrotum. Jack bounced the weight of Emily's breasts in each hand, fingering a nipple now and then. He may not hold on for much longer; this girl was beautiful for other things, besides looks.

'Stop,' Jack cried, 'let's go to the bedroom!'

Emily's mouth rose from her play tool, her tongue having to remove surplus saliva. 'But I'm having fun,' she muttered, her one hand now clasping the play tool to slide up and down. 'And besides...' Her words came loud and clear. 'He'll last a bit longer later, when he fires another bullet.'

Jack could not disagree, especially when Emily's mouth returned to motion up and down on him. He just hoped he could fulfil her expectations later.

Emily knew in an instant that she was someone else. And as clouds in her strange vision cleared, in a wardrobe mirror she could see she was a man; a young man, his face pale, his body sitting up and naked in bed. But as she pulled away the bedclothes to look down upon his private parts, there was nothing... no penis... no scrotum... nothing. There was not even a scar... a sign of some operation? Emily felt herself frown and inside the man grimaced, feeling so distraught.

Looking about the strange apartment, Emily felt a sudden cold grip the man's body to prick up hairs on his skin. His white body lay bright within the darkness of the room and she could see his nibble fingers reach for the comfort of the bedclothes.

But something grew in the shadows before she could make out a mist. Through the man's eyes, Emily watched petrified as a black, spectral figure swayed overhead, the phantasmal shape now defining to form a head and outstretched arms. Soon the hands grew mystically out from arms of dense mist, until elongated fingers reached for the man's legs. Emily could not hear the man scream but knew he had, as now he (and she) could make out bulbous, staring eyes that infested a malevolent glare beneath the darkness of its black hood. She had envisaged this thing before.

As the Dark Ghost grabbed for the man's feet, he kicked back. But soon around him came figures; ghosts of departed souls, crying, some laughing in hysteria, some of them begging to be freed, but most cursing offensive language to the man. It was then that the Dark Ghost grasped his ankle, after which, Emily felt his body twist and break.

Emily awoke in an instant, her body perspiring. The repulsive vision of watching some young man get tortured was too much. And through the silence of it all, it was as though she had been him; experiencing the tormenting souls as his breath came choked, his body twisted to angles until it came mutilated beyond repair.

She pushed herself up, wiping tears from her wide eyes as they searched the room. Emily's feverishness did not subside until she noticed Jack asleep alongside her. And then her heart still pounded loudly in her chest. For a while she took deep breathes, again realising she had been subjected to another nightmare. Or was it one of her silent visions; some silent movie cast in brightly shifting clouds?

Whatever it was, she could not shake the man's face from her mind.

After her sweat had transpired to grow cold, Emily moved to comfort herself beneath the bedclothes, but remembered the man's grasping hand. She wiped her face all over before considering visiting the bathroom, but her mind was still giddy, her vision of the man still clear.

Knowing she had started to keep her sketchpad nearby, she reached to grab it and a pencil from her bedside cabinet. With the only light cast from a half-lit moon and a distant streetlamp, Emily started to etch her pencil against the paper. She did not need good light to draw the man's face; her mind somehow controlled her hand, her eyes still dreamy and unfocused, with a misted light still surrounding her.

She did not stop when a bedside lamp lit up the room.

Jack sat up in bed and rubbed his bleary eyes to watch Emily drawing frantically. He had never seen anyone sketch so fast and precise. For a while he observed the strange talent of his new girlfriend, but eventually had to ask.

'What the...?' Jack rubbed again his eyes. 'Miss Emily, my Ems... what on earth are you doing?'

Jack received no answer and looked perplexed as Emily's hand moved freely over the paper, a drawing of head and shoulders now taking form.

'Emily... Emily, please,' he pleaded, 'what are you doing?'

For a number of seconds Emily's hand did not stop, her eyes unfocused, her head not turning to acknowledge Jack.

'Stop it Emily, what the...?'

Suddenly Emily's rigid frame relaxed and her hand flopped down against her sketch.

'Are you alright Ems my dear?' Jack looked close into her eyes, watching them go from being wide and unfocused, to narrow and rational.

'Why... I'm okay I think,' Emily spoke soft, but unsure. 'I had the most awful dream... no a vision... a man being tortured to death.'

'And you start to draw?'

Emily looked down knowing she had picked up the sketchpad, but not realising the result of her handy work. 'Why it's him.'

'Who,' Jack asked, fumbling with the bedclothes, sliding down to go back to sleep, 'who's he?'

'The man in my dream,' Emily explained softly, turning to Jack to show her confusion, 'a man in my vision. He had no private parts. He got killed by some...'

'Sounds like you've been watching too much daytime television,' Jack interrupted whilst trying to find comfort in the bed again. 'I thought it was the other sister that had strange habits.'

'Gifts I think they be called my good man,' Emily whispered, her eyes regarding Jack with contempt. 'You not know the history, or any of the others.'

'What's it you say Miss Emily?' Jack muttered to ask beneath the bedclothes.

'Oh, nothing Jack,' Emily looked back at the sketch of the man she had drawn, 'you'd just better go back to sleep my dear.'

Aroused by a knocking noise, Emily turned over in bed. She faced Jack but could see that he was fast asleep; somehow undisturbed by the sounds coming from the front door. Emily slid over to check her wristwatch from her bedside cabinet. It read 10:40.

With mouth open, Emily sat aghast upon her side of the bed, soon awakening to realise what time it was. And then the knocking at the front door resounded again. She slid from the bed to quickly find her bra and pants, and discovered that Jack's oversized t-shirt would do. Again she heard heavy rasps at her front door as she exited the bedroom. Gingerly she paced down the hallway to open the front door.

At first all Emily could see was the bright light of day, but gradually detected a figure standing outside. As her eyes accustomed themselves to the bright morning sunlight, she could see Detective Nathan Lawrence looking her up and down. She edged closer to the door, hiding behind it after realising how exposed her legs were. With one hand she held tight the door, the other pulling down the t-shirt.

'Oh, sorry Miss Emily,' the detective looked away from Emily's curvaceous figure and naked legs to concentrate on his task, 'but I call this morning because I had no answer last night.'

'We were out detective,' Emily tugged again at Jack's t-shirt, not knowing if it revealed too much. 'Jack and I had a trip to north of London to trace my sister.'

'Ah, well that explains why no answer.' With Emily's nakedness the detective came indisposed but wanted to explain things in private. 'Can I come in as I've things to discuss?'

Emily stepped back into the hallway to retrieve a nightgown from the bedroom upstairs. Watching Jack turn over, she dressed to find him still asleep. She found the detective in the hallway after tying the robe's belt about her waist. She watched the detective turn after closing the door, his eyes now fixed on her after searching the room. She waved him into the lounge and followed, but stopped to look at him expectantly.

'Well as you're probably tired after yesterday and have...' He coughed; realising that the word 'we' meant that she still may have company. 'I'll cut to the chase, as you did ask about anything regarding your mother's death.' Quickly the detective looked sorrowfully at the floor. 'For that Miss Emily, my condolences by the way.' He watched Emily nod in acceptance and so continued. 'We have no real lead to why your mother should be killed... or murdered to how you said. However, in the way in which she did, all we found was the hospital window broken, some sign of a struggle and a mutilated body on the car park.' He saw how Emily's face grew pale. 'I'm sorry to bring all this back for you Miss Emily, but as you asked...'

'It's okay,' Emily waved her hands before pulling the robe about her more tightly, 'really it is. I need some sort of closure, whether it be bad news or not.'

'Well, the thing is,' the detective paced around the lounge as if unnerved. 'There is an account leading up to your mother's death that seems particularly odd.'

'Odd,' Emily questioned, 'in what way?'

'Well it comes from a nurse who attended your mother's ward the night she was killed. She was on the reception desk not far outside the room.'

'Did she see who killed her?'

'Not exactly,' the detective stated, leaning against the fireplace to look at the artificial coals before turning to continue. 'I think it be better if I read out her statement... would you mind?'

'No, of course not,' Emily conveyed as she sat down. 'Sit down if you want. Do you want a drink?'

'No mam, I'm okay,' he said, but changed his smile in grimace to read from the document he had unfolded. 'Shall I continue?' He asked, seeing that an attentive Jack had entered the room.

'Yes please do,' Emily stated turning her head to acknowledge Jack, a forefinger put to her lips to order him to be quiet.

I woke up a little before midnight. I must have nodded off but a scream woke me up. At first I noticed how the reception area was unusually cold, as if freezing air was passing through. Anyways, I got up to investigate and noticed how all lights down one corridor were all off, yet behind me, down the corridor opposite, all lighting was on. I heard more screams and noises and deduced that they came from Miss Layton's cubicle. So I ran to get in and see, but the door was locked solid and the metal handle freezing. I heard another scream and the sound of braking glass but couldn't get in. I banged on the door, even shouldered against it. After all went quiet, I stood baffled to watch the door open by itself.

'They don't have locks those doors to those cubicles, do they?' Emily enquired.

'No, strangely they don't;' the detective admitted, 'only the on-suite bathrooms are lockable for privacy.' The detective held up a hand to gesture. 'Shall I continue?'

Emily nodded as Jack joined her to sit on the sofa bed.

I went inside S21, Miss Layton's cubicle, to find it freezing cold. Observing the broken window, I then saw that the patient's bed was empty. You may think me crazy, but I swear on my husband's life, that I saw out the corner of my eye, a dark like figure... a thick, black mist that seemed to disappear through a nearby wall vent and under the door of the washroom. I swear, before screaming to see the poor patient in the car park below, it was one of the creepiest things I ever did see.

'That's it,' the detective cleared his throat before folding the document back into an envelope. 'That's the only witness we have, seconds before your mother was found on the hospital car park.' In his other hand, the detective folded back his notepad. 'This nurse has worked years at the hospital and is known to be quite creditable. She's about to have some promotion, so surely there can't be any doubts.'

Emily looked at Jack, knowing he had a question for the detective.

'Well don't the hospital wards have closed-circuit television,' Jack stood to emphasise his question. 'Surely they'd show something the nurse might not have seen?'

'It was one of the first things we checked, as it could have shown the killer, or at least what –'

'Did they reveal anything?' Emily interrupted, her hands clenched tight with impatience.

'We can only go on what the nurse said in her statement,' the detective paused to scratch his chin. 'But the recordings before opening the door are weird.'

'Weird,' Jack intervened to ask, 'weird, how?'

'Well both cameras, as I was told, are on the same circuit... the same power supply.' The detective again cleared his throat. 'The camera monitoring the reception desk and ward beyond worked fine the time in question, yet the camera pointing towards your mother's room and the corridor beyond, well...'

'Well what?' Emily asked, staring at Jack and then back at the detective.

'Well the camera went off the time just before the incident; it didn't even record the nurse trying to enter.'

'Went off,' Jack asked as he sat, puzzled. 'Went off how?'

'Well at first we have the camera recording everything fine, but just before your mother's... before the nurse woke to try and get in the room, the fluorescent lights from a distant tent to flicker until all lights go off and then as most of the corridor is recorded in darkness, it is hard to tell.'

'Hard to tell,' Emily wanted an answer. 'What is hard to tell?'

The detective turned and paced before answering; his hands all over his face in frustration. 'The camera seems to have recorded something of a dark shadow moving to your mother's room before the video goes fuzzy and eventually blank.' The detective spoke with open arms. 'I know it sounds absolutely crazy, but it ties in with what the nurse said she saw.'

'No, it sounds quite ominous,' Emily said softly looking at a stunned Jack.

'And the camera was dead after that?' Jack continued their discussion.

'No Mr Torrance,' the detective spoke resolutely, 'that's what makes it even weirder.' He stepped to stand above them. 'A minute or two after poor Sarah's death, the camera came on to record everything fine... the corridor all lit up again and everything back to normal?'

TWENTY—EIGHT

JACK HAD FOUND THE SMALL hire car quite claustrophobic, but had to admire Emily's driving. Not only had she never travelled across the English Channel by ferry, but had to adjust her driving for Europe. And as Jack's car was in for servicing too, they had no choice but to take the small Renault to Amsterdam. As he had postponed a number of commitments to help Emily, he just hoped his car would be ready for lecturing students next week.

Jack regarded the outer suburbs of the city as if they were still in Bristol, but somehow this place was different. Indeed centrally, the city had more rivers; their subsidiaries transporting long, narrow boats that weaved their way beneath low bridges, the traffic above somewhat less tranquil. Jack chuckled to himself; appreciating to how much cleaner the streets looked to those back home, the people more organised and disciplined in their lives.

And thinking of someone disciplined, he glanced at Emily, her eyes flicking constantly between road and street map. He had offered to help navigate through the city, but she wanted to do this alone. As she had disclosed, it helped her concentrate on her driving.

They reached another cross junction; straight, narrow streets either side reaching for at least half a mile, each bordered with light grey terraced houses. Emily stopped the car in the centre of the junction to ponder on her position, but was hooted from behind by a following car. As the driver revved the car up in anger to navigate round them, Jack noticed the driver express some sign of displeasure. Maybe the Dutch were not as admirable as he first thought.

'I can't get the road,' Emily stuttered with agitation, 'I mean the street... it's supposed to be down here?'

'Here let me,' Jack announced, taking the street map from Emily's hand. 'Let's check it out whilst you park alongside that kerb there.' He had noticed another car stop behind them. 'I'll check the street names whilst you drive.' Before Emily could pull over, again Jack noticed another unpleasant sign from the driver behind as he steered around to pass them. 'Fucking idiot,' Jack whispered, but saw Emily stare questionably at him after parking.

It took another ten minutes for Jack to negotiate the street layout of the housing estate, and with a little more luck than navigation skills, he found the narrow terraced house sandwiched between others like some tightly shelved book.

'Is this the one then Jack?'

'Yes, according to the address on that postcard,' Jack thumbed in direction of the house they had managed to park alongside, 'this is the one.'

'I hope you're right,' Emily frowned as she lowered her head to look past him to view, 'those at that café were not very helpful.'

'That's because they only spoke limited English my dear.' Jack opened the door, but hesitated to exit for Emily's approval. 'Shall we?'

'Well I've not drove all this bloody way for...' Emily got out the car, her determination now driving her on. But for a long moment she rested her arms on the car roof, her tired eyes staring at the house, tentative to find what this house would disclose.

Disturbing her thoughts, Jack asked, 'Coming?'

Emily smiled and paced around the front of the car to clench Jack's arm for comfort. Or was it reassurance? She was certainly glad he had come along. Meeting Effie was one thing, but Ellen seemed somewhat an opposite; this sister working in some strip joint... some gentleman's club in a city such as Amsterdam? This was too shameful for words.

Nervously Emily paced behind Jack, her arm almost losing its grip around his as he strode up steps that lead to the front door. For some reason, she had reason to believe that something here was wrong. However, it was probably that she had been disconcerted by driving in a different country or by trying to talk with people who did not understand her. Maybe it was just the nerves of finally meeting her youngest triplet sister?

After rasping his knuckles against the dark red door, Jack pulled Emily around to see apprehension in her eyes. 'It'll be okay, my dear, you'll see.'

A girl opened the door to give some Dutch greeting, but Emily stood oblivious, hiding behind Jack, refraining to talk.

'Do you speak English?' Jack asked slowly.

'Yes, a little, but not great,' the girl said, but paused to notice Emily stare at her from behind Jack. 'What is it you...?'

'We're looking for –'

'You are looking for Ellen,' the girl deduced, her eyes fixed on Emily. 'You are sister?'

'Yes,' Emily moved close as the girl opened the door a little wider, 'yes I am.'

'You look like her, but how did you know...?' the girl smiled, but frowned soon after. 'I didn't know she had a sister, she never spoke of having one.'

Emily leaned forward to give the girl the postcard from the rented accommodation in north London. 'We found this after paying her landlord's rent and so came here.' She watched the girl take the postcard and smile. 'And your Beatrice, I know,' Emily pulled a photograph from her handbag that was slung over one shoulder. 'I recognise you from this.'

Beatrice took the photograph from Emily and her smile widened somewhat. 'She must have left these when came over.' The girl's smile changed to express regret. 'But she be not here anymore. Ellen left months ago.' Beatrice stretched out her arm to hand both items back to Emily. 'I afraid we had a little fall out.'

'Fall out,' Jack questioned, 'What about?'

Emily took Jack's arm to pull him aside.

'Look Beatrice, I know you were once Ellen's friend,' Emily played nervously with the photograph and postcard, 'so please if you can just tell us where she went?'

'She left in a huff, as you say in English.' The girl's eyes glistened with the start of tears, her cheeks quivering. 'But she be not here now, and that all I know.'

Jack stood back to let Emily take charge of the situation, he knew how determined she could be, especially to locate her youngest sister. But as Emily was to question again the girl, he noticed a man come behind Beatrice and feel her up and down, his hands reaching under her t-shirt to grope around her breasts before finally sliding down the girl's waist to rest on her buttocks. Moving into daylight, Jack and Emily noticed the man kiss Beatrice on her neck and nibble at her ears.

'Come back to bed,' Jack and Emily heard him whisper, his eyes cloudy and unperturbed by visitors at the door. And then he noticed them.

'What do you want?' the man leaned unsteady against the doorframe, his eyes unfocused as if intoxicated. 'Hey, she looks like...' With one hand the man turned Beatrice's face to look at him. 'What has she come back for?'

'Look,' Jack intervened, not liking how the man treated Beatrice, 'we're just looking for my friend's sister here.'

The man went to step forward to observe Emily more closely, but stepped back, his legs somewhat unstable. 'No, it isn't... but she looks...'

Jack was again about to question the couple, but found Emily's hands pulling him back. She poked him hard in the ribs and ushered him around to face her. Confused to why she had turned him away from questioning, Jack saw Emily pull out another photograph. Squinting at it in bright daylight, he watched Emily point to the man in the picture with Ellen. It was the man at the door. It was Robbie.

For a moment Jack stood bemused, but Emily grasped what had happened. She swivelled Jack around to explain.

'Don't you see Jack,' Emily's voice was but a whisper. 'That is Robbie, Ellen's boyfriend... or at least, he was.' She could see that Jack was still confused. 'Ellen must have found out that Beatrice wanted Robbie all along, or vice versa. And so she left...' Emily twitched her head in Beatrice's direction. 'In a huff as you say in English.'

'Yow, what's this about keeping us talking on our doorstep, people?' Robbie's English accent was obviously more fluent to that of Beatrice.

'As we've asked already,' Jack answered Robbie, his patience tested somewhat, 'we just want to locate Ellen... this is Emily, her sister!'

'Well the bitch isn't here man,' Robbie waved his hands to move them off his property. 'She's gone off with some Russian lesbian bitch, so now fuck off!'

'Well there's no need for...' Jack controlled his anger but advanced.

Before having the door slammed in his face, he saw a hand swipe the cheek of Beatrice as Robbie pushed her into the depths of the hallway. Jack was enraged and went to bang aloud on the door, but Emily caught his hand just in time.

'Jack, it's not our business,' Emily shouted, 'let it be, please!'

Jack turned and stormed off down the concrete steps, his fingers eventually pulling on the passenger door car handle. Emily rushed to him to try and calm him.

'Look, I don't like it any more than you,' Emily stared at Jack with conviction, 'but at least it's Beatrice and not my sister!'

'No girl deserves a scumbag like that one.' Jack pulled back his hair in frustration, his other hand resting on Emily's shoulder. 'Best your sister got rid of him, that's all that I can say of the matter.'

Suddenly Emily was turned by another grip. Beatrice had escaped Robbie to apologise.

'Look I so sorry for losing Ellen.' She looked at each of them in turn, but focused finally on Emily. 'Your sister good friend and I make mistake?'

'Well that's life my dear,' Emily said quietly before raising her voice. 'History is history as I'm concerned... I just want to trace my sister. I want to find Ellen!'

'You do look like her.' Beatrice gazed fervently at Emily.

'If you know anything about her whereabouts,' Emily insisted.

'All I know, maybe she still with Russian friend,' Beatrice raised her hands in question. 'Ellen stay with her or something... got her working at some club?'

Hearing her name being shouted (along with profanities), Beatrice swivelled round, disturbed to see Robbie shouting from the front door. Emily looked over the girl's head to see her boyfriend smoking a joint of some description, his voice calling for her to stop talking to them and get back inside.

'I sorry... really I be, but...' Beatrice turned to hurry back, but half way she faced them to shout, 'Fallen Angels... Fallen Angels!'

Jack stepped around Emily, again angered to the way Robbie lashed out at Beatrice before eventually dragging her inside.

'Jack,' Emily shouted as she restrained him, 'it's none of our business!'

'No,' Jack responded angrily, 'but that scumbag needs teaching a lesson in manners!'

'Yes I agree, he does,' Emily clenched hard to Jack's wrist. 'But let it go.'

'Let it go?'

'Yes, at least we have a lead.'

'We have a lead,' Jack removed Emily's grip. 'What do you mean... a lead?'

'What that girl shouted.'

'What... *Fallen Angel*,' Jack ridiculed, 'what's that all about?'

'No the plural... Fallen Angels,' Emily explained stepping to get in the car. 'I believe it's the name of that club.'

Jack joined Emily inside her car to ask questions.

'How can you know the club is called that?'

'Coz I saw some post on that social media site,' Emily smirked. 'Some Dutchman told that I... or Ellen that is... does great, live shows there.' She paused to wait for Jack to stare back from the house they had visited. 'I bet you my bottom dollar that in Dutch, *Fallen Angels* translates to something like Gev...allen Eng...allen, or something like?'

'Translates to what?' Jack frowned, but realised it was Dutch. 'Well we can check it out at that restaurant... apparently they have internet access. You can check it out online... on your laptop.'

'Well if it's a positive match, I want to check out the club after.'

'Yes, but if it's the type of club I think it is, well they'll probably won't open 'til midnight.'

'Well at least we could locate it.' Emily started the car engine. 'Maybe ask around if possible?'

'Well count me out... it's been a long day,' Jack said rubbing his stomach. 'Besides, I'm famished. You can drop me off at the café.'

'You're not coming with me?'

'No, can't we just check out that translation and go tomorrow.' Jack waved his hands aloft to gesture. 'Besides, we've no place to stay yet.'

'Fine,' Emily gritted her teeth, 'Fine. You get stuffed and find us a place to stay, but I'm going to check it out before nightfall, no matter how sleazy the place may be.'

Sleazy may have been the wrong word for it, but as Emily walked from her parked car towards the street corner, she noticed the nightclub. It was a tall, dark building at the end of a line of retail buildings, its brickwork on one side decorated in purple and black where a metal staircase gave access to a small door above – some sort of second storey, staff entrance. It was then that she noticed the cartoon-like artwork overhead. Highest was painted the face of an angel, all innocent, haloed and white; the other beneath, some wicked girl, her head crowned with devilish horns, her lips pouting and glistening red.

But it was around the corner that Emily came convinced she was at the right place. Above the main entrance was decorated the sign: *Gelvallen Engelen*. Although she incurred some problems with translating the words back at the café, her laptop proved the Dutchman's post to describe *Fallen Angels*.

Did her youngest sister really work *here*?

Even in the daylight it was dull; the letters almost dark like the painted brickwork behind, the windows blacked out. But at night, Emily imagined the place to look somewhat different; the lights of the nightclub sign would be bright and flashing red in its attempt to allure wealthy gentleman.

Emily looked left and right and leaned to one side to check her car in the distance. She stepped back to admire the large entrance that arched overhead, but became disturbed to imagine what depravation such a gentleman's club did inside. She stepped forward to cautiously test the door. Grimacing she found it locked. She turned in direction of her car, but hesitated to think whilst checking her wristwatch; if the door at the top of the metal steps was locked too, maybe it would be better to join Jack back at the café – find out what accommodation he had booked, get some sleep and return next morning.

Suddenly, as Emily was about to go, she heard a key turn in a lock and some latch scrape open. Then, as a fat woman bumped her way out of one of the main entrance doors, Emily noticed her mop stale get wedged in the frame above. Emily deduced that this was some cleaner who had probably finished her shift, and so grabbed her opportunity. She rushed to open the door further, but it was stiff against the pavement below. Using her weight, she held open the door in order to pull down on the mop head that had got jammed. Although grateful, the cleaner was somewhat surprised to have such assistance, but thanked Emily (in Dutch) before brooding over her cleaning utensils in a bucket. The cleaner winked and again said something in her language before pointing at the signage. Emily gathered from her actions that the cleaner was moaning about a difficult cleaning task. Leaving the cleaner gobsmacked, she grasped the opportunity to get inside and so slid through the nightclub entrance.

It was dim inside, the only lighting from small spotlights that stretched along the ceiling and into the club. Gingerly Emily made her way along to what she assumed was some doorman's kiosk. From here the corridor widened, a heavy door with a keypad to her left and a passage falling down to her right. Bewildered in which way to go, she continued forward, somewhat pleased to see brighter light ahead. As she meandered her way between tables and chairs, to her sides she could see alcoves, areas set back with leather couches and red cosy seating that looked firm but bouncy. However, most modern furnishings were in shadow, the lack of lighting making her observations indistinct until she reached a bar area.

Emily looked above, her eyes following a row of lightings set into the top of the service area, noticing the bar circle around to a stage, or was it just some raised level in the floor. She crept forward, her fingers sliding over the marble surface of the bar, her hand a reassurance of stability; God forbid should she trip over something. Anyhow, she asked herself, what *was* she doing here? In her head a voice whispered to answer... by the likes of it, you're trying to find some slut of a sister.

Emily had almost reached the end of the bar, when she saw something brightly lit up from a single spotlight. She vaguely made out other spotlights pointing towards it as these were all off and did not shine against the sturdy, silver pole standing vertical from floor to ceiling.

Suddenly Emily's heart jumped as from behind a voice shouted. She squinted against the light above to notice a large figure in a doorway. Again the voice called something in Dutch, the man's voice deep.

'Helan,' it seemed to call, or was it 'Helen?' The man's voice called again in Dutch but later changed to speak simple English. 'Helen, is that you?'

Emily moved aside to observe the man better. He was a large man, not so fat in belly but plump around the neck, his eyes piercing bright as they widened to see through the dim of the room.

'Helen, is that you,' the man called, trudging around to view Emily more, 'you look different... your hair?'

Emily froze to the spot. If this was the nightclub manager, it was obvious that he could not make her out properly. Did he mistake Emily for 'Ellen', or was it he thought she was this *Helen* girl? At first she managed a wave and then nodded to acknowledge her identity, but when he asked to why she was there so early, that she was not due to work until midnight, Emily had to respond.

'Sorry sir, but...' She raised the tone in her voice hoping it would pass inspection. 'I forgot my phone... forgot where I put it.'

'Well it not be down here,' the man grunted, 'my girls are not allowed this, you know that... it be the rules.'

'Sorry, then where be my stuff?'

'You have a cold my dear?' The man disregarded his first question to interrogate with more vigour. 'Your stuff... you not know where changing room be by now?' The man edged forward to squint at her more intensely. 'Are you on drugs again Helen?' The man chuckled but found he was snorting. 'Stronger ones they must be if you not know y' room.' He regarded her with distain. 'Anyways, I told you to use outside stairs.' Emily kept quiet. 'Forgotten y' key have we?'

Emily nodded. 'The cleaner let me in.' Somehow she was getting away with being this *Helen*, but was this her sister, did he mean Ellen in his foreign accent? Nonetheless, she was obviously being mistaken and so thought she could find out more about Ellen – find out what exactly she did – maybe check out her room?

'What should I do at midnight... tonight?'

'Strip of course girl, like y' always do.' The nightclub manager pointed and then waved his forefinger. 'But do not get too close like last time. That guy got the idea he could take you home.' The manager chuckled. 'But I know why he get excited. You tease like some English Britney in that school uniform.' He slid to lean against the bar. 'But you earn me good money my friend.'

'Where's my room?' Emily asked softly.

'Oh, do not jest anymore my girl,' the manager sniggered, 'you serious need to give up bad stuff. Good money I give, but not for drugs. But it be your life.' The manager thumbed behind to point. 'You know where changing room be... back door and up from toilet.' The manager again chuckled before filling a tumbler with a measure of vodka from a near empty bottle. His face changed to that of concern as he stepped around the bar. 'Shame so young ones get fixed on that stuff.' He looked at the drink in his hand. 'Better to stick to old friend, no?'

Quickly Emily skirted around the nightclub manager as not to get questioned any further. She raced past several private booths on either side, nearly knocking stools over to reach what she gathered were the back toilets. She paused to look apprehensively up a flight of wooden stairs, questioning whether she would have to examine every room. Suddenly she noticed a girl come out the toilet. She was dragging a bundle of clothes stuffed into a black, plastic bag.

Emily felt the urge to use the toilet, the nervousness of dealing with the manager somewhat pressing. But after noticing the state of them as the girl brushed past, she declined. Besides, the knowledge of her sister's whereabouts was more important.

'Excuse me,' Emily held the girl back by her arm, 'do you speak English?'

'A little,' the girl said, 'some I learn at school.'

'Please tell me what room is Ellen's?' Emily thought again, 'or maybe Helen?'

'Not know a Helen,' the girl stuttered, dumbfounded. 'Is she new here?'

Emily pondered to think, watching the girl drop the bundle to light up a cigarette.

'Maybe,' Emily remembered the conversation with Beatrice. 'But a girl, a Russian girl who works here, do you know her... she be with my sister?'

'Ah, yah, ruskie,' the girl chortled, 'you mean Monika, she share room with girl.' The girl rolled her eyes. 'Be more than friends... you understand?' The girl winked at Emily before blowing smoke into her face. 'Monika is room three.' Emily watched the girl drag the black, plastic bag out from being jammed between the toilet door and frame to trudge upstairs.

Slowly and carefully, Emily followed, ascending the creaking staircase, its worn wooden steps reverberating hard beneath her shoes.

'You need some help?'

'No, I okay,' the girl turned to reply.

Eventually as she reached the top, Emily stared down a long corridor to notice the girl make for the door she deduced was the one she saw from outside. She could not help but turn her nose up at the unwelcoming smell drifting through the corridor. Slowly as she wandered on, she restricted her breathing somewhat, the foul stench now scathing her nostrils. Was it nicotine, alcohol, perfumes, body odour from sweated costumes, urine, or a mixture of all? Whatever it was, it made her wince.

'I leave door open for bit,' the girl said, pushing her bundle into the light, 'fresh air we need... but you close after, yah?'

Emily nodded, but was more concerned in finding room three. Understandably it was the third up on the left.

Changing room three was unlocked and so she entered. Emily paused to examine the room, or was it that she heard voices?

It was relatively small, especially for two girls when changing. Large wooden wardrobes stood either side of her, and in front was a long, white dressing table, its square but elongated mirror surrounded by miniature light bulbs. From where she stood, Emily could see the reflection of her waist.

The room was littered here and there with items of clothing, the dressing table piled with an array of perfumes and makeup. The only thing that showed any sign of tidiness was the stool buried underneath the dressing table, some sort of a diary placed on top. It was the first thing Emily reached for.

Reading the diary, Emily could not understand the language (however, deduced it was Russian), but recognised drawings of her sister placed near the rear. Along with sketches this Monika had done of Ellen, Emily found a chart drawn near the back that detailed some timetable; probably that of both Monika's and her sister's routine – times to when they performed, changed or had free. With her left hand holding tight the diary, Emily searched the draws of the dressing table, having to wrench them open as they were stiff.

The top draw contained a mixture of bras, knickers and tights, some bikinis and short skirts, but mostly skimpy underwear. The left of the next draw down was packed with masks, folded hats, cosmetic jewellery and cut-off t-shirts. On the right-hand-side of the draw rolled several play-toys, two differently shaped dildos, butt-plugs, and a black-leather double ended dildo.

For a minute Emily stood tall in amazement, her eyes continually assessing the items before finally being disgusted at the unkempt ashtray on a shelf before the mirror. The whole surface was littered with ash burns and scores from uncaring haste. How could anyone work in here, let alone two young women? Closing her eyes to turn away and examine other things in the room, Emily glanced at a photograph held between the frame and mirror of the dressing table. She prised it free to study it closer. The picture showed Ellen with what Emily construed as Monika, both entwined in laughter beneath the Eiffel Tower in Paris. The city of love and romance,

Emily mused. And then she realised to what that scumbag Robbie had said about Ellen: *she's gone off with some Russian lesbian bitch.*

Abruptly the door opened and swung in to bang Emily's rear.

'Who the fuck, are you?' a girl's voice cried. 'What the hell do you think you're doing?'

Emily spun around. Being suddenly startled, she stepped back until her buttocks hit the dressing table. She was amazed to see an almost identical reflection of herself in the girl staring back. The girl, somewhat unkempt and more bedraggled than Emily, was about to wail abuse, but silenced to stand aghast.

Ellen was dressed in tight, black leggings, her hips and thighs slightly less profound than Emily's. Her body was slightly slimmer too, but no least less sensual beneath the flimsy t-shirt she had knotted together above her waist. Pulling back strands of hair that fell over her eyes, she stared at Emily, her black hair highlighted at the ends but separated into two pigtails that overhung each ear. Her eyes were not hazel like Emily's, but ejected a dark, unwelcoming stare nonetheless. At first neither could speak, both perturbed by each other's similarity. It was Emily that took lead to apologise.

'Look, I'm sorry to invade your privacy but,' Emily stuttered, her eyes continually scrutinising her sister all over, 'but you're Ellen aren't you... Ellen Louise.'

'My name is *Helen* and get away from my stuff.' Ellen rejected the fact that Emily looked just like her. 'Who are you, some copy-cat detective woman, searching for dope?'

'No, I'm Emily Rose... your sister.'

'I have no sister,' Ellen voiced angrily, moving towards the dressing table and pushing Emily aside. 'I have only one friend and this is our place.'

'Yes, I'm sorry about...' Emily paused to examine Ellen sideways as she picked up makeup knocked to the floor. 'But I came from England to find you... traced you here from Robbie.' She showed Ellen the photograph, but she pushed back her hand after recognising it. 'And you have another sister, Effie.'

'Look, are you some copycat woman like that film... Single *something* Female or what?' Ellen noticed the diary in Emily's grasp. 'Hey, bitch that be my friend's diary, so give it back!'

Emily had hardly outstretched her arm before Ellen snatched it from her grasp.

'I was only trying to find a way to trace you.' Emily stepped sideways, not liking the way Ellen looked at her after checking Monika's diary. 'The three of us were born –'

'I told you lady... it's only me Helen and my friend Monika now,' Ellen interrupted, 'we have each other and she be the only person I need.' Ellen slammed shut all the draws that Emily had failed to close. 'You can tell that Robbie to go fuck himself for all he did!'

'I know,' Emily described to what she construed, 'I guess him ditching you for that Beatrice was something you hadn't imagined. To leave everything and go all the way to –'

'How comes you know all my business, copycat?'

Emily had lost her attempt to take things calmly. 'I'm trying to get all my sisters back together after our poor, fucking mother got *murdered*!'

Maybe the harsh attitude of her youngest sister had been infectious. One minute with Ellen and she was seething herself. But thinking back of Robbie and all that Ellen must have gone through, Emily kept her sympathies reserved.

God knows why, she thought, *haven't I been through as much, if not more? Why should I apologise to this ungrateful person... her face grotesquely plastered in heavy makeup, her lips coated black and her eyes dark and bloodshot...? If she didn't reflect in that mirror, I'd say she was some fucked up vampire!* Emily's mind paused to contemplate on its unusual hard attitude. *Because she's your sister*, a compassionate voice answered.

'Look I got Effie back... found her in some place for loonies. I don't want to go through that shit again!'

'Then leave woman,' Ellen leaned over to place the diary back on the stool beneath the dressing table. 'I have no relation to any *sisters*. There's just me and Monika now!'

Emily hardly had time to notice the falling tears tattoo beneath Ellen's ear, but almost scraped her stud earrings from her lobe as she reached to grab Ellen's t-shirt at the neck. She pushed Ellen forward towards the mirror, now grasping one of her pigtails as leverage. She then saw the ring pierced through Ellen's nose.

'Look you heartless bitch, take it or leave it,' She flung Ellen forward to make her look up at Emily through the mirror, 'but if you were christened Ellen Louise and you're a Layton-Aston, then you be my sister... a triplet from our Sarah.' Ellen tried to knock away Emily's grasp, and Emily realised that this girl was strong, but with rage Emily shook her. 'Look at me and tell me that we don't look the same... just look me in the eye and deny it!'

Still holding Ellen's pigtail, Emily lunged down so her cheek was smack against her sister's. Somehow Emily felt emotion she had never beheld. She turned Ellen's face so that they stared at one another in the mirror. 'Deny it if you want Ellen, but you're still my flesh and blood. We're Effie's flesh and blood, and that of our mother, Sarah. We're triplet sisters... now do you believe me?'

'Get away you fool,' Ellen eventually fought her way free, standing to push Emily away. 'Fucking bitch, what you know about me?'

Emily retaliated, knocking Ellen against the dressing table; her backside perched precariously on the right, the left of the furniture piece almost lifting.

'This is *my* place,' Ellen shouted, 'mine and Monika's, so leave me alone!'

Somehow Emily felt a weakness in Ellen that only she could sense. She deduced that below all the 'macho' makeup and hard character, Ellen had not suffered half the pain as she had. Yes it was true, she had been betrayed by some scumbag lover and had changed to become bisexual, but it seemed to Emily that her sister was just some sheep in wolfs clothing, some girl that had resorted to drugs to nullify months of rejection, lowered her self-esteem to strip for money to get by. Maybe to her and this Monika, it was easy cash? But who could live like this? Surely her sister could do better?

'Get away from me before I call the manager,' Ellen shrieked, 'he'll see you who you are... some imposter!'

'But you must come back,' Emily screamed, watching Ellen scramble out of the changing room, 'we're all in danger... but mother said we can fight as one.' Emily ran after Ellen to see her lean against the corridor wall, sliding along and struggling to reach the open door to the metal staircase. Had Emily unintentionally hurt her? 'Maybe you have some gift like we do, Effie and me?'

Emily leaned against the doorframe of the changing room, thinking her task had failed, thinking Ellen would not stop. But suddenly, as her sister reached the lowering rays of the daylight from outside, she turned to peer at Emily from the doorway, her eyes annoyed but inquisitive.

'What do you mean... some kind of gift?'

TWENTY—NINE

Inquisitively Emily stared across the table at her newly found sister. Ellen was nibbling on a handful of peanuts she had grabbed from the café counter on her way in. Emily grimaced; it was as though Ellen hadn't eaten in days. Maybe she hadn't? How come this girl wanted to be known as Helen and not Ellen? Had she changed identity due to past convictions – had some run in with police over drugs? And why the gothic look; surely it turned men off, not aroused them? However, what Emily had learned from her first day in Amsterdam, over here, things were quite different.

'I only come, coz you said you'd buy me something.'

Emily never took her eyes off Ellen, but looked as if oblivious to anything her sister said.

'Ems, I *can* call you that can't I?' Ellen glanced at Jack at the counter and then back at Emily, her hard grin changing into a mischievous smile. 'Your boyfriend *is* going to pay for my order, isn't he?' Continually she popped peanuts in between her black matted lips. 'Ems... it's a good short for your name you know.' Ellen frowned, realising Emily had snubbed a reaction. 'Not been here before. I hope the food is good.' Ellen winked before her eyes searched the café for activity.

Emily studied Ellen for a while, reflecting on the difference between her and her sister back home.

'I ordered chicken,' Ellen continued, her wide grin somehow displeased Emily. 'Here in Amsterdam they call it –'

'When was the last day you ate exactly?' Emily interrupted, her hand shaking to put down a jug full of water after filling her glass.

'Last pay day.' Ellen refused to be scorned, her self-preservation strong. 'Or was it *last* night the manager gave me a little bonus for my Britney show?'

'And you get good money in that line of work?'

'Oh no, sorry,' Ellen had pretended not to have heard Emily, 'he's yet to pay me for that, so I couldn't refuse a free meal now could I?'

'You like that line of work for such money?' Emily repeated to belittle, knowing her approach to this sister would need to be different.

'Like I said before Ems, it's like any other job... it's just a job that pays money and you get used to it.'

'Are you sure it's not some way to get back at men for the failures of a past relationship?' By her sister's expression, Emily knew that she had broken some of Ellen's outer shell.

'I gather then that you've never indulged?' She twitched her head in Jack's direction. 'I guess boyfriend over there would disprove of such a performance.'

Emily looked at the table, its checked pattern of white and red squares somewhat disparaging.

'In fact he said I be a smash at such a thing.' Emily looked up and past Ellen, her eyes dream-like, staring into the darkening street beyond.

Ellen spoke aloud to break Emily's pondering.

'So Emily,' Ellen mused. 'Or should I stick to Ems?' She licked her fingers, the last of the peanuts devoured. 'What is your line of business, exactly?' At first, with her mind elsewhere, Emily did not respond until Ellen repeated her question, 'So, what is it that *you* do Emily?'

'I work as a media journalist in Bristol,' Emily paused to reflect. 'A job my foster parent got me after promising to look after me... after...' Emily tried to picture the photograph she had seen of her father. 'Carl was Mike's best friend and our biological father, but he got murdered.'

'Seems like I'm not the only one who's had problems,' Ellen voiced.

Emily was not sure whether Ellen had spoken justly or had conveyed some type of cynicism.

'Past is past,' Emily said quietly, 'but you must want to know what happened, Carl was *your* biological father too?'

'Like you said, past is past.' Ellen searched again to locate Jack. 'But I bet you had a better upbringing... bet that you had it good as a child.'

'Good,' Emily snapped, 'you call visiting mother in some mental institute, good?'

'But I thought you said you were adopted, like me?'

'It was our mother's friends that brought me up, Mike and Rachael.' Emily looked down again to pinch at the tablecloth. 'Our mother Sarah had been convicted of attempted murder... well until recently... and then she...' Emily shook the memories from her head; she wanted to know more about her sister, not recite the past. 'But tell me more about you Ellen, what's your story?'

'That too is a long story, and *Helen* is not going there.'

'But surely you want to know –'

'Forget it sister,' Ellen snapped. 'If you'd been slung from place to place like I was, then maybe you'd not...' Suddenly Ellen saw Jack approach with three coffees on a tray. He handed one to each of the girls and sat down to stir his own.

'Ellen, this is Jack.'

'Your boyfriend I presume,' Ellen mocked, 'as he wouldn't be ordering me the chicken, would he?'

Emily smiled thinly, thinking Jack would introduce himself, but curiously he cut to the chase.

'Have you mentioned to Ellen what happened to your mother... that she missed her funeral?'

'I was about to, but thought she'd want to know more of the past.'

'Look, the name is *Helen*, and as you said, the past is past, so –'

'I was trying to be friendly,' Emily barked, rolling her eyes at her newly found, but already insufferable sister. 'We call them manners back home.'

'Well,' Ellen glanced aside to look at the activity at the café counter, 'I must confess... I only come for the meal you promised.'

'You not want to know Emily's history... what happened to your mother, or know that you have another sister?' Jack quizzed somewhat astonished.

'Look there's only me and Monika now,' Ellen said, wriggling in the small chair, 'she's the only family I have now.'

'What about Beatrice,' Jack tested, 'what if this Monika turns out to be the same?'

'She'll not want to be with men,' Ellen snarled, 'especially bastards like that Robbie!' Again Emily saw a part of Ellen's hard shell crack and fall as her sister came rattled. 'She'll play them along but... what do you know about it anyway?'

'That's how we traced you here.'

'What, that stupid postcard?'

'Yes, and photos Emily found. Who knows, but this friend of yours could be...' Jack was trying to persuade Ellen to come back home, but felt Emily clench his arm.

'I think things have changed since then,' Emily said quietly.

'What do you mean?' Jack turned to face Emily.

'Well let's say,' Emily patted Jack's hand, 'some of the things I found at the nightclub and in Monika's room, were things only two girls can enjoy... you understand?'

At first Jack sat back in bewilderment, watching Ellen push her tongue between two fingers and lick up and down. But shortly after, Ellen stopped her provocative gesture to show resentment.

'Well its more to whom you can trust.' Ellen glared at Emily. 'You might be my so-called sister, but I live with Monika now and we know everything about each other. Yes, we have arguments... once she even threw me out, but we are, even if you dislike it, together!' Ellen mused to observe the couple look questionably at each other, her anger slowly diminishing. 'But you two look cosy. How long you been together?'

Emily blushed and feeling her cheeks inflame, stood to excuse herself. 'Sorry, I must visit the toilet.' Quickly she turned but tapped Jack on the head. 'We haven't been together that long, have we my dear?'

Ellen smirked somewhat, watching Emily step in the direction of the ladies toilet, but her grin widened when she saw her food arrive. Without unravelling the knife and fork from their encompassing napkin, Ellen grabbled with the chicken drumsticks.

'Yes, we've only been seeing each other properly for a few weeks now, but I've liked Miss Emily a lot longer.'

'Get it while you can, coz it might not last,' Ellen winked at Jack, her black lips now shining a slippery wet. 'But you two look cosy, maybe it was meant to be?'

'I hope so,' Jack leaned forward, his elbows on the table. 'I used to watch Emily... waited for her to go on lunch, her and her friend would come out of work on the hour, as timely as a cuckoo-clock bird. I'd follow her to the shops... watch her eat on the benches and...'

'Fucking stalker,' Ellen joked. 'I'd have you arrested.'

'No it wasn't like that, not by any means,' Jack protested. 'I'd never hurt the girl. It's just she seemed the perfect one for me. And coz of that, I'd always back out of talking to her, or asking her out.'

'You want someone with a bit of...' Ellen played with the chicken bone, sliding it in and out her mouth, entwining her tongue about it and then licking around her lips. 'She might look like me, but I bet she's not as... stimulating?' Ellen dropped the chicken bone onto the table, but Jack watched her now suck her fingers provokingly. And then she questioned, 'You two had sex yet?'

'Why yes, but what's it your business,' Jack stuttered, almost choking

'Just seems that you'd be interested in me... looking like Ems and all?'

'I thought you and Monika were...'

'She's lesbian, but I'm well... undecided after...' She sucked on more chicken from her plate, her biting into the meat almost an indication of the vigorous lovemaking she could do. 'Well not all men are... bastards. And sister Ems has picked a good one I think.' She paused to wink and play more with her fingers. 'Some of them would certainly like you.'

'Some of who would like me?' Jack had never felt more intimidated but aroused.

'Girls I know at the nightclub of course.'

'You'll get indigestion gobbling that lot down after nothing much else.' Jack turned his eyes to his coffee, trying to ignore Ellen's seductive performance. *Is she always like this*, he thought, *or is it just something that comes with her job? Maybe like Robbie, she's had something to get her high?*

Ellen stopped eating and looked at Jack in a strange way; not provocatively or in hunger of sex, but a yearning, a want of different man – someone honest but compelling, trustworthy and yet endearing.

'Eating like that, you'll be sick if you've got to work tonight.'

Ellen smiled at Jack, her fingers picking at her food, still playing with it to excite him. But then she stopped to frown.

'I take it my so-called sis has filled you in on my job?'

To reply simply, Jack nodded.

'Well maybe you'll come to watch,' a board smile stretched across Ellen's face. 'Monika and I do a special performance for guys on their Birthdays and such like.' She had finished playing with the chicken, but found the fries long and teasingly good. 'You could pretend it's your Birthday.'

'I'm with Emily,' Jack told before turning the table of question. 'What happens should you get asked out, at this nightclub of yours?'

'My work... or should I say our work, well it's just a performance. We get our pleasure from each other behind closed doors. We'd do no more whatever they pay, as some girls have, after a promise, well... gone missing, let's say.' She paused to swallow a mouthful of fries. 'But one girl from the Czech Republic, I guess if *you* asked, well she'd take y' money for a more *private* experience, should I say.'

'I wouldn't do such a thing,' Jack insisted, 'especially not after finally getting Emily.' He did not want to express his dislikes about Ellen, but needed to dowse this girl's fire. 'Besides, should the girl be like you, or look nothing like Emily, well I dislike that dark makeup, those tattoos on a girl and such heavy piercing.'

'What's the matter Jack,' Ellen snapped back after downing her coffee, 'don't the guys in England like this shit... sorry to disappoint!' Ellen slammed down the coffee cup before protesting. 'Why's it she wants me to go back to England anyhow... give up my life here, my job, me fucking partner... just to play happy families?'

'She wants to honour her dead mother, Sarah... your biological mother. We believe that she was murdered and Emily...' Jack needed to compose himself. 'And Emily believes that all three of you, all triplet sisters have a joined purpose, something –'

'I tell you my purpose here.' Ellen stood in anger. 'I say that I am thankful for the meal, I wish you the best Mr Jack, and tell that Emily to look after herself.' Jack stood up to respond, but Ellen shushed him to continue. 'Sister or no sister, I have no intention to leave Amsterdam, or my friend Monika.' She turned quickly, but Jack noticed a tear leave an eye. 'I'm sorry man, but I leave now, goodbye!'

'No Ellen, don't leave, please,' Jack stepped out from the table to follow. 'Emily's going to be so...' He considered paying for the bill to run after her, but... 'Stay longer to talk... talk with Emily please?'

But as soon as she had stormed through the café door, Ellen was gone.

Jack sat down, his elbows on the table and his hands all over his face with frustration. Or was it that he was genuinely tired? He rubbed his eyes whilst considering another coffee when the inevitable question came.

'Where's Ellen, or *Helen* should I say?'

Jack looked up at a stern-faced Emily, her arms folded tight and handbag swinging from its strap. Jack sat back, now needing to massage his head before speaking.

'Well, see, I'll put it bluntly.' Jack hesitated to watch Emily's eyes open wide, noticing on this occasion how they lost their beauty to stare in horror. 'I don't think Ellen is going to come back, no matter how many meals I buy her.'

'Why not,' Emily scraped the chair back to sit down, glancing at the remains of Ellen's meal before staring back at Jack, 'she said she'd listen if we bought her that. And maybe she'd give some address... maybe her email?'

'You can't expect the girl to uproot herself just because you've arrived.' Jack could tell by Emily's face that this was going to be difficult. 'She's got a job here, and a friend... sounds like they're close.'

'Yes, close enough to be fucking each other!'

Jack sat forward, perturbed that Emily swore so loud. 'Keep it down babe.'

'No, why should I?' Emily slammed her handbag on the table, Jack having to reset the condiments that had toppled. 'All I wanted was her to visit us, meet Effie back home, maybe get all of us on a picture... it's not much to ask now is it?'

'I know you're upset,' Jack was playing with fire. 'But you can't expect –'

'Why did you let her go?' Emily wriggled fretfully in the chair. 'How come you didn't stop her before my return?'

'She shot up out of here so quick only enough to wish us the best.'

'Best, the best,' Emily slammed the side of her fist against the tablecloth. 'She not know what shit we've got back home?'

'She's not interested Emily,' Jack muttered. 'Besides, it's only that you imagine this Amanda woman has plans to kill you.'

'I just wanted her to...' Emily's anger erupted into tears, her head bowing, her hands clenched tightly together. 'If only she could've left a phone number or something?'

'Don't cry Emily,' Jack stated, his hand on top of hers. 'I hate to see a girl as pretty as you, cry.'

'We'll go visit her again tomorrow.'

'We don't have time,' Jack instructed, 'our ferry is booked and it's a long enough drive to –'

'Then we'll cancel it and get her number instead.'

Jack felt tired and weary but hated to see Emily frail.

'Look Ems... as she calls you,' Jack smiled, hoping to cheer her up. 'Ellen, or should I call her *Helen*, well according to that manager you met, she performs tonight doesn't she?'

'Yes, but I'm not going there,' Emily declared adamantly, 'not to see her do such things... all those men staring at her!'

'Well then, I'll go, and try to catch her after her shift,' Jack lifted Emily's head to show conviction in his eyes. 'Maybe I'll get her number or something?'

'You sure that's not all you're going for?'

Jack secretly bit his lip before trying to convince his girlfriend otherwise.

'Ellen is with her girlfriend right... she's bi-sexual... has her lesbian girlfriend?'

'It's not them I'm concerned with.' Emily turned away as if to hide something, as if jealousy had never been something she had experienced before. 'They'll be lots of them stripping... to God only knows, how and why?'

'Then come along and keep an eye out whilst I meet our dear Ellen,' Jack had reached a level of resistance. 'Experience the cultures of this European city?'

'I think not,' Emily said coldly as she turned to glare at him. 'You do what you wish, but I have not unpacked anything yet. Besides I'm tired and it's already so late. We leave tomorrow.'

THIRTY

AFTER PAYING FOR ENTRY AT the kiosk, Jack stepped gingerly further into the nightclub. The first thing he noticed was how dark it seemed compared to the bright, flashing lights over the entrance outside.

Walking slowly through a puddle-lit corridor, Jack eventually reached a circular service bar where alcoves lay either side; squared recesses with elongated seating that surrounded low marble tables. In one he saw a couple getting intimate, but glancing back, he noticed only the woman moving, her buttocks gyrating in front of a man's face. In what he could make out of the man, the business guy simply sat and smiled from within the shadows.

It was not long after Jack had ordered a drink (somewhat difficult in English with his speech drowned by loud music) that a blonde girl approached to slide her fingers down the long sleeve of his shirt. She said something but Jack simply smiled after voicing Ellen's name. The blonde girl was unperturbed and after looking at Jack curiously, said some sentence he presumed was Dutch. She fingered with his hair and then slid the top of her forefinger down his jawline. Jack moved away to follow the bar around to an area engulfed in lights. Above him he watched a mirror-ball swivel as spotlights beamed coloured lights about a high-level in the floor. From its couple of steps up, he now recognised this as a black-matted stage; the lights now glimmering against a thick, metal pole at its centre.

Jack stopped just short of the stage to rest against the end of the bar. He noticed now how the whole area was decorated in a marble effect. He sipped his whiskey and coke, swirling the couple of ice cubes around that the large barman had dropped into his drink. It was then that he felt long fingernails run up his shirt from spine to shoulder. As he turned to identify the blonde from before, she again said something incomprehensible. But by her seductive expression, Jack fathomed the girl's intention. Again he voiced the name *Ellen*, and then twice *Helen*, but the girl stood perplexed, her eyes fixed only on handsome money. He heard the girl voice one English word, *play*, but misheard a monetary figure. At one point Jack found the blonde quite alluring, her grey eyes glimmering from the light from above the bar, her ample, exposed cleavage quite inviting. But as she persisted, he again exclaimed the name Ellen, and then Monika.

'I come to see *Ellen*... or maybe *Monika*...?' Jack gazed at the blonde's dumbfounded expression, her fingers now flicking back her hair in disapproval, her eyes narrowing before she retreated. He watched her reluctantly disappear into the shadows of a corner, but noticed her pointing at the stage.

Jack looked around in disarray; although it was past midnight, the nightclub was virtually empty. He shielded his eyes from the spotlights to observe the odd man being entertained in distant cubicles. And further past the stage, into a larger area beyond, he could make out another activities of private entertainment. It was then that a voice grunted at him from the other side of the bar. Jack hardly heard the bulky man speak, but deduced that this barman was indeed the manager. He too was pointing at the stage.

'You Englishman?' he chortled, flinging a towel over his big shoulder. 'Then you like Monika... she ruskie... they like Englishman.' He tapped Jack heavily on the shoulder as if intoxicated and unsteady. 'You like Britney... then you like Monika!' He swung round to place glasses aside, his heavy chest bouncing with snorting laughter.

Jack stood dumbfounded, even enough to sip his drink. But then came the bumping beat of a deep drum; a rhythm he recognised from over a decade ago. And although it had been years since he had heard the tune, he distinguished the track from the start. In time with the beat, stage spotlights twirled into action, but suddenly stopped to shine against the dance pole, as a figure stepped up and onto centre stage.

Was this Monika, Ellen's Russian friend pretending to be Britney?

As the rhythmic, bumping beat gave way to the first verse, the slim girl stepped forward on stage, the whole of her body exposed by bright light. Looking the best to resemble her role-model, Monika was dressed in dark shoes, her slim, athletic legs tightly covered in black, but laddered, fishnet stockings; her red and pleaded, cotton skirt was the best to envisage some schoolgirl uniform, as too was her white blouse with a striped, red and white tie hanging freely around the neck. Attractively hiding Monika's little breasts below her blouse was a pink, woollen cardigan.

Jack looked her up and down as she stepped to the beat of the music. Her reddish hair was pigtailed but circled against her head either side. As she removed pink, furry headbands, her pigtails flopped down beside her ears, her eyes blinking innocently as she examined the room. Although somewhat disparaged by the scarcity of audience, the Russian girl stepped through her routine. After undoing the top buttons of her blouse to expose a little cleavage, Monika undid her tie to slide through the blouse collar, and then turned to remove the cardigan. As she swung around the pole and played provocatively with her tie, she kicked off her shoes. This gave her opportunity to mount the pole in full, her thighs tight against the shiny metal, her legs extended towards the ceiling. She swung several times around the pole before jumping off to land on all fours. Squatted down with legs open, Jack could see red knickers between her taut thighs. She rolled backward into a cartwheel to mount the pole again, the music now voicing the distinct chorus. Jack gulped at his drink, but almost swallowed an ice cube from the manager nudging his shoulder from behind.

'She good yah?' the nightclub manager shouted. 'Ask for private dance later?'

Jack shook his head to decline, but could not take his eyes off the young girl's performance; her little breasts now bouncing beneath the stretched blouse, her nipples detectably erect. And although this Monika was almost as thin as Effie, the erotic and elaborate way she motioned her legs and hips, he recognised her athleticism. Jack thought although she was thin, she had thighs that would ride a saddle strong.

Lowering herself to the ground, her buttocks tight between the metal pole, Monika camel-toed whilst undoing buttons on her blouse. With her chest now open, her little breasts bounced to finally come exposed. She slid her chest against the pole, her blouse now stripped and fallen away, her body moving up and down the pole.

She kicked herself away from the pole, leaning forward to tease the exposure of her buttocks beneath the skirt. And then Jack noticed Monika turn her head back to smile and wink at him. With her legs taught and buttocks tight, she winked again before lowering her pleated skirt; the rosy cheeks of her buttocks bare each side of her red knickers. Next she kicked off the skirt before taking time to tease her audience in rolling off her fishnet stockings. All but for her red, frilly knickers, Monika was naked and exposed by the one spotlight; her body made even more sensual by the fast moving lights and the colours they ejected onto her skin.

Jack could feel the music travel through his body, its vibration almost persuading his erection to last; as watching this girl's performance, it was difficult for his organ not to get aroused. He took his eyes off Monika to notice other men gawping at the Russian, his mind trying to convince himself that Emily would never do such a thing. But his imagination teased him. Emily would look so... sexy doing such a performance.

Gradually Jack found the music pumping to its end and gazed at the Russian doing more topless moves. Was she to remove the knickers too... some sort of finale?

As he stared about the nightclub, trying to ignore the bounce the music made in his head, he recognised a figure not far away – someone else admiring Monika's performance. But this was another girl, one he now knew. Unperturbed by all the music, lights and activity Jack wondered over to who he now knew was Ellen.

'Ellen... *Helen*,' Jack yelled as she tried to walk away after seeing him, 'she's good isn't she your friend?'

'Yes, she copies my act well.' Ellen yanked back to free herself from Jack's grip. 'I did the same last night, see.'

'So have you thought anymore about coming back?' Jack gulped the last of his drink and slammed the glass on the bar.

'Back to where,' Ellen shouted sarcastically, 'nasty England... where there's hardly any of *this* work... where you can't get good stuff on the street? Go back there, just to play happy fucking families?'

'No,' Jack affirmed, his grip now tighter, 'a place where your sisters want to see you home... know that you're safe!'

'Well, Ems has seen me. You have seen me. I'm safe here with Monika, so take y' ferry tomorrow and get the fuck out of my life!'

'But Emily wants you back... I promised her I'd help?'

'Then *un-promise* it man. She knows the score. I stay here with her!' Ellen pointed to Monika as the infamous Britney track finished. 'She's with me and I'm with her, simple!'

'But at least talk about it.' Jack released her arm after seeing a doorman approach. 'Give me a chance to say why Emily is so keen... why she's so impatient to get you home?'

'I've told you before that this place is my home now... how many times?' Ellen rolled her eyes and then turned abruptly to see Monika finish with a split, her hands already applauding her friend.

'Then give us five minutes... just five to explain.' Jack pleaded, applauding also.

Seeing a bouncer approach, Ellen twitched her head in a direction for Jack to follow. Swiftly they stopped short of a lobby where Ellen glanced at toilets below a stairway.

'Bouncers were eyeing me questionably,' Ellen winked as she chewed gum. 'I could've had you thrown out.'

'But you know I don't mean to –'

'I know that,' again Ellen winked, 'but they don't, do they?'

'Please, if I can just explain why Emily –'

'Yes, she said, something about a crazed woman,' Ellen interrupted, her eyes searching the stairway, 'some woman she said killed her mother and is out to get her... oh and me... and oh, the other one too, what's her name again?' Ellen stepped up close to face Jack, her eyes staring wild. 'Be another reason not to go back to *Great Britain*.'

'But there's more to it than that,' Jack tried his best to convince. 'Emily believes that together you...'

Suddenly a girl bounced out of the toilets and ran between them, her head turning first to greet Ellen. As Jack looked down upon the loosened pigtails and red hair, he deduced the girl to be Monika. But surely she had not had time to get changed already? Ellen's announcement broke his line of thought.

'Monika this is Jack,' Ellen grinned somewhat. 'He's come with Emily... a girl who thinks I'm her sister.'

'Are you?' Monika asked as she acknowledged Jack. 'You not have sister, I told?'

'Hello,' Jack said slowly, 'you are Russian girl... girl who just did...'

'Yes you like?' Monika said twirling her body, opening her heavy leopard skin coat to reveal her Britney schoolgirl outfit beneath. 'You want special or something?'

'Yes, you was very good, it was original.' Jack stuttered to watch her close tight her thick overcoat. 'But you've got the same things on as... surely you're not going home in...?'

'It my last show of night,' the Russian girl exclaimed, opening her coat to reveal again her seductive outfit. 'This be Helen's idea... but she much better than me.' Monika seemed exhilarated, maybe by physical endurance, maybe by drugs? She turned to question Ellen. 'I get no dance like you after... no men want special? I hoped your friend here pay good money... I do private in this again if he want?'

'Here's not here for that my friend,' Ellen informed.

'Man come to club and not want dance?'

'No, see this man, Jack,' Ellen turned to see Jack step back slightly, 'he come to only talk... with me about the girl I met here earlier... girl who said she was my sister.'

Monika smiled and paced slowly towards Jack as if intoxicated, the deep green in her eyes revealed more by a bright, overhead light. Jack was enchanted by the Russian's small face, the tenderness of her young skin and pretty freckles that decorated her nose. But for some reason Jack pitied her. Why should such a gorgeous, young and athletic girl have to travel across Eastern Europe just to live in a city doing this kind of work?

'You have Helen's sister as girlfriend?' Monika asked, frowning.

Jack nodded. 'Her name is Emily.'

'She has just one sister?'

Jack shook his head. 'She has two.'

Monika searched Ellen's face.

'The other is named Effie,' Ellen exclaimed. She brushed Monika aside, but held her hand whilst confronting Jack. 'This Effie, does she have some sort of special gift too?' Ellen looked back at Monika, her friend pulling on her hand. 'Emily said she has, but never said what...'

'Look,' Jack held his hands aloft, 'all Emily wants is you to come back to England, even if it be just for a while, maybe get a photo done. Surely that wouldn't be difficult?'

'Are you sure that's all she wants, coz it sounds like she's in trouble.' Ellen again felt Monika pulling on her arm. 'Something to do with that crazed woman she mentioned. I'll have no part in that kind of thing.'

'Then just give us a contact number,' Jack pleaded, trying best to play innocent, although his charm did not always work. 'We have no address, no phone number... couldn't she just have your email?'

'I'll have nothing to do with some woman if she did what Emily said she did.' Ellen was finally pulled back a few steps.

'Helen, please, can we go now,' Monika leaned against Ellen's back, her arms folded around her shoulders to meet at the front. 'I'm so tired after that show... me not have anything since we got up.'

Watching the two girls step along the corridor to go out of the nightclub, Jack followed but was stopped by a doorman. Jack called to the girls just in time before the doorman pulled him aside.

'Hey Ellen... Helen,' Jack pleaded, 'don't leave this way, I promised Emily I'd have something for her... even if it just be an email?'

The doorman looked at the two showgirls who had stopped to look back; he obviously did not understand Jack's words of English, but held him there so not to follow. Ellen returned to tell the doorman that Jack was her sister's friend and that he could follow them out. For a moment the doorman stood puzzled by the fact that Helen (as he knew her), had a sister. And during that moment, before being released from the bouncer's grip, Jack stood bemused at Ellen's fluency of the Dutch language. Somehow, in the short time she had lived here in Amsterdam, she had picked up the language so rapidly. It was impressive. But what was it that Emily had said?

Jack left his thoughts behind to exit the nightclub.

Eventually he caught up with the girls, Monika struggling somewhat to keep slippery shoes on a wet pavement.

'Please Ellen,' Jack clenched her arm, 'talk with Emily before we go back tomorrow?'

'Look, I got you loose from that bouncer, what more you want?' Although it must have hurt, Ellen snapped back her arm with vigour. 'Besides, the name is Helen, remember? And I live here now!'

Jack looked to the floor as if he had no other card to play. It seemed every hand he dealt would never win over the game. As he considered turning to walk away, suddenly he heard Ellen ask Monika to fetch a bottle of red wine from a nearby shop, but as Monika described, she had hardly any money; that was why she had not eaten since morning.

'Has he not paid you tonight?'

'No, he pay tomorrow,' Monika told Ellen. 'He disappointed as no specials.'

For a while Jack watched the girls check what money they had in their pockets before approaching. He looked again at Monika; sympathetic at how the large leopard-skin coat engulfed such a spindly frame.

'Here have some from me,' Jack said offering Monika a note of his foreign currency. 'I'll only have to change it back home anyway.' He saw Monika reach out her hand but hesitate to take it. 'What, isn't it enough?'

'It's plenty enough,' Ellen said snatching the note and turning towards the shop. 'And thanks man.' She turned back to grab Monika's hand but left her alone to announce sarcastically to Jack, 'Don't think we owe you a favour for this or something... as we don't do threesomes.' Twice he noticed Ellen wink before entering the shop.

Jack turned again to walk away, disgusted by Ellen's arrogance as she left Monika to follow.

'Do not forget Helen,' Jack heard Monika shout, 'get me food, I hungry.'

He glanced back at the lonely Russian girl, her body cowering to the cold night air, her face solemn. He had to have a last word. At least try one more time?

'Please, Monika,' Jack stated, clenching hold of Monika's hand as she started to walk, 'with that money, at least make sure Ellen... Helen gets you some food.'

'I ask, but think, she will not.'

'Then have this,' Jack whispered, winking whilst giving her some more money. 'But keep it under your hat.'

'But I do not wear hat?' Monika frowned.

'Keep it a secret between us,' Jack chuckled, his hand pushing the money into her delicate fingers.

'I should not have stranger money without...' Monika blinked, slowly curling the money into her overcoat pocket. 'I give you special next time?' She smiled thinly but winked back at him. 'You come again to visit?'

Jack shook his head. 'I doubt it.'

Again he took pity on the Russian girl after feeling her little fingers so cold and wondered if beneath the coat she was shivering. But why did she not change properly in the nightclub?

It was then that he saw her open a handbag she had hidden beneath the thick coat and pull out a pen and some business card. As she started to write something on the back of what was a promotion card for the nightclub, he looked her up and down.

'I'm sorry I shouldn't say this, but... why such a cute girl like you be lesbian?'

'Life be difficult back home... men be harsh,' she replied glancing up at him now and then. 'Helen help me travel... so I help her here. We have special relationship. We tease men.' She handed him the nightclub promotion card, a mobile telephone number written clearly. 'But I feel you different... you cute also... nice English man.' Monika smiled thinly but looked inwardly sad as she stared at the wet ground. 'Helen good... I look after her... she look after me.'

'She was christened Ellen you know,' Jack explained whilst examining the card, 'Ellen Louise.' He squinted at the number written on the back. 'Is this your number?'

'Yes,' Monika smiled, 'my mobile, but not tell Ellen... only to me text, promise?'

'Yes we keep both things secret,' Jack said, lifting Monika's head to kiss her forehead. 'I keep this secret, you keep money for food.'

'You good man... not many here at club like you.'

'I just want the best for Emily,' Jack looked into Monika's sad eyes. 'She just wants her sister back... her family.'

'I understand,' Monika gasped to take a deep breath. 'I lost only sister many years back... I still miss her... remember as child.'

'I'm sorry,' Jack stood baffled trying to decipher her story, 'but what happened?'

'She fell into river... drowned.' Jack could see memories flooding those green, tearful eyes. 'I not able to help. Not save her, as I not swim.'

'Ellen's sister, Emily,' Jack said, trying to remove her sadness, 'she good swimmer, maybe teach you someday if Ellen keep in touch?'

'Maybe,' Monika looked in the direction of the shop, 'Maybe not.'

'You are not doubt a real good friend to Ellen... Helen.'

'Yah, but we argue always... she the clever one.'

'The clever one, how?'

'She learn speak Dutch quick and so my language. I still have learn English good... Dutch also. She have special talent. Learn all language fast. Russian not easy to English I told.'

'Indeed, I hear it isn't,' Jack agreed.

'She pick up language fast, and how you say... dialect?'

'She knows a lot of bad language too,' Jack joked, but saw Monika frown. 'She swears a lot in English, doesn't she?'

'Oh yah,' Monika now understood and started to laugh. 'Curse and swear, yah.'

'What's so funny?' a voice asked as they turned to see Ellen return with a bottle of wine.

'Nothing,' Jack responded, 'Just making friends.'

Ellen eyed both of them curiously before taking Monika by the hand.

'You not get me food?' Monika pulled Ellen back.

'No, we have rent to pay soon, remember?'

Seeing Monika glum, Jack took her other hand and slotted another note between her fingers.

'But you already –'

'You need to be fed,' Jack stated, tapping Monika's hand, 'everyone needs to eat.'

'She's not a charity case you know,' Ellen snapped.

'I didn't say she was,' Jack asserted. 'Call it a tip for such a good show earlier.'

Monika smiled to see Jack wink at her.

'Fine, but we're going,' Ellen stated dragging Monika by the hand, her friend's eyes still fixed on Jack. 'We'll get pizza on the way.'

Jack put his arm around Emily's shoulder. He realised that she was admiring the view of the continent gradually disappearing. But looking closer, he could see tears swelling in her eyes. Maybe it was from the cold of the sea breeze that swept up around them as they leaned over the stern of the ferry.

Jack squeezed Emily tight; he hated heights such as this, especially travelling high above water. He refrained to lean as far as Emily to watch the churning, foamed water, but found that she was indeed crying, disappointed in them not convincing Ellen to come back home. He slid his hand about her waist, the heat of his palm warming Emily's exposed stomach. *Why wear denim shorts in such an exposed place, where the grip of winter would soon be upon them?* His thoughts continued. *And her back exposed with her shirt tied just below her chest?* But he had to admire that her hips and legs were more voluptuous than that Russian girl. Even Ellen hadn't got Emily's admirable shape and curvature although they looked more alike than Effie. *Maybe she had not packed enough in such hurry? But that was unusual for a girl like Emily.* He pondered more. *Maybe it was just her way to nullify emotion with being as cold?* But seeing her distraught, he had to ask, maybe take her mind off things?

'Miss Emily,' he cleared his throat, 'why is it you wear denim shorts on such a cold journey?' He paused, but there was no reaction, her eyes frozen like her body to gaze upon the distant coastline. 'I know you said you would've loved to stop on the beach longer, but surely to come –'

'Does it matter?' Emily snarled; her eyes still fixed on viewing the last glimpse of the continent. 'Even staying another day in Belgium didn't help.'

'But you liked that beach, the hotel, that shop of curiosities?' There was a pause but no reply. 'I had to phone about postponing that first lecture. Luckily my colleague had it covered.'

'I'm sorry to disappoint,' Emily glanced aside to peer at him. 'Maybe I should've come alone?'

'Of course not,' Jack said, showing no regret, 'I wouldn't have missed this trip with you for the world.' He gripped her body tighter, leaning down to touch his cheek against hers so there faces were alongside each other. 'To share such an admirable view together… it's priceless.'

Jack felt Emily's face etch a smile.

'Your hand is as warm as your heart Jack, that's why I think I'm falling for you.'

'Only think?' Jack chuckled, but felt another tear run down Emily's cheek and wet his. 'Have you not already?'

'I can't, not until all this…'

Jack pulled away. It was not what she had said, but the fact that he saw the rough, churning water from such a height. And then he noticed tears running down both her cheeks. *Was this real concern to survive a relationship or was it that she had failed to persuade her sister?*

'Sorry Ems, but I got nervous, the water,' Jack realised to what he had said. 'Blimey, I'm calling you Ems like Ellen did. Must be contagious?'

Emily turned slightly to stare at him. 'Quite a contagious person, wouldn't you agree?' Jack nodded in agreement. 'And obnoxious, ill mannered, deceitful, foul-mouthed…' Jack took Emily hands to hold at the wrist. 'And what's with working that kind of club, being bi-sexual with all that stupid makeup?'

'Calm down Ems.'

'See, even you've picked up her contagion.'

'Miss Emily, it's me Jack, remember?' Jack pulled her near and swung his arms about her. 'Sorry my dear, but I did try to get her to come, even just to visit. She is quite obnoxious.'

'Probably best I don't see her again then isn't it?'

'It's not all doom and gloom.'

'No?'

'No, coz her friend Monika gave me her mobile number, but to text only… a secret between us. Maybe she'll give Ellen's mobile?'

'Oh yes, I bet that is not the only thing she's after!'

'She's lesbian remember?' Jack held Emily close to stare with sincerity. 'Apparently Monika does the shows to get back at men, something to do with her past. Not like Ellen, she was into men before, well up until that Robbie anyhow.'

'I don't think that the girl will give away Ellen's number as they're too close.' Emily tried to turn away, her thoughts elsewhere. 'I bet you'd love to go back to that club and try though.'

'And why would I do such a thing?' Jack noticed Emily hunch her shoulders and exhale her doubts. 'Why would I want that when I got you?' He held her shoulders strong, one in each hand. 'I didn't tell you this as you'll think I'm some stalker, but as we know each other already…' He paused after seeing that beautiful glint in Emily's hazel eyes, a harsh and questionable look, but somehow endearing. 'I used to follow you and you're friend. Angela her name is it not?' Emily nodded but blinked as if puzzled. 'I wanted so many times to talk with you… ask you out, but failed every time. You only had to turn and look my way and I would hide. Until I got more confident that is. George helped me.'

'Who, the guy who owns the jewellery shop?'

'Helps to run it,' Jack corrected. 'He's no manager.'

'And that's why you pretended… why you showed me that necklace?'

'Yes, and it took every inch of self-confidence to do that.'

'But you seemed quite…' Emily held Jack's hand that gripped her shoulder. 'Actually, thinking back, I guess you *were* nervous.' Emily etched a smile, 'Just a little.'

'And so through all that, do y' think I'm going to let y' go now?'

'Hold me again Jack.' Emily turned; disappointed to see the horizon had nothing but sea. 'It's not that I'm cold, but hold me again… please.' To Emily's satisfaction, Jack granted her request. Emily was cold. Jack felt her skin silky cold, like marble.

'Make love to me Jack.' Jack tried to pull away, but was held by a strange strength in Emily he had not yet felt. Instead she pulled herself up to him, anchored by her arms encircling his neck.

'Make love to you here,' Jack chortled, his mouth nibbling at her ear, 'what with people coming on deck?'

'No you fool,' Emily giggled, whispering a low, sexy voice into his ear, 'later when we get back. Before Mike brings Effie back.' Now Emily nibbled at Jack's ear, hoping it would quash her playful mood until later. 'But I want such tender sex this time; make it memorable… not like they have in those dirty clubs.'

'But the girls only dance for the money in there.'

'Yes Jack, I'm sure they do.'

THIRTY—ONE

EMILY GLANCED UP FROM HER laptop screen to see that Jack had returned. Quietly he stepped around her, considering whether to take his morning newspaper into the kitchen to read. Hovering above the sofa bed he hesitated to sit, but then realised Effie was back in the kitchen preparing her favourite soup and toasted baguette. Reluctantly he sat, but placed down the newspaper to swivel his mobile phone between fingers. Several times he glanced at Emily before she caught him studying her.

'What's with you being so nervous?'

Jack did not respond, but put down his mobile phone to open the newspaper. He lowered the open pages to peer over the top at her. He could clearly see that Emily was eyeing him curiously.

'What's wrong Jack?' Emily somehow knew by his actions that something was bothering him. 'Effie didn't wake you last night again did she?'

'No, she did not.' Jack fiddled with the newspaper before deciding how to tell her. 'It concerns more to do with your other sister.'

'Ellen,' Emily said with distain, 'that one?'

'Well I know that you probably lost hope in her, but…'

'But what?' Emily squinted at him as she put aside her laptop.

'Monika text me last night and told that Ellen has agreed to give us her email.'

'Is that so,' Emily turned back to the laptop, responding to comments posted to her social network profile. 'What makes her change heart all of a sudden?'

'I don't know, but Monika said she'd like to see pictures of Effie.'

'Well why didn't she come over with us last week and see her for real?'

'Like you said,' Jack replied, 'maybe she's had a change in heart.'

'She's changed from being not so bloody cold you mean?'

'Well do you want me to forward it to you or not?'

'Yes, yes of course,' Emily sighed, thinking that if Ellen could change from being some hard bitch that she could too. Besides, Effie had never seen her, and she had been all but curious. 'Forward her email to mine. Maybe we can get Effie and her to swap photos at least. But I'd rather not rush into…'

Suddenly Emily's mobile phone rang and vibrated from within her handbag. She reached past her laptop to dig deep into her handbag to find it.

It rang again. It was Angela.

'Hi Ange, see that your off on a trip this weekend.' Angela asked to how Emily knew this. 'Like everything, you've posted pictures of the place already. That spar place looks nice though.' Emily smiled at her friend's naivety. 'What's up anyway, you're not supposed to be online during works time?'

'Well it concerns that woman you hate. I didn't want to log any comments on there.'

'Who, that Amanda woman,' Emily snapped, her attentiveness alerted. 'What about her?'

'She's been into the office again and asked something about you, had words with the manager about that role she pretends to be interested in. I recognised her from your drawing. The resemblance is striking, especially when you said you hardly –'

'What did she want?' Emily snapped, but diluted her aggression to see Effie walk gingerly into the room, dipping a toasted baguette into her cup of soup. 'You didn't let her know anything about me did you… where I live?' Emily tried to keep her tone soft, as she knew Jack and Effie could probably hear.

'No Emily, I would never do that.' There was a pause and Emily heard Angela rustling paperwork. 'She and the manager asked to where you were, but I just said to them that you were on leave… something about visiting family.' She paused and then asked with concern, 'I've not done wrong have I?'

'No Ange, it'll be okay, but where's the drawing, she didn't see it did she?'

'No, I've hid it in your bottom draw, but…' Emily deduced Angela was pondering on whether to tell her something else. 'But it was something she said with that horrible smirk of her face.'

'What did she say Ange?'

'She told of how reporting such a murder must be hard to take sometimes. But I explained that we only covered media journalism; fashion, beauty, celebs… that kind of stuff.'

'What murder?'

'I don't know exactly. It has something to do with a gay councillor getting murdered, his body brutally distorted like your… The guys over the other end of the office mentioned it. The next thing I know, she ignored me to explain to the manager how her city apartment was not far, but that she was renovating some large house east of the city… somewhere in the country.'

'Did she give you any idea where her apartment is?'

'No, but I think the manager was holding a copy of her details.'

'Could you get her address from that Ange?'

'Why, what for?' Angela stuttered somewhat nervous. 'What if I can't get in to check, or the manager…?'

'You do the errands don't you?' Emily interrupted, 'coffee for meetings and such? Why, use your initiative girl.'

'It might be difficult.' Emily heard Angela sigh. 'You owe me big for this, and I can't be sure if I –'

'You'll do it girl. What are friends for?'

'What you want her address for anyhow?'

'Tell you later Ange. But please, it's important. See you, Ta.'

Emily disconnected the conversation to look up and see both Jack and Effie staring at her.

'What?' she said in query. 'I have my reasons.'

'What, to get people at your work to do your dirty work,' Jack spoke slowly, watching Effie look aside, the bashful sister pretending not to have eavesdropped.

'But that's not where it ends,' Emily leaned forward to crawl on hands and knees towards Jack. Suddenly she pushed down Jack's paper. 'I need a favour from you too my most gorgeous boyfriend.'

'What?' Jack barked, snatching back the newspaper. 'I don't think I'm going to like this much, am I?'

'If Ange gets the address of this woman, will you check out where she lives for me?'

'But why Emily,' Jack folded the newspaper before slamming it down next to him, controlling his anger as Effie was standing by. 'What's this going to achieve?'

'Well I know you're still sceptical but hear me out.' Jack peered over at Effie who was now hovering by the fireplace. He then looked back at Emily to give his full attention. 'I have a hunch that the woman visiting my work, the one Angela has just seen, is able to conjure some evil to do her bidding.'

'What?' Jack dismissed. 'Look, I know that some things you've said about this I've listened to, and have indeed wondered about myself, but this Amanda woman being some sort of mistress of Black Magic?'

'Look Jack, even Effie agrees to things that have happened. She's heard things spoken that even I didn't know?'

'What, voices of dead people telling her things?' Jack was reluctant to look at Effie; he knew her hard-staring eyes would be boring holes in him. 'But come on, I know things we've discussed lately have a lot to explain, but this Amanda summoning evil, it's a little ludicrous. She's just some talented solicitor, lawyer, whatever she is. Not some… evil conjuror?'

'That Amanda woman was cavorting with that doctor, the night he got killed at his own mansion; someone Mike said did this stuff. Although Carl, my father, tried to warn Mike, he didn't believe him until it was too late.'

'What do you mean, it was too late?'

'Well, Mike could only save Sarah; my father was lost in the fire.' Emily paused to reflect. 'In letters my Great Aunt sent to my father before his death, she warned of this doctor's power, and that he was evil… that he could control evil. Letters kept show that he was indeed my father's father. He had taken advantage of my Great Aunt's sister and they despised him for it.'

'I'm sorry, I'm getting confused… this is too much. Your Great Aunt's sister?'

'It's what Mike gave me in that shoebox.' Emily sat close on the sofa bed to try and explain. 'They're somewhat confusing themselves, but what I believe is that this doctor took advantage my Great Aunt's sister, which gave birth to my father, who was later adopted by a Reverend.'

'This gets even more –'

'No hear me out,' Emily pleaded. 'What is more, is that my father attained, or conceived you may say, strange psychic powers from his mother, my Great Aunt. He told Mike things that would happen.'

'And did they?'

'Not always, Mike disbelieved. But I believe that my father was gifted with some power that could prevent evil things from happening.'

'Like the death of Sarah?'

Emily sat quiet for a moment until Effie touched her shoulder. 'Tell him,' Effie said, suddenly finding herself overwhelmed with self-assurance, 'tell him more.' But Emily remembered the image of her twisted mother, her body broken upon the hospital car park. 'Then I'll tell him.' Emily reached to grab Effie's hand from her shoulder, a scared look in her eyes. 'Emily tells of having the weirdest of visions, things that she said happened in the past.'

'And I suppose, as her sister, you believe her implicitly?'

'It runs in line with what the voices have said.'

Jack looked upon Effie with ridicule, and she knew he was thinking her absurd.

'But you have no facts,' Jack urged, his eyes searching both of theirs. 'You can't just go and accuse this woman of murdering Sarah. I know you've not had… well, some sort of condolence but?'

'The man wants facts,' Emily angered, her eyes staring wild at Effie. 'Well, let's tell you what *I've* learned.' Emily nudged up even closer to her nice but cynical boyfriend. 'Like how some colleague of that Amanda got killed, a man apparently linked to that doctor years back, now as Angela just told me, some wealthy, gay councillor gets murdered in the same way... a disgustingly horrific murder that I bet resembles what happened to Sarah. My mother, if you remember me telling you, despised this Amanda even more than I, and now I'm beginning to know why. Surely these connections can't be but coincidence?'

'This story,' Jack searched beneath where Emily sat, 'it would be in this morning newspaper, wouldn't it?'

'The man who knew Amanda was killed by his own doing.' Effie said coldly.

'How do you know that?' Emily stared up at her sister as Jack fumbled with the newspaper.

'It was told to me by the voices.'

'But you've been on medication haven't you... I gave you that stuff to make you sleep myself?'

'I'm sorry Emily, but I hate being so vulnerable when they visit. Mostly I've spat them out.'

Emily was clearly annoyed, but came intrigued in what her sister could be hiding. 'So what have you learned from these voices?'

'The voices are from dead people... invisible ghosts that whisper to me the truths they have learned beyond the grave.' Effie held Emily's shoulder as if nervous and unsteady. 'Like how young Charlie told me about his murderer, that Daniel is cursed and regrets to have delved into such dark magic.'

'And these voices you hear, they tell you things that may happen?'

'No they don't.' Effie ignored Jack's question as she deemed it sarcastic. 'The voices tell that dark forces are being tampered with and that we should be prepared.'

'Prepared for what?' Jack asked.

'To combat evil,' Effie told, 'like how Aunt Evelyn said?'

'But how did you know our Great Aunt's name was *Evelyn*, I haven't mentioned it yet have I?' Emily looked as dumbfounded as Jack, and Jack recognised her surprise. 'You've not being prying in my shoebox have you Effie?'

'No, Aunt Evelyn told me when she warned of evil being summoned again, that she wants us to be prepared.'

'Us,' Jack questioned, 'what do you mean by *us*?'

'Three sisters reborn to deter this evil from happening...'

Emily stood up beside Effie and interrupted. Suddenly the visions she had had, made her realise what one letter her Great Aunt Evelyn had sent her father, meant. 'Yes, this Great Aunt sent our father a letter suggesting their sisterhood would be reborn to balance good against future up rises in evil... but our father wanted to stop it himself. Maybe it is nature's way to combat such dark forces.'

'And you believe this sisterhood to be you, the three of you?' Jack's tone had a hint of cynicism. 'That's the real reason why you want Ellen back here with you, isn't it? So you all can cure hunger and develop world peace?'

'No, the voices tell different.' Effie muttered turning away, disparaged by Jack's continued sarcasm. 'The voices say that this is true evil... evil that hides itself away to overshadow the good in all; that a natural good should balance such evil.' Effie wandered about the fireplace to look at framed pictures on the mantelpiece.

For a long moment all three were quiet.

'So is this what became of that councillor,' Jack asked, breaking the silence, 'because he had a disagreement or something with that Amanda?' He pointed to the story in his now open but folded newspaper.

Effie turned from admiring the framed pictures to face Jack, her eyes darkened by lack of sleep. 'That councillor was murdered by dark forces, ones most likely summoned by that Amanda.' She paused and then looked at Emily. 'The voices of the innocent want these murders to stop; they want our help.' Effie turned away; her head drooped to look at the floor in sadness. 'The same voices told that mother was killed that way too.'

'Is that why they're always so... crippled, broken... somehow petrified?' Emily asked, her voice faltering.

'It was just how she fell, wasn't it... out of the window?' Jack surmised. 'After all, it was the third floor, wasn't it?' He paused to reflect. 'However, there's nothing to explain how she got there.'

'I believe the voices have told me things for a reason,' Effie said, circling in front of the fireplace. 'I believe mother wanted us to all inherit such gifts to help the innocent.'

Suddenly Emily grabbed the newspaper from Jack and searched the story. The one thing that made her sit back on the floor in amazement was a photograph of the councillor before his murder.

'Stay here both of you,' Emily instructed sternly. 'You want evidence Jack... facts that prove were not both stupid?'

Both Jack and Effie looked at each other as they heard Emily messing through stuff in her bedroom. And then they both flinched at hearing a cupboard draw slam shut.

Soon they both looked towards the door, Emily bouncing in the room with drive.

'Here's your evidence Jack.' Emily threw both the newspaper and a folded piece of paper at Jack. 'Check the photograph with my drawing.'

Slowly Jack unfolded the drawing and compared it with the councillor's photograph. 'But you've never...'

'No, but that was from my weird visions, something you disbelieve.' Emily pointed a finger at her drawing. 'I drew that the night probably just before he got killed. Maybe Effie is right. We have gifts but don't know how to use them?'

Jack could not discount the evidence. He had seen her drawing frantically that night after having some frightening dream. He just thought it was her way to release the grief of losing her mother.

'So if you warned this man straight after drawing this, you could have saved him?'

'Maybe, but how was I too know, by the time –'

'He could not be saved.' Effie interjected. 'Such evil would not stop until...'

'But surely such a gift like this could save...' Jack stopped to see Emily smirk.

'I thought you said this *gift* of mine was just an emotional glitch?'

'But this is evidence, you can't surely have known...'

'And Effie,' Emily poised to question; 'you disbelieve the voices she hears are just some sort of lunacy?'

'I didn't say it that way.'

'But you implied?'

Effie grinned after hearing her sister's defiance.

'But this, well,' Jack was dumbfounded, but tried to reflect the need to be rational. But maybe he changed the subject to elevate his own guilt and embarrassment. 'But does that detective know about this...? No of course not, you've just...' Again Jack studied the overwhelming likeness between the newspaper photograph and Emily's drawing.

Emily turned to see Effie grin before looking again at the pictures scattered above the fireplace.

THIRTY—TWO

JACK SAT IN THE DRIVER'S seat in silence. He had left the engine running for a while but decided to switch it off, not knowing how long he should stay. It had been raining heavily on the way and following Amanda from the courtrooms had been a rather gruelling task.

Thinking of how Detective Lawrence would take Emily's identification of the murdered councillor, Jack thought of him as some private investigator, following this woman to her hideaway. But gradually he questioned to what he was doing there.

The rain had subdued somewhat and so Jack opened the window half way. It had been stuffy in the car and the cold flow of early night air helped him concentrate. In his mind he retraced the journey after recognising this Amanda woman from Emily's drawing. Indeed, he had to admit, the likeness was somewhat scary.

As he stared up at the apartment, he noticed lights go on through the house, including what he deduced was the bathroom. He had caught the woman opening a bedroom window before the bathroom light went on.

Job done, he thought, but let's just take note to where the place is in my street atlas. He opened the dashboard compartment and retrieved the booklet, switching on the overhead light to locate the correct page. He pencilled a line from the street where he was parked back to the city centre. That's enough to please Emily, he assumed. But I better phone her, tell her that I've followed this Amanda woman back to her city apartment.

Jack dialled Emily's number on his mobile phone.

'Jack, is that you?' Emily asked a tone of desperation in her voice. 'Have you managed to find out where –?'

'I'm here, parked outside,' he interrupted, presuming her request. 'That Amanda's apartment is in Victoria Street. It's quite impressive.'

'Well it would be for someone in her position.'

'What a solicitor, or is she a lawyer?'

'I'm not sure, one of the two.'

'Well, where the place is, and its size, her job must be paying her more than well.' Jack swivelled his head to look further down the road behind him. 'Her car's not a cheap one either.'

'Can you get inside?'

Jack froze, amazed at Emily's audacity. 'Are you kidding girl. I've located the apartment, even marked it in my street atlas. But not for one second am I going in there. I'm no private investigator you know, I'd probably get –'

'I'll marry you,' Emily interrupted, but paused to reflect on whether such a commitment was rather severe. 'Well, at least I'll get engaged.'

'Are you kidding me Emily, because that's nothing to jest about?'

'No please Jack, this is important.'

'Important enough to make you promise to marry me?'

'For me and my sisters Jack,' Emily sounded anxious, her voice croaking. 'That woman has got to have some evidence that she is delving into the occult, documents or something on witchcraft.'

'And you want me to…'

'Yes, get whatever you can. Photograph it on your phone.'

'And you'll marry me if I do this?'

'Well, I'll think about it.' She paused, realising what she had said to encourage him to investigate. 'I do love you Jack... you know that by now. If you can just do me this one favour, I promise… well, I at least owe you one.'

There was silence at Jack's end of the call and Emily got fretful. 'Jack, are you still there? Please, after what happened to mother, you said you'd help me and my sisters get justice for her murder.'

Still there was a moment of silence, Emily poised for a reply.

'I believe she's having a shower,' Jack finally responded, 'and has left the bedroom window open. Maybe I could get inside, but it's going to be tricky.'

'Why, can't you get up to the bedroom window?'

'There's a terrace of some sort that circles around, but first I need to get on top. There's a tree nearby, but…'

'Do you think you can do it?'

'It'll be slippery coz of the rain. Everything is wet... soaking wet.'

'Please, if you can get any evidence at all?'

'Well, I suppose I could try at least.'

'Please Jack; I'll love you forever if you do.'

'Yah,' Jack bantered, 'probably have to visit me in jail for breaking and entering though.' He sniggered a little before deciding, 'But what the hell.'

'I owe you Jack, and love you. Be careful.'

Jack disconnected the call and looked up at the house. Suddenly with his new task in mind, the apartment looked more ominous, the half-open bedroom window somehow foreboding.

As stealthily as he could, Jack locked his car door and crossed the street, keeping low and quiet until he reached a brick wall. Luckily the apartment lay in the dim between streetlamps, which stood each way, further down the road.

He lifted himself up to sit upon the apartment's adjacent brick wall and kicked over his legs, his backside becoming wet from absorbing fallen rain. Nervous that he was now on the property, he edged nearer the building, examining the tree he had noticed from within his car. It did have a substantial branch that could carry him up towards the veranda, but how would he reach it?

He noticed that some maintenance work had been done between the apartment and its neighbouring building. Searching the leftover materials, he noticed a thick length of timber about a metre in length. He deduced that its end would carry a foothold if he secured it at an acute angle. Slamming the timber down between roots, Jack pivoted the plank at an angle against the tree truck. With a powerful lift he managed to balance one foot on the timber and grab the one main branch that twisted towards the veranda. By swinging his other foot upon the ledge of the veranda, he surged his bodyweight to swing upon it. For a moment he lay along the narrow veranda, feeling his clothes cold and wet. With caution he crawled upon all fours and carefully made this way past the bathroom window to the bedroom.

It was not long before he was inside, the room dim with the only light cast from a laptop that lay on a distant desk. The only other light shone as a beam across the room from a partly open door, this room Jack deduced, was the kitchen. Carefully he closed the window behind, trying best to return the opening to how it was before. Slowly on hands and knees, he crawled to the desk. Surely if this Amanda had documents, they would be on the desk or within its draws?

As he passed the closed bathroom door, he could hear Amanda under the noise of the shower, muttering words and her short attempts to sing. He crawled on to examine the draws of the desk; quickly rummaging through, hoping his noise would not be heard. Out of what he examined, he only had time to look through one strange book found in a bottom draw. It was some old testament; a diary record bound in cracked, dry leather, with drawings, sketches, lines of undecipherable text etched in ink on aged paper. It was not until he pulled it along the carpet to photograph it with his mobile phone camera, that he saw how burned its edges were and how it had been somewhat repaired. Quickly he turned the pages, taking only enough time to focus for the camera to detail the images and text. And then, keeping his mobile phone low and away from the direction of the bathroom, he turned the pages one by one, photographing each page as steadily as he could. But for some reason, his hand was nervous, his fingers shaky to see each flash ignite brightness against the walls.

He replaced the old book to the bottom draw, his mind trying to ignore the contents of it. *What were those drawings, symbols, lines and verses of ancient-looking text?* He neglected his curiosity to continue searching the other draws, but there was nothing of relevance. He peered up over the desk to ensure Amanda was still showering, but gazed upon the bright laptop screen at eye level.

Nervous and constantly looking back the bathroom, Jack examined files on Amanda's desktop. Amongst the array of neatly positioned folders, Jack noticed one entitled *Daniel's Research* and another folder called *Research Documents*. Quickly he opened each folder and browsed their contents.

Suddenly Jack heard the noise of the shower cease; replaced by a nervous feeling of uncertain quiet. Neglecting the eerie silence, he presumed Amanda's laptop had internet access as he noticed its wireless functionality. Quickly Jack realised he could send Emily Amanda's files by email and so initiated an email to Emily and attached each folder. In the email Jack simply typed, *Hope these are useful, will delete sent email.* Jack hit the *Send Email* button, but saw that the email was taking time in the *Outbox*.

Suddenly Jack glanced to see the bathroom door open. Slowly Amanda came out, her hands fixed on drying her hair with another towel wrapped tightly about her breasts. Jack squatted down upon his knees, only his eyes peering over the desk and past the laptop to study her. For one moment she stopped and looked as if right at him, but was probably only confused to why her laptop had not timed into a sleep mode. Gradually she decided to retreat to the kitchen where he heard her rummaging through cupboards.

Jack rose up to glance at the laptop. Still the email was in the *Outbox*, the file size of the attachments taking time to send.

He swore under a breath. 'Come on, come on y' bitch, do it,' he whispered, not noticing Amanda exit the bathroom and wonder over to the bedroom, sipping at a large glass of red wine. Quickly he ducked down again behind the desk, hoping that the woman would not come over to examine her laptop.

Amanda stopped again to look over, but was now holding her mobile up to her ear. Jack struggled to make out her conversation, but then watched her continue to the bedroom after sipping again at her wine. Once he had seen her enter the bedroom, Jack glanced again at the laptop. Luckily the *Outbox* was empty and a new email logged in the *Sent Email* box. Kneeling at a precarious angle, Jack poked at the keyboard and slid a finger over the mouse pad until he could delete the email he had just sent. Sitting down on the carpet, his back against the desk, job done he thought. But there was one problem: Amanda was still in the bedroom… his only exit.

It seemed like an eternity before Amanda came out to refill her glass, her body now dressed in casual wear. But still Jack hesitated, waiting for her to disappear into the kitchen. As soon as she was out of sight, he scurried like a little mouse as fast as he could on all fours to the bedroom, the stretch of light from the kitchen illuminating him for a second like a searchlight exposing an escaping criminal. But he was now in the bedroom, seeing Amanda's clothes and towels littering the floor. He had no time to observe her dark lingerie and revealing nightdress, or that she had some luggage case half packed; he had to be through the window like lightening.

And he was just in time. He had closed the window, although not properly, and was squatted down with his back against the pebble-dashed wall. He looked down to the safety of his car in the distance; suddenly realising Amanda was staring out the bedroom window after frowning to why it was extensively open.

Jack kept quiet and still after seeing Amanda's reflection in the tilt of the window. But then the light went on and illuminated all the ground below, his direct escape route floodlit. Luckily, although now leisurely dressed, Amanda closed the curtains to only leave a frail expanse of light stretching along the ground below. This was Jack's chance and he took it.

What a relief it was to get back in his car, although his jeans were wet around his backside and spine. Quickly with the adrenaline from his secret escapade, he phoned Emily. As he waited for a reply he felt his breath short and his knees quivering, but wallowed in an internal pride; the fact that he had done this for the girl he loved.

'Jack, you okay?'

'Jobs done babe.' Jack smiled although Emily could not tell, but by the tone of his voice she knew he was relieved but proud. 'Check y' email Miss Emily,' he continued, a hint of impudence gathered from his venture, 'there's probably a lot to look through.'

'But I thought you only took photos?'

'I have. Of some strange book,' he added, 'but will send them to y' laptop after. For now, open this email girl. And then you can marry me.' Jack chuckled.

Emily paused for a while, but Jack could hear her giggle before shouting out orders for Effie to start up her laptop. 'Thanks Jack, I owe you, maybe I will marry you some day,' Emily smirked. 'Let's get all this shit behind us first and then I'll think about it.'

'Only think my dear, I heard you promise.' Jack grinned. 'I'll get the engagement ring just in case.'

'You'll propose, properly that is, sometime soon?'

'I'll think about it my dear.' Jack's grin stretched wider.

For a moment there was quiet between the two, until Effie opened the email and Emily's curiosity overwhelmed her. 'What happened in there Jack? How on earth did you get to email me this stuff?'

'That stupid woman left her laptop on,' Jack chortled, 'just had to see what stuff might be useful.' He paused to see lights switch off in Amanda's apartment. 'I deleted the email after it was sent, so there's no chance of her knowing.' He took a deep breath, his relief from the task evident. 'Never played detective before, quite scary I must admit, but quite exhilarating.' Jack hardly heard Emily's reply, her attention directed to Effie who was browsing the emailed folders. 'You've got the email okay?'

'Yes Jack,' Emily confirmed but came somewhat distracted, hovering over Effie who sat browsing the opened folders. 'This stuff's weird. All of this will take some time to examine. By God some of this will take some understanding.

'Yes, maybe like the book I photographed,' Jack explained. 'There were all weird drawings and the language...' Jack stopped to talk, his eyes catching movement outside Amanda's apartment.

'What about the language, Jack?' Emily asked, suddenly becoming worried to why he stopped in mid-conversation. 'Jack, are you still there?'

'Yes Emily,' but Jack stalled again, 'it's just that Amanda is closing her front door... she's carrying a luggage case, must be going somewhere.'

'I wonder to where's she –'

'But of course,' Jack interrupted. 'I heard her talking to some professor guy about meeting him at her house in the country.' He paused momentarily. 'But I didn't think she was going there tonight.' He glanced at the dashboard clock. 'Then again, I suppose it is still quite early.'

'Jack can you follow her?'

'What, you are kidding right,' Jack snapped. 'Don't you think I've done enough for –?'

'Please Jack,' Emily interrupted, 'just do this one other thing for me.'

'I just cannot believe the audacity of this woman.' Jack talked to his ego, but openly to convey his sarcasm.

'This woman, Mister Jack Torrance,' Emily interjected slowly, 'could be your future wife.'

'But if her house is in the country,' Jack queried, 'it could be miles away... in the middle of nowhere?'

'Look, I'll pay to fill up your tank if need be.' Emily turned to acknowledge Effie, her sister's study of the folders giving surprise. 'And I'll make it your worthwhile when you get back.'

'Really,' Jack shunned, 'how?'

'Rachael is picking up Effie later. She wants to know more from Mike about our past.' Emily felt a glare look up at her. 'We'll have the place alone... for a couple of hours at least.'

'She's just pulled away,' Jack changed the subject. 'That car could easily out run me in country lanes?'

'Please Jack,' Emily pleaded, 'if you can just find out where else she lives.' She continued in a seductive voice, 'And then, when you come back, I'll be waiting.'

'I can't believe this,' Jack fretted, curling back his hair with his fingers, 'what a man has to do for love.' He then started the engine, pulled out his car and turned it around to follow Amanda. 'This had better be worth it my girl.'

Jack had followed the sports car for some time, managing to keep Amanda's suspicious eyes at a distance. Constant evening traffic on the main roads had helped him stay undetected, but now she had turned off on to a side road and so he had to be more vigilant; ensuring he did not lose sight of her tail-lights whilst navigating the dark countryside lanes.

It was several minutes before Amanda's sports car took another left, the lane meandering through woodland to reach a dark and ominous building, its tall structure only visible from the roof glistening wet from fallen rain. Jack stopped at the junction, squinting through the darkness to see her fading taillights, but suddenly they brightened to brake and stop. Slowly he observed the lights reverse as if to park and then all lights disappeared.

Jack turned his car full circle about the junction, and after seeing enough room down the lane, decided to park in sight of the house. He just hoped that in darkness, the woman had not seen his headlights. After climbing a small ridge, he peered over bushes that ran alongside the lane. Although somewhat afar, Jack could make out Amanda's figure, her body and face illuminated as she locked her car with flashing indicator lights and a high-pitch bleep.

He could barely see Amanda now, but watched her silhouette cross an expanse of gravel driveway before ascending some stairs. He glanced back at his car, trying to remember if he still had that flashlight in his dashboard compartment. Yes, he remembered it there when he replaced the street atlas, but would it still work?

He looked back towards the house after hearing distant voices. And then he saw another figure walk from its parked car to join Amanda on top of some stairs; the two figures now standing to talk, lit by wall lamps either side of an arched stone entrance. After watching both figures disappear into a partly lit hallway, hastily Jack descended the verge in order to retrieve his flashlight. Unfortunately, after testing its dim beam against the ground, he found the batteries almost dead. He banged the head of the torch several times, thinking it may have hidden power, but its light faded still more. He swore under a breath and glanced around after realising how exposed he was in the light of the open door. After grasping the fact that he could use this mobile phone to light such a brief stroll to the house, he threw the flashlight onto the passenger seat and locked the door.

He started trudging through undergrowth, but paused to hear sounds that he thought were footsteps. Gradually Jack became conscious of someone watching him from within the dark reaches of woodland. Maybe it was just his imagination, or that his nerves were already on edge, but he was convinced someone was studying him.

But then it dawned on him, why am I doing this? Emily only wanted to know where the house was, not a full investigation. But maybe Jack had to surpass his first attempt of playing detective, but more importantly, what if he heard this woman confess in murdering Sarah, or at least have played some part in doing so? Maybe he could get Emily answers from inside, like who was the strange visitor that had met Amanda on the entrance? Was he that professor on her phone, got there before the master of the house? Jack's curiosity was certainly teasing him, especially when he noticed one half of the arched entrance door ajar.

From the edge of the gravel driveway, slightly obscured by undergrowth, Jack poised to stare at the open doorway. But what if Amanda and this professor were there talking in the hallway, surely he would be seen? He hesitated in anticipation, his nerves chilled by something more than the sharpness of the cold night air. And then he heard something again, a rustling in the bushes, a crack of a branch underfoot. If someone was following him, who could it be and where were they?

He dashed for the entrance, not sure to how long the one door would keep open, but had to calm his exhilaration once he got there. Inhaling air through his nose in long and steady intakes, Jack steadied his breathing to peer at the hallway through the gap. Although having enough to cast shadows upon walls, he noticed the scarcity of light, only battery lamps scattered about the long room. Jack pondered; no electricity? But then he remembered the professor question the place in his conversation; that the place had been brought for renovation. But this was no time for reflection, Jack had to be inside and quickly, hidden somewhere in a nearby room to hopefully hear a revealing conversation between the two other occupancies.

Jack raced in and slid into an adjacent room, checking quickly that it was in darkness. From the partly open door he observed and listened, but something else niggled at his mind. It was not just that there was something strange about this Amanda, but the things Emily had spoken about her; things she had said coming from her and her mother. And of course there was Mike's recollection of the night this woman tried to poison Sarah, dressing in a nurse's uniform to go undetected. What type of person would go to lengths to do such a thing? Why on earth did she want Sarah dead? Surely it was the other guy Emily had spoken of, who wanted revenge; a paralysed and incapacitated man. However, Jack contemplated; death was a bit serious, even if she had been accused of assaulting him. But it was he who had entered Sarah's house to go on some false pretence whilst three defenceless babies lay asleep. But maybe in all of what Emily had told, she had left things out, stuff about her past that he considered incredible. And now Emily wanted justification against this woman for her mother's demise. That was understandable. But to believe her (and Effie both) that this woman practiced Black Magic to command evil to do her bidding, it was ludicrous. However, Jack had to agree, some things were certainly difficult to explain. *Trust me to fall for one so weird*, he contemplated, *must be the sacrifice for getting such a stunner*.

Jack's thoughts were distracted after hearing distant voices come from the other occupancies, and so he crept from his hiding place to decipher more clearly their conversation. He paced stealthily along the hallway to stop at the bottom of a newly renovated staircase, the aroma of wood arousing his sense of smell first, regarding the workmanship in the encircling balusters and staircase up, the next. It was now after studying the floor that Jack noticed most of the area had been renovated too. Evidently most of the house had been subjected to some renovation programme.

He slid past a cellar door and on to see cupboards rebuilt beneath the staircase above. Soon he reached a scullery and kitchen area, where, after passing a large hallway mirror, he could see Amanda talking to a white-haired man, Jack listening to them from the depths of some pantry.

To what he heard, he was right that Emily and her sisters should fear this woman.

The professor, who Jack squinted at to make out his grey-white beard and spectacles, told Amanda of only seeing two sisters at Sarah Layton's funeral. And so he denied the possibility of all three combining to oppose her power of the Black Art. But Amanda expressed that, as long as the third was alive, the three could join as one. And like the old prophecy that the doctor had researched, they could demean her power. The professor discredited Amanda's continued research into the doctor's work, neglecting the possibility that three creatures of Mother Nature could counteract her evil summoning; that three divine animals would be reborn in human form so mankind will not see, hear or speak of evil. In the professor's words, the prophecy was preposterous.

However, the professor could not discourage Amanda from wanting Emily dead; the woman thinking the eldest triplet could learn of the prophecy, that the three triplet sister's had each inherited a third of a divine gift during birth, and that when each was combined, it could compromise her power over evil.

The professor huffed at her, thinking the idea mad, but after detecting the obsession in her eyes, knew he could not dispirit her from following this belief. He waved his arms in disarray, wildly accusing her of murdering people without due cause, asking to why she did not just go ahead and kill all three sisters. But Amanda muttered something that made him go quiet. Hearing what he did, a cold chill ran down his spine, and it was not from any draft.

'But surely I have only to dispose of one and their chances of... are none?'

The professor did not speak for a while, but circled the room in the shadows. 'But surely, even if what you believe is true... if these two sisters have yet to be united with the third, then –'

'Then I must be sure they don't!' Amanda snapped; her right hand outstretched as if her fingers were to claw the professor. 'See, by killing one, then they have no chance of all... have they my dear professor.'

As Amanda came into view and faced him, Jack could see the fixation in her eyes. He had seen the same scary glint in Emily's eyes, but this was something different; a dark, loathsome hate that bore a hole into whomever she stared at.

'But surely if only the two are together, at the moment that is,' the professor tried to change the subject, not wanting to look at Amanda's eyes as she stood in the shadows, 'surely we can get on with what the coven wants to do here?' He paused a little, to survey the building, its undecorated walls and ceilings, the place bare of furniture. 'Surely we can start the ceremonies soon.' He faced her to ask, but could still not look at her eyes. 'I could get secret meetings for our coven up and running by tomorrow if you would like?'

'Not until this business is sorted my dear professor,' Amanda circled the man like a predator stalking its prey, 'and besides, now I've had to dispose of that non-believer...'

'He was our thirteenth member, an additional wealth to our corporation.' The professor held his hand to his forehead. 'What are we going to do without a thirteenth –?'

'He was a liability my dear Grayling,' Amanda barked.

'Then we cannot proceed,' the professor muttered, his head drooping. 'Not until we find –'

'No, so stop bothering me about it,' Amanda interrupted. 'Find someone else more worthy... someone more committed.' A wide grin etched along her face as her dark eyes glinted in the shadows. 'In the meantime, I have some female 'wise monkey' to dispose of. I guess it doesn't matter which one, but...' Amanda's sentence trailed off, her attention directed to a strange feeling that someone else was listening.

Her dark eyes squinted directly towards the hallway, but Jack was in hiding; only half of his head peering around the door, enough to see the glint in her eyes vanish. She looked at the professor as if to study him like some biological experiment.

'Then it is done my dear professor,' Amanda told, steering him in sight of the hallway door and that of the main entrance. 'If you can get someone else for our little society,' she wagged a finger at him whilst ushering him along, 'someone a little more... reputable, may I say, and then we can have things move on around here. Obviously I'll have to have them vetted before we proceed, but, well, I have other things to do.' The professor turned to her for second as if with another question, but continued a slow walk towards the main entrance. Amanda stepped briskly in the other direction, pretending to exit the large room through another door, but crept back through the door to re-enter the room slowly and quietly.

Jack squatted down further upon knees, his haunches now numb as he watched the professor walk past. But soon he was up and after stretching his legs, crept steadily behind the spectacled man, watching how the professor's receding white hair got swept about as he opened one main entrance door. Although he had stopped to observe the visitor half way along the hallway, Jack could feel the sudden rush of a cold, damp breeze race in from outside. Jack heard the professor slam back the large wooden door, the booming sound against its heavy twin, uncomforting like that of a prison. But this was just some old and renovated house. However, as that Amanda had commandeered it, Jack pondered on its use, probably for her own malicious intent and that of this secret society of hers.

Jack stepped toward the main entrance, trying to observe the last of the professor as he climbed into his car. But until he eventually found a window to peer though (one in the room he had previously entered), Jack saw the professor's car disappear down the lane and into the darkness. It was then, as he turned, he caught sight of the silhouette behind him. But then something heavy hit his head.

Amanda was still cursing at Jack's weight when she had seated him on the floor and was tying his wrists together around a thick, wooden post. She had gagged him first with duct tape and wrapped it several times around his ankles, not wanting him audible or mobile if he awoke. But the intruder's wrists where difficult to tie together; Jack's hands falling either side as she struggled to keep hold of the tape. It was then that a pounding came upon the doors; the main entrance, right above that part of the cellar. With her hands shaking and struggling to wind tape around jack's wrists, she fretted to hear another set of rasps against the door. *Who the fuck could that be*, Amanda thought. *Surely the professor had not left anything behind? Maybe he had returned after seeing this man's car parked somewhere down the road, and come back to warn her?*

'You're too late professor,' she murmured, 'I think I know who this baby is.' She stood tall to take breath, her task to secure Jack against the post somewhat exhausting. 'He'll be just what I need for leverage.'

Again, knuckles hammered on the door above.

Quickly Amanda checked her hands and ran up to the hallway, but by now was greeted by nothing but silence.

Slowly she opened the one half door of the main entrance to see the silhouette of a man walking across the gravel driveway and back to his car. The man turned as if by intuition, somehow knowing Amanda was peering out from the door. Or was the place as creaky and noisy as it had been in all its years previous?

'Yes, hello sir,' Amanda played sweet on the outside, but inside she was seething, 'can I help you at all?'

The man turned fully and gently wondered towards her before pausing to climb the stone steps up to the main entrance.

'Yes madam, I think you might.' The man advanced carefully up the stone steps, but stopped on the top step, his face not coming fully into view from light cast either side. 'I followed a man to these premises, a man who has some suspicion about you. Well actually, it'll be his girlfriend.'

'And you are?' Amanda looked at her dirtied hands and so became conscious of the cleanliness of her face.

'I'm Detective Nathan Lawrence miss. I was following a Mr Jack Torrance. I caught up with him following you from your apartment. I believe he and his girlfriend have some fixation that you know something about the death of her mother?'

'Her mother,' Amanda played innocent but inside her stomach churned over, 'what mother?'

'A Sarah Layton,' the detective had his small, coil-bound notebook at hand but did not once glance at it. 'She's the deceased mother of an Emily Aston-Layton.'

'Sorry Mr Lawrence, but I have no idea of who those people are.' She tried to play her innocence by giving gesture. 'Maybe the man you saw leave was Professor Grayling?'

'No miss,' the detective told, 'I know the professor, and yes, I did see him pass me in his car.' The detective frowned. 'But how do you know the professor?'

'He's a friend... he's been a friend for a long time,' Amanda described. 'We're both members of an astrological society.' She remembered what the doctor had told her to say from all those years back.

'But there's another car parked back up the lane to this house.' The detective thumbed back, pointing along the drive behind him. 'I believe it belongs to the man I followed here.'

'Is there?'

'Yes, just as you turn into the lane.'

'Oh, that's probably... yes,' Amanda pretended, knowing it was most likely Jack's. 'That's probably the electrician.'

'An electrician?' the detective sneered.

'Yes, the guy's been doing work about this old house,' her pretence was admirable, but then again it was Amanda Burley, a woman who could conjuror up more than a hellish evil. 'You see it's just been renovated but the electrics, plumbing and so forth still need to be done.'

'And he's still here?'

'Maybe, I'm not sure,' she pretended ever confidently, 'Maybe he was the one you saw around here... maybe your other man, this Jack guy you describe, maybe he has already gone... disappeared?'

'But I've not long followed him here. I'm sure that's his car parked back there?'

'Probably that of my electrician; pulled over to complete his survey, maybe of the grounds, the house structure?' She pressed the old doorbell as evidence of it not working. 'I don't know about these things, obviously.'

'Yes I tried that when I first came.' The detective looked puzzled. 'But I saw no man in the car, it was locked?'

'Maybe he's still doing his survey?' Amanda smiled falsely, hoping it was enough to convince.

'I doubt any electrician would survey a house in this darkness, never mind the grounds.' The detective again frowned. 'I'm sure that car back there belongs to the man I followed here.'

'Well, as I said Mr Lawrence, sorry detective, I wouldn't know about those things.' It was getting harder for her to present such a convincing smile. 'Why don't you go and wait by the car for when he returns.' Amanda shook her collection of house keys for him to see. 'I will probably be leaving soon, but by all means if you want to wait around...'

'What was that noise?' The detective asked.

Amanda came stunned to hear Jack making some retaliation against being confined in the cellar; he had probably knocked over a chair she used to bind him.

'It's probably this old house,' Amanda looked up at its tall structure, ignoring what maybe going on below, 'might still need some structural work, never mind renovation.'

'But that sounded like...' The detective paused to listen. 'Is someone in the basement... do you have a basement?'

'A cellar, quite a big one...' Amanda had to find something convincing, she had to get rid of this pesky detective. And then it came. 'Why it might well be that electrician guy working down there after all.' She rolled her eyes to express her stupidity. 'Guess I'll have to check on him before I leave.'

'As I'm not pressed for time, maybe I...?'

'No Mr Lawrence, please if you don't mind, I've got a lot to get through tonight before I go back to the city and work tomorrow.'

'So just to sum things up for me, you've only seen the professor and this electrician tonight Miss Burley?'

'Yes, that'll be it, now if you don't mind...'

Amanda slammed the half door against its twin and the detective heard a bolt and a lock turn. He hovered for a moment to scan the grounds of the old house and then proceeded towards his car.

Inside, Amanda leaned against the large wooden doors, trying best to calm her nerves. Again she could here noises from the cellar. Under a breath Amanda swore before stamping across the hallway to the cellar door.

'Wait until *Miss Wise Monkey* finds out what I have to bargain with.'

THIRTY—THREE

EMILY HAD PICTURED A GLOOMY place like this before. But poised in the shadows of some spooky woodland, she was not sure where she was. But then she noticed the silhouette of a house, it melancholy in the dark of its eerie grounds. And even more foreboding was one of its main doors, ajar and inviting, its entrance hiding some mysterious blackness. Confused by how her vision jumped ahead like some jerking projector film, Emily's body trembled as she stood to watch one twin door open wide.

Puzzled to why she was suddenly close to the house, she glanced down at her shoes after feeling them crunch against gravel. And now she knew sounds were coming from within the house. Yet in visions there was no sound, no speech; only feelings of cold and dread, like silently observing the strange mist that flowed thickly just below her knees, its spectral fingers swirling about her legs to obscure her feet. Shivering, she watched how it rose to cover the stone steps of the main entrance to flow inward through the gap between the twin doors.

Emily's vision shot forward again. She had entered the house after pushing wide the already open door. And inside, at first she saw nothing but darkness. But after examining the gloom of a hallway, she noticed a large wooden staircase, its base spreading wide in a circular construction to meet the floor.

Suddenly Emily clutched at the main balustrade to keep her balance, but quickly retracted her hand after sensing someone in danger. Encased in the eerie silence of her vision, it was harrowing to know that Jack's muffled calls came from beneath the floorboards. But as Emily shot past, what she deduced was a cellar door; she now perceived his silent screams were coming from elsewhere.

Unnerved by not knowing where he was, abruptly Emily found herself staring at her own reflection in a large and tall hallway mirror. Perturbed after being scared at her own image, Emily studied herself. It all seemed so surreal. But now she knew Jack's voice did not come from beyond the cellar door, but from within the depths of the mirror. She squinted to observe a figure kneeling in swaying mists beyond her own reflection.

As her vision jerked again, it was then that Emily recognised Jack, his head locked down against some wooden altar, the structure resembling some wooden platform, all black and ominous within a murky landscape. His face now twisted to call to her, but his gaping mouth motioned in silence. And then as she looked upon the triangular guillotine above him, she screamed; only she heard nothing of her own cries... all she could remember was Jack's desperation to be freed as tears began to flood her eyes.

👁 👁

Emily shot up from being sprawled against the keyboard of her laptop. Through blurry eyes she recognised the files she had been examining. She felt her arms numb and her skin cold from perspiration, yet her body flushed with heat. Another vision she presumed. Only this time it had been more evident. Jack was in trouble.

Emily rubbed her eyes as she scoured her desk for her sketchpad. But by the time she whisked the pencil across the page and started etching, the vision was fleeting; the envisaged house a scrawl, along with the hallway mirror, the staircase, the cellar door, and the guillotine. And then there was Jack's gaping mouth, his bellowing screams contorting his face. She tossed the sketchpad to the floor; her eyes even more tearful than when she had awoke. For some reason, after that first vital moment of seeing bright light all over the page, she knew her gift had gone, the sketch just some hopeful misconception of her vision.

Emily started to weep heavier. The one time she needed to use her gift, she could not procure it, as now, she was certain Jack was in danger. How was she to save him now?

Emily did not see Effie walk gingerly into the room, her sister's eyes fixed on the floor to observe the thrown sketchpad. Effie picked it up and flattened the page to see clear the drawing. The youngest sister had spoken but Emily was hammering at the keyboard, typing in Amanda's address into some map search, desperately hoping she would find Jack at Amanda's city apartment.

'If he's been caught,' Emily fretted, 'I hope it's there and not the country place...' She stopped to realise how stupid she had been in asking him to do such a thing. 'Why on earth did I ask him to follow... an evil bitch like that as well?'

'You not answer me Emily,' Effie asked warily. 'What's with the drawing?'

Emily had now heard her sister and hastily wiped the tears from her eyes. 'Oh that,' she mused, 'just thought it might locate Jack.' She turned to look back at the laptop screen. 'But it's just a bunched up mess of scribble.' With her eyes still streaming of tears, Emily hit more buttons and moved her finger irritably across the mouse pad.

'Why it's a house, with an over big door and inside there's...' Effie turned the drawing about to scrutinise it more. 'There are steps up, another door, a figure inside a square with a...'

'It's a mirror and it shows that Jack's going to get his head sliced off if I don't do something.'

'You had another vision?'

'Yes, but that thing won't help me save him, will it?'

'Why not,' Effie turned it around to another angle, 'the house has two large spiral chimneys?'

'Yes, but how many country houses circling the whole of Bristol have such construction,' Emily snapped, not knowing her unease made her sister nervous, 'let alone having such a staircase and some stupid fucking mirror?'

'And that is Jack,' Effie murmured to enquire, 'the face below the –'

'Yes Effie, it is Jack,' Emily interjected sharply, 'and he's in trouble. Don't ask, but that drawing told me so. My vision told me so. But I can't do nothing but hope to find him at that other address.' She waved her arms in protest, revealing her dismay. 'What was I thinking... sending him out to... oh...? I'm such a fucking idiot!'

Effie turned away from hearing Emily swear, not liking to see her sister so ill tempered. She sat down to study again the drawing. Compared to the others Emily had done, she had to admit, it was unconvincing. She peered over, annoyed to hear Emily mutter more swear words. But now it was because her elder sister was having difficulty in printing some map to the device on her desk. She looked again at her drawing and of the man in the mirror.

'Of course, you,' Emily barked, 'we could use you, or at least your friends?'

'My friends,' Effie scrunched up her nose with apprehension. 'What friends?'

'The voices,' Emily bounced out of her chair to snatch her map printout, 'the people you speak to? Surely they'd tell us where Jack is before I go searching for him?'

'It doesn't work that way.'

'Well, in what way does it work, Effie?'

Effie did not like her sister's cynical tone and moved away as Emily sat beside her. 'I do not call on them.' She faced Emily, her eyes full of worry, knowing Jack was dear to them both. 'I wish I could help, but they come when they...' She paused to reflect, her eyes glancing down to watch her hands nervously rubbing each other. 'I could ask the next time they... but some are mischievous, liars... not all are good or family... sometimes they be wicked.'

'I see,' Emily took a deep breath after realising she had upset her sister, 'then I guess I'll have to try this way.'

'Is there nothing on those files we looked at earlier?'

'No, nothing about that bitch's country house,' Emily said with wrath, getting herself up to sit again at the laptop. 'It's just all weird, this stuff... drawings, palms and verses in some language like Latin, ancient looking symbols... especially the stuff that Jack sent... the photos of that book.' Emily paused, her face somewhat paler than before. 'That's the last time he was probably alive.'

'You must not think like that.' Effie got up to stand beside her sister, stooping over Emily's shoulder to look at the laptop. 'You felt that *we* were still alive, even though you didn't know where we were?'

Emily reached to grab Effie's hand but only managed to clasp her clammy fingers. 'Yes, and Jack's helped me both times, to find you and Ellen.'

'Well didn't Jack say Ellen was good with languages?'

'Yes, but how's that going to help Jack?'

'Maybe it won't,' Effie tried to use her newly learned skills on Emily's laptop to open her sister's email account and copy in Ellen's email address. 'But you try and ring Jack again and I'll get to do this.'

'But you don't know this stuff?'

'I had some lessons in that institute,' Effie admitted. 'I wasn't always bad. I only drew blood pentagrams all over the floor because some evil ones used to visit.' Emily looked up at her sister with pity in her eyes. 'Don't be worried about that now, I've grown up a lot since you and Jack helped.' She nudged Emily aside to sit down. 'You try Jack again and I'll get in touch with Ellen on here.'

Emily smiled. As she got up to watch Effie poke away at the keys, she felt suddenly proud of having a little sister, someone to love and trust, and help. And although she could not shake her nervous feeling about Jack, she took comfort in her little sister. Circling the lounge Emily called Jack's mobile several times, but on either occasion, like twice before, he failed to answer.

'I'm going to that bitch's apartment,' Emily affirmed, waving the map printout above her head as she grabbed her handbag. 'I need to do something to try and see if Jack's still okay.'

'Are you taking your phone?'

'Yes, of course stupid,' Emily frowned. 'Jack might call.'

'Then do this texting thing you do,' Effie asked, scratching her head. 'Message that Monika that I am sending Ellen an email with this stuff. Maybe she'll make something of that Latin you said it was?'

'If she has another change of heart, maybe she'll help us?'

Effie was not sure whether Emily was being sarcastic, or in fact hopeful. 'I'll try my best to persuade her,' Effie voiced watching her sister grab her car keys. 'See you later Emily, and please take care.' Emily smiled thinly before heading down the hallway and out her front door.

Effie was quite confused by the laptop software, but most of the technology installed was not much more different to what she had learned in the institute. In addition, she had watched how Emily had used social media and forwarded emails, and after a few dummy practices she had picked it up quite quickly. Effie browsed the *Sent Email* folder in Emily's email account and located the email Jack had sent from Amanda's apartment. Reopening Jack's email, Effie clicked *Forward Email* and poised as what to write.

> *Ellen, this is Effie, sister you not yet met. Please, I beg you to help. Emily so worried as Jack is missing, fears him dead.*
> *Amanda woman is evil. Jack tracked her but Emily had vision he in danger.*
> *Please help to understand files as she be in danger too. We all are.*

With the folders already attached to the email, Effie hit the *Send* button, but left it in the background to be sent. At first she detached the power cable to sit with the laptop upon the sofa bed and play a number of games; ones that the wardens back in the institute had told her were relaxing. But after five minutes, she looked again upon the files now copied to a desktop folder.

Effie had distinguished most of the language as some type of Latin, but some looked Celtic, even Hebrew. But it was the drawings that interested Effie. And after examining some of the diagrams etched by this past doctor, she regarded the sign of the pentagram with caution, knowing although it helped her in her early days to dispel evil; it was also used for evil enchantment. She browsed the files, each picture, each photograph more interesting, but she knew she was growing tired, her eyelids heavy. But with what had happened to Jack and the fact that Emily had gone and left her alone, surely she could not sleep.

Suddenly a bleeping sound came from the laptop and Effie closed all windows except Emily's email account. It was a reply from Ellen. The highlighted email instructed Effie to click on a hyperlink and how to talk with her live. Effie glanced around the room as in doubt. But the place was empty, and she was alone. Surely talking to Ellen, even if only online, she would feel less lonely? She might even forget her woes, well at least until Emily returned. Effie hesitated before clicking the emailed link. After watching a chat room box appear, Effie eventually typed.

Ellen, is that you here. This is Effie.

For a minute there was no reply, and then came a short, sharp sound.

Yes, sis, it be nice to see pics of you. Email some girl!

I have only a few, most from institute. Ask Emily to do one of us together?

There was another short delay.

Yes, be great, but what's all this. It took ages to download?

Please, want to talk but I fear things bad with Amanda woman.

Effie sent the reply but typed another message immediately after.

We believe woman have power to summon dark forces and kill people. She has murdered people already.

Again a delay; Effie presumed Ellen was examining the files.

Such stuff is nonsense sis... get that stuff out of y' head. You be back in that place that Emily said you were in!!!

Please believe, Jack not believe before until now. We showed him proof.

You have proof girl?

Effie paused, realising she had only forwarded Jack's email and had not sent the photographs of the doctor's book from Jack's camera.

Check files on email. I send another of photographed book. Then believe?

Effie drafted another email to how she had seen Emily do, attached the folder of photographs, and then came Ellen's reply. Effie minimised the email window to observe the live chat room account.

I'll have a look sis, but this stuff will take time. Serious shit here!!! Why ask my help on this?

Jack said you good with languages. You have strange gift like me?

Is that so? Maybe I just have strange affection to the written word?

Jack said you pick up speech quick too?

What's this got to do with what you send?

Check language in book and research in folders. I think they be some type of Latin, or language like Celtic.

You know something about it girl?

I learn stuff at school before I went to institute, but learn some in there as well.

My snobby parents paid for all shit like that at school too, but I know that's not why I read languages and speak them so good... some sort of gift, like you say?

Effie stopped typing, her thoughts going back to the institute and young school days before her final and decisive assessment. Soon her memory recollections of being institutionalised were broken.

This is weird stuff. Where you get this serious shit... it's wicked.

Please just give us some help, if only translating the language. Emily wants to know what Amanda is capable of.

Right, will do... Take care, sis. Don't forget those pics.

Those of Emily and me you mean?

There was no reply.

I've emailed book ones already.

But as she hit the *Send Message* button, the chat room connection was closed.

Just in case Ellen would reconnect, Effie minimised the chat room window to browse more of the files. She again examined the descriptions that surrounded the pentagram sketches, but could not decipher any of the language. Only some basics in Latin did she recall from her previous schooling but that was years ago.

She glanced up, the silence about the place suddenly giving her the realism that she was alone. Uncontrollably she shivered and so pulled her cardigan around her. Finding a folded blanket perched on the arm of the sofa bed, Effie unravelled it to wrap around the upper half of her body. Now, with only her hands poking out of the comfort and warmth of the blanket, Effie could examine the files more. But with her eyelids heavy, maybe tonight, although alone, she would get a natural night's sleep or at least just a little before Emily returned.

Effie awoke on the sofa bed, but the laptop and her blanket had gone. The room was somewhat darker than before and it had become quite cold. But Effie recognised what was happening, especially when a distant voice called her name. Lethargic, as if weighted by some supernatural gravity, she got to her feet and padded slowly towards the hallway. With eyes open and glazed, she paused before hearing a voice call again, this time from her little bedroom.

Effie turned and walked slowly down the hallway before pausing to enter her bedroom.

'Yes, who is it?' The warmth of Effie's breath exhaled into mist from the chilling temperature of the room. 'Who's there... is that you little Charlie?' She entered her bedroom, her pale and numb body somehow unperturbed by the now freezing air. There was no reply as the voice had faded. 'Charlie I cannot play tonight. Please don't be sad, but I am worried.' Effie turned to sit on the bed, her eyes fixed and glazed, but her face scrunched with worry. She searched the bed for the cosmetic mirror, but in her torpor could not find it. 'I fear that someone dear to me is dead, and like you, unnecessarily so.' Effie sat in the icy cold of her bedroom, her ears pitched to the silence around her, her other senses somehow anesthetised. 'Please, I know it be wrong, but my sister...'

'I know,' a soothing voice spoke. 'We know of Emily's dismay my child.'

'Who is this?' Effie showed fear in her voice, patting the bed about her in search of the little round mirror. 'Have we spoken before?'

'Why, yes dear Effie, once before. Or would it be twice now?'

'Aunt... Aunt Evelyn,' Effie's eyes swelled with tears. 'Is that you Evelyn?'

'Yes my dear child, so you have no reason to fear.'

'I am sorry, but Charlie tells that...'

'Your young friend has been taken by dark forces my child.' The voice paused as if remorseful. 'Justice has not followed the young boy's death.'

'But he's been gone for...' Effie tilted her head forward, a small tear escaping each eye. 'I thought he had more time?'

'His soul has been influenced to gather justice by other means my dear.'

'But he said... I told him I'd expose the man... his murderer.'

'It be too late now, you have not been listening of late.'

'It's my medication great auntie, please, we have difficult times and...' Effie tried again to find the cosmetic mirror, but somehow knew this was the real voice of her great aunt and did not need to see if her shadow was white.

'I know my dear,' the ghost of Evelyn spoke soothingly, 'so please not cry from what has come of Charlie, but lift your head as you have your sisters.'

'He is lost to us?' Effie croaked, her question unanswered. She sat in silence for a minute before finding courage to ask things she had never before dared. 'Aunt Evelyn, how can I save Mr Jack, Emily and I too fear that he is dead?'

'He not be dead,' the voice whispered, 'that is all I can tell.'

'But how can we...?'

'Never mind that my child,' the ghost of Evelyn instructed, 'you must all be strong for what future darkness comes... you must be prepared.'

'Prepared for what?'

'Like the sisterhood before us,' the voice told earnestly, 'and the one we learned in ourselves, you must combine your forces to be one, as dark evils are being sought.'

'What forces Aunt Evelyn, what are they?'

'Your gifts of nature my dear,' the voice seemed to be humoured, 'gifts especially strong in each of you that can diminish the evil men do.' Effie sat up with interest, but was somewhat confused. 'You yourself have one... a gift to hear from those to help dispel evil.'

'You mean I was too late to bring justice for Charlie?'

'Yes, it is something like that.' The ghost of Aunt Evelyn paused as if distracted. 'But remember my dear, unlike ours, a sisterhood power such as yours can prevent mankind from seeing, hearing or speaking of such despicable evil. And such a sisterhood can eradicate such evil.'

'But how,' Effie cried, tears streaming down her cheeks, 'we just only got to know Ellen?'

Effie sat again in silence, her head twisting side to side to hear intently.

'Aunt Evelyn, please, I know not what to do!'

'The sisterhood will find a way.' The ghost of Aunt Evelyn announced, before it began to fade. 'Remember, your mother is watching over all of you...'

Effie's eyes were already open when she saw her bedroom. At first she looked about sheepishly, but then studied her reflection in the dressing table mirror. She saw that had been crying. And still, tears fell over her cheeks to soak her dress below.

She glanced down at her twitching hands to notice how she trembled. But this was normal after a talk with the voices; her ears now reverberating some high-pitched whistle, like that for a dog. And by observing her sitting in her bedroom, it was obvious that again she had sleepwalked from the lounge. Maybe, she thought, this was where Aunt Evelyn thought she would be most safe.

Effie sat for a minute or two, her face placid and pale, but behind her expression, her mind was churning over all that her great aunt had said. She remembered every word of it, although a lot confused her. And then she grinned in the reflection of the mirror. The one thing Effie was glad about was the fact that Emily, Mike or Rachael had not seen her sleepwalk again.

THIRTY—FOUR

ELLEN POSITIONED THE MOUSE POINTER over the confirmation button to book her flight ticket, but hesitated to click it. She glanced up, alarmed to notice Monika bounce back into their apartment with yet another pizza, her girlfriend sharing loudly her past midnight experiences at the club. The last couple of nights Ellen had pretended not to have being well enough to do her shift, but Monika had covered her performance schedules; the Russian girl's body exhausted, but her eyes wide with excitement to the tips of money she had earned.

Instead, since messaging Effie a couple of nights ago, Ellen had been subdued by some other drug. This was no smoke, powder or pill of some physical description, but an investigation into some occultism sect that mentally provoked her. She had examined closely the emailed photographs and browsed most of the attached files. And having some uncanny talent to decipher the text, Ellen found them more than interesting. She had even stayed up all one night to explore the possibility, and more importantly the authenticity, of a Doctor Schroeck's historical research. Effie's excuse to Monika come morning, was that her girlfriend needed rest from all the exhaustion of her double shift, but the Russian was curious to her English friend's motive; that she knew Ellen was not really ill, but had become obsessed with what her sister had sent.

Ellen never liked to lie to Monika; they had always exchanged banter and argued things out. But this was something she wanted to keep secret. Maybe it was what she had discovered about this doctor's research that had proven decisive, the corrupted man's interest in using the Black Art for his own interests, mastering some malevolent occult society who sacrificed animals (and even the rumour of people) to summon evil at a bloodletting ceremony.

At first Ellen thought it all some joke, but then considered the doctor's society as a shield to cover dubious financial dealings. Then for some reason, as she delved into the research, her heart began to race, her eyes tired of reading but her mind eager to learn more.

And then there was this Daniel, his and this Amanda woman's own interpretation of the research, both relentless in their quest to discover such dark power.

When she first read the attached files, Ellen had ridiculed the possibility of controlling such evil power; this was not the Dark Ages, but a decade into the twenty-first century? But after deciphering most of the ancient Latin text using her extraordinary talent, she came obsessed with the photographs that Effie had sent of the old book. She herself could not believe she was beginning to accept her sisters' belief in all this, but only minutes ago, Emily had emailed to tell her that Jack was still missing and that both she and Effie were worried sick.

Ellen had pondered to why this Amanda woman would want to harm her sisters, or Jack for that matter, but she had learned from the doctor's notes that Mother Nature would create a sisterhood to counteract such resurrected evil; that three humans, females derived from early primates, would be born as a righteous sisterhood to dispel such evil.

Ellen had become fascinated by her new study. She had not been captivated by anything like this since quitting university and that was before she met Robbie. She heard Monika ask about the pizza, but simply mumbled to her Russian friend for her to save her some for later.

And now Effie had emailed again, her sister's plea for help intense after a visit from some great aunt of theirs. After confessing her ability to hear voices from the dead, Ellen knew now why Effie had been rehabilitated. At first Ellen regarded Effie as still unstable, but discovering Emily had visions too, Ellen considered whether each of them *did* have supernatural talents? She had to admit that her own skill to decipher languages and speak them so fast was abnormal. And according to what this dead doctor had predicted, a sisterhood would be born to dispel his discovery of dark power. Maybe Ellen and each of her sisters *had* been born with talents to negate such evil; that they could stop others from using the doctor's power, prevent them from seeing, speaking or hearing evil in the future. But then again, Ellen had to admit; all of this seemed so incredible.

'It go cold if you not have now the pizza?'

'Okay give it here,' Ellen replied seeing Monika stand with her one hand outstretched to offer the shallow box. The Russian girl looked slightly off balance with her legs crossed and her other hand on hip. 'I forgot the microwave is broken.'

Monika span around, her eyes rolling as Ellen took the box, her knee-high stockings having more laddering than Ellen could remember, her leg muscles more tight and thin. But Ellen still fancied every inch of her body as well as her bubbly and seductive personality. She watched her Russian friend sip a mug of tea from a distance, a gentle smile etched on her face as she stood to lean against the breakfast bar area. But Ellen knew too well how inquisitive her Russian friend was.

It was time to declare her intention.

'Monika, please don't get upset, but I've decided to go and see my sisters.'

'You go England?' Monika asked; her face now glum as Ellen nodded. 'But you say you not want sisters, there be only me, us here in this city doing…'

'Yes, I know, but…' Ellen maximised the browser window to confirm her flight booking ticket to England. 'This is important to me… they are in trouble.' She watched Monika turn away to walk in the bedroom. Ellen slid from the stool to follow.

'It's about time I grew up from all this pretence. We hardly have anything here.' Ellen stood in the doorway, Monika's eyes glaring at her half-packed suitcase. 'This place is not the best. Demoralising work at the club, our pay up and down… struggling to make ends meet?'

'What about me?' Monika cried, turning to reveal tears streaming down her cheeks, the rivulets darkened by absorbed makeup. 'After all we go through? I pay you back for travel and get you job at club?' She paused to wipe the tears from her eyes, glancing in dismay at the top of her hand, seeing it dirtied with smudged makeup. 'We have life here, me and you, we be friends… lovers.'

She waved her hands up in question. 'You not want that anymore, you grow bored of me?'

'No, of course I don't girl,' Ellen replied, pulling down her jogging bottoms to reveal a tattoo just above her shaved genital area. 'You think I'd get your name tattooed here in Russian if we not be together... forever.' Ellen winked to try and restore faith. 'Besides, you're the only one who goes down there... your tongue is the best!'

'But these be your sisters,' Monika babbled, pointing at Ellen's suitcase. 'They want you to stay, you will stay... I know you will.'

'They are in danger my girl,' Ellen went to grasp Monika's arm but the Russian flinched to back off. 'Once they are alright and we all are safe, I'll come back, I promise!' She grasped Monika's wrists so that she had no choice but to look at her. 'You do the same if you had chance to be with *your* sister again.'

'That be not fair.' Monika shed tears now of anger. 'You know I not save my sister, we only children back that time.'

'But think if you could have the chance of being with her, even if only for a short time?'

'Cruel thing say,' Monika pulled her wrists free, 'you promise not mention as you know it upset me.'

'Yes, but you not listen to me, to how important this is. Not just for me to meet sisters I thought I never had, but I believe something is wrong... they are in danger from some evil woman. They reckon we all are. And I believe we can do something about it.' By the ease on Monika's struggle, Ellen hoped her friend was less irate. 'I can finally do something that is not demoralising, degrading... stop from being such a bitch.'

'You cruel at times, but no bitch,' Monika pulled her wrists free but smiled thinly. 'Well, not such a bitch, not like Oleyssa.' Again Monika fretted to wipe the tears from her eyes. 'You will come back, you promise cross heart?'

'It'll be just for a couple of days, I promise,' Ellen reassured, taking a nearby cloth from her bedside cabinet to wipe clean Monika's cheeks. 'I'll bring something from England back for you.'

'English ragdoll with ribbons in ponytails, the one I see online?'

'If I see one, but now you're asking.' Ellen started to mess around within her suitcase. 'Maybe we could both visit England one day… you could meet my sisters, once I've met them first. And if we get on after all this that is?'

'After all what?' Monika had been intrigued all along to why Ellen had been on her laptop and still believed she was owed some explanation other than some crazed and dangerous woman.

'I'm not sure of anything yet, but I believe my sisters are in danger from some evil woman. My sister Emily believes she could've murdered Jack.'

'Jack, nice Jack,' Monika showed true concern, 'Mr Jack who give tip for Britney dance?'

'Yes, and I know you like him,' Ellen teased, knowing how far she could humour Monika. 'I thought you only like girls… one like me?'

'Jack be charming man, not horrible like men at club.' Monika rolled her eyes again, her clean and vibrant skin glowing against the haze of the bedroom lamp, her ribbon-tied pigtails making her look ever young. 'But men not know how treat girl special in bed. Not like you… toys or no toys.' Monika smiled mischievously before frowning. 'But you go now, this moment… and for how long?'

'The flight is about ten in the morning, it'll take an hour or so, but then I got to find Emily's place in Bristol.' Ellen left the bedroom to disconnect the laptop and cable from the two-pin electrical adapter. She brushed past Monika as she obstructed the doorway. 'I'll see these girl sisters of mine, help them with whatever and be back in no time.'

'But I be alone in apartment,' Monika muttered sadly as she sat on the edge of the double bed. 'Do more shift at club to pay way?'

'Look, we'll just probably get this woman arrested for murdering people… locked up for being strange… using magical ways to avenge people she dislikes.' Ellen placed the laptop and cable in a rucksack and pondered on clothes littering the bed. 'But Emily believes she killed Sarah purposely this way… magic that can set evil upon someone.'

'I do not believe in such.' Monika wriggled on the bed, pulling down on her ponytails as she was now more distressed to hear of her girlfriend's mission. 'But you have proof... sister show evidence on laptop?'

'Yes, newspaper described a man who this Amanda befriended as getting unnaturally mutilated.' Ellen flung some extra underwear into her suitcase. 'Emily said our mother, Sarah, got killed that way too. Effie tells that all of us are in danger.'

'You say mother,' Monika pondered, 'this Sarah be your real mother?'

'Yes, but she is dead now. Apparently she was murdered.' Ellen froze, her body suddenly overwhelmed with guilt. Monika glanced up at her friend; she had never witnessed Ellen so solemn. 'And I never even got to know her. Effie said she wished me at her funeral.' Ellen stood for a moment like a statue cast in some pose, a silence of thought shared between both girls.

'You make me worry more for you now,' Monika mumbled, her eyes again swelling with tears. 'But I not understand; how can you believe this woman evil?'

'Look, I didn't believe in all they told me at first, but,' Ellen stopped nervously packing to face Monika. 'We have to face up to things, even if we don't always like them. Remember I told you how Robbie betrayed me and took my then best friend?' She shut the suitcase lid vigorously and pulled anxiously on the zips. 'But if all that hadn't have happened, then I wouldn't have met you now would I?'

'And I be kind more than Robbie,' Monika murmured. 'He be like all men.'

'Apart from our friend Jack, that is?' Ellen winked.

'Yes, he good man, have good heart.' Monika stared at Ellen's suitcase, her bright green eyes enlightened by her smothered dark makeup. And then she saddened to remember Ellen's quest. 'You will take care, you promise me?'

'Yes of course girl, don't fret.' But Ellen was nervous of something other than the flight. 'Nothing ventured, nothing gained as they say.'

Monika frowned. For a while she sat bewildered on the edge of the bed before her eyes widened and her voice announced seductively, 'You have time for licky?'

Ellen simply nodded before crawling along the bedclothes to kiss her girlfriend's cheeky smile.

THIRTY—FIVE

'THAT WAS A FUCKING WASTE of time,' Emily shouted after slamming shut the front door and storming into the lounge. 'He's been missing now a third night and all they do is to ask you to phone round.' Emily glared at Effie with anger after tossing her car keys into a circular, glass ashtray on the coffee table, 'As if I haven't tried that already?'

'Maybe it is too soon to go to the police?' Effie muttered, somewhat scared of her sister's reaction after observing her temper.

'You think so little sister.' Emily stamped her feet to circle in front of the window like a lion about its cage. 'I've filed a missing person's claim, but what else is there to do but phone everyone we know?'

'Did you try the university again?'

'Yes, this morning and afternoon.'

'What about George... that guy you said worked at the jewellers... wasn't he Jack's school mate or something?'

'I visited the jewellers yesterday, but he said that he had heard nothing.' Emily played agitatedly with the black curls of her hair whilst staring out of the window. 'But he did give me his number; maybe I could try it again?'

'I heard your mobile ringtone, but by the time I –'

'You stupid girl, didn't you pick it up?' Emily interrupted angrily. She searched her handbag to realise that again, she had left it elsewhere in a hurry.

'How was I to know that you left it here?' Effie was clearly upset with Jack's disappearance too. 'It went off by the time –'

'And you only tell me this now?'

'Why, you have *two* mobile phones now do you?' Annoyed, Effie stood up from sitting on the floor, her game of cards now totally abandoned. 'How was I to get in touch?' She stormed past her sister to pace loudly down the hallway to her bedroom. 'I don't have one of those things, and if I had, I don't have anyone's number, or know how to work it. They didn't allow them in there!' She sat in frustration on the bed, glancing at her shaky hands.

'Then where is it?' Emily called from the lounge, but went without reply. 'Effie, where's my phone?'

'It rang from somewhere in your bedroom,' Effie shouted agitatedly, and then spoke calmly as if within a second her personality had changed. 'If you remembered where you put it, instead of bawling at me, then you might even find it.'

Effie rubbed her throat anxiously with trembling fingers. She had never shouted like that since sessions in the institute. That was before she had learned that all voices were not bad. But she remembered how some tried to manipulate her, pretending to be a relative, a lost and lonely soul, or a friend to be.

She looked sadly into the mirror. Although Emily had made her look ever so pretty, she felt that she had lost some of her individuality, her sensitivity, and for a while, had felt an overwhelming oppression. Maybe it was just what had happened to Jack, or that it was now that she regarded Ellen as a lost cause. Emily had been viciously irate; she had lashed her aggression out, her temperament so wild, so oddly uncompassionate. But now she thought it understandable, especially as Jack was now a boyfriend, her lover, even a potential future husband. And Emily did truly love him; she had openly confessed it to Effie the night before.

Effie shuddered to suddenly see Emily appear at her bedroom door.

'It's from Jack,' Emily announced with glee, her voice croaking with delight. 'He's left a voicemail message!'

'What's a voicemail message?' Effie asked, but was unheard, her sister rushing excitedly back into her lounge. 'What's it say? Is he alright?' Effie enquired as she followed Emily into the lounge.

'Shush,' Emily instructed; her hand waving at Effie to be quiet as she tried to listen to the recorded message.

'What's he say,' Effie persisted to ask. 'Where's he been?' She paced into the lounge to tug on Emily's cardigan. 'Tell him we've been worried sick!'

It was not Emily's angry voice that silenced Effie, but the whole blank expression on her now paled face. Effie also noticed her sister's mobile fall to the floor. Emily stood like a frozen statue, her anger and disbelief mixed together in some sort of paralysis.

Effie reached to grab the phone by Emily's feet, but saw her sister fall back against the sofa bed.

'What's the matter Emily?' Effie pained to ask, her throat tensing as bile clumped there. 'What's happened to Jack?'

But Emily did not reply; she just sat there, her eyes fixed on nothing, her mind lost in disbelief.

'He's not...' At first Effie could not speak the word, but had to know. 'He's not dead is he?' Tears swelled in her eyes and one escaped to fall down a cheek as she tried to continue, 'He's not been murdered like mother?'

'No,' Emily said coldly. 'No, he's not dead.'

'Then what is it? Why are you so... pale?' Effie cried, trying to push the mobile into Emily's hand. 'Tell me what the voice says!'

At first Emily sat unperturbed, a moment of shock preventing her reply. But Effie persisted to know what her sister had heard.

'Emily, please,' Effie shook her sister's arms, the mobile again falling to the floor. 'I can't work your mobile, you know that. Tell me please, what's happened?'

Effie stopped in shaking her sister; her vision blurred by tears, her sudden emotional discharge causing her head to ache. And then, as she slouched to sob, Effie heard her sister mutter something.

'He's been kidnapped,' Emily's voice announced emotionlessly. 'Kidnapped and held by that evil woman.'

'That woman Amanda,' Effie repeated to affirm, 'the woman who does the evil?'

'Yes,' Emily told, her eyes fixed in a glaze. 'He is her prisoner. And unless I meet with her, she'll kill him.'

'She'll kill Jack, but why?'

'Well, I guess it's me she really wants.' She turned slowly to notice Effie's wide eyes. 'It must be some trap, something to prevent me from...' Emily paused to think of how she could save Jack. It was near midnight already and the call had been missed for at least an hour. 'But I've got to try and save him, he's done so much for me... for us.'

'But you said it's a trap?'

'Then I'll be extra cautious.'

'What about the detective?'

'Amanda told to meet her alone, that she'll kill Jack if I tell the authorities.'

'Then I must go,' Effie commanded with newly found confidence.

'No,' Emily replied adamantly, 'I can't risk the both of us from –'

'But Aunt Evelyn said that without all three of us together, we wouldn't be able to stop such evil?'

Suddenly Emily realised to why she had misinterpreted the doctor's research; that a united sisterhood could possibly fulfil the doctor's prophecy and prevent his evil from occurring. But was this doctor's ancient dark magic the same as what Amanda could now do? Emily had no doubt that her mother had been subjected to the same horrible death as the councillor, but what of this Daniel Whittaker? Being wheelchair bound, he surely had purpose to avenge her mother, but why would this Amanda want her mother dead; and now, maybe her herself? With the convergence of all that had happened, Emily had not thought things through straight. Never mind comparing facts and ideas, and trying to relate her mother's death to this strange woman, she had also become obsessed in finding her sisters. And with Jack's abduction to put the icing on the cake, it had become all too much. In addition, Effie had found her voice, she was insistent in coming.

'I'm going alone,' Emily barked. 'The three of us aren't here... I'm going alone!'

'But, what if...?'

'He's my boyfriend and I'll save him myself if I have to!' Emily snarled as she reached down to retrieve her mobile phone. But quickly Effie snatched it from her grasp. 'Give it back here now!'

'Not unless I go too.'

'Stop acting like some spoilt brat and give it back!'

'Jack's my friend too,' Effie stated fervently, pushing away Emily's hands that grabbed for her phone. 'You're not having it back unless I go too.' Effie squabbled with her sister, but found that Emily was giving in, her emotions too distraught to endure. And now she started to cry. 'Look, I can take calls... just in case something happens.'

'You don't know how to use it,' Emily babbled, sobbing. 'You said so yourself.'

'I can learn, surely,' Effie eyes widened, 'if only to pick up a call?'

'Pity you didn't earlier,' Emily conveyed with a mix of cynicism and regret.

'Then why did you get me out of *that* place if I can't be of help now?' Effie stared wildly at her sister, but gradually composed herself to see Emily cry. 'You know I only want to help... Jack is also a good friend to me.'

Emily wiped the tears from her eyes, knowing she had to be strong. If Effie was prepared to stand up against this woman to save Jack, then surely she should. She smiled thinly, her glazed hazel eyes widening to look on her sister with pride instead of scorn. She got up and gazed down at Effie, who studied closely her mobile phone, watching her examine the device. Seeing Effie glance up to acknowledge the correct button to take a call, she pouted to lay down the law.

'You come... you stay behind me,' Emily pointed at herself to express instruction. 'Only I do the talking, and you do everything as I say, agreed?'

Effie nodded to agree but accidentally dropped Emily's mobile on their haste to the car, the screen of the device now fractured as it lay on the path to Emily's home.

THIRTY—SIX

'IT'S BEEN TEN MINUTES SINCE we left the car,' Effie fretted, trudging through the undergrowth to follow her sister. 'Are you sure this is the way?'

'This is the right track,' Emily stopped to study the pathway between trees, her penlight illuminating the darkness, her sister huddled close behind. 'It's the one according to my map in the car... the one that that bitch described.'

'But I'm falling everywhere?'

'You wanted to come,' Emily stressed. 'You said you'd be no problem?'

'I know but,' Effie cowered to look into the darkness around her, 'it's the first time I've been out in this kind of place... especially with it being so dark.'

'Keep walking, you'll get cold,' Emily stated. 'I know I am.'

Effie watched her sister's breath exhale into a soft mist before the beam of the penlight was again directed to the floor of the woodland.

Effie cringed in hearing the distant cry of a fox. Screeching owls calling about the darkness in the trees above had already agitated her. A couple of times she wandered askew and stumbled into overgrowth; her grabbing onto Emily to balance herself made her sister swear under breath.

'Watch where you're going,' Emily instructed, seeing her sister look anxiously at the darkness above. 'Look to the path... and follow my penlight.'

For a while they plodded along the meandering path through ever thickening woodland until they came to a staggered junction.

'How much further is it?' Effie questioned, dejected at how her plimsolls slipped against the slippery mud.

'The clearing should be straight ahead. But this junction, well it's...'

'There,' Effie called to point at where firelight flickered in the darkness, 'just ahead and to the left... between those trees.'

Momentarily the girls studied the distant flame to come increasingly scared of their mission, but cautiously Emily crept on, her sister now holding on from behind as she bravely switched off her penlight.

The firelight in the middle of the clearing came evident as the sisters traipsed near. As they crept towards a wood fire circled by stones and rocks, they paused to glance about them, hoping to catch a glimpse of Jack. But he was nowhere to be seen.

What the sisters saw that worried Effie particularly was the blood-spattered sign of the pentagram, as this was not only in the doctor's book and research, but she had attempted to draw signs like it in her own blood. And for a long moment Effie trembled, thinking that she had just woken from sleepwalking the corridors of the institute.

What caused Emily alarm was the tall, black candles flickering alight at each point of the marked pentagram, as if placed in accordance to those doctor's drawings. But was the sign actually drawn in blood?

Effie stooped ahead to touch it, but quickly retracted her hand after confirming it was real blood. Was this blood of an animal, or was it human? More importantly, could it be Jack's blood?

'Jack,' Effie called wearily and then repeated in all directions. 'Jack, are you here. Where are you Jack?'

'Shush Effie,' Emily ordered, although also impatient to know Jack's whereabouts. 'Try and get him on my phone, we may hear it ring.'

'But it isn't here,' Effie stressed, trying to search her dress pockets and then her woollen cardigan. 'I can't find it.'

'But you had it off me,' Emily voiced angrily but tried to keep her voice down. 'You said you'd look after it while...'

'I can't find it Emily,' Effie interjected fretfully. 'I'm sorry but it must have...'

'Why you stupid girl,' Emily scorned, 'I should've kept it when –'

'Lost something have we my dear?' a voice called from a distance. 'Brought little sister along for company have we Miss Emily, or is it that you're too scared to face me alone?'

Emily and Effie huddled together whilst both of their heads turned to locate the voice, but it just seemed to echo about the trees. Whether it was the reassurance of light or the comfort of warmth, slowly they edged closer to the fire, their faces stern in studying the darkness around them. It took a while before Emily found enough courage to speak.

'Where's Jack?' Emily asked, turning her head at all angles, ushering Effie to be close behind. 'If that's you Miss Burley, I believe your skirmish is with me and not my boyfriend.'

Apart from the crackle of burning wood and a rustle in the treetops, for a moment there was nothing but silence.

'My name is Amanda,' the voice announced somewhat closer by. 'But then again, you should know that.' As the girls searched the trees that circled them in light of the fire, the voice paused. 'Don't worry about your boyfriend, he's safe... a little dreamy and tied up at the moment.' The humour in Amanda's voice turned slightly grave. 'But I don't know how long he'll be alive for?

'Let him go,' Emily commanded, Effie stepping gingerly along behind her. 'If it's me you want then let him go...' Both sisters stopped when they saw a figure of a man slumped against a tree trunk, a binding of ropes encircling his body to clasp it there. 'Jack has nothing to do with this,' Emily spoke out bravely. 'If you have any qualms it's with me. You killed my mother... our mother?'

'And you, I believe, burst my tyres,' Amanda announced somewhat childishly before asserting the main issue. 'But that be nothing to what I have gained from the man your so-called mother disabled. Daniel died of his own stupidity, but your man here will be an example to see the power I have gained.' Amanda paused as her silhouette appeared from behind the tree to where Jack was bound. 'I may not be as powerful as that doctor but...' The sisters cringed to observe Amanda swivel a large pointed dagger that glimmered against the firelight as she toyed with it. 'You'll see for yourself soon my power, as your friend here...' Amanda's grin stretched wide across her face.

'Daniel's paralysis wasn't Sarah's fault. I now believe we did it to protect her.' Emily's declaration made Effie frown. 'We have powers too. We had such powers even as babies... that's what your master...'

'Yes, I do believe the doctor was right,' Amanda interrupted vigorously. 'And now I know why Daniel went to kill the three of you... sacrifice you before you had chance to deter his power. Your pesky father did the same at the doctor's mansion, although somewhat unknowingly... saving your mother to give the three of you, life... stopping the sacrifice of your unblemished souls to preserve the prophecy.'

'You're wrong Miss Burley,' a voice announced from behind Amanda. As another figure holding a flashlight appeared from out of the woodland, Amanda's crazed eyes turned to despise him. 'Yes, I heard that Sarah Layton was saved by Carl Aston, their father, but it was a Mr Mackenzie who rescued her from the fire.' Detective Nathan Lawrence pointed his flashlight in Amanda's direction. 'I've discovered that unscrupulous dealings were done at this doctor's mansion, and *you* were a young accomplice who helped him to avenge differences and oversee horrific murders just to be some part of...'

'Oh, and you know so much about it do you, detective?' Amanda spat her words at him as if she could spit snake venom.

'Yes, in fact, I've been doing some interesting homework,' the detective spoke calmly but with a hint of sarcasm. 'If you dig deep enough to see what's beneath that masquerade of yours, you've not changed one bit over these years?'

'And how's that Mr Detective?' Amanda questioned, glancing at first to see if Emily and Effie were still watching, her eyes gleaming in the firelight. For some reason the two sisters began to smile. Had the cavalry arrived just in time before this bitch could hurt poor Jack?

'Well, to cover up your unscrupulous ways using some sham of an astronomical society is somewhat...'

'It's an astrological society if you must know.' Amanda's face was now full of malice.

'More like a bunch of malicious money launders,' the policeman derided. 'Trying to continue in the boots of the old doctor are we Miss Burley... kill off anyone who offends or may spill the beans?'

'The name is Amanda,' she corrected with spite, but calmed in respect to the knowledge and power she bestow, 'and I know nothing of what you assume detective... my person and the accounts of my business are altogether forthright.'

'But Miss Burley, you ridicule me,' the detective grinned. 'I've been listening to your conversation with my friends here.'

'Then I take it, you know all too much for your own good.'

'That'll be true,' the detective announced as he pulled out his mobile phone, 'I've definitely heard enough to convict you.' He pointed his flashlight to illuminate Amanda's anxious face. 'Miss Burley... Amanda Burley, I am arresting...' the detective paused to concentrate on his call to his colleagues in authority.

Amanda was on top of him like a flash; she had lunged at the detective from some distance. And having increased strength to assail the man like some demented maniac, he went down heavy against the woodland floor. It was only when he hit her away by reflex, that he noticed the dagger in his thigh. And as he recoiled to crawl away, the frenzied woman struck again, plucking the sharp blade from the first wound to plunge down to inflict another.

Although Emily wanted to help, she held Effie back from going to the detective's mercy. And when they watched Amanda hold up the squirming detective's hand to cut deep between thumb and forefinger across his palm, both sisters froze. Emily pulled Effie close, huddling her to back away from Amanda, watching the woman now stand and hold the blade up towards the night sky. Amanda grinned to watch the detective's blood ooze down the blade and upon the handle where it gathered in shallow recesses. The sisters shivered in their dismay, not knowing what they could do.

Emily considered trying to rescue Jack, but paused to watch the detective crawl painfully towards his assassin, the man's face pale but eyes bulging with animosity. Amanda turned to show a last glimpse of pity as she recognised the abhorrence in the detective's glare, knowing that soon his stare would change into a fixation of terror.

As Amanda dripped blood into the fire, at first the sisters observed the hissing steam, but then heard the crazed woman holler words, her arms extended up towards the dark sky.

It was not until Emily moved her eyes away from pitying the detective that she grasped what was happening. Effie too looked at her sister with apprehension, but was pushed back by Emily who needed to try and stop Amanda from casting her spell. She knew that her Latin words would surely summon some ancient evil.

Emily charged at Amanda but the older woman had seen her coming and simply threw her off. After Emily rolled against woodland debris to come sprawled upon the muddied earth, she heard Amanda approach to speak.

'Think wisely of your choices my dear lady.' Amanda said grinning whilst she pointed the blood-stained dagger at her. 'I was going to use your man to exemplify my power, but first I need to do away with this pesky braggart.'

Amanda returned to the centre of the pentagram to turn the knife in the flame of the fire and chant more words. Emily recoiled as the night air grew cold, a wild breeze had disturbed the treetops and a sense of foreboding had fallen upon the clearing. She flinched after crawling back some distance; Effie had grasped hold of her as she kneeled to join her sister. They glanced at each other, terrified to what they may see. Could this thing that was about to be summoned be the creature that murdered their mother, that journalist... killed Daniel?

Perturbed by the strange words bellowing from Amanda's mouth, the sisters slid away but heard branches braking nearby. Effie hoped it would be some of the detective's back-up team, but Emily trembled to think it was some invoked devilish creature, trampling branches underfoot with its talon-like feet. Effie sensed someone was looking back her, at them, was watching the grisly actions of Amanda's performance. But then Effie was hauled forward by her sister.

'We've got to do something,' Emily fretted, 'even if we just get Jack out of here?'

'He's tied to the tree and we've nothing to free him,' Effie replied, her voice frantic but strengthened with hope. 'Maybe police will come... maybe they'll trace the detective's call and...' Again she was dragged by Emily as she glanced back to where she sensed someone watching. Soon she joined her sister to gaze upon the horror that came.

From behind Amanda, and in between two large trees, a mist assembled to circle in a grey coloured vortex, dark shadows within glimpsing out like anguished faces eager to escape. As the mist reached high towards tree branches and thickened, its centre glowed as if a lighthouse had shone through a foggy coastline. And soon, all around, the mist flowed freely, its spectral tentacles covering the woodland, almost touching the terrified detective that crawled frantically away.

It was then, after Amanda had finalised her summoning spell that a dark figure stepped from the cloudy assemblage. At first it flowed much like the mist, but shimmered in the light of the wood fire, its ethereal shape gradually congealing to form a monk's habit, the heavy hood concealing the face, it now just some deathly blackness. As the phantasmal creature glided towards the detective, Amanda turned to watch its arms and hands form, as if dark strips of tattered cloth were being magically weaved together whilst it moved. As the ghostly figure stopped and hovered, nearly double Amanda's height, its defined shadow faded before the cloaked spectre turned its head towards her. It was then that the sisters partially glimpsed its stony face.

Although withered to the bone in the shape of a human skull, the face had pale skin that shone an insipid white under the black of its hood; its nose and mouth were intact with black, downward arching lips that revealed jagged teeth as it grinned to wait instruction. Amanda bellowed out Latin words and pointed at the detective, its face suddenly indistinctive as it turned between observing the detective and its conjurer.

Emily and Effie watched with horror as the Dark Ghost approached the detective. As they saw the man kick out in desperation, they saw the phantom's hands grow, its claw-like fingers elongated to reach for the wounded man. Emily cringed to witness the detective get mutilated like her mother, but saw the Dark Ghost had retreated somewhat, its bulbous eyes staring at Amanda, its expression seething at the sight of a crucifix that the detective had taken from beneath his collar to hold aloft.

Amanda shot forward and quickly snapped the necklace from the detective's hand, the chain of metal braking and slipping from the man's grip. Without delay she tossed the necklace to the corners of the clearing and repeated to issue her commands. She pointed to the detective before ridiculing him.

'You'll need a lot more faith for that to work you stupid bastard,' Amanda barked, 'now die, like all that will try to defy me!'

As the terrified man gazed back at the phantasmal creature, he noticed it open its cloak and pull up extensively one arm. Beneath the blackness of its cloak and body came tortured souls, faces of demented and nefarious people that laughed hysterically, or was it because they were condemned to so much pain? As the Dark Ghost closed in on the detective, Amanda chortled to watch the spectral shapes shoot about and inflict torment and injury to the petrified man, his limbs pulled to extremes, his head and body twisted, his bones pressured to snapping point.

Emily and Effie could not look any longer and turned their eyes away from the screaming man. Effie held her head in her hands as she could feel the sounds intensify, her mind capturing the malicious torment even more than her ears. Emily too felt sick, but the rage that built up within her provided enough for her to encompass bravery. She pulled Effie hands away from her head and stared at her sister in commandment, her open hand gesturing for her to stay.

Effie watched as Emily crouched to race across the woodland clearing to recover the crucifix she had seen Amanda throw aside. Luckily, as the evil woman was absorbed in finally experiencing the results of her new power, Emily returned unspotted, the silver crucifix dangling from her clenched fingers. The girls huddled together again trying to dismiss the last deathly cries from the mutilated detective, but then heard Amanda curse English words at them.

Quickly Emily hid her newly retrieved necklace and skirted with Effie around the clearing to save Jack. But as they squatted in fear to how far Jack was from them, they cowered to hear the evil woman announce more instruction.

'Look at you two pathetic souls,' Amanda ridiculed, facing them after knowing the detective was now dead, 'you have no more power than that policeman.' She pointed the dagger at them after cleansing it with a cloth. 'And you shall come to be like him. And it will all be over. Then there will be nobody who can defy my power!'

The two sisters squatted further down on their haunches; their attempt to save Jack might only get him killed. Surely this woman had become seriously infatuated with such power, and with that, she would do anything?

In the undergrowth the girls tensed to watch the woman stand close to the fire again and spout out Latin words, some replication of what she had done before. Behind her the Dark Ghost hovered at the edge of the clearing. It had retreated from the detective's body, its play toy now sapped of its soul – the policeman's body just some empty husk.

'Trying to save that precious boyfriend of yours are you Emily?' Amanda shouted at the girls. 'I'd have this blade in him before you even got near.' She twisted the knife so it gleamed against the dwindling firelight. 'Besides, it should be your own pretty faces you should be worried about.' Amanda grinned to reveal a bottle from her pocket. 'You know what this is girls?' Amanda smirked to watch the sisters peer questionably at one another. 'Or should I say, to whom it belongs?'

'Let Jack go and I'll pretend we know nothing about any of this,' Emily shouted valiantly.

'But you're already part of it Emily,' Amanda said strong and slow, 'you and your so-called sisters.' She paused to pour blood from the small medical bottle so it ran down the dagger blade and collected at the handle. 'This'll be your mother's blood Miss Emily. And as your poor mother has already departed from us, well I do believe you're the next of kin... the next in the bloodline.'

'Why be so horrible to us,' Emily jabbered to ask. 'Why be so nasty and such an evil bitch? Let Jack go!'

'Argh, but I thought you understood. Maybe I was wrong. But I can't take any chances you see.' She paused to angle the dagger so the blood trickled down the blade and into the fire. 'Maybe I should enlighten you before...' She paused again to watch the last of the blood singe in the fire. 'The doctor foretold of three witches being born to defy his power, each having the virtuous power of three wise monkeys. And my guess is that, although you've found your gifts, you have no influence...' Amanda paused to reflect, her wicked grin ever wide. 'And besides, only two of you... that be no danger to me... I only have to kill one for the other to be useless.'

'You can't do this, you have no reason,' Effie found courage to shout, but Amanda was now chanting words of the doctor's ceremony in ancient Latin again. 'You'll go to hell like those horrid voices...'

'Then see if you two puny bitches can defy the Dark Ghost?'

Amanda turned to renounce her presence with the dark entity that hung in a wavering mist some distance away. She again bawled out commands in the ancient language before pointing at the sisters hiding in the shadows. 'One or two of you, it doesn't matter... without you and your influence, I have redeemed the great doctor's power. And from here it's... goodbye.'

Effie pulled on Emily to crawl away, but her sister resisted staying in the path of the oncoming phantom. It was just as the Dark Ghost revealed its hellish glare upon them, that Emily preached words, kissed the crucifix and moved it across her chest in the sign of a cross. For all that was in her that was morally good and virtuous, Emily held out the crucifix in sight of the phantom. As she closed her eyes and prayed, she tried to recall all her Christian belief. But the spectral fingers of the Dark Ghost were almost upon her, somehow the grey mist engulfing them so the creature's evil glare would not see the crucifix. Effie looked about frantically, terrified to see the grey mist thicken as it glowed and flowed about them. And then she saw something so unusual it made her wince. Emily's nose was now bleeding, but the fog had retreated to where it had been seconds ago, the Dark Ghost having to approach again.

Emily's visions felt like they were breaking her skull. The first was of the crucifix held out in her hand; the second was pushing back the fog, and thirdly, the retreated position of the evil apparition. It was as though the apparition had been pushed back, enough to save them of its malicious touch – its spectral fingers having to extend again to their elongated form, the crawling mist cleared somewhat. But the dark shadow advanced once again, and like the glowing mist, it was soon upon them. Emily's vision cleared the evil's advance once more, but now both of her nostrils oozed blood.

Leaning against her sister, Effie almost toppled in losing her balance. It was not just being amazed at the repetition of time that pictured out before her, but she now understood her sister's gift; that although Emily was terribly in pain and bleeding, she was neglecting the advance of such an evil. So what if she joined her? Maybe she had no choice but to help her sister? And what was it that Aunt Evelyn had said, and that which Amanda had just admitted; that only together would all sisters be influential?

Quickly Effie clenched tight her sister's hand and muttered, 'I am with you Emily, we be as one like the voices say.'

Flinching somewhat, Effie could now feel her sister's pain, but somehow felt it shared between their bodies. She saw Emily come somewhat reprieved, her eyelids flickering as she turned to her sister to grin in approval. But the evil shadow now towered over them, its power increasing and intensified, its bulging eyes glaring at them with sharp menacing pupils below the darkness of its hood, the pale of its skeletal face defined to exemplify its intent. The wavering apparition began to raise its spectral cloak and from under its body were heard voices of torment and loathing.

But suddenly Effie heard other voices, people who she recognised, some recent, some from years ago in the institute, all overwhelming her mind to block out the hollering agony and torment that spilled out from beneath the phantom's cloak. And now Effie could see into Emily's vision.

At first Effie saw dark apparitions of evil souls swirling about them. These deranged faces flew spectrally before the tall shadow of the Dark Ghost as its black lips stretched in a deathly grin to expose pallid, jagged teeth. But as the swirling evil souls flew at them to inflict pain, Effie heard voices defy their hollering torment. And now, as Effie could see her sister's vision clearly, Emily could hear the voices. But as the hellish torment increased with evil souls mocking them, both sisters were losing senses. Emily's vision of her crucifix was now failing to neglect and push back the phantom's advance. Effie's hearing of voices was gradually being muted against hollered abuse. Both sisters were wavering to hold off the affliction of such an evil.

At first Effie did not feel the hand slide into hers until the cold of it cooled her palm, but when she envisaged the figure as a bright apparition in the distance, she could hear Ellen's voice call. And it was so surreal to recognise someone she had only chatted with online. But now she realised her younger sister was there, physically by her side.

And now all three could see what Emily saw of the evil adherent; all three could hear the voices that had now revitalised their attempt to neglect the evil. And as all three sisters joined hands that clenched tightly together, the vision of Ellen came forward, leading another bright figure. This taller, more mature bright apparition, felt virtuous, almost holy as it held out a candle before it.

At first Amanda was amazed to see the young woman appear from the bushes. But when she glimpsed Ellen's face as she took hold of her sister's hand, Amanda grimaced to realise who she was. She stood perplexed, not knowing whether to snatch the crucifix from Emily's hand or to accost the newcomer. But she knew she could herself get caught up in the battle that raged between the sisters' minds and the evil that stood before her. Amanda raged with disappointment to see the Dark Ghost retreat slightly, and to how the evil souls now flew about cursing their victory. She felt like running to all three sisters and slitting their throats, but surely this powerful evil had yet to establish its power over such charmed but sceptical witches.

With a desperate and last attempt of revenge, Amanda clenched the dagger with one hand and cleansed it with the bloodied cloth before clambering towards the large tree. But by the time she reached Jack, he had already awoken to free a hand against the binding of ropes. Without remorse she plunged the dagger down against his face and although he dodged her somewhat, it sliced his hand. But it also sliced into the binds that restrained him. He gazed in fear to watch Amanda now clench at the dagger with two hands, its impact into the bark deep enough to need two hands to prise it free.

Jack writhed like a fish out of water. He pushed all his weight against the rope although the binds bit into his hand and opened his sliced wound. But it was a test against time. He needed to use the blade to cut the rope further. If Amanda had another thrust at him, she could strike somewhere more vital. He pushed his wrist up and down against the blade, cutting the rope between, but then Amanda dislodged the dagger.

Again Amanda arched back with the dagger above her head to trust down on to Jack, but his binding had snapped and he parried the weapon away. To Amanda's dismay, again the sharp blade dug deep into the oak's thick bark. Frantically the woman tugged at the handle and Jack glanced about to realise his opportunity. He pulled again against his binding until another rope snapped. It was then, when his wrist was free, he struck Amanda's cheek.

The stunned woman fell into a collapsed heap aside of the wide tree truck until she came dazed upon the woodland floor, her body lying feeble and her eyes foundering. In a state of panic from his bout, hastily Jack pulled free of the ropes binding him. He stumbled forward from his confinement, his legs weak but energised by shock, his eyes staring down in revolt against the woman squirming on her back.

Jack turned to lean clumsily against the tree, his senses still wavering, wanting to pluck the dagger from the bark. But it was no good. Either his strength was too weak or the blade was stuck fast into the wood. It was when he took another long breath before attempting to remove the dagger, that he heard the commotion. He glanced around the truck of the large oak, his hands gripping the bark to support his unsteady legs.

Jack stood aghast to see three women crouching, their hands in each other's, the first with her arm outstretched to hold up a crucifix. And although a thick mist twisted about them, he recognised all three sisters but could not believe his eyes. Holding his wounded hand with his other, Jack staggered forward, ignoring the pain to observe the towering shadow that hovered above them like some mystic monk. His eyes turned to Emily and inside his heart prayed for her to win this supernatural battle. *Emily you have the strength, I know you do*, he shouted in his mind. *And now you have the sisterhood you wished for. They are with you to defeat this thing... this thing I never believed you said was true.*

All three sisters could now see the Dark Ghost glare down at them as the evil souls flew mystically about them. And although Ellen's touch had invigorated their power to oppose the evil, all three were now faltering. For some reason the bright figure of Ellen had dimmed to disappear, the image enfeebled to the hellish phantoms constantly hounding it. But behind was another brighter light, a figure holding out a candle. And this intensely white apparition drifted towards them, its face angelic, its body virtuous and holy.

This image was of Sarah, their mother. And unlike at burial, she was uncorrupted, not twisted or tormented by the hellish evil that now plagued them. She smiled at her daughters, her face emphatic to see all together and proud to how they were all attractive. But as her eyes drifted to notice their predicament, Sarah's face came enshrouded in doubt and unease. She glanced back at her sisters after catching sight of the evil towering over them, seeing how Emily was near to dropping the crucifix.

It was then that all sisters ignored the image of the evil standing overhead, to look on their mother with desperation and hope. They all watched Sarah's lips move as if mouthing words to them, but all they could hear was the bellowing evil chants from evil souls.

It was Ellen that first heard her mother.

'Fear not my children,' the bright apparition of Sarah told. 'With all three daughters charmed as virtuous souls of Mother Nature, we shall together deny this evil that murdered me anymore existence.'

Emily and Effie now looked onto their mother's apparition after hearing her words. But now, as the Dark Ghost retreated at noticing Sarah's ghost, her apparition was issuing instruction for them to repeat her words. But the words were of some foreign language; an ancient Latin to that Amanda had used to summon the hellish creature. And after being feverishly subdued by the Dark Ghost's power, Emily and Effie closed tight their eyes as well as their clasping hands.

'My daughters, my children,' Ellen translated from her mother's ancient Latin words, 'repeat these Godly words and with your powers you shall combine in spirit and souls to dispose of this summoned evil.' Ellen listened intently to her mother repeat a sentence of ancient Latin, something Holy to oppose the evil that hovered close.

Again the bright apparition of Sarah repeated the sentence of ancient Latin until Ellen was copying her. With the Dark Ghost poised in dilemma, Emily and Ellen looked fervently towards their youngest sister after hearing her speak. With all still encased by Emily's vision, the three sisters repeated the sentence of ancient Latin although somewhat abstruse. Slowly Emily and Effie repeated their sister's words and came more confident with pronunciation.

It was then, as they shouted to repeat the ancient Latin sentence, the sisterhood saw orbs of light detach from Sarah's candle flame to capture the evil souls that flew about the woodland. Instead of meandering briskly the air to inflict torment on the sisterhood, the evil souls now tried to outpace the bright orbs of light as if launched missiles pursued them. And when such bright light engulfed the phantasmal, angry faces, the soul was released; a placid floating cloud drifted free of torment, anguish and suffering. This soul had been forgiven for its corruption in life or during its haunting death, one that had suffered enough under the command of the Dark Ghost. And with every soul that was released of torment, the Dark Ghost flinched with anger, its size diminishing with every sin redeemed.

From the other side of the clearing, Jack could hear the three sisters bellowing out the words of a strange language, a sentence repeated that was to him, totally incomprehensible. But to his delight, the dark shadow that once towered above them had now diminished in size as it retreated into a thicker mist behind. Flickering balls of light sped about the darkness of the treetops to engulf phantasmal faces that contorted with alarm. Astounded by the conflict that raged in the woodland before him, Jack stood petrified but came transfixed by the sisters' energy and determination. He gazed upon Emily with emphatic admiration.

Suddenly there was an intense light that shone dramatically before the three sisters. For a second it glowed bright enough to light all darkness beyond the clearing and then shot towards the dark shadow that began to dissipate like the retreating mist.

As the ghostly dark shadow began to dissolve into a thinning mist, it came ruptured by an intense orb of light. Jack put his arm up to protect his eyes, he could hardly observe what had happened until all that existed in the woodland clearing was a grey glowing light and a quickly fading mist. Slowly this swirl of foggy assemblage faded to leave the shadow of the woodland clearing, the sisters only illuminated by the fading light of the wood fire and fallen candles.

Jack staggered toward the girls as fast as his legs would carry him. He opened his arms to clasp Emily, but saw all three girls collapse to the ground. He stumbled a little before looking upon Emily's face, his balance unsteady from kneeling. She was half unconscious; she was totally fatigued, her nostrils and mouth clotted with streams of blood. But by her heavy breathing, she was alive. And so were her sisters.

Emily did not know how tight Jack had hugged her, but neither of her sisters knew how he hugged them too.

EPILOGUE

'How's the hand Jack?' Emily asked whilst frowning.

'It's tight, but after visiting the hospital again this afternoon, I'll live.'

Effie smiled at Jack whilst watching him press awkwardly the bandages wrapped around his hand. And then she looked across the lounge at Emily who was pouring cups of tea.

'I visited somewhere else this afternoon,' Jack disclosed, pulling a bag from his pocket. 'I've been to see my friend George Louis.'

'The guy who works at that jewellery shop,' Emily interjected glancing up at him, 'The one on the high street that's not far from my work?'

'Yes my dear, that's the one.'

'So what you got there my friend Jack?' Effie became excited by the three small parcels wrapped in glistening silver paper.

'You have one each, but please let Emily open hers first.'

'Well, which one is mine?' Emily asked, putting down the teapot to wander over.

'It doesn't matter,' Jack said offering Emily one of the packages. 'They'll be all the same, but precious to each of you.'

'Something precious for me,' Ellen asked cautiously as she walked into the lounge after visiting the toilet, 'what ever could that be?'

Effie glanced up at Ellen as she hovered over her, both impatient to watch Emily unwrap Jack's gift.

'Why it's the crucifix that I wanted to buy when we met,' Emily's face shone with gleeful recollection. 'Jack pretended to be a shop assistant just to ask me out.'

'It wasn't easy,' Jack mused, 'believe me.'

'Do we all have one then?' Ellen leaned over to take the parcel Jack offered.

'Yes, and by, well what happened the other night, well... I think it's somewhat appropriate, don't you agree?'

He regarded each of the sisters in turn and then heard Effie agree, 'Yes Jack, you disputed me and Emily but...'

'I must admit,' Jack leaned back into the comfort of the sofa bed, 'I had to disbelieve you at first... anyone would. But after seeing...'

'I didn't,' Ellen muttered, retreating to stand behind the sofa bed to unwrap her parcel. 'I came convinced when I read that stuff.' She paused to reflect on her arguments with Monika. 'Obviously at first, what with Monika disbelieving, I too thought that such things couldn't happen... that evil forces could be conjured. But after reading more into that ancient language and all that history, it gets to you like some obsession.'

'Well hang that thing around your neck for protection,' Jack intervened, 'that's why I brought all three for each of you.' Jack looked at how Ellen observed the silver crucifix held up against the light. 'Emily said it's a good job you came when you did.'

'Yes,' Effie turned to view the youngest triplet, 'how did you get so convinced to come over when you did?'

Ellen was about to speak when Emily intervened, 'What I want to know is *how* you knew where to find us, exactly?'

Ellen pulled Emily's mobile phone from the back pocket of her jeans.

'I found this when I arrived at this house.' Ellen held up Emily's mobile phone and turned it against the light. 'I remembered its decoration of lily flowers from the café in Amsterdam that afternoon because Monika likes lilies too.' Ellen looked from admiring Emily's mobile to see all in the lounge interested in hearing her story. 'Well as I noticed the screen was cracked, I tried to operate it. With the screen paused on that last message, the one from that evil woman, well I replayed it you see.' Ellen stepped close to Emily to place the mobile phone down beside her oldest triplet sister. 'Just glad I found the place in time for you guys.'

'So are we,' Emily affirmed, taking the mobile phone to caress it. 'So are we.'

Printed in the United States
By Bookmasters